PEREGRINATION SERIES

BOOK 4

WATER

Peregrinate - V. To travel over or through an extensive voyage.

WATER

Peregrination Series Book 4   S.G. Boudreaux

ISBN   978-1-7339636-4-0   (paperback)

ISBN   978-1-7339636-5-7   (digital)

Zanchier Publications
PO Box 12936
Lake Charles, La. 70612

Sgboodro2@yahoo.com
www.SGBoudreaux.com
www.zanchierpublications.com

Peregrinate: To leave one's homeland and wander for the
love of God; to travel especially on foot.
(v.) to travel over or through something.

Glossary

Capped letters are the annunciated parts of the word, whil[e]
bold letters receive the long sound.

Vashti Mayer (VA shti M**A** yer)
Toren Pascal Degare' (Tor en Pas cal De GAR **A**)

<u>Book 1: Earth Glossary</u>

Dragoman (DRA -go-mun) – was, or is, an actual profession.
They served the kings of empires as interpreters in
Turkish, Arabic, and other Persian speaking countries.
They were men who were skilled in many languages and
political information about other countries, and served as
a sort of consultant. I just elaborated on their abilities for
the creativity of the storyline.

Peregrine (PER-e-grin) – Noun derived from Peregrinate - Made
up for the book. A person who travels over time, through
storms doing work for God.

Scroll of Rubric – made up for the story. However, a rubric is
simply a code or instructions for something.

Staff of Moses – This is an actual item from the Bible, used by
Moses, whom God used to perform many miracles. My
research concluded that it has never been found.

Goddelikheid Crucible or Divinity Crucible – the name
Goddelikheid is a translation of divinity in a foreign
language. However, a crucible is a bowl like item that is
used in distilling or separating metals for the
purpose of refining.

Portal – a hole in time created by generating a large amount of
energy, either naturally or mechanically, that Peregrines use
to time travel.

Garganthera – a fictional land of giants made up for the storyline.

Barriers Edge –a veil that separates dimensions of planes, also fictional thing made up for the storyline.

Bermuda Triangle - most of us are familiar with the strange tales
that come out of the Triangle. I just elaborated and
explained why.

Reader's Island – a fictional place created for the story that exists in
the center of the Bermuda Triangle. At least, regular people
can't see it, only Dragoman and Peregrines.

<u>Book 2: Wind Glossary</u>

Bakrashan (Ba kru SHAN) Fictional city in a fifth-
dimension plane on Zanchier.

Carpasmere (Kar pas MEEr) Another region or city in
Zanchier.

Catamount (CA ta mount) *Gorge:* Fictional river and cliff
area in the Xantifal Mountains.

Kabihanxu (ka bi HAN <u>ju</u>) The firebird's scientific name.

Pagorinx (PA gor inx) Mythical large wildcat residing in the
Xantifal Mountain range in Zanchier.

Scaithers (SK**A** ther) A band of cutthroat outlaws that reside
on Zanchier.

Tarphamor Horn (TAR fa moor) horn of an animal resembling
a ram native to Zanchier.

Xantifal Mountains (ZAN ti fal) Where Oz's home is located on
Zanchier.

Zanchier (Zan **KEER**) Fictional country in a fifth-dimension plane
somewhere in the universe.

Some of the storms that are listed in the book series are factual
storms that took place throughout history. Some places in the book
are actual places and researchable. Some places are fictional and are
made up for the benefit of the storyline.

This book series is a work of fiction. Although it is based upon
some biblical truths, all characters are fictional and in no way
represent any living or deceased persons. Any similarity is purely
coincidental.

Author's Note

First, welcome to any new readers who may be beginning with this fourth book in the series. I encourage you to go back and read books 1, 2, and 3 to fully understand who the characters are and what the books are all about. Also, a big shout out to all my loyal fans who have returned to read the ongoing story entitled the Peregrination Series. I hope you've enjoyed the last three books, Earth, Wind, and Fire, and that you will find even more fun, intrigue, and perhaps a few new favorite characters within these pages. The next and last book in the series will be titled *The Final Battle, Battle of the Beasts*.

As per the first three books, I will introduce to you more about the characters that you have already been reading about. Book 4 will begin with an introduction to some of the back-stories for the Dragoman known as Vashti Mayer, and the Peregrines Ezekiel Davis, Nadia Bonhomme, and Timothy Johnson. Their stories both past and present are woven into the current situations and are once again joined by all our past friends, and some new and forgotten characters. I hope you enjoy this, the fourth book *Water*, in this five book fictional series entitled the Peregrination Series.

Prologue

The Peregrines have located the first two pieces of the Armor of God — the Belt of Truth and the Breastplate of Righteousness — and are back on Reader's Island awaiting the next location of the third piece, the Shoes of Peace.

Bridget and Dominic have returned from their accidental peregrination to Zanchier, and Dominic is still healing from the wound inflicted on him from the demon's poisoned arrow.

The tension between Sean and Timothy over their mutual feelings toward Kristen is growing, especially since she has chosen Sean.

The Dragoman have made an error concerning the marks for the twelve tribes of Israel, and it has caused some hard feelings for two of the Peregrines who just recently discovered that they are not included in the final battle. The two who have taken their place in the battle are relatively new Peregrines, and this information fuels the anger within Uriah even more being one of the displaced.

There is also new information concerning underwater portals that no one knew existed until recently. During their trip across the Mediterranean Sea aboard a ship to find the Breastplates of Righteousness, Sean was washed overboard during a storm and discovered a portal. Once before on Reader's Island, the glow from the underwater portals were seen by some of the Peregrines from high atop the island's mountains, but they weren't sure at the time what it meant. Now, back on the island, the Dragoman are searching the archive books looking for anything that may tell them as to why these portals exist, and if they are to use them and how to do so. They now have recovered the stolen key but are still uncertain as to whom the betrayer and thief might be.

We now continue the story with Book 4 in the Peregrination Series.

In all this you greatly rejoice, though now for a little while you may
have had to suffer grief in all kinds of trials. These have come so
that the proven genuineness of your faith-of greater worth than
gold, which perishes even though refined by fire-may result in
praise, glory, and honor when Jesus Christ is revealed.

1 Peter 1:6-7

Chapter 1

Reader's Island, Late summer, Present Day

Vashti Mayer quietly stood watching the scene before her with
interest. She had been a Dragoman for twenty years and a Peregrine
for three years before that, and she loved this lifestyle. She was the
only person that she knew of, or ever read about, that started as a
Peregrine and then was called to be a Dragoman.

The earlier announcement by Petra about the two young
Keepers suddenly appearing on the front lawn from a portal, after
having been missing for three days, had everyone in an uproar.
Everyone simultaneously questioned them, wanting to know what
had happened to them, where they'd been and why they hadn't
returned instantly. She also noticed that two people were not present
at their reappearance.

Uriah and Timothy seemed very angry and hurt over not being
included in the Chosen Twelve to fight in the final battle.
Technically, they were chosen but then replaced. Her concern was
that they seemed to blame everyone else for this instead of trusting
God's plans. None of the Dragoman or Peregrines had any control
over this decision. God chose each one of them, marking them
accordingly with a tribal symbol for one of the twelve tribes of Israel.
Uriah and Timothy had marks, but they were marked for the two
tribes listed in the Bible as defiling themselves. Because of their

defilement, God did not include those two tribes in future battles, choosing to replace them with two other tribes. This recent revelation had set the scene for the remainder of the searching, and it wasn't going to be a pleasant one. She and Uriah had never been particularly close, but Timothy Johnson, like Ezekial Davis and Nadia Bonhomme, was one of her Peregrines. She would try and possibly speak with him later.

The Peregrines, especially the main twelve, were already dealing with their own internal and external battles within the large traveling group. There was always going to be conflict amongst some people within a group this large, but these developments, or further tests of the spirit, were going to complicate things even more.

As she stood musing through her thoughts, her attention returned to the chatter and bombardment of questions of the two recently returned teens. She noticed that Timothy finally appeared outside, a forced grin upon his face. Uriah was still not present; probably hiding in the privacy of his room, stewing over the new development.

She might have to try and speak with him later or have Malachai to. After all, she had known Uriah for some time now, at least the last thirteen years. After Hiram's coo years ago, Malachai Harel had taken over as Dragoman for Uriah, and Vashti and Malachai were very close. She had heard all about Uriah from Malachai and they had prayed for the man often over the years.

Vashti watched Malachai amongst the group. The two of them had shared a special bond from early on. They were dear friends for the first five years or so, and then their relationship had blossomed into something more. It had taken nearly the whole first five years of Malachai's flirtatious endeavors to convince her that they were meant to be together. Especially since she was almost four years his senior and from a completely different background than him.

Malachai was of Jewish descent from the late-fifteen to the early sixteen-hundreds. Vashti was from the old country of Germany. Her father had been German and English, and her mother had been of English and Jewish descent. Vashti had been raised very German minded with a strict upbringing and not a lot of playfulness, for it was considered in her home as foolishness. Therefore, she and Malachai were an unlikely pair, for he was a very playful, fun-spirited individual. When she first met him, she thought him arrogant, childish, and rude. It hadn't taken her long to see that her first impression was completely wrong. Malachai was just the opposite. He was just so interested in her that he applied all his efforts into winning her heart. It took them a few years to become close friends, then without his even trying any further, just by being himself, she fell hard for him. When she finally revealed her feelings to the extremely patient man he was overjoyed, and they vowed right then before God alone, that they would be bound together until death took one of them. They had as formal of a ceremony as two people without a priest or rabbi could. They kept it secret, just like everyone else had that lived this way and formed attachments over the years. They didn't hide the fact that they preferred each other's company and often spent much of their time together. They just had never displayed affection for one another in public. Now that open relationships seemed to be acceptable, especially with the pre-peregrination husband and wife team of Seth and Caroline Jager, she wondered how she and Malachai's relationship would now work. They could display affection in public without judgement, or their friends concerns of warning them of the dangers of growing that close to someone. Things had certainly changed over the years. Her and Malachai's relationship wasn't the only secret one, she always knew that, but she was certainly surprised by Wendal and Prisca's secret marriage. Prisca had suffered for thirteen years of not knowing where Oz had disappeared to, or if he was ever coming back. Prisca had never once mentioned to her about their relation-ship, and they were very close friends. But then again, Vashti had never shared about her and Malachai's relationship with anyone else either. Not even with Prisca. It was just the way things were back then. For everyone's safety and peace of mind, you just kept that sort of thing to yourself.

Malachai looked over at her and smiled broadly, the feelings of elation at the kids return overtaking everyone with joy. She warmed inside like the sun was glowing deep within her soul. The man still could give her butterflies in her stomach. He walked over to her and amid the chattering, planted a kiss on her in front of everyone. Only a handful of people were paying attention to them.

Simon just smiled at them and said in passing, "It's about time." Which meant that he obviously knew of their affection toward one another.

"I agree sir." Malachai grinned at Simon and then Vashti, wriggling his eyebrows at her.

Vashti giggled at his antics, swatting at him sheepishly out of habit. When he didn't relent and step away, she smiled heartily at him. This new feeling of openness with their personal lives felt strange. It would be nice not to have to hide certain things. Although they'd hidden them for so long it would likely take her a while to get used to it without feeling like she was doing something wrong.

The large group of people moved to the patio area to sit and listen to Bridget and Dominic regale them with their tale of being stranded in Zanchier and the adventures that took place while there.

Jason was curious about Dominic's wound. "Mind if I take a look at your shoulder, Dominic?"

"No, go right ahead," Dominic answered. "Although, it feels just fine now. Every so often it'll ache a little." He pulled his shirt over his head as Jason, and now Safra, inspected the wound.

Jason and Safra exchanged glances. It appeared to be healing well, but there was still some discoloration around the wound's entry point. Jason placed his hand over the area and prayed, hoping to draw out whatever poison may be left. The wound's appearance didn't change much.

"I'll be right back," Safra told them. She went inside to get an herbal cream, returning and handing it to Dominic.

"This may help with any aching," she said. "The wound is old, and therefore must be harder for Jason to heal as some tissue has already died. Jason was unable to do much, but this may help with the healing process."

Jason answered, "There may still have been some poison in the wound that needed to be drawn out to allow it to heal further. Hopefully I was able to pull the rest of it out and it will be able to heal quickly now."

"Thanks," Dominic said to both of them. "It sure is nice to be back with everyone. If it hadn't been for Bridget, I would have died for sure." He glanced gratefully at Bridget.

"Well, I suggest you rest for today and try to give your body a chance to mend itself," Jason said.

"Okay." Dominic smiled. "I could do with a break. It's been a crazy three days. Especially yesterday with that Marnor character and his cronies."

"Well, the two of you won't have to worry about them anymore." Jason smiled.

"Maybe not, but Bridget has had quite a shock. She's handling it well enough, but she might need someone to talk to about it."

"Really?" Jason queried. "What about exactly?"

"I'd prefer it if you'd ask her about it. It's kind of personal. She might not want to discuss it at all. She's had enough bad family ties in her life." The look on Dominic's face indicated that he feared that he'd said too much.

Safra followed Dominic inside to apply the cream to his shoulder, get him some food, and make sure he stayed in his room to recuperate.

Jason watched Bridget animatedly talk about Zanchier but could see the look of exhaustion on her features. Caroline obviously noticed as well.

"All right, everyone. I know you're all curious and excited, but she looks beat," Caroline stated. "Come on Kid, let's get you some food, a nice hot shower, and some rest. She can give you all a recap later."

"That sounds heavenly." Bridget sighed. "I must tell Ryan thank you for creating the Portgens and that home button feature. It truly is a lifesaver."

"I couldn't agree more," Simon chimed in from behind her. "God has truly gifted us with a very talented young inventor." He smiled broadly.

Jason watched as Caroline and Seth escorted the young woman inside. He wondered what Dominic could have meant by Bridget having *"enough bad family ties in her life"*? He might mention it to Caroline since she was closer to Bridget than any of the others. Then, perhaps Caroline might inform him. He needed to know if this new development might somehow influence their future missions.

He walked inside as the crowd dispersed to see if he might catch Caroline alone for a minute. He didn't want to let on to anyone else about Bridget's new discovery without her consent.

After grabbing a quick bite to eat, Caroline and Bridget walked up the stairs to the second floor. Bridget went to her room for some clean clothes, as Caroline ran her bath. Jason took the opportunity to speak with her.

"Caroline, can I speak with you privately for a minute?"

"Sure," she said a bit confused. "What's up?"

"Dominic mentioned that Bridget had some sort of shock back on Zanchier. He didn't say what, but that I needed to speak with Bridget about it. I figured since you were close to her, that it'd be best if you asked her about it."

"Certainly. So, Dominic didn't say what it was that was so shocking to her?"

"No, only that she *"had enough bad family ties in her life,"* whatever that means. He seemed to think that privacy was important here."

Caroline looked confused by this. "Sure, I'll see what I can do."

"Thanks, and if you don't mind filling me in, I'd appreciate it. That is, if Bridget is all right with you telling me. Any information could be pertinent to our missions."

As Jason turned to walk away from Caroline, Seth was coming down the hallway from the opposite direction.

Seth watched the strange exchange between Caroline and Jason, gaining his curiosity.

"Seth," Jason nodded as he passed him in the hallway. Seth nodded back in reply.

As he approached Caroline, Bridget stepped from her room headed toward the bathroom.

"What did Jason want?" Seth asked his wife.

"Oh, nothing really. Just wanted me to make sure that Bridget was all right."

"That's it?"

"Yes," Caroline stated, not wanting to say anything just in case Bridget wanted to keep whatever experiences she had to herself.

Bridget looked up at Seth as she approached them. "Did you need something from me, Seth?"

"No, Bridget. Just to tell you that we're glad you're home. My wife here has been going crazy with worry."

Bridget smiled up at them. "Thank you. Well, if you will excuse me, I'm quite a mess. Oz's treehouse sort of has running water, but it isn't hot or even warm, and I'm a bit sore. We've been traveling all morning."

"Yes, excuse me. I don't mean to hold you up." He smiled at her, then turned to Caroline. "I'll talk to you later." He leaned down to kiss her cheek.

Seth left the upper hallway and went downstairs, curious about the exchange between his friend and his wife. It was certainly nothing to worry about, but Seth felt as though he were a bit jealous. Why he didn't know. He fully trusted Caroline, and he had no reason to not trust Jason, but Caroline was a very attractive woman. Jason had even commented on the fact a time or two. Seth shook himself from his thoughts. He was being silly if he thought Jason had a thing for Caroline. Jason was in love with Memnah. He said so himself, but Memnah was a good distance away and he couldn't see her daily like Seth and Caroline could. There he was, analyzing Seth situation again. He was being ridiculous. He shrugged the feeling off and went outside with everyone else to see what their plan was next.

Seth found Simon, along with most of the other leaders and a few of the others, sitting beneath the veranda.

"Hey," Seth said to no one in particular as he approached them. Several of the others greeted him in kind.

"Any plans yet as to where we head to next?" he asked, sitting down on one of the chairs.

Simon answered, "Not yet. I believe the next piece to search for is the Shoes of Peace. I was looking through the *Book of Armor* last night and discovered some ancient maps in the back of the book that said where the pieces were supposed to be found. However, I believe them to be very old indeed. The maps showed the armor pieces that we've already found to be located somewhere else entirely. Not where we found them at all. Whoever wrote these books must have done so a very long time ago. Some of the information is outdated, such as the armor's location."

"So, the separation of the armor took place after these books were written?" Zeke asked.

"I would say so. We have no idea how old these are? I haven't come across any dates yet within the book. The only one to give dates is the *Book of Lineage*. It tells of some Peregrines and Dragoman who lived almost a thousand years ago," Simon stated.

"Really?" Odessa stated excitedly. "I'd like to look at it if I may?"

"Certainly," Simon answered her.

"So would I," Seth chimed in.

"Me too," Nick interjected, as well as some more of the others.

"All right then," Simon said, standing. "I'll get the book and meet you all in the archival library in say, ten minutes?"

"Sounds good to us." Odessa beamed with excitement.

The men all looked at each other and grinned, still surprised by her excitement over most things.

"What?" she asked as they all looked at her in amusement.

"Nothing," Alec stated, as all the men shook their heads.

"I can't help it that I get excited about life." She grinned.

"We just find your excitement, refreshing," Alec replied.

Odessa smiled at him and his ability to always put her at ease about any possible insecurities. Alec truly was a good man. She wasn't likely to find a better one. But was that reason enough for a relationship?

Odessa, Seth, Zaccai, Alec, Nick, and Oz all went inside the library to look over the ancient *Book of Lineage*. The outside was stunningly decorated, and the gilded pages were just as impressive. As they all sat at the large table, jumbled together to get a good look, Simon flipped page after page, reading aloud the names, dates, and status of each recorded person of interest.

Somewhere in the center of the book, something caught Seth's attention. "Wait," he said, as he stared at the portrait of the man who stared back up at him.

"What is it, Seth?" Simon asked.

Seth was quiet for a moment, still unsure that what he was seeing was real.

Caroline happened to walk into the library at that time.

"What are you all looking at?" she asked, approaching the table.

"Seth?" Simon asked again, as he watched Seth's expressions as though he were searching his memories for something.

"Simon, I don't know how this is possible, but the man in this picture strongly resembles what I remember about my father."

"Are you sure?" Simon asked, stunned by this revelation.

"My mother used to keep a photo of him when I was younger. I used to catch her looking at it from time to time. When she died, I never saw the photo again. I don't know if my grandmother hid it from me or if my mother did?"

"Simon," Caroline questioned, "is it possible that Seth's father was a Dragoman or a Peregrine? Do you think that is why he never saw him again?"

"Well, anything is possible at this point. His father was most definitely one of them. Further reading should disclose one of those as truth. The traits which we all possess that have led to this lifestyle were thought to be random by choice. Now I'm not so sure that we were correct in that thinking. Perhaps some of us do have family that ties us to this life? Bridget certainly does. Her father was a Dragoman and now she is something new all-together. I haven't found anything about Keepers in any other archive book. These new, well actually old books, are the first mention of them. Perhaps that is why they were hidden away until they were needed."

"Well, it would certainly explain why he never returned home to us," Seth said, staring at the portrait.

Simon read the name. "Toren, Pascal Degare'. Does that sound familiar, Seth?"

"I remember my mother saying my father's name a few times. And then screaming it when she would have nightmares about his leaving us. His *name was* Toren."

Caroline spoke up, "But what about Seth's last name? Jager?"

"Back in those days, if a man and woman weren't married, then the child was given the mother's maiden name," Simon stated.

"I do believe that Jager was my mother's maiden name. My grandmother had the same last name, and I just never made the connection that they were never married."

"Well, now you know why your father likely left and never returned. Perhaps he couldn't?" Caroline wrapped an arm around Seth and leaned into his embrace as his arms engulfed her.

"It's strange to think that my father actually lived a thousand years before I did. Or was born that far ahead." Seth was still a bit shocked at the revelation.

Nick spoke up next. "I wonder if the rest of us could also have similar ties, like Seth's, listed somewhere in these books?"

They all looked at the massive archival library.

Simon answered, "Well, anything is possible apparently. But to find out, you would all have to know your family history very well. Seth here is just lucky to have recognized his father's image from this portrait. Unless there are others among you that have never met or barely remember your mother or father?" Simon asked curiously, glancing around the table.

Everyone else shook their heads no to Simon's question.

"Well, while you're all talking to the others, try to broach the subject to see if anyone else has a similar past. Perhaps we have answers for them here in the archives."

They read the listing about Seth's father and found out that he was one of the very first Peregrines to ever be chosen for peregrination. He was indeed listed as a Peregrine who studied under a Dragoman named Wrathburn. As they looked through the archive book for a while longer reading up on anyone of interest, they came across the Dragoman once known as Wrathburn. The book didn't reveal very much about their personalities, only their service dates, ages, history, missions, and who they mentored or were mentored by. The book contained about one hundred such listings; much like the Dragoman archives they now kept. The main difference was that this old book had drawn portraits to go with the listing. Along with the listings were mentions of battles, wars, and betrayals, but no other details.

"Hmm…" Simon pondered. "I wonder if any of the other books tell of any details concerning the events mentioned here. It looks like I and the other Dragoman have our work cut out for us."

"Well, I fer one 'ave had enough. We've been sittin' here fer over an hour goin' through this book. I think I'll go get in some exercise. Maybe a bit a sparrin'? Any takers?" Oz stood and stretched his back.

"I'll take you up on it, Oz," Nick answered. "I could do with some movement myself." The two men left the library as several of the others filed out behind them.

Caroline followed Seth out of the room, leaving only Odessa and Simon still searching the book. Caroline was a bookworm also herself, but she was too concerned with Seth and his recent discovery to leave him to himself at the moment.

"Seth, are you all right?"

"Yes. I think so. It certainly clears up a lot of questions about my father abandoning us all those years ago."

"And your certain that Toren Degare' is your father?"

"No doubt. It's shocking to think it's true, but he was definitely my father." Seth sighed. "I think I want to burn off some pent-up energy as well. Are you up to sparring with your husband, Beautiful?" A devilish grin split his lips.

"Sure thing, Handsome. Just try to keep up with me. That is, if you can?" Caroline grinned back with a raise of her eyebrows by way of a challenge.

Seth chuckled loudly, grabbing the attention of several of the others. They watched in interest as Caroline and Seth raced out the door, pulling weapons and starting to spar already. The others decided that this was going to be fun to see and ran outside to watch with several of the others engaging in battles against one another. The sparring lasted the better part of the afternoon until fatigue set in and showers were needed. Afterward, dinner was eaten, Bible study was over, and relaxation time was at hand.

Uriah finally appeared at dinner time but really didn't speak to anyone. He took his food and went somewhere else with it. He didn't make an appearance the rest of the night.

Simon, after clearing it with Seth, brought up the discovery they had found in the new ancient archive books concerning Seth's father.

"You really found out that your father was a Peregrine?" Sean asked.

"Yeah. Much to my surprise," Seth answered.

"Can we see the picture of your father in the book?" Kristen asked.

"I don't see why not. Simon, what do you say?" Seth questioned.

"Certainly. Whoever would like to view the book, come with me. You can wait in the library while I retrieve it." Simon left for the secret hiding place they now used to avoid any more thefts, returning soon to a room full of people.

"Goodness, you're all a curious lot." He grinned teasingly.

Simon opened the book to the page listed as Toren Pascal Degare'. Everyone took turns looking at the image and comparing the looks of the man in the portrait to Seth. Many claimed to see the likenesses between the two of them, but it was Alec who pointed out the similarities between Seth and Jason to the image of the man in the portrait.

"Alec," Jason stated from across the room, "you're out of your mind. Seth and I look nothing alike." He made his way across the room to view the portrait which suddenly had everyone's attention. Those close to it looked at the portrait, then to Jason, then to Seth. As Jason stepped up to view it, he abruptly stopped. His face grew still with a look of astonishment across his features. Jason was speechless.

"Seth," Jason said clearing his throat, "are you certain that the man pictured here is your father?"

"Positive. My mother had a photo of him when I was young."

"I'm not sure what's going on here, but my mother had a polaroid photo of my dad when I was young too." Jason looked sideways at Seth. "This portrait is of the same person that my mother told me was my father. Only, I never met him. He was gone before I was born."

"No way," Seth said, an eery feeling shaking his very core. "Do you mean to tell me that we are actually…brothers?"

"I believe we are, half-brothers at least," Jason said, stunned.

Simon sat in the armchair closest to him, his head reeling from the discovery. Could Seth and Jason truly be half-brothers? Did Toren Pascal Degare' travel throughout time, taking up with women from all over the world and time period? It appeared that he had with at least two such women, both from vastly different eras. And if that were the case, then he either somehow managed to travel into the future, or he was still alive somewhere, because Jason and Seth were separated by more than one-hundred years as far as what time period they were from. The earth's current time period was the year 2018. They weren't able to travel past the current age in which they truly lived. So, if Toren Pascal Degare' was in a book and listed as living and being a Peregrine over one thousand years before, he must have been able to travel into the future, which is an age that they all thought to not have been written as of yet.

"Just as one or two questions get answered, more mysteries are thrown into the mix," Simon mumbled with an exasperated sigh.

I am your servant; give me discernment
that I may understand your statutes.

Psalm 119:125

Chapter 2

Seth and Jason both stood there, shocked by what they had just learned about one another. Neither could believe that they were actually brothers. Bound by a father who was also a Peregrine but who lived a thousand years earlier.

It was beginning to look as though the whole Peregrine gene might actually be something that *was* passed from parent to child. Or this was all really some odd coincidence, or an unusually odd plan orchestrated by God.

Simon didn't believe in coincidences. He believed that everything was planned according to God's will. He looked at the two men whom he had been mentoring.

"I wonder, Seth, if this is the reason that the two of you had the portal connection the first day you arrived? Jason was the one who found you, and you both arrived in the same storm portal from completely different places in time."

Seth shrugged his shoulders as Jason replied.

"It makes sense, Simon. Nothing like that has ever happened before. Perhaps it was God's way of confirming what we just learned?"

"Yes, that very well could be the answer to that puzzle," Simon said thoughtfully.

Seth grinned at Jason. "You know the really funny thing about all of this?"

"What's that?" Jason asked curiously.

"Even though I was born one hundred and thirty-eight years before you, you're older than me." Seth smiled from ear to ear.

Jason smirked at Seth's analysis. "Well, since I'm the older brother, then that means you have to listen to me."

"I'm not so sure about that," Seth teased back.

The two men looked at each other and smiled.

"Well," Jason said, "I think that's enough excitement for me today. I think I'm going to go back outside to relax. Seth, you and Caroline care to join me? I figure we have some catching up to do."

"Sounds good to me, Jason." Seth grinned at him, then grinned down into the loving face of his wife who smiled back.

Many people followed them outside to join in the conversation or to have one of their own.

Kristen decided to seek out Timothy —who had been very quiet and scarce today— to see if he was all right. He had quite a few things lately that hadn't exactly gone his way, and she wanted to make sure that he knew she held no ill will toward him. She may have chosen Sean as a significant other, but she still considered Timothy a friend.

Sean noticed her leaving. "Kristin, where are you going?"

"To find Timothy. I really think we need to talk about a few things."

"I don't think that's such a good idea, Kristin?"

"Sean, I'll be fine. We all still have to work together here. It's not like we'll never see him again. Besides, he hasn't really stepped out of line or anything. I just think we need to clear the air."

"I'd say he knows where you stand. I'm sure he can figure it out on his own. What's there to explain?" Sean said a bit irritably.

"A lot actually," she said defensively. "Not only did I not choose him, but I have replaced him as one of the twelve to fight in the final battle. He has a few reasons to feel resentful toward me, so I just feel like we need to talk things through."

"Fine, but I'm coming with you," Sean stated.

"No, Sean. I don't think that would be a good idea. I can handle Timothy. Besides, I'll make certain we talk where we can be seen by others, not off in private somewhere."

"Fine. But I'm going on record to say that I don't like it." His jaw clenched.

"Duly noted." She smiled and kissed him on the cheek. "I'll come find you a bit later before bed."

Sean watched her go, knowing full well he couldn't stop her. Kristin definitely had a mind of her own and he wouldn't change her for the world. He just didn't trust Timothy Johnson as far as he could throw him.

Kristen found Timothy sitting beneath the porch in one of the chairs next to the wisteria vines that were growing up the side of the house.

"Hey," she said as she slowly approached, "can we talk for a minute?"

"What for?" he said irritably.

"Tim, I think we need to settle a few things that stand between us." She stood still, waiting to see if he would take her up on it.

Timothy looked at her for a couple of seconds and motioned to one of the chairs nearby.

Kristen sat and took a deep breath, trying to think where to start.

"Tim, I just wanted to say that my choosing Sean had nothing to do with you."

"Obviously." He smirked, looking at her.

"And I'm sorry if you got hurt. That was never my intention. If I led you on in any way, I never meant to."

He just looked at her with a questioning brow.

"I mean," she stammered a bit, "I've had feelings for Sean for a little while now. I just wasn't sure what kind of feelings they were until we were in Solomon's Copper Mines. It wasn't until I almost died that I realized how much I cared for him."

"Yay for the two of you," he stated sarcastically.

Kristen took a deep breath, realizing that this probably was futile, like Sean had said. But she was going to finish regardless of what he said or how he reacted.

"Next, about the chosen thing. I had no idea about any of that. If I could give you back your place as one of them, I would. I don't even want to know what is expected of me during this Final Battle. Frankly, it's a bit frightening."

"Well, I suppose neither of us have any control over that either. Apparently, it's God's choice and for whatever reason I don't measure up with him either." He crossed his arms over his chest and stretched his long form out in front of his chair, crossing his feet at the ankles.

"I'm sure it has nothing to do with you personally, Tim. Perhaps God's plans for you are greater than fighting in the Final Battle. After-all, he did call you to this way of life. So, he must see something in you; something greater than any of us could imagine. You did tell me that you were saved, right?"

Tim cracked a small sneer-like smile at her attempts at cheering him up. "Yeah, I did." Tim stood up, "As far as the rest of it, I guess I'll just have to wait and see just what His plans for me are. Now, if you're finished, I think I'll head off to bed." He turned and walked away from her without a word or a backward glance in her direction.

Kristen wasn't sure what she had expected from him. Perhaps a bit more civility, maturity, or understanding? For a man who was thirty-one years of age, he was behaving like a wounded teenager. Maybe Tim never had to grow up? Perhaps all of this was part of his spiritual tests? Either way, Kristen had done her part and apologized for any misgivings. It was getting late into the evening, so she decided to call it a night and headed to bed, first going to find Sean as she had told him she would, saying goodnight to Jason as she passed him by.

Jason nodded a goodnight to Kristin in passing, but instead of heading off to bed, he decided to take this opportunity of being on the safety of the island to chance a visit with Memnah. Simon had given him his blessings, as long as they were at the island and not on a mission. He set his Portgen for 1840 Israel and disappeared into the night for the next several hours.

The next morning, Odessa awoke after having had another dream. Although, she was extremely confused by what she saw. She found Simon sitting at the kitchen table, coffee cup and breakfast plate in front of him.

"Simon, I've had another vision or dream. I'm not sure which because I really didn't sleep well last night." Odessa grabbed a cup of coffee and sat down beside him at the table. "The strange thing about the dream was that it only showed the water surrounding Reader's Island, and portals glowing below the surface, like the kind that Sean described when he was washed overboard the ship while we were in the Mediterranean Sea."

Simon watched her with interest, listening as she described her dream, the wheels of his mind spinning in thought and reflection.

"Odessa, are you sure that was all you saw in your dream?"

"Yes, Simon. There was nothing else given, not even what piece of armor for which we are to look. It only showed the surface of the water and portals glowing beneath it."

"Hmm," Simon mused, "that is odd. When we were here on the island last, when all the kids took a hike up to the mountain peak, Kristin and Sean reported seeing portals located beneath the surface of the waters surrounding the island."

"Really?" Odessa stated in surprise.

"Yes, quite shocking. At the time, I had no idea what to make of the information. We never knew about the portals being there before that day. No one had ever seen them before that. Probably because no one ever took an adventure up to the top of the mountain peak before." Simon's brow furrowed in thought.

"What do you think it means?"

"I believe that one of the pieces that we are searching for may be located somewhere underwater. Or, more importantly, perhaps a city located beneath the water's surface, kind of like how Atlantis has been described throughout history. You know, a thriving, lost, civilization somewhere on the ocean floor." His face lit up animatedly.

"Well that would be quite an adventure!" Odessa's excitement and wonder evident across her facial features. "Do you really believe that one of the pieces could be located beneath the water's surface in some ancient underwater civilization?"

"I do believe so, my dear. God seems to be leading us in that direction as of late. With Sean being washed overboard during that storm and seeing a portal, and Kristin and him also discovering the portals located beneath the surface here at the island, I'm almost certain that's where we're being directed to next. However, until I get further confirmation about this leading, I don't want anyone going near the portals beneath the water's surface. We need to make certain that it's safe, and that it's truly where God is leading us." Simon finished with a warning.

"All right, Simon. As you wish. I suppose we'll just have to wait and see if God gives us more information." Odessa grinned and shrugged.

"Perhaps we shall ask Safra to pray about it and see what God lays upon her in a vision," Simon offered by way of an answer.

Odessa stood to get her a plate of food to go with her coffee, now a little annoyed at Simon. She always felt like her premonitions or visions weren't enough for Simon to accept as truth for what was happening or needed doing. It seemed like he always had to defer to Safra's abilities to make certain that what Odessa was telling him was what they needed to do. It made her feel a bit like he didn't trust her visions or her gift from God. Odessa shrugged off the feeling, grabbed a plate of food, and returned with her plate to her seat beside Simon. They chatted through breakfast as others appeared and joined them.

After breakfast, the Peregrines decided to take to the grounds to practice their God-given skills and their battle strategies.

Bridget, Dominic, and Wade all went to the gun range to practice shooting, led by Alec and Zaccai. Zaccai decided that they needed practice with a bow as well, not just a gun, just in case they ran out of bullets or only had a bow.

Seth, Caroline, Jason, Oz, Bridget, and several of the others decided to find Simon after breakfast to discuss missions, finding him in the stables.

"Simon," Oz yelled to catch the man's attention.

"Yes, Oz? Do you need something?"

"Me an' some a' the others were jus' wonderin' if ya had any idea where we might be goin' to next."

"Well, Odessa had another dream last night, but it was of the underwater portals located around the island here. I'm not certain what this development means, so I ask you all not to say anything to anyone else about it just yet. I don't want people trying to swim out to the portals to see where they go. The Portgens may not work underwater and going through a portal that we aren't certain as to where it goes may not be safe. Plus, if the portal closes, it isn't like a storm will likely appear to bring anyone home."

"Well, I can see that bein' dang'rous. Ya hear that?" Oz turned to everyone with him. "Yer not ta tell another soul 'bout this yet. An' if any a' ya' take ta' the water ta try anythin' stupid, you'll deal with me." Oz stared them all down.

Most everyone there simply smiled at the large, burly man's words. They knew he would make good on the threat, but they also knew him to be a big softy. None of them planned on doing anything stupid anyway. Exploring underwater portals without proper scuba equipment was not something any of them wanted to try anyhow.

Simon commented again, "I will check with Ryan to see if there is a way to make the Portgens water-proof. While we are waiting to hear from him on that, several of you can go into a city and see about getting some scuba equipment. Just purchase the needed supplies from a store. Just four sets for now. We will fit everyone else later if we see that we need them."

Jason stepped up. "Sure thing Simon. Me, Seth, Zeke, and Oz will take care of that." The others all nodded their agreement with Jason's decision.

"All right then. Nothing further about this until I speak with Safra about praying for guidance. Not even with the scuba gear. I just want to have it on hand if we decide to use it."

Simon looked at the group before him, realizing there was something that needed to be done. The artifacts that they had gathered over the last six months or so were still sitting in his private hidden artifacts room back at his safe house at Barriers Edge at Garganthera. Simon realized that he needed to go back to his home and bring those artifacts to Reader's Island. He had an urging that they may need them very soon.

"Seth, Jason, how would you boys like to take a trip back home to my safe house?"

"Sure. I'm up for a trip back home," Jason replied.

Seth grinned. "Sure thing, Simon, I really miss your place. It's no Reader's Island, but it's still one of the only homes that I've ever really had."

"Good!" Simon smiled. "I may need your help. We need to go back and gather the artifacts that are in my hidden room."

"Why do we need the artifacts, Simon," Seth asked.

"I feel God urging me to bring some of the pieces here. Anyone else care to join us?" he enquired of those standing around him.

"Sure," Caroline said. "I would love to see the place where Seth first peregrinated."

"All right then," Simon said, "someone grab a Portgen and let's go."

The group of five, which included Simon, Seth, Jason, Caroline, and Bridget, all walked through the portal to Garganthera and Simon's safe house at Barriers Edge. Bridget and Caroline were overtaken by the sights before them. They had seen large things in Zanchier, but nothing like the people in Garganthera. Everything there was large, the buildings, the people, the carts, the horses, the cows, everything was huge. And the barrier that surrounded and separated the dimensions was different than that on Reader's Island. They had never seen the barrier like this before. Simon noticed the looks on their faces and he figured it had to do with what they were seeing, so he decided to explain.

"Different looking isn't it?"

Bridget spoke next as if from a dream. "I think I vaguely remember something like this from my childhood."

"You just might, Bridget. You were about the age of three when you first passed through a portal. I'm certain your father crossed the barrier with you many times."

Caroline, unable to take their eyes from the scene replied, "This is so much different from Reader's Island."

"Yes, at most of the safe houses Barriers Edge only separates the realms, or dimensions in time. You can only get to Garganthera through the barrier here. The island offers a multitude of selections. The other Dragoman homes are much like my own here. They also reside at the edge of the barrier in whatever realm or time period they chose. You know, it never dawned on me that the two of you had never seen the barrier like this. Other than Reader's Island, the two of you have only ever been in the first dimension. Isn't that correct?"

"Yes, I suppose so," Caroline answered. "Unless of course, Zanchier is in a separate and unknown dimension?"

"My dear, we know so little about that place that we aren't even certain where it resides amongst the planes and dimensions. It is something that I am hoping to remedy soon enough. It keeps popping up in our lives, so there must be something of importance still there of which we have need."

Simon suddenly stopped in front of his home. Something was very wrong here. Simon's eyes raked over the dwelling he had called home for the last thirty years. The front door had been kicked in and was splintered and barely holding to its hinges. They all pulled their weapons and slowly approached the house, trying to walk through the mess as quietly as possible.

The front room was a complete wreck. The maps, charts and papers Simon had attached to the walls were all strewn across the floors and tabletops.

"It appears, Simon, that whoever did this was searching for something," Jason said as he looked about the room.

"Not someone, Jason. I do believe the demons have been in my home. And if they've been here brazenly searching, then they must know that we are close to finding whatever it is we need to begin the Final Battle."

Simon suddenly started realizing that they were probably here for the artifacts that he had hidden. He went through another demolished door that led into his living area. The furniture was shredded, stuffing lay everywhere, and the books were all strewn about as bookcases had been knocked over. All of Simon's belongings were destroyed.

The large beautifully carved oak doors that led into the wardrobe room were splintered and tattered, the beautifully carved trees almost unrecognizable from the beating that they took. As they walked into the wardrobe room everything was strewn about laying everywhere. It was utter chaos. Most things were unrecognizable, and the beautiful tapestry curtains that he had hanging in the arched inset walls on the edges of the room had been ripped from their places and thrown along the floor.

"At least they didn't find the hidden artifacts room," Simon stated gratefully as he walked over to the wall, removed the stone, and pulled the handle allowing the door to pop open inward. As they walked through the door, the lights beyond automatically came on.

Caroline and Bridget were amazed by what they saw inside the large room. Caroline had been to museums and seen many collections in her day, but never had she seen a collection like what Simon had. The room was very large, and except for computer space and cleaning stations in the middle of the room, almost every inch of wall or floor held an artifact.

Seth was shocked at the utter and complete destruction of Simon's beautiful home. It angered him to think that anyone could do such a thing. But then again, they weren't dealing with human beings, this was the work of demons bent on stopping them at all costs.

" Simon," Seth said, "why would they do this to your home? What is it that they could be searching for; if that was what they were doing?"

"Well, Seth, surely it was the artifacts. Remember when I told you that some of these artifacts would be needed somehow for the final battle, or leading up to it?"

"Yes, I recall you saying that."

"They would stop at nothing to stop us from winning that battle. Satan desires that no one be saved. He seeks to ravage the earth and all that lives within. I believe that if we manage to win the Final Battle, then his reign of the earth and all other realms will be much lessened. Whatever evil plagues us now, will be significantly reduced."

Bridget spoke next. "Simon, what exactly in this room do you think it was that they were after? And, how do you know how to use these things, or that they'll even work?"

"Well, Bridget, since we found the key that was stolen that opened the last book, I found some passages that relate to instructions on what to do concerning the Final Battle. Within those instructions it not only tells us *how* to use certain artifacts that we've been collecting over the years, but it also gives detailed instructions about it."

"What key are you speaking of, and who stole it?" Caroline asked curiously.

Oh my, Simon thought, *me and my big mouth. I had forgotten that not everyone knew about that key. I hope I have not opened a can of worms here.*

"Well, Caroline, when Seth returned from Zanchier with the odd creature sting on his arm, they also returned with the key that opened the last locked book. Unfortunately, it went missing but was recovered recently."

"How could something like that just go missing? Did someone take it for some reason?" she asked, feeling like Simon was leaving out some important details.

"Well, since neither of you are a suspect, I suppose we can tell you. There is a thief and a betrayer amongst us. We don't know who it is, or what their purpose is, only that they stole the key so that we could not open the last book."

"And you've known this ever since that night?" Caroline asked, a little irritated about not knowing.

"Yes. However, we didn't want to alarm anyone and cause distrust within the group. The bonds created on Reader's Island several months back, were, and still are, very important for the search. We did not want to destroy that camaraderie by having everyone mistrust everyone else. That is why we only told a handful of people. Only the group leaders knew about it. They and they alone are to continue searching for the thief. Do you both understand? You cannot tell another soul about this. Not even after the betrayer is found. I don't want everyone going around thinking they were all suspects and that they aren't trusted. It is meant to look like a coincidence when the culprit, or culprits, are captured."

"We understand Simon," Caroline said, as she and Bridget looked at each other, both shaking their heads in reply. Although Caroline had to wonder if her husband knew all of this. She knew that his leadership position may have forbidden him telling her, but as his wife she felt somewhat cheated that he knew of something like this but did not bother to inform her. Caroline didn't like secrets, and Seth had been keeping one from her almost since the time they were reunited.

Bridget and Caroline walked around the artifacts room glancing at the beautiful things that Simon had collected over the years. They noticed that he was taking very few things with him, placing them all in duffel bags and handing them off to Seth and Jason.

"Simon, how do you know which artifacts to take?" Bridget asked curiously.

"One of the books is, as I said, like an instruction manual. It has shown me what items we would need so that is all I am taking for now. I shall seal the room and conceal my home better so that the demons may not find it again. If we need anything else, we'll come back for it later."

"What exactly is it that you are taking?" Caroline asked curiously.

"The Scroll of Rubric was mentioned to work like an instruction manual. The Goddelikheid Crucible is meant to be used for refining of some precious metals we must still locate, and the Staff of Moses, well, it really didn't say how we are to use it, only that we would need it."

"The actual Staff of Moses?" Caroline asked, surprised. "I can't begin to imagine how that's going to be used."

"Indeed," Simon said, his surprise matching Caroline's.

Simon glanced around the room, sadness lining his features at the thought of leaving the rest of his beloved collection behind.

"Perhaps when the Final Battle is over, I can come back and collect all of these things for posterity. Our future generations need to know of our past. Especially with the collision of all the world's once the battle is won and the veil between worlds falls, and all is exposed for everyone to see."

As they left the artifacts room, Simon sealed the door once more, casting a protection spell over the entrance so that it may not be discovered. Once that was finished, and they were leaving his home, even in the horrible state that it was in, he cast another protection spell vowing to one day return and set his household to rights.

They opened the portal and walked through it back onto Reader's Island. Simon took the artifacts into the archive library to show Nuncio and the other Dragoman there. He explained that they were to be used somehow either in the final battle or leading up to it, and that they must protect them. All the Dragoman agreed that they would place the artifacts in the same area where the books were being held for safekeeping.

Simon filled the other Dragoman in on the destruction of his home in an apparent attempt to locate the artifact pieces and destroy them. With this knowledge, the other Dragoman decided to return to their own Barriers Edge homes to see if the same had been done to their safe houses.

Vashti's and Malachai's homes had been destroyed as well. The artifacts that they had collected from past missions, destroyed by the demons.

At each dwelling, they all stood and mourned the loss of all the work, the loss of lives, and the history, soon to be forgotten by future generations.

Fortunately, Prisca's home had yet to be discovered by the demons. Simon placed a protection spell over the dwelling in hopes to conceal it from a possible future attack.

"I'm not certain how long this spell will last, but it will afford some protection for a time."

"Some is better than none, Simon." Prisca looked worriedly at her home.

"Are there any artifacts here that need to be brought to the island?"

With one last look at her home, Prisca answered, "None that are important to the Final Battle."

Simon's mind was a whirlwind of thoughts as they walked back through the portal onto Reader's Island. They would not need to return to their homes again unless God chose to send them there. With the armor pieces being collected, the Final Battle was soon to be at hand. The demons were growing more agitated and causing more problems and destruction than ever before, and they now moved in larger groups.

They would all have to be even more careful than before while traveling in any of the dimensions. The demons no longer feared stepping through to the fourth. The only truly safe place for them now was Reader's Island.

"This is what the Sovereign LORD says: When I make you a desolate city, like cities no longer inhabited, and when I bring the **ocean** depths over you and its vast waters cover you,

Ezekiel 26:19

Chapter 3

Somewhere in the Sea of Crete

Annabelle awoke, slightly disoriented from the large hurricane that had hit the city of Hawaii's coastline just hours before and the orphanage where she had lived most of her life.

Annabelle was all of ten years of age and had lived in the orphanage since she was three years old. Her parents had perished during a storm off the coast of Hawaii one day while out fishing. She had stayed with a neighbor and friend while they went to work. Her father normally had friends and co-workers who helped him with the fishing, but that day, no one else was available so her mother had gone to lend a hand. Annabelle never saw either of them again. The neighbors couldn't take her in permanently and she had no other living relatives who were in any shape to take in a toddler.

Annabelle sat up and looked around at the odd city and the strange way in which the people here dressed. She certainly was no longer in Hawaii. The storm must have carried her off, but to where? It looked as though she had been deposited on a dock by the water, thrown down into a large coil of ropes and nets.

"Hello there."

She heard the craggy voice and a strange accent from somewhere behind her say. She sat up straighter, hoping to find the owner of the voice. As she turned back toward the water's edge, she saw an older man sitting upon one of the pilings at the dock's edge, leaning upon a cane, watching her.

"Are you speaking to me?" she answered back.

"Well of course I'm speaking to you. Do you see anyone else nearby? Perhaps you think I'm speaking to the fishes?" the old man asked her.

"I suppose not." She clumsily stood amongst the large ropes. "Do you know where I am?"

"Well, where are you from?"

"Hawaii, and I'm pretty sure that I'm no longer in Hawaii." She looked around her at the odd but beautiful city.

"You would be correct. You definitely are not in Hawaii." He chuckled lowly.

She turned to look at him. "Should I be afraid of you? I'm normally not afraid of people, but at the orphanage they taught us to beware of strangers."

The man laughed heartily at her honesty.

"No, there's no need to fear me. God sent me to get you. Do you believe in God?"

"Oh yes sir, very much. I pray to him each night to take me from the orphanage and find me a family."

"Well, either he answered your prayers, or he has a much bigger plan for you than either of us can imagine, little one." The man smiled in her direction. "What is your name, girl?"

"Annabelle."

"Just Annabelle?" he asked her with raised eyebrows.

She smiled at him. "Annabelle Celeste Ellis is my full name."

"Well, Annabelle Celeste Ellis, my name is Dekker Smit Vandenberg, and it is a pleasure to meet you."

Annabelle smiled slightly and bowed a bit to the man. "Nice to meet you as well, sir."

"How old are you, Annabelle?"

"I'm ten years old, Dekker, sir."

"Goodness, you're awfully young. Well," Dekker said, standing, "Why don't you just follow me, Annabelle, and we'll get you cleaned up and some food in your belly, hmm?"

"Yes sir. Since God sent you, I'm sure I'll be just fine with you." She beamed at him, sensing that something was very different about him. When she looked at him and he at her, it was as though he didn't really see her.

"Mr. Vandenberg, sir?"

"Yes, Anabelle?" He smiled at her politeness.

"Are you blind?"

"Yes, somewhat. I am mostly blind. I do see some shapes and colors, but my sight is very limited. And you can just call me Dekker."

"Okay, Mr. Dekker." She grinned at him and took his left hand with her right.

Dekker was a bit taken back by such a trusting gesture. He smiled down at her and squeezed her right hand ever so slightly as he led her through the streets of the city to his small hovel at the edge, not too far from where God had sent him to find her.

Lord, Dekker thought, *I sure don't know what your plans are for one so young, but I know that your ways are not my ways. And I sure don't know why you brought her here to me. But I'll do as you ask, just help me lead and guide this little lady how you want me to.*

Annabelle continued to search the strange city for any signs as to where she might be.

"Mr. Dekker, where are we?"

"We are in an ancient Greek city known as Akrotiri."

"How is that possible? Greece is so very far from Hawaii, isn't it?"

"Yes, it is. But with God, all things are possible."

"So, God really brought me here?"

"Oh yes, Annabelle, he did. And as I said before, he has great plans for your future. We'll discuss it further once we get to my home." Dekker reassured her.

They walked just a few blocks further to a small, second story apartment tucked within the side of a building made with large, whitish-colored stones. There were many such buildings and they were tightly placed near each other. It appeared that there were about six windows in each level that she could see, and since Dekker's apartment had two windows on one side and two on the other, she assumed that the other ones each had four as well. Probably making about eight apartments in each building.

Dekker noticed that she was suddenly quiet, probably taking everything in.

"The people here dress strangely." She observed, looking out one of the windows.

"That is because we are in another world, Annabelle." Dekker sat down at the table, placing a glass of cool water and some bread, cheese, and fruit on the table for her.

"Really?" She turned to look at him, watching him sit at the table and walked over to join him. "Thank you for the food."

"You are welcome."

They ate in peace for just a bit before resuming their conversation.

"What did you mean when you said that we are in another world?" she asked between the nibbles of food she now took.

"Well, Annabelle, as I said before, God has chosen you for something very special. He brought you from your homeland in Hawaii to this place here, Akrotiri. Just as he brought me from my homeland, the Netherland Antilles, many years ago."

"But why did he bring us here?"

"I believe it is to find something that is very important to him, and then give that item to someone else."

"What are we to find, and whom are we to give it to?"

"I believe we are looking for some ancient armor pieces. I believe that I have found them, but they will not be easy to acquire."

"Who do we give them to once we get them?"

"That I'm unclear about. God will reveal the person or persons when the time comes. It is our job, however, to figure out a way to acquire those pieces. I believe that is why God brought us both here."

"How long have you been here, Mr. Dekker?"

"Almost five years. My lack of sight makes it a bit harder for me to do certain things, but it also affords some other benefits as well.

My other senses, and my walk with God, are much better than when I could see well with my eyes."

"Did you come here like I did? Through a storm?"

"Yes, I did. But unlike you, I was very sick for the first three or four days. One of the kind villagers here found me and tended to me until I got well."

"Were they brought here for the mission too?"

"No. She is from Akrotiri. Her name is Heba."

"That's a pretty name."

Dekker smiled at the girl. "Yes, it is. Much like Annabelle."

Annabelle smiled at Dekker. "Thank you."

Dekker could hear the smile in her voice. "Now, let's clean up the dishes and go for a walk. I need to show you around Akrotiri and maybe even show you where to find the pieces of armor. But remember, this is a secret mission that only the two of us can know about. Don't speak to anyone else about it unless I tell you it is all right to do so."

"Yes sir." Annabelle smiled, excited to be involved in a secret mission for God. The orphanage had been an okay place to live, but life there was very boring. They had so many children and not enough staff that they tried to keep order constantly, so playtime was nearly nonexistent. And even though she was surrounded by other children, it was hard to make friends. As soon as you got close to someone, they left for placement in a temporary home or were adopted.

This felt like a very fun game, even though she knew it wasn't one. Annabelle was very happy to be here, and she hoped that God wouldn't change his mind and send her back to the orphanage, however far away that may be, after his plans for her were finished.

"This place is odd looking," she stated curiously, looking around at the strange buildings, symbols, and clothing that the people wore.

"Well, Annabelle, we *are* in an ancient city."

"Ancient? Is that why everyone's clothing looks so strange?"

"Yes, I believe so. I remember learning about a city long ago that was buried beneath a volcano, after which, a Tsunami hit the coast where it had been located. I believe that this city, Akrotiri, is that very same city."

"How is that possible? Wouldn't the volcano's eruption have destroyed the city?"

"Normally yes. But for whatever reason this city was spared. It is, however, not in the same place in which it began. I believe that it is now in a different location. Somewhere beneath the surface of the earth."

Annabelle's eyes grew round with surprise. "That sounds awfully strange. I can't see how it's possible."

"Yes, it does. But take a look up. Do you see the sky?"

Annabelle's facial expression changed to confusion as she looked up and saw only a mist far above them. "No, I don't see the sky. I don't see anything but fog."

"That is because we are somehow living underground. The entire city, except for a few of the highest areas that are now a jumble of ruins, was transported here."

"Well, why am I here? I didn't live in Akrotiri. And, neither did you," she asked, still confused.

"God brought us here to find the pieces of armor I told you about."

"What would He need me for? I don't have any skills. I am only an orphan, and just ten years old," she stated plainly and honestly.

"You are far more than that, Annabelle. If God called you here, then he needs you for something very important. You may have been an orphan back in Hawaii, but you are also a child of God."

Annabelle grinned up at Dekker, his words brought comfort to her. She had never thought of herself as belonging to God. As being his child, or anyone's for that matter. She felt very important indeed.

Annabelle's expression became confused again. "Mr. Dekker, how did God bring me here?"

"Well, was there some type of large storm where you lived right before you woke up here?"

"Yes. A hurricane hit the island and the orphanage where I lived."

"Then that, dear one, is how you came here. I'm not sure how it works, but God uses intense storms apparently to move people and places," he said, motioning around them, "to wherever he chooses."

"So, God put this city underground?"

"Well, I don't know about all that. Let's just say that mother nature may have moved this city, but God provided a way for its people to survive the imminent destruction of their civilization. To hear the locals tell of the history and legends is all very interesting." He smiled down at her.

"I would like to hear them," she replied, smiling back.

"Then we shall go to Heba and have her tell you all about it. She speaks Greek so I will have to translate for you."

"You can speak Greek?"

"Oh yes, I had to learn out of necessity."

They walked the city and Annabelle asked questions about where they were and what she saw as Dckkcr tried to describe the city, the people, and their strange customs to her.

She saw large stonc columns that seemed to reach all the way up into the misty air on the front and sides of most of the larger buildings in the city. The people all wore long, flowing, gowns of colorful fabrics with tasseled ropes at the shoulders and waist ties. Sandals adorned most of the people's feet. As they walked, she saw men on horseback and in chariots with thin, tight-fitting shirts of white, skirts of pleated split leather pieces, shaped liked neck-ties which hung from a thick leather waistband. Across their shoulders, flowing red material tied on the right side, and the upper bicep of each man was ringed with a tasseled band that matched their skirts. Their feet were shod in an armored-type shoe, and their heads all covered in an interesting looking helmet with wings near the back of the skull on both sides.

Annabelle watched as the men trained in combat. There were several men, all who looked to be in charge, which wore similar outfits, but had slight differences. The helmets and the shoes were slightly different than most of the other men.

"Why do those men's uniforms look a little different?" she asked, pointing to them.

"I can't see what you're asking on, Annabelle, but I believe I know of what you're speaking. There are a group of elite warriors that lead the rest of Akrotiri's army. Within these elite, are twelve that are considered the strongest, fastest, and best at fighting. These twelve men are the ones who now wear the armor pieces that we must acquire. "

"How are we ever going to do that?" she asked in surprise.

"That, I'm unsure about. We will have to pray and see if God will supply us a solution as to how to accomplish that task."

"If he brought us here to do it, then surely he will let us know how when the time comes."

Dekker looked down at the blurry image of the young girl. Her faith and trusting innocence gave him a bit of shame.

"You are absolutely correct, Annabelle. I forgot that for a bit. Thank you for the reminder. God shall supply all of our needs."

They continued their walk around some of the city with Annabelle exclaiming about all the marble statues, fountains, colors, and architecture of the place. They soon came to Heba's home where Dekker introduced Annabelle, explaining that she was brought by their God to Akrotiri as well. They all sat down as Heba began to tell Annabelle the ancient story of how Akrotiri had fallen beneath the water into the bottom of the ocean.

As Heba spoke, Annabelle sat glued to her seat as she watched the woman's facial expressions change with the story. She listened closely to Dekker translate so she wouldn't miss a thing.

"This story has been told by the elders of the city for many years. My grandfather told it to me and now I tell it to you." Heba smiled. "Long ago, Akrotiri was a beautiful, ancient, thriving city which dwelt on the coast of Crete. It's leaders and people flourished for many years. We were a people who honored the gods and kept the ways, culture, and rituals of our ancestors and followed the ancient ways. Years came and went, and as Akrotiri grew and prospered, so did its people. Many years passed with the people growing vain and selfish, no longer giving the gods the respect they commanded. The people became a greedy race which turned from the worship of our gods. This went on for many years without repentance. Until one day a prophet came to tell our people that they must turn from their wicked ways or they would all suffer. The people ignored the prophet for a while until his constant badgering of them made them resentful and irritable and they killed him. Soon after the prophet's death, the sleeping mountain began to rumble, and smoke began to bellow from its top. The emperor at the time said that the people had angered the gods of Olympus and that they were punishing our people for their evil deeds. The gods opened the mouth of the sleeping volcano and it let loose its rage upon the city. But, in the wake of the rumbling of the mountain, at the same time as the molten rock spewed forth from the mountain, the god of the sea saw the fear and trembling of the Akrotirians and heard their cries of remorse and pleadings of forgiveness. The sea god had compassion on our people and brought forth a wave to save our people. The water and lava collided as the top level of the city was buried beneath the hot rock. The bottom levels of the city fell and sank into the ocean, surrounded by some sort of magical shield which protected our people and the rest of our city. The god of the sea pushed our city into a special hole at the bottom of the Mediterranean Sea, where our city now sits. We were saved from death but are destined to live alone here in this place as a punishment for our forgetfulness of the gods."

"Where is here, Heba?" Annabelle asked.

"Well, many men over the years have explored the area around where our city sits. The reports all say that it is a large cavern with a dry pocket inside the very mountain and volcano that cast us into the sea. We now live in solitude at the bottom of the volcano. Many men have ventured out through many different paths to find a way back to the surface above, but few have returned. We are unsure as to whether the others died on their journey, or if they found a way out and left the rest of us here to perish."

"What do you mean perish? Your city seems very much alive and well."

"Our city is alive, and people continue to live, but we live a half-life down here. The lack of sunshine makes it hard to grow crops. We have light of some sort that comes from somewhere above, but our people are unable to find the source. We can only assume that perhaps it is the underside of the lava that casts the light. We live in fear that one day the volcano may spew again, and perhaps this time, finish the job it was meant to do a thousand years ago."

"That seems awfully scary," Annabelle said. "I don't know about your gods, but my God can do anything. Perhaps if your people were to ask him, he would help."

"Perhaps, little one." Heba smiled with a small chuckle. "Perhaps your God was the one the prophet spoke of so many years ago. The people rejected him because he spoke of a one true God. When he called our gods false, the people took up arms against him."

"Have there ever been others here visiting?" Annabelle asked her.

"We have never had any visitors to our city before you and Dekker." Heba fondly looked at the man.

Annabelle noticed the woman's look of longing as she smiled at Dekker. *Heba must like Mr. Dekker,* Annabelle thought.

"Annabelle, Heba wants to know if you would like something to drink?"

"Yes, thank you." .

"Thank you for the story, Heba," Dekker spoke in Greek.

"You are most welcome, Dekker. Anytime you need anything, you only need ask it," Heba stated back, a look of sincerity in her eyes. But Dekker could not see the woman's face well enough to see the feelings written there. But Annabelle certainly could. Heba turned to get Annabelle and Dekker some water, then asked them to stay for dinner. They accepted her invitation and spent the evening chatting and getting to know one another better.

Annabelle decided that once they left Heba's home, she would tell Dekker of the woman's obvious feelings for him. But for now, while they were here, she would watch and observe her surroundings, and try to learn some of the language that Heba and Dekker tried to teach her.

Annabelle was truly happy for the first time in a very long time. This adventure she was now on, in this beautiful underwater city, with the very nice man Dekker Smit Vandenberg and the Akrotirian woman named Heba, was far beyond anything she could have ever asked of God. She would do her very best at whatever task that God had for her.

In Him we were also chosen, having been predestined
according to the plan of Him who works out everything in
conformity with the purpose of His will.

Ephesians 1:11

Chapter 4

Reader's Island, Present Day

Shortly after returning from the safe houses, Jason, Seth, Oz, and Zeke, all left for a modern city somewhere in the first dimension to purchase the scuba gear that Simon requested them to obtain.

They stepped onto the 2017 Bahamas coastline in late summer, into an area the current maps showed as wooded. The storms due to hit in the near future would destroy many of the islands, and they needed to make sure they could obtain the necessary equipment Simon requested.

The islands weren't large, so walking to the nearest coastal town to get the equipment wouldn't take them long from where they entered from the portal.

As the men got closer to the beachside cities and resort areas, the amount of people they encountered grew larger. Women in scantily clad swimsuits milled about the shoreline and the sidewalks of the tourist filled shops.

The men couldn't help but notice the excessive show of skin that literally bombarded them from every direction. Not to mention the smiles and looks they themselves were getting from those very same women.

Zeke turned and smiled as he watched a woman walk by as she turned and eyed him in appreciation as well. They smiled at each other just before Zeke felt a slap against his left arm, snapping his attention back to the task at hand.

Zeke turned to see Seth looking at him with amusement. Zeke smiled with a shrug of his shoulders.

"What?" he asked with a big grin. "I'm not attached to anyone."

"Right…" Jason dragged out. "What about Zaccai?"

Zeke's voice grew more serious. "What about her?"

The men all smiled at each other over Zeke's sudden nervousness.

"We all know that you and Zaccai are, shall we say, forming an attachment?" Seth said, using his own words against him.

"Is it that obvious, Mates?" Zeke asked.

"Yea' it is. And lookin' at that there, will cer'ainly lead ya' inta a world a' trouble, Mate," Oz stated matter of factly, gesturing over his shoulder with his thumb.

"Looking never hurt anybody. Besides, I may like Zaccai, but we aren't officially in a relationship, and I ain't dead yet." Zeke smiled at the men.

"True," Oz replied. "but if Zaccai sees ya' lookin' at another woman like that, you can bet yer' buddin' relationship will be cut off real short."

"Yeah, you're probably right, Oz. Boys, I suggest we get that equipment and get out of here real quick," Zeke said, as another woman walked past and caught his eye. He shook his head in appreciation as Jason, grinning at Zeke's obvious enjoyment, pushed him into a nearby shop's interior; Jason leaning back to take another look himself.

The men were able to purchase the needed equipment, then find an abandoned, storm-ravaged, building from a previous storm years earlier, and opened a portal to Reader's Island.

They took the scuba gear to a supply room located within the rear of the mansion, then went in search of Simon and the other Dragoman. They found them in the usual place, the archive library, looking through the ancient archive books for guidance.

"Hello, boys. You're all back quickly," Simon stated, stopping what he was doing to speak to the men.

"The Portgens make quick work of time-travel," Jason stated.

Simon smiled at them over the rim of his glasses.

Oz questioned Simon. "Any more progress with these here ancient books?"

"A little, yes. We think we've discovered that the undecipherable *Book of the Keepers* may have been written in an ancient Greek language of some sort."

"How in the world did ya' fig're that one out?"

"A little help from Merlin, and I had Ryan run a search for ancient civilizations that disappeared suddenly throughout history, like with a natural disaster. He found several as a matter of fact. But one in particular stand's out from the rest. However, because there weren't a lot of records kept back in those days, it is hard to determine if the language is the same."

"How ya' gonna' find out?"

"I'm not sure. We're still working on it. Ryan can find some amazing things with his technological abilities. Let's just hope he can find the correct language we need."

Jason changed the subject. "When do we start exploring the portals beneath the waterline here around the island?"

Seth added, "I have to admit, I'm really curious to know where something like that might lead."

Simon looked at him. "Yes, so am I. However, I'm a bit fearful of them as well. For one, we aren't certain that they are always open. According to what Kristin and Sean saw when they were up on the summit of the mountain, there are about ten in all surrounding the island. They were just glowing areas beneath the surface. We really aren't even certain they are portals. Portals are created when storms are present. These were seen at night. We've never seen them during daylight hours."

"Sounds more like the passable safe windows of Barriers Edge than storm portals. Like the ones at Garganthera," Seth stated.

Simon had an *aha* moment. "You are absolutely correct, Seth," he said excitedly, "I believe that is exactly what they are. Perhaps we need to investigate this further before we venture out into the water? It would make perfect sense as to why they are there at the bottom edge of the barrier. But first, we need to see if Ryan can make the Portgens waterproof. I don't want anyone getting lost below the surface of the water. That is unless any of you are hiding a set of gills?" he finished teasingly.

They all grinned at his humor.

Jason said, "Isn't that what the scuba gear is for?"

"Yes, but we don't know what or where you'll end up on the other side of the window," Simon reminded him. "So caution is of the utmost importance."

Malachai spoke up, "Perhaps we should take another night expedition up to the mountain's peak and check this out for ourselves?"

"That may be a good idea, Malachai," Simon stated. "We need to chart where these portals are on a map of the island. It may also help us to determine where they could lead to, based on their location, direction, and longitude and latitude placements. We can have Ryan run cross searches for any cities that may have disappeared that are near those coordinates and direction."

"Sounds like a plan," Malachai smiled. "Looks like we are going camping up top of the mountain. Who wants to join us?"

Vashti perked up at the sound of Malachai's excited voice. "Count me in. It's been years since I've gone camping and not had to worry about mission minded things. Well, except for marking a few spots on a map that is."

"Caroline and I will go too," Seth volunteered.

"Sounds like fun," Zeke stated.

"Not me. I'm not climbin' the side a no moun'ain unless I have to. 'Sides, I had my fill a' moun'ains back on Zanchier."

Simon and the others chuckled at Oz's exclamation.

"You'll need to see if Kristen or Sean will go along. They can show you where they were when they saw the areas in question," Simon stated.

"I'm sure that won't be a problem. I remember hearing Kristen talk about how she loves that sort of thing," Seth said.

"Yeah," Zeke smiled. "And wherever Kristen goes, I'm certain young Doran will follow."

The others all laughed at Zeke's statement. Jason even cracked a small smile until his thoughts returned to Memnah. All the new couples forming around him and fate had thrown him the most difficult kind to have. Being in love with a woman who could never join him in his life here. They were separated by time, barriers, wars, demons, and destiny. It was a very hard place to be but giving up on their relationship was not something Jason dared to entertain. After all, God was the one who brought her into his life, didn't He? Or was this one of his spiritual tests? Was he supposed to give Memnah up? They could never actually build a life together, could they? Perhaps this was something he would have to strongly pray about.

As everyone separated and went about preparing for the excursion up the mountainside, they all yelled to whoever they passed along the way asking if they wanted to tag along. Kristin and Sean agreed to go and be the guides, and several of the others agreed to go as well, stating they had never seen that part of the island and were very curious. They decided to leave that very afternoon so they could see the barrier's portals during the night and chart the locations on the map.

The company included Malachai, Vashti, Seth, Caroline, Zeke, Zaccai, Kristin, Sean, Alec, Odessa, Nick, Nadia, Gabriele , Dominic, Wade, and Bridget. Jason agreed to tag along, just in case anyone needed medical attention. Besides, sitting around here just made his mind wander and he needed to keep busy. Jason asked Shannon, the head housekeeper, to pack some food for them to take with them as well as any other necessary supplies. As Shannon left to take care of the request, Simon approached from behind.

"Jason, perhaps this little excursion could shine some light into who the betrayer might be as well." Simon's hushed tones echoed between them as he looked around to make certain no one could hear them.

Jason looked around as well. "I'll see what I can do about that, Simon. But none of the people coming on this trip are real suspects. I still have my doubts about Sofia. Too many coincidences happen around her. It just seems strange to me."

"Yes, I see your point," Simon said thoughtfully. "Perhaps I need to have this conversation with Oz since he has spent more time with her than anyone else. I truly don't believe it is her, but I was also wrong about Hiram before. Perhaps he can get somewhere with those who are staying here."

"Good luck with that," Jason said as he and Simon parted ways.

Jason went to gather his backpack and bedroll, taking his Portgen and laying it on his bedside table. He looked at the device, reluctant to let it go.

They really don't need me on this hike. I could take this time to go and see Memnah instead. He shook his head to clear his thoughts. "I can't keep going back every time I think I have a few hours to spare," he said audibly. Every time he went back it became harder and harder to leave her. He was only making things worse for himself. His jaw tightened in determination as he shoved the Portgen in the side-table drawer, grabbed his pack and bedroll, and left the room in a hurry.

He met up with the rest of the hiking party in the archive library where Simon was handing Malachai a folded map of the island and some pencils to mark where the barrier glowed. Jason put on his happy face for everyone else's benefit.

"Everyone about ready to go?" he asked, approaching the growing number of people.

Seth answered his friend, "I think so. Looks like everyone's here."

"Good."

Seth added, "Kristen said that the hike up took them about three to four hours last time, so we should get going if we want to make it before nightfall."

"Good idea." Jason turned to address the group standing and conversing amongst themselves. "Is everyone here?"

They all looked around and either shook their heads yes or chimed a reply.

"Great, then let's get this show on the road."

Shannon appeared from the direction of the kitchen carrying the pack of food supplies.

"Thanks, Shannon." Jason smiled.

"Of course," she said with a bright smile. "You all try to enjoy this trip. No battles, artifacts, or hurry to return. Take your time and relax, pray, commune with nature and God." She patted Jason's arm before she turned to leave.

Jason smiled, knowing that she was talking to him in particular. It was no secret about him and Memnah, and it was also no secret that he missed her terribly and took every opportunity to visit her. Jason knew his friends here had been praying for him and he truly appreciated that. He needed all the help he could get when it came to her. She had truly captured his heart like no other woman ever had. He shook his head again, realizing he was chasing another rabbit down a hole.

"Let's move out, everybody," he yelled.

Kristen smiled from ear to ear as the group of sixteen headed for the highest point of the Island's mountain. She joined in as they all chatted excitedly about the adventure they were going on, just for fun this time. Yes, the hike was meant to plot coordinates, but that was an easy task that only took a few people and very little time. The rest of the trip would be heavenly. She missed the camping trips she used to take with her father when she was younger. Trips like this brought back so many memories of her parents and her happy childhood. Her last trip up this mountain had ended with her conflicted between two men. This trip, she would be able to enjoy her and Sean's time together without interference from Timothy. As they left the house, she could see Timothy and Uriah out on the front lawn practicing.

Timothy and Uriah had spent the morning sparring, trying to work out their frustration and hostilities toward recent events and decisions which affected them. Decisions they had no control over, and no input.

Timothy watched the others walk behind the mansion and disappear as they rounded the house toward the mountainside. He took another drink from his canteen as Uriah noticed the direction his attention had turned.

"I don't know why you concern yourself with everyone else's business. They don't deserve your concern or caring." Uriah took up his stance against Tim, his sword raised and ready to do battle.

Tim sat his canteen back on the ground and raised his sword again, looking at him. "Perhaps, Uriah, but we are all still in this fight together. Whether we are part of The Twelve or not, we still have to do our part. Besides, it isn't that easy to just get over someone. Haven't you ever been in love?" Tim stood ready to spar.

Uriah and Tim battled as they continued their discussion between strikes.

"Sure I have. I just don't let my emotions rule my head." Uriah grunted against the strike. "Besides, I don't think you are really in love with that girl, just infatuated."

"Why do you say that?" Tim's reply was strained.

"Because you always acted like you wanted to control the situation more than you cared for her. It seemed more like a competition with Doran than you really trying to win her over." Uriah struck Tim's shield hard.

Tim looked at his friend. Uriah may be an unconventional man in a lot of ways. One who harbors some very strong feelings toward some of the others, but what he said did strike a nerve. Could he be right? Were his feelings for Kristen born more out of winning than what he actually felt for her? He had been a lawyer, and a good one. He rarely lost a case, and in those days, he did whatever he needed to do to win. Maybe this thing with Kristen and Sean was just that, the old him trying to win.

"Maybe your right, Uriah," Tim offered, ending the conversation. They spent the next half-hour sparring. Afterward, they cleaned up and met under the veranda for dinner, along with the few others who stayed behind.

Uriah and Tim sat at the far end of the table and watched the Dragoman all gathered around the other end, talking about the ancient books and their contents, with Safra, Oz, and Sofia joining them.

Uriah looked at Tim as he ate his dinner, trying to gauge his level of agitation at the situation they both found themselves in.

"So, what do you think about all of this *Chosen* stuff?"

"What do you mean? There isn't anything we can do about it. God's the one who set The Chosen. I'm not going to argue."

"Imagine that. A lawyer who won't argue," Uriah said sarcastically. "Are we supposed to just go along with it? I don't know if I can do that. We've been doing this much longer than either one of the girls have."

"I know that, as well as everyone else. But still, what can we do about it?"

"I don't know. But I've been thinking about it a lot."

"Uriah, you're just making yourself miserable by dwelling on it. Me, I'm trying to forget it and move on. It isn't easy, but you know, it may be a good thing not having to fight whatever it is that is required in the Final Battle."

"I don't believe that. Don't you remember the prophecy from the *Book of Armor* that Simon read when he first opened it? About how the Chosen will rule the nations when the battle is over? After all the years I've spent living this life, I deserve to be one of those rulers, and so do you."

"How do you know that we won't still rule. We are chosen for *this lifestyle,* Uriah. Maybe that was what the prophecy was talking about?"

"I don't know. All I know is that we deserve to have that sort of respect as well. And If I can do something about it to make sure we get it, I'm going to."

Timothy looked at the man with a bit of concern. Uriah had always been a hot head, but lately he seemed to really be taking offense at everything and everyone who he thought stepped on his toes in some way.

Simon and Nuncio noticed that the two men had been distancing themselves from everyone else ever since yesterday's announcement that they would not be in the Final Twelve. Simon exchanged a knowing glance with Nuncio. They both knew that they would have to talk to the two men soon. It didn't bode well for there to be this sort of discord in the group. Perhaps they could each take them aside separately after dinner and speak with them privately. This would be the perfect time since the rest of the group was up the mountain.

"Nuncio," Simon said. "Why don't you take Uriah and have a discussion with him while I talk with Timothy."

"Certainly. I'll chat with him here on the patio."

Simon stood and approached the men sitting at the other end of the table.

"Good evening gentlemen," Simon said with a grin as he approached them.

"Simon," they both replied.

"Timothy," Simon said, "I wonder if I could have a word with you in private?"

Timothy looked at him. "Sure," he answered, a bit skeptical.

"Great," Simon smiled again. "How about we go into the kitchen for a cup of coffee and some of that wonderful cinnamon cake that Clancy made for dessert?"

"Sounds good," Tim said, standing to follow Simon into the kitchen. Just as they were walking away, Nuncio approached Uriah and sat down beside him at the table.

"Uriah, do you mind if we have a chat as well?"

"Do I have a choice?" Uriah asked cockily.

"Certainly, but I would appreciate if you would allow me to speak with you," Nuncio said, still sitting.

"Why not." Uriah sighed, leaning back in his chair.

"Thank you," Nuncio said. He called to Simon as they were walking away. "Simon, could you have Petra bring each of us some coffee and cake as well?"

"Certainly," Simon yelled back over his shoulder to him.

Uriah watched the old man get comfortable, adjusting in his seat with a small wince of pain due to the hip injury received years before.

"Uriah," Nuncio began, "you surely know what I wish to speak with you about. I and the others are very concerned over your anger about the selection of The Twelve. You do understand that it was not our choice that you and Timothy be replaced?"

"Not really, no," Uriah said, crossing his arms across his chest.

"We all thought that we had found The Twelve which included you and Timothy. That's why we never checked the others for marks. All we were searching for after Gabriele and Kristen arrived were the signs for Issachar and Judah. We assumed we had the symbols correct."

"Perhaps that was your mistake. Assumption," Uriah said aggravatedly.

"Yes. You are very correct in that. We certainly did make a few mistakes there. But if it had not been for Lord Rawthorn's list, we would have sent the wrong people into the Final Battle, and that could have been horrific for all of us. If The Chosen, selected by God, are not sent into the Final Battle then the whole of the earth, and all the worlds within it would perish. God made that decision, not us."

"I don't understand how God could choose two girls to take the place of seasoned warriors. I've been working for God for sixteen years, Nuncio. And now suddenly, I'm not good enough to fight whatever He has for us at the end? Those two girls only have about three years of experience between the two of them." Uriah fumed.

"I don't know why He chose whom He did. Only he knows the reasons. Isaiah 55:8 says, "For my thoughts are not your thoughts, neither are your ways my ways, declares the Lord." We can't know what His plans are or who he will use to accomplish His will. We just have to accept where He has us," Nuncio finished, realizing that he didn't seem to be getting through to Uriah. He continued as Petra sat the coffee and cake in front of them.

"You know, when I was first injured thirteen years ago, I was still in the best physical shape of my life, even at my age then. I assumed that my injury would heal completely, but much to my chagrin, it didn't. I kept waiting for God to take the pain and burden away, figuring that He still needed me to do His work. For years I was angry at God for taking away the life that He gave me. I loved going on missions with my Peregrines, battling demons, and finding adventure wherever God chose. Then, in one single battle, it was all over. I was suddenly resigned to accept the fact that I was unable to do the things that I once could. For whatever reason, God had settled me here on the island for the duration. I couldn't understand why. I often complained while praying," he said with a stiff, shamed smile, "asking what I did wrong to make Him remove me from the life He had called me to. Then, one day, I was searching the scriptures for answers and God brought me to the passage in Genesis 32, when Jacob wrestled the Lord and the Lord touched the socket of Jacobs hip. Then, again in Psalm 38, where it speaks of feeble and brokenness. God does things for reasons unto Him alone. I have learned to accept my place here. I have received many blessings by being the Dragoman to live on the island and manage things. Blessings that I would have missed had I not been injured. God removed me for His reasons. I may not know them all, but He has graciously shown me a few of them. You see Uriah, what you see as a punishment, or a shunning, is likely a blessing in disguise. And you will only understand it and see it if you stop being angry at God and your friends and start looking for the plan He has for you."

Uriah looked at Nuncio, remembering the man he once was and recalling the aggravation he once displayed with his current situation. He realized that Nuncio had put all of that in the past, he just wasn't sure that he could do the same. Nuncio was much older than he was now, and Uriah wasn't ready to be put out to pasture so to speak.

"What do you expect me to do, Nuncio? I understand what you're saying, but I can't just turn off my anger and feelings."

"I understand that, Uriah, but it is up to you how you handle and react to the situation. You need to take time and pray, study, and seek God's leading. He will help you to overcome your feelings. But you must be willing to give him the opportunity."

"I hear what you're saying," Uriah said standing. "I'm going to head on up to my room and think about what you have said. Thanks for the concern, Nuncio." With that, Uriah left and walked inside for the comfort and solitude of his room.

Simon had found Petra and gave her Nuncio's request. Then, he and Timothy sat at the edge of the counter in the now clean kitchen. Everyone else had already left and they had the room to themselves.

Simon pointed to the counter. "Have a seat my boy while I get us some coffee and cake. How do you take your coffee, Tim?"

"One spoon of sugar and a little milk," he said sitting and waiting on Simon to return. When Simon placed the cake and coffee in front of him, he said, "Thanks, Simon."

"You're welcome." He returned with his own cup and plate, and sat next to Tim. "I do so enjoy Clancy's creations." He smiled as he took a bite of the delectable cinnamon confection.

Timothy grinned slightly at Simon's obvious enjoyment. After taking a bite himself and sipping some of the hot liquid from his cup, he said, "Well, what's this talk all about?"

Simon looked at Tim, seeing he was not one to beat around the bush.

"Well, Nuncio and I were just a bit concerned over how you and Uriah were taking yesterday's news. I know it had to be a shock to hear that the two of you weren't counted amongst The Twelve."

"Yeah, it was. But what difference does it make how we feel about it? There isn't anything we can do about it anyway."

"True, but if you need to talk or get anything off your chest, I understand and am willing to listen."

"I just don't understand why two inexperienced girls were chosen to fight over two men who are far more capable and much more experienced."

"Perhaps that is the very reason why," Simon pondered.

"I don't get what you mean." A confused look clouded Tim's face.

"In the Bible, it talks often of how God chose the most insignificant of people to do the most extraordinary things. So that men could not boast of their own deeds."

"All right, well why not leave Seth, Jason, Oz, or any of the other men out of the equation? Why give us marks if He didn't want us to fight? He could have just left us unmarked."

"I don't know why God chooses whom he does. Perhaps it has to do with matters of the heart, or your spiritual walks and trials? Or, perhaps, He just chooses the strongest people that can handle what you might consider to be rejection, He may consider it a compliment, a testament to your ability to withstand. I just know that God has not abandoned you, or Uriah. He surely has great plans still for the both of you, as well as the other Peregrines who were never marked at all for the Twelve Tribes. Surely, they wondered about their purpose and destiny just as you do? The prophecy in the *Book of Armor* mentioned that each champion, The Chosen, would rule over the earth, not just The Twelve. God doesn't mince words, Tim. Just remember that all right?" Simon looked at him for reassurance that he understood.

Tim sat in silence a minute as Simons words settled into his thoughts.

"Maybe. I never thought of it like that." Tim looked at Simon who looked at him over his spectacles. Tim couldn't help but grin at the man who grinned back.

"Now, let's finish this cake so that we can have another piece." Simon smiled devilishly making Timothy chuckle. The two men sat and chatted amiably about what the glowing, underwater, portals might mean. Timothy remembered seeing them and described the image to Simon as they did indeed have another piece of cake and another cup of coffee to wash it down. They talked for the better part of an hour before Simon decided to head to bed, citing his age and inability to hang like he used to. The two cleaned up their dishes and parted ways for their rooms.

Timothy took what Simon said to heart, deciding to pray about the situation and maybe have a look in his Bible at those whom the world saw as insignificant, but God saw as useful. He wondered if Uriah had the same reaction to Nuncio's chat with him. Knowing Uriah, Tim seriously doubted that he swallowed his pride well enough to accept what he was told.

Sing joyfully to the Lord, you righteous; it is
fitting for the upright to praise him.

Psalm 33:1

Chapter 5

Reader's Island, Mountain Peak

Kristen and Sean led the expedition up the mountain side at a decent pace. It was dusk when they made it to the top of the mountain where they had last camped, and where Kristin had discovered the underwater portals. The area at the top of the mountain was plenty large enough for the group to camp.

"Did anyone bring tents?" Caroline asked.

Kristin grinned at her. "We don't need tents here on the island. The weather is always perfect, there are no bugs to irritate you, and it never rains."

"Yes." Bridget smiled. "The animals won't bother us either."

Caroline grinned back. "I guess I'm so used to living in tents, that when we aren't at the big house, it's become a habit to think we need one."

Everyone tossed their packs and bedrolls on the ground and walked over to the rock, on which Kristen had already climbed to the top, to see if the underwater portals could still be seen. They were all anxious to get a look at the portals themselves.

Sure enough, out in the water, was a faint glow just below the surface in what appeared to be the same places as last time.

Kristen smiled down at the others who were gathering around the base of the rock.

"You can see them. They are faint, but visible," she said, climbing down from the boulder's top to allow Jason to have a look.

"Isn't that something?" he said. Pulling a pair of binoculars from his side bag, he took a closer look at them. He turned, looking at all of the underwater portals, being careful not to step too far either way on the rock.

"Just like Kristen had stated, there are portals all the way around the island just at the base of Barrier's Edge below the water. Which means it must pass through the water instead of ending at the top like we all thought."

Seth jumped up next, followed by Malachai and Vashti. Everyone took turns climbing the rock and looking out over the scene below.

While the rest took their turn looking out over the water, the others began building a small table of sorts from fallen wood so that they would have something solid to spread the map out on and mark the plots.

Jason's digital binoculars had a compass and coordinate marker within his visual area, enabling him to be able to call out the exact place to mark each one of the portals or gateways.

Malachai decided what he believed them to be.

"I truly think that these are windows or gateways in the barrier, not portals, like Seth suggested before. If the top of the barrier will allow us to dial up a certain era, and decade, then where in the world could these underwater windows go?"

Vashti offered her opinion. "Perhaps they aren't windows at all but perhaps anchors for the barrier itself?"

"I don't believe so. If that were the case, why would they be glowing? No, I think they lead to places. What places, I am uncertain."

Zeke smiled excitedly, "It sure is going to be interesting to find out."

Zaccai agreed. "Yes. To see an underwater city would be a thing to behold. *If* such a thing does exist?"

"Zanchier exists," Caroline stated. "If God can make a place like that, and that city outside of Simon's called Garganthera, then he certainly can make cities that survive and thrive beneath the vast surface of the oceans."

Seth looked at her in earnest. "True, but whether or not *we are* meant to survive and thrive below the surface is another thing all together. I don't know about any of you, but my super-power doesn't include breathing underwater."

Sean smiled. "Neither does mine, and I can control the water to some degree. I don't think I could move an entire ocean though."

Odessa chimed in. "No, but the Staff of Moses quite possibly could, with God's blessings of course." She beamed excitedly.

Alec grew excited at her words. "Of course! Maybe that is why we were to acquire it on a mission?"

Seth and Jason looked at each other and smiled. Things were beginning to make sense; *if* that was how they were to use the object.

Jason peered through the binoculars again, calling out another set of coordinates.

"Malachai, when do you think Ryan will finish that computer search for ancient cities that disappeared after a natural disaster?"

"I'm not sure, why?"

"I'm curious to know if any of them might line up with any of these latitudinal and longitudinal points of the underwater windows."

Bridget giggled with excitement, clapping her hands together. "This is all getting very exciting. Although, I'm still not completely comfortable with being in the water. I *can swim* now thanks to Dominic and Wade, but not well enough to travel underwater." She suddenly had a sobering thought. "I must say, some of my excitement is beginning to vanish."

Everyone chuckled or smiled at her declaration. Zeke answered her.

"I doubt you'll have to. Surely, if God put those windows there, and He wants us to pass through them to somewhere, he'll provide a way."

Malachai answered, "I believe, like Odessa said, that the staff of Moses may be the answer to that question."

Caroline asked, "Yes, but wasn't the staff just a tool? The staff itself wasn't what parted the Red Sea, God did."

"True," Odessa replied. "But we were supposed to collect it for a reason. Surely this is why?"

Zaccai shrugged. "Perhaps the artifacts were to be collected for posterity purposes only?"

"Maybe," Odessa answered again, "but why would Simon feel pressed to bring them here to the island then?"

"That is a good question. I suppose the Dragoman, Safra, or one of your dreams, Odessa, will afford us with an answer," Zaccai stated.

Dominic sat and drew the scene before him. Quickly sketching out the people and where they stood, the top of the mountain, the stars and constellations that shone brightly in the darkening night sky, and the glowing of the windows beneath the water's surface. The darker the night grew the brighter the windows glowed.

Jason called out another coordinate as Malachai and Vashti made notes on the map and on separate pieces of paper to be added to an archive book when they returned.

"They are definite fixed points. The motion of the waves doesn't upset the position of portals in the least. They have to be part of the barrier."

Sean answered, "That's what Kristin and I thought. We noticed that as well."

Nick asked, "Any idea when we might need to check these portals out?" The aspect of underwater voyages did not appeal to him in the least. Traveling by ship three days back had made him nervous enough. Now, he may have to travel an extensive amount of distance underwater. He wasn't too happy about the prospect.

Malachai answered, "We have to make sure the Portgens are capable of working underwater before we allow exploration. We don't know what, or where, is on the other side of these portals, so letting anyone pass through without a way to get back, especially since it is underwater, is not an option. There are many precautions we must take first."

Wade spoke up. "Is underwater where we're supposed to find the next piece of armor?"

"We really aren't certain yet, Wade," Malachai responded.

"I did have a dream last night about the gateways, or portals, beneath the water that surround the island," Odessa stated.

"Really?" Caroline asked curiously.

"Yes, but that really was all. It didn't show any armor pieces or anything else. And I haven't had any other premonitions since then."

Vashti replied, "Perhaps this is all that God wishes us to concentrate on for now. You have all been going non-stop for three to four weeks and have had some very serious demon wars in the process. Perhaps the Lord is giving you all a little break to rest and restore."

Sean grinned broadly. "Hey, I'll take it if he's offering."

Alec grinned at Sean's attitude. "Me as well, my friend. I could do with a petites vacances."

Wade leaned over and whispered to Gabriele. "What's that mean?"

"It means little vacation, in French." Gabby smiled at him.

"Well why didn't he just say that?" he whispered back.

Gabriele just shook her head in amusement at the young man, not bothering to answer his rhetorical question. She pulled her ukulele from her pack and began to pick and strum, entertaining her group of friends while they busied themselves with setting up camp.

Jason, Malachai, and Vashti were still engaged in the plotting of the gateways to precise coordinates so they could find them during daylight hours.

Nick said, "I'll go gather some firewood to start a campfire."

"I'll help with that," Nadia stated.

"Me too," Wade jumped up to help.

Jason yelled over his shoulder while maintaining his gaze on the open ocean. "Since you're building a fire, Shannon packed us some coffee, powdered creamer, and sugar if anyone wants it."

"I do," Odessa quickly stated, many other takers also chiming in. She gathered the necessary items while waiting for the fire to start, humming along with Gabby as she played and sang.

Caroline, Kristen, and Bridget started unpacking the food the kitchen staff had packed. There were fruits, vegetables, and sandwiches for their dinner so no heating would be necessary. They also had put dried meats and other snack foods, as well as one of Chef Clancy's wonderful desserts. Made into carrying sized portions of course.

Sean, Zeke, Zaccai, Seth, and Alec unfurled the bedrolls. Everyone placed theirs next to whomever they wished to sleep beside. Dominic stayed still and drew, watching the activity in camp and trying to capture the images quickly on his sketch pads. Simon and Nuncio had agreed that his sketches would make wonderful additions to the archive books, especially since they found the very ornately designed ancient archive books, and the extraordinary details the pages held.

Jason, Malachai, and Vashti finished the plotting just as dinner was being handed out.

Jason took a plate and sat down on his bedroll, thanking Caroline for the food. "We'll check the coordinates again in the morning, just before sunrise to make sure nothing has changed."

Malachai answered, "Yes, I was thinking we needed to do the same thing. Shall we say blessing everyone?"

The murmurs of agreement passed and Malachai prayed over their meal, their time spent together, and the wonders that God was soon to reveal to them.

The rest of the night was spent in joy as they sang, laughed, joked, and even danced beneath the open skies of the mountain top.

Caroline decided to take this opportunity to speak with Bridget about what Dominic had told Jason upon their return from Zanchier.

"Bridget, can I speak with you a minute?"

"Certainly, Caroline. We haven't been able to chat in ages with just the two of us." Bridget smiled brightly at her.

"I have a question to ask you," Caroline said, as she settled in beside Bridget.

"Of course, anything."

"Well, Dominic mentioned something about you finding out about more bad family ties and having some shock of some sort?"

Bridget's smile deflated quite a bit as she took a deep breath. "Yes. I've been meaning to discuss that with you anyway. I'm just not sure how to go about starting the conversation."

"Well, just tell me what happened." Caroline encouraged her.

"Well, all right. I found out that that awful Scaither-man, Marnor, is my half-brother."

"What!" Caroline asked, shocked.

"Yes. Apparently, his mother, Mary Draiwood, and my mother Mary, was one and the same."

"Goodness, what a shock you must have had."

"Yes. It's simply dreadful, and yet not so much so, all at the same time. I must admit, it's nice to know that I actually have family alive somewhere. That I'm not really alone. Even though we will never be like a real brother and sister, he *is* still my brother regardless. Caroline, why would God give me such a mess of a family like I have? Or, *had* anyway," Bridget asked in confusion.

Caroline wrapped her arm around Bridget's shoulder.

"I don't know, Bridget. But regardless of who or what your family was, or is, you turned out brilliantly." Caroline smiled at her young friend.

Bridget smiled brightly at her. "Thank you, Caroline. I'm so glad God chose to drop you into my ditch in Dover."

"So am I, Bridget." Caroline giggled, hugging her again. The two of them joined the group of revelers once again, enjoying an evening of care-free fun.

Alec sat down next to Gabriele to join her in song, the two of them smiling at one another and belting their hearts out.

Odessa felt a small pang of jealousy over seeing him so animated and thoroughly enjoying another woman's company. Gabriele was different than that tavern girl back in Tintagel. If Alec and Gabriele chose to, they *could* have a life together. Odessa shrugged off the fleeting feeling. They were friends, and working companions, nothing more. Besides, Alec was ten years Gabby's senior. Still, Gabriele was by all definitions a woman. And not just any woman, she was a Peregrine. A very beautiful, talented, strong younger woman.

Stop it, Dee! She admonished herself quietly. Why was this bothering her so much? Alec had done as she had asked and let her be about the subject of her feelings for him. Perhaps he had given up waiting for her to make up her mind? Why would she even *need* to make up her mind? If she had true feelings for him, wouldn't she already know that? She had never experienced jealousy before where Alec was concerned. Perhaps it was because since his declaration of love, she couldn't help thinking about it every time she looked at him. He was beginning to dominate her every thought and that could be very dangerous indeed. She needed to focus on what God had called her to do, not whether she was in love with Alec Chevalier.

Jason watched all his friends congregate around the fire, couples all sitting next to each other while the others piled in around them. Jason was happy for his friends and their ability to find someone they could love, especially with their lifestyle. He just wished he had the same fortune. At least he wasn't dealing with Alec's problem. Alec had been in love with Odessa for the last eight years apparently. Jason couldn't' imagine waiting that long to be with someone, only to be rejected when you revealed your feelings. At least with Memnah, he knew she loved him in return. The irony of it all was the fact that they couldn't be together anywhere except Timna Valley, and only when he could sneak away to see her which only happened when he was on Reader's Island. The last time he snuck off to see her when not on the island, a demon war broke out, people got hurt, and Bridget and Dominic disappeared for three days.

Jason sighed audibly, drawing the attention of Seth who sat next to him.

"What's bothering you, Brother," Seth stated, feeling an odd sort of elation at having a brother, especially a man like Jason Marshal.

Jason's head snapped around to look at Seth. His words caught him by surprise. A small smile was evident on Jason's face.

"You know, that sure has a nice ring to it." Jason grinned.

"Yeah, I agree. I've never had any siblings. I barely had a family at all growing up." Seth smiled back.

"I had two half-brothers and a half-sister back home," Jason stated, "but it sure is nice to actually have someone I can call family right here."

"Well, God saw fit to give me that on both sides of the spectrum here," Seth said, motioning with his head to Caroline who sat next to him, engaged in a conversation with Zaccai.

"Yeah," Jason said, a bit more soberly. "You're very lucky, Seth."

"Jason, I know you have very strong feelings for Memnah, but do you really think you can keep up the relationship with the way we live?"

"I don't know, Seth. It's something that I've been praying about a lot lately. I just don't know if it's fair to either of us. Not knowing if we can ever truly be together. It makes me wonder why our father lived the way he did. Did he deny the life God asked him to live, and instead, jump from time period to time period, taking up with a different woman each time? Never truly being able to stay in one place and love just one woman? Who knows how many brothers and sisters we could actually have out there?"

"Yeah, I've had the same wonderings myself." Seth grinned.

"I could never live that way of course. But this life does get lonely, and I can never bring Memnah here with me." Jason threw a piece of wood he had been fidgeting with into the fire.

"No, you can't. But, maybe after all of this is over, you can go back to Israel to live with her and her people?"

"Who knows how long that could take. Besides, I don't think that will be possible either. Remember the prophecy?" Jason looked at Seth. "It said that the Chosen would rule over the earth and all the dimensions. I don't think that I will be given a choice in the matter."

"Maybe not, but we can hope and pray that you will get to pick where you choose to reign." Seth patted Jason on the back.

"Or, whether we want to reign at all."

"Have *you* had much luck in denying God's will for your life?" Seth asked with a small grin.

Jason chuckled lowly. "Nah. You?"

"Not a bit. I tried, but it made me miserable." Seth chuckled back.

They laughed a little more before Seth's attention was once again taken by Caroline, and Jason was left to his thoughts. Jason leaned back against an obliging rock, watching his friends enjoying a truly relaxing evening, without a care in the world. He hadn't seen everyone so animated and joyful in a long time. He smiled to himself, realizing he loved his life. If he could only figure out how to incorporate Memnah into it, he would ask for nothing else.

Lord, Jason prayed silently, *you gave me a heart for her. Please, show me a way that we can be together. And if that isn't possible, show me how to deal with letting her go.*

His attention was drawn back to the crowd of people who were singing and clapping, as Sean and Kristen started dancing to the quick tempo of Gabby's ukulele. They were soon joined by others as they lost themselves in the peace of the island and the brief carefree evening that they rarely got to experience.

Main house, Midnight

"The others are growing very suspicious. Simon and Nuncio watch everyone very closely now ever since the key went missing."

"Yes. We are also watched on missions. I lost the key when demons attacked our camp at Tintagel. I had it out, looking at it when the attack started, and quickly shoved it in my pocket. When I checked later, it was gone. At least that will keep them from opening the book."

"I don't think so. I believe it was found by someone. I overheard Simon and Nuncio talking about being able to open the last book now."

He sighed. "You haven't found where they've been hiding the books and keys?"

"No. They are very careful not to let anyone see them putting them back in hiding. Of course, when they are out during the day, I can catch glimpses of the opened books as they are studying them. But, I have yet to see them open the last book."

"Just keep your eyes open for when they do."

"I'm a little frightened. I feel like the others are growing suspicious of me. I'm not sure this is all worth it."

"You listen to me, you volunteered yourself for this, you're going to stick to it. If you betray me now…"

"I won't. You know I love you, and I'll do whatever I can to help you. I'm just nervous, that's all."

"Good. I always knew I could count on you. Don't let me down now, Petra."

"I won't, Uriah."

The two embraced in a kiss, hidden in the shadows of the trees and thick shrubs. They soon parted ways, Petra running to the house first, looking in every direction for anyone who might be out at this time of night.

Uriah watched her go. They had had a relationship on and off over the last ten years or so, but they had grown closer since they had all become permanent residents of the island. Uriah liked Petra.

She had been a very useful woman and ally over the last few years. He wasn't in love with her as she professed to him, but then again, Uriah never really loved anyone. There had been a time when he thought that he and Prisca were growing close, only to find out that she was in love with Oz. Even before Oz had disappeared everyone knew that he and Prisca had feelings for each other. Even still, Uriah was just as shocked as everyone else, except Simon of course, to find that they had been secretly married for years before Oz had disappeared. He had tried to be a friend and a comfort to Prisca then, but she would have none of it.

That explained why Simon had always tried to discourage him from declaring his feelings to Prisca all those years ago. Simon could have at least told him back then that she and Oz were married.

Everyone he had ever loved or cared for was either taken from him, left him, betrayed him, or didn't care for him at all. It was time that Uriah took matters into his own hands and finished what he, Hiram, and several others had started years ago. It was time someone else took over. The Dragoman were antiquated, and their beliefs just the same. Hiram may no longer be here to lead NKRO, *the New Kingdom Rulers Order*, but Uriah could move forward without him. He still had an alliance with the demons that Hiram had made years ago. Perhaps Uriah could use that to his advantage? He may not be an all-powerful Magus, as Hiram had been. But his gift of electricity could very well come in handy. Plus, he had been practicing the little magic that he had been learning under Hiram's tutelage. He was tired of not being good enough for God, and tired of being told what to do by these new Peregrines. He was ready to take over, and he might just have a new ally in Timothy.

Timothy stood looking out over the way the shadows danced upon the ground as the island breeze stirred the treetops. He was unable to sleep for some reason, so he had ventured onto his balcony to enjoy the quiet of the night and the half-moon that barely lit the island.

Timothy noticed someone running across the yard to the house. It looked like it was Petra, but he wasn't entirely certain. He stepped away from the railing, into the shadows of the overhead roof. As he stood there pondering what she would be doing out at midnight wondering around the island, he then saw Uriah leaving the same stand of trees that Petra had come from just a minute earlier. There was no mistaking that who he saw was Uriah. The man had a walk about him like no other. It was made from years of pent-up anger and frustration. A deliberate, forceful, walk, one that showed that Uriah was never at peace.

"Well now, Uriah, it looks like you've been having a quiet little tryst of your own."

Tim smiled to himself, wondering how he could use this information to his advantage. He liked Uriah, but he knew the man was only out for himself. If the man was making friends, like he had been with himself, then he had an agenda. Tim wondered just what Uriah was up to?

From another balcony just a few doors down from Timothy's, Oz and Prisca also stood on the balcony enjoying the beautiful half-lit skies of the quiet island night.

"Priss," Oz said, grabbing her attention. She opened her eyes from where she had been leaning against him, reveling in the feel of his arms around her. Happy that he was home for a spell.

"Yes, what is it?" she asked, trying to follow his gaze as he directed her attention to the woman skittering across the lawn.

"Does 'at there look like Petra ta' you?"

"Yes, it does. I wonder what she would be doing out this time of night?"

"Whatever it is, it prob'bly isn' good."

"I can't imagine what she would be doing roaming the island at night," Prisca stated curiously.

Just then, Uriah appeared.

"Same thing Uriah mus' be up ta'," Oz stated, worry lacing his words.

Prisca's surprised face turned up to look at Oz. "Perhaps they are just lovers, hiding their feelings like we all have for years."

"They could do that indoors," Oz stated. "What could they be discussin' outside that they need ta hide? 'Sides, why hide their feelin's anymore? No one else is."

"Yes, it is different now. But not everyone is comfortable with that yet," Prisca said, trying to rationalize the tryst.

"Maybe. But maybe there's more to it 'an that? Maybe they're up ta som'thin' worse. Maybe, we jus' found our thieves."

"Surely not. Do you really think that Uriah and Petra could do such a thing?" She was certain they were innocent.

"If ya' remember, we didn' think Hiram could do th' things he did either. An' with th' way Uriah's been a actin' lately, I'd say he's the best candidat' we 'ave. He's been stan'-offish ever since Hiram left years back. I always did suspec' Uriah. Now, I'd say I 'ave a good 'nough reason ta' keep a real close eye on 'im. And you an' the other Dragoman need ta keep an eye on Petra." He and Prisca watched the man carefully slink back to the house.

And it shall come to pass afterward that I will pour
out My Spirit on all flesh; Your sons and your
daughters shall prophesy, your old men shall dream
dreams, your young men shall see visions.

Joel 2:28

Chapter 6

Mountain Peak

The next morning, Jason, Malachai, and Vashti rose earlier than the others, before daybreak, to check the plotted points of what they now called underwater gateways. The gateways were still in the same places as they were the night before. And with the tide being out they were a bit more visible with less water covering them. The task took the three of them fifteen minutes from start to finish.

Jason and Malachai took to building a fire while Vashti got coffee and breakfast ready. As the three of them worked, everyone else began to stir from their sleep.

Bridget sat up, stretched, and with a big grin said, "Good morning, everyone."

Jason grinned at the ethereally happy girl. "Good morning to you, sunshine."

"Good morning, Jason," Bridget sang, grinning even bigger if that were possible, quickly jumping up to help Vashti prepare breakfast.

Jason watched the young girl. He smiled again at her happy demeanor. It wasn't very often that Bridget became saddened by something, and when it did happen, she seemed to get over it very quickly. He wished he could take what the world threw at him with such grace and acceptance. He would be much better off if he could.

The rest of the group began stirring awake just as dawn broke across the mountain top. The sun's rays flashed across the sky in shades of pink as the water's surface sparkled in the morning light. Glistening specks of gold danced on the soft ripple of the ocean's gently lapping waves.

Jason breathed deeply of the cool air and the scent of flowers wafting along on the breeze as he stood there gazing out over the beauty of the lower island and the easy movement of the water.

Alec walked up behind him. "Good morning my friend." He slapped Jason on the shoulder.

"Morning, Alec. How'd you sleep?"

Alec smiled from ear to ear, stretching his long thin frame. "Like a baby in his mother's arms."

Jason smiled at Alec's description. "Sounds peaceful."

"I think," Alec started, "it is because we don't have to worry here. We can sleep without fear. And it was good to unwind last night. We haven't had that kind of fun together in a while."

"Yeah, I know what you mean. Too bad it all has to end this morning. We need to get everyone up and moving. I hate to say it, but we have to get back down the mountain and back to work."

"Slave driver. Can you not even let us enjoy our breakfast first?" Alec joked, pulling Jason over to the fire to grab a plate of pre-cooked biscuits, hard-boiled eggs, and bacon that Bridget and Vashti pulled out of the food baskets.

After a quick breakfast, Bridget, Wade, and Dominic quickly packed their bedrolls and spent some time playing with the island animals; testing some new commands to see just how far the animals would go when asked to do something.

Everyone else finished eating, packed up, took care of extinguishing the fire, and got ready to hike back down the mountain.

Kristen inhaled deeply of the clean island air. "I wish we could stay up here for another night. I love it up here."

Sean grinned at her. "I know. Me too. You're making a regular camping and hiking addict out of me."

"It's not me." She smiled. "It's nature. How could you not love being out here in all of the glory of God's creation?"

"I didn't care for it before, but I truly didn't know what I was missing," Sean stated, looking out over the edge of the mountain and down into the flower laden valleys below that stretched out to the water's edge.

Kristen smiled at him. "I'm glad you enjoy it, or else we'd have to take separate vacations."

The two of them laughed over her joke.

Odessa packed, watching Alec and Gabby chatting away while she did. She shoved her hoodie into her bag a bit too forcefully, drawing Caroline's attention.

"Hey," Caroline said, walking over to her, "are you okay?"

"Yeah," Odessa shrugged. "Why do you ask?"

"You seem a little out of sorts this morning," she said, taking note of where and who had captured Odessa's glancing attentions.

"No, not at all. Just ready to get back to work."

"Odessa, is something about Alec bothering you? Seth and I have both noticed over the last several weeks that something is happening between the two of you. I haven't known either of you for very long, but Seth says that the way you two have been acting toward each other is very out of character for both of you. If you ever want to talk, I'm here. Even if it is just to vent. No opinions offered unless asked for."

Odessa looked at Caroline. True, they hadn't known each other long, but Odessa had come to like and respect the woman over the last month.

"All right," Odessa said, standing up and tossing her bag to the ground. "Alec revealed to me a few weeks back that he was in love with me. I told him that I truly didn't think that I felt the same but seeing him with that tavern girl back in Tintagel, and then watching him with Gabriele, well, it just irritates me for some reason." Exasperation oozed from her clenched teeth.

"Do you want my opinion?"

"I don't know," Odessa looked at her intently at first, then she broke into a small grin. "Yes. I suppose so."

"Well, have you ever been jealous of Alec and anyone else before?"

"No. But, it isn't like we were ever around other people. Our lives before the island were very secluded. We were only ever around others on very rare occasions. It has always just been Me and Alec, then Jason and Seth."

"Perhaps, you took your relationship with him for granted. You never had to think about your feelings for Alec before, because you never had to worry about other women. Now, you are faced with a myriad of possibilities. He's told you how he feels, and you've rejected that…"

"No," Odessa interrupted. "I didn't exactly reject him. I told him I needed time to think." She picked up her pack and slung it across her back as the group of people began the hike back down the mountain. The two of them falling in step beside each other.

"Isn't he giving you that time?"

"Well yes. But for some reason, I can't help feeling irritable about him enjoying the company of other women."

"I think, my dear Odessa, that you are in love with Alec as well. If him laughing or joking with another woman bothers you that much, then I'd say it's because you are afraid that he may decide that waiting for you is taking too long. You're afraid of losing him to another woman. If it was just friendship you felt, I don't believe that you would be having these feelings."

Odessa sighed heavily. "I know you're right. But I'm so afraid that it won't work between us. We are very close yes, but so close that we argue often over things. I'm afraid we'll fight too much as a couple."

"I think, that the two of you are so comfortable with each other, that even if you did fight; which is inevitable in any relationship; that you'll be able to work out your problems without fail or worrying about driving the other one away."

Odessa looked at Caroline, realizing that what she spoke was truth. She smiled at Caroline and playfully jabbed her arm with her elbow.

"Thanks, Caroline. I think you're right, but I'm still not ready to tell him that I feel the same way. I'm just so hard-headed and stubborn," she finished looking at Caroline, defeated. They both laughed at Odessa's revelation.

Caroline playfully jabbed back at her. "I think you'll be able to work out the details soon enough. You're a smart, brave, capable woman, who has nothing to lose by telling him either way. You'll either be miserable without him by not telling him, or you'll be miserable if he turns you down because his affections have changed."

"You have a very valid point there." Odessa smiled as the two women giggled slightly at her words.

The hike down the mountain went smoothly and quickly with the group reaching the main house by eleven a.m.

Simon walked out of the library as he heard the hikers returning, all in great spirits.

"Well, hello everyone," he said with a smile. "It appears that you all enjoyed your trip."

"Very much so," Malachai answered. "It was very refreshing."

"Did you find out what we needed to know," Simon questioned him.

"Absolutely. I'm going to go stow my pack, grab a cold drink from the kitchen, and then I'll meet you in the library in about ten minutes."

"Wonderful." Simon smiled broadly.

Simon greeted everyone as they passed by, listening to all the congenial chatter between them. He smiled at the strong relationships they had all built as of late. His thoughts soon returned to the conversation Oz had had with him at breakfast about seeing Petra and Uriah late last night. If it were just a tryst, then there wouldn't be any problems. If, however, Uriah and Petra were found to be the betrayers and thieves, then that would definitely change things. The only good thing about Uriah possibly being the guilty party was the fact that he hadn't formed any ties to anyone else in the group. He doubted that many of them would take it badly if he did turn out to be the thief. Uriah's hot-headedness, and inability to follow orders or respect the newer Peregrines had become a real problem. One that he hoped Nuncio's talk had helped with last night. Simon felt that he himself had gotten through to Timothy, at least a bit. He only prayed that Uriah had taken what Nuncio had said to him to heart as well. With Oz's revelation at breakfast he hadn't had the chance to speak with Nuncio about how his talk had been received.

Timothy had appeared at that moment from the kitchen, having a late breakfast today due to the lack of people here at the house. He seemed to earnestly be happy this morning, even chatting and joking with the others as they came inside; several of them telling him how he missed out on a great night. Simon noticed Timothy glance at Kristen and Sean, his mannerisms changing to seriousness before he was back to being jovial again. Simon hoped that he could get over Miss Wright quickly so that they could work amiably together once again. A thought suddenly came to him and he realized that Timothy and Uriah had been spending a lot of time together lately. He hoped that wouldn't pose a problem if Uriah was found to be the guilty party.

The large group of people scattered in different directions to unpack and hit the showers. Some changed and went out to get in some sparring and practice using their gifts as they waited on the Dragoman to decide what they wanted to do with the information they compiled on the underwater gateways.

Simon and the others decided that they were indeed gateways within Barriers Edge. They just had to figure out where they went and how they were going to determine that. As the Dragoman sat in the library looking over the map of the island with the plotted gateways, they formed a plan.

"Simon, your Peregrines had to acquire the Staff of Moses on a mission. They seem to think this is why that piece had to be found, to be used for water travel with these gateways," Malachai stated.

"Hmm, that could be the case. Only, the Staff isn't magical, the power was from God himself. The Staff was only a tool," Simon answered.

"Yes, but our gifts are also only tools. Tools given to us by God to accomplish the task that he has laid before us all."

"Yes, I see your point. It is very possible, but until Odessa or Safra have been given any further visions, we must wait or form our own plans of exploring the underwater barrier."

"So, what do you suggest we do then?" Malachai asked.

"Well, several of the men went to buy some scuba gear. Four sets to be exact. Now, we can either send them down to see what's on the other side or wait to hear from God."

Nuncio grew a bit nervous. "I say we wait. We have no idea what's down there. Surely God will give us an answer soon."

"Perhaps, but maybe we are to figure this one out on our own?" Simon argued.

"If we are wrong, someone could get hurt or disappear again," Vashti offered.

Simon sighed. "You are right of course, Vashti. But sitting here waiting, knowing that the demons are moving, even to the point of destroying our safe houses, and that the Final Battle is growing so close that I'm having dreams about it, is beginning to wear on my nerves."

Nuncio's ears perked up at Simon's declaration. "Simon, why did you not mention that you were having dreams? They could be very important and need to be analyzed. The answers could lie within them."

"I've thought of that, but they really make no sense at all. Just a jumbled mess of strange scenes that have no bearing on anything that we are discussing."

"Such as?" Nuncio asked.

"Well, if you must know, I see creatures. Strange creatures like I've never seen before. They seem to match the description of the animals Bridget has talked about back on Zanchier. I figure my subconscious is creating them from her description."

"Well," Nuncio urged, "what about the dreams? What did you see?"

"Well, all right. Let me see if I can remember," Simon said, sitting up straighter in his chair. "I saw Bridget and Dominic riding the backs of flying beasts. I believe it was the one Bridget called a firebird or Kabihanxu. Wade was also riding the cat creature she described, the Pagorinx I believe is its name. However, they weren't riding for pleasure, it was more like they were in a battle. I couldn't see who they were battling, but I could hear the clash of metal on metal, and gun fire. I'm assuming that meant the others were there as well. That's all there is to tell. I just keep having a recurring dream about that particular scenario; not often though, only a handful of times."

"I would think that it means something, Simon. We need to remember this just in case it is a needed message to be useful at a later date," Nuncio stated.

"Yes, you're right, of course," Simon replied.

Malachai got them back on track with the current situation. "So, what about the underwater gateways?"

"Let's go see Ryan about the waterproofing I asked him about yesterday and see if he's figured anything out," Simon said standing, followed by the others. The group of five headed toward the computer room where the young man spent the majority of his time, working, searching, and inventing more devices that were very useful to them and the Peregrines.

"Ryan, sorry to bother you, but we were curious if you found a way to make the Portgens waterproof?" Simon entered the room, the others behind him.

"Hello, Simon," Ryan said not looking up from his workstation, bent over some new device he was designing. He soon pushed away from the table and stood to face them without really looking at them. "The Portgens are al...already waterproof for traveling p..purposes."

"Yes, I understand that Ryan," Simon replied, "but will they handle underwater travel? They would become completely saturated with water, not to mention the pressure and depth to which they might be subjected."

"I'm n..not sure about th..at. They would h..have to be tested to s..see what would happen. I c..could maybe figure it out after t..testing." Ryan said, somewhat shyly.

"Well then, we'll take a few of them out with the diving equipment, and I'll let you know the results. Thank you, Ryan. We'll let you get back to your work." They left the room as Ryan turned immediately back to his tinkering.

As they walked the hallway, they discussed today's plans.

"Let's find the others and get started with our experiment." Simon and the others left the building in search of the Peregrines who were getting in some time sparring and using their gifts. They found them all out on the front lawn, near the stables, in an area they had created for just such a purpose.

"Seth," Simon called as he was the first person he saw.

"Hey, Simon, what's up?" Seth said, breathing hard.

"We're going to try out the scuba equipment and Portgens underwater. Can you and some others grab the scuba gear from the supply closet?"

Seth grinned. "No need to get anyone else, Simon. I can handle it alone." Seth left and headed inside the house as Simon and the others gathered the rest of the Peregrines to explain what they were about to do. Seth returned shortly, effortlessly carrying all four of the scuba bags and tanks. He had one thrown over each of his shoulders and carried the other two, one in each hand. They appeared to be no heavier than rags to him. Seth loaded the equipment onto the four-wheeled ATV for the groundskeeper to haul for the two mile walk to the shoreline. The ATV squeaked and groaned under the weight of each added bag and tank. Some of the Peregrines smiled at the scene, knowing full well the heaviness of just one bag and tank. As everyone walked briskly, eager to see the experiment's results, the ATV teetered and tottered just ahead of them, its suspension system groaning in protest to the excessive weight with each little bump or turn.

Once they reached the water's edge, Sean excitedly asked, "So, who's going?"

"Well, Zeke, Oz, Jason, and Seth acquired the equipment so, they'll be the ones to dive. Besides, Jason is an experienced diver, and they may need Seth's strength down there."

Oz spoke up, "I'll defer ta som'one else if they wan' ta take my place."

Sean quickly answered, "I'll go!"

"All right then, Sean, you can take Oz's place. But no funny business," Simon admonished him. "Jason is in charge down there and we are only testing the Portgens, not the gateways," Simon quickly added.

Sean nodded his understanding of Simon's warning, and the four men suited up and went into the water with their Portgens. They swam out near the gateways just to get a look at them from beneath the water's surface. Not to mention, the further out from the coast they went the deeper it got.

Seth noticed that the gateways appeared much larger beneath the water than they did from above, and that the color of the gateway was harder to make out. The depth of water to the bottom was about fifteen feet where the barrier existed. Seth looked at his Portgen, checking to see if it was still working. The display screen was still reading functional.

Jason swam out past the barrier, curious to see how deep he could dive. When he turned back, he noticed that he could still see the others. They were still within the protection of the barrier, but he was now in the first dimension where, if he swam topside, he could be seen by others traveling by. He swam down to the bottom of the ocean floor, another fifteen feet deeper than Seth, watching the screen of his Portgen. His screen suddenly went blank letting him know that the Portgen couldn't handle the pressure or the water. As he traveled back upward to swim back through the barrier into the third dimension of the island, something caught his attention just off to his right. As he turned to look, a large shark was swimming toward him. Jason reached out and pushed the shark away from him. He swam quicker, hoping to reach the barrier before the shark could return, but once again it was swimming toward him. Jason's brain hurried to rationalize a plan, when suddenly the shark was caught up in a swirling mass of water which carried him away from Jason. Jason scanned the water, searching for an explanation, when he saw Sean controlling the mass of swirling water which placed the shark far enough away for them to swim safely through the barrier. The shark looked frightened as it swam quickly away from where the swirling water had deposited him. Jason gave Sean a thumbs up as thanks and the two of them swam back through the barrier and toward the beach.

As they exited the water, the four men handed their Portgens over to Simon, Malachai, Vashti, and Prisca who tried to get them to work.

"Well," Simon said deflated, "It appears that being underwater for that length of time has finished them all. None of the Portgens will even turn on. It appears that we may have a problem on our hands."

He turned to address everyone there. "It appears that you will all need to turn your Portgens over to Ryan soon. We'll need him to see if he can figure out how to make them all waterproof. I'm not keen on exploring the underwater portals without a safe way to return. You can all go back to whatever it was you were doing until further notice."

Jason walked over to Sean. "Hey, Sean, thanks man. I would have been fish food if you hadn't been out there."

"No problem, Jason. I'm just glad Oz backed out of going. I just felt that I really needed to go on this dive."

"You and me both, man. And thanks for listening to the urgings of God." Jason slapped him on the shoulder. The group dispersed as the groundskeeper again hauled the equipment back up to the house in the four-wheeled ATV.

Uriah watched everyone walking back, and he decided this would be a good time to speak with Bridget. He had been wanting to talk with her. She may have some important information concerning Hiram's last days that might help him to implement the plan they had made years ago. Bridget might also take to her father's work, eventually. If she knew what her father had in mind for man kinds future, perhaps she would join him? She was, after all, Hiram's daughter.

"Hello, Bridget," Uriah said, walking up beside her.

"Hello, Uriah. Can I help you with something?"

"No, not at all. I just thought that you might have more questions about your father that you may want me to answer," he offered.

Bridget thought for a second. "Well, could you maybe tell me how my father and mother met?"

After finding out about Marnor, she figured she should learn a bit more about her parents to decide whether or not Marnor had been telling her the truth. Of course, he had no reason to lie to her about such a thing, but she still didn't trust the man.

"Let's see what I can remember." He smiled down at her. "Your father was an intriguing man. He was always studying charts, maps, storms, and time travel. He was fascinated at how it was all possible. Everyone tried to tell him not to over think it all, but he was certain that he could figure out a way to find new places. He always said, that with all the places we had already discovered, that there had to be hidden planes somewhere within the dimensions. He monitored storms and their strengths and made meticulous details about them. He soon discovered that any storm that reached a particular strength, under the correct circumstances, would open a portal within a portal. That was when he discovered Zanchier. He wanted to pass through and see what was there for himself. When the conditions were right, and a storm was imminent, he waited inside the portal without passing through to the other side, and it led him to Zanchier, where he first saw Mary. He told me that the first time he had seen your mother, he was instantly smitten."

Bridget smiled brightly at Uriah.

"He said that she was the most beautiful woman he had ever seen. You resemble her a lot you know."

Bridget smiled even more. "Really? I don't remember mother very much. Father never spoke of her."

Not wishing to shut her down with depressing conversation, Uriah continued. "Your father spoke of her often. And, now that he had storms figured out, he went back to see her as often as possible."

"But how did he get back from Zanchier so easily? The only way out of there was through the dustbowl which was hundreds of miles away from Storm Valley."

"Well, in one of his earliest visits to Zanchier, he met a man that knew he was a stranger from another world. The man then explained to him how to leave by way of the valley instead of the Dustbowl."

"How?" she asked curiously.

"I'm not certain. He never really gave me that information before he disappeared. I'm sure the answer lies somewhere within his books."

Bridget thought about her father's books. She hadn't looked at them since they came to Reader's Island. Perhaps she needed to study them further.

"Anyhow, back to your father and mother," Uriah said, trying to keep her on track with where he wanted her. "Hiram fell madly in love with Mary and continued to visit with her over the course of a year. They were soon married when Hiram thought that he had figured out a way for Mary to pass through the portal. You know the rest of the story from there."

"Yes, Unfortunately," Bridget said woefully. "Uriah, did my mother have any other children?"

"I think so. I remember your father mentioning her having a son, but he said the boy was belligerent, willful, and didn't like him much."

"Do you know how old he was then? The boy I mean."

"Well, maybe about thirteen or so I think. Why do you ask?"

"I was just curious whether she had other children. I did live there for a while, so it just made me wonder." Bridget decided not to ask any more questions. She didn't feel like discussing Marnor right now. She didn't want everyone to know that she had yet another bad person in her family tree.

Oz watched nonchalantly from a distance as Uriah quietly spoke with Bridget. The two of them walked and chatted congenially all the way back to the main house. Oz decided he wasn't too keen on Uriah getting friendly with his sweet, little, Bridget. He would have to chat with her about Uriah very soon. He wasn't sure what he would tell her, but he would warn her somehow about getting too close to the man without letting on about him being watched. None of the others except for the group leaders and Dragoman knew there was a betrayer. They had all done a good job of concealing that fact. He wasn't planning on blowing the whistle just yet, besides, the Dragoman had instructed them to make it look as though the discovery was a surprise to everyone. And, technically, he had yet to find proof that it was Uriah. But for Oz, Uriah was the obvious choice. He fit the profile, was trained by Hiram, and apparently had it out for everyone. Like Hiram, Uriah had let all his past disappointments along with all the new ones take root and darken his very soul. Oz had a feeling that Uriah was up to something, and he was going to figure it out and stop him if it was the last thing he did. He would not allow anyone to harm his friends again like Hiram did thirteen years ago.

If any of you lacks wisdom, you should ask God, who gives
generously to all without finding fault, and it will be given to you.

James 1:5

Chapter 7

Akrotiri, Underwater City, Sea of Crete

Dekker and Annabelle got up early the next morning and walked the
city streets of Akrotiri. They ventured to the city courtyard where
Dekker explained to Annabelle what they were doing as she
watched the guards in training. After which, Dekker took her to the
docks to watch the fishermen bring in the day's catch. Annabelle had
never seen fish like some of the ones they hauled in. Some were *very*
strange looking, like something out of a science fiction story.

After watching the fishermen haul in their catches, and the
market merchants coming down to purchase the fish to sell at the
market, they purchased a few small fish from one of the fishermen,
stopped at the market to purchase some fresh loaves of bread and
some fruits for a late lunch, then returned to Dekker's home to have
a bite to eat.

Annabelle smiled appreciatively. "These fish may look strange,
but they sure do taste good," she said contorting her face in
confusion at the long, spiky, bluish-green colored fish.

Dekker smiled at her remark. "Yes, they are very tasty.
Sometimes they're hard to clean and handle because of the spikes,
but you learn quickly if you want to eat," he chuckled along with
Annabelle.

"Mr. Dekker, what do you do to make money here?"

"Well, that is a good question. Some days, I help a friend at the
market with his booth. When needed, I also do blacksmith work for
carts and weapons. Other days, I work at the community gardens,

planting, tilling the soil, and watering things. There is no rain here, so we often distill the sea water at a distillery to use for watering the plants. There are a few freshwater pools back up on the edges of the city that we use for drinking water."

"Don't plants need sunshine as well?"

"Normally, yes. But whatever light we receive from whatever source seems to be enough to help the plants grow. They do struggle more than they would above the ground, but they do well enough to feed the city."

"It's strange to think that we are somewhere beneath the ocean's surface. Do you think we will ever see the sunlight, or grass again?"

"I'm not sure, Annabelle. All I know is that God called me here for a reason. Wherever we end up after our purpose is fulfilled is up to God."

"I suppose you're right. I'm glad to be here. I just don't want to go back to the orphanage."

Dekker smiled at her. He tried to see her as clearly as he could, but all he could make out was a blurred shape.

As she sat chewing her food, the wheels of her mind continued to turn, causing her to ask, "What is a blacksmith?"

"It is an occupation where I take metal and heat it with fire. Then I beat it with tools to shape it into whatever I need. I make cart-wheels, swords, horseshoes, buckles, fish-hooks, boat anchors, and whatever else is needed."

"I would like to see you make something."

"I think that can be arranged, right after we finish lunch."

They finished eating, cleaned up, then left the building and walked to a small wooden shed just around the corner from Dekker's home. Inside the wooden structure was a large stone fireplace, a large anvil, several hammers, large tongs, and other tools, large tubs of oil on the floor beside the anvil and a huge stack of wood and coal against one wall.

Dekker opened the large swinging doors on the front and two shuttered windows on each side of the shed. He then started a fire, stoking it to heat quickly. He took a sword that he had apparently been working on and laid it in the fire.

Dekker explained to her each step as he did it, so she would understand why he did them and why they were necessary. She sat and watched him work on the sword for the rest of the afternoon.

"How do you do blacksmithing if you can't see, Mr. Dekker?"

"Well, I used to do it before I lost most of my sight. Now I rely on my other senses and memories to help me. It is mostly by feel. I can tell what I need to do by the weight and balance of the object that I am working on. After it cools, I can tell by touch."

Annabelle was fascinated that the man could do something like this without being able to see properly. It gave her hope for her own abilities and future.

Before she knew it, it had grown late in the day, which was hard to tell since the light outside did not change all that much. The light did wane some which was a sign of the hour, but it never truly grew dark. They closed the shop and headed back to Dekker's home to get a good night's sleep.

At some point during the night, Dekker was awakened by a dream. He saw a large group of warriors entering Akrotiri, yet they were entering peacefully. They weren't charging in and their weapons were sheathed. He assumed these people were warriors for most of them were clothed like that of a warrior. Their clothing, however, was more modern than that which the Akrotirians wore. Could these people be invaders of Akrotiri? The Akrotirians had seen no one else since their descent beneath the water. Dekker's arrival years ago had the entire city concerned and had caused the king to initiate the training of the guards at a more regular schedule and rigorous pace. That was when Dekker had first seen the armored pieces. When he first came to Akrotiri, his sight had been good, but over the last five years of being here his vision had declined. He didn't know why, but there was nothing he could do about it. What confused him most about the vision was his ability to *see* the details of his dream. He saw the people, their clothing, their weapons, the colors of the fabrics, their hair, skin, and even the color of some of their eyes. They were of every race and age.

Dekker knew this dream had to be a sign for him to get ready. He decided that he would go to the markets this morning and get enough food and supplies to feed and house them all. He didn't know if he would have enough room in his small home, but he could put some of them up in his blacksmithing shed. He knew this dream meant that his time here in Akrotiri was coming to an end. He just wasn't certain what it meant for Annabelle. Was he to take her with him when he left? Surely she wasn't meant to stay here all alone; one so young, in a place like this? He prayed that God would reveal all he needed to know soon.

Reader's Island, Bermuda Triangle

Ryan was working diligently on a way to make the Portgens able to withstand going underwater. Malachai and Vashti helped him to quickly assemble the four damaged ones for retesting the next day. Some of the Peregrines stood and watched them work, amazed at Ryan's knowledge and abilities to design, and invent things very quickly. Sean, Kristin, and Jason were among those that quietly watched.

Sean whispered a question to Jason. "How does he figure things out so quickly?"

Jason shook his head with raised eyebrows. "I have no clue. I just know that he has always done this sort of thing. Even before he was called to be a Dragoman."

"Ryan's a Dragoman?" Sean asked, confused.

"Yeah, technically speaking,. Jason shook his head again. "I mean, he doesn't really guide any Peregrines, but when he was first called, Simon knew he wasn't meant for peregrination. So, Simon gave him the label of Dragoman because there were no other titles back then. Now, with the Keepers being a new type of Chosen, I figure there must be a title for Ryan other than Dragoman."

"I'm curious about something, I've known people like Ryan; you know, autistic; before I peregrinated. I don't think they would have understood the whole PS thing, if that had happened to them, or living like this. How did Ryan handle all of that?"

"Well, from what Simon told me, Ryan never experienced Peregrination Sickness. He didn't even appear here. Simon had a dream about Ryan, where he was told to travel to Scotland to retrieve him."

"Really?" Sean asked perplexed. "Why do you think that the Keepers and Ryan are the only ones to never experience PS?"

"Well, they aren't the only ones. Safra never experienced it either. But she can't pass between worlds without one of us being with her. I don't understand how or why all of that is the way it is, but God does, and I guess that's all that really matters."

"I wonder how Ryan reacted the first time Simon came for him?" Sean grinned, tickled by the picture in his head.

"I asked Simon that same question once. He told me that Ryan was waiting for him. Ryan told Simon that God had spoken to him and told him that he would be visited by Simon, and that he was to go with him and do as he asked."

"Wow. Now if I had had that kind of warning, it might have made it easier," Sean stated smiling.

"I don't think so," Jason said. "I doubt I would have believed it myself. I probably would have thought it was just some crazy dream, *even though* I was a believer before I peregrinated. And, if someone came to me and told me to follow them because God told them to come get me, I would have thought they were nuts." He smiled broadly. "The faith of the innocent is so much stronger than ours. We let ourselves become jaded as we grow older, to the point to where we barely hear from God at all. I'd say God knew exactly what he was doing when he brought us all here through the storms without warning."

Sean smiled. "Yeah, I guess you're right about that."

They continued to watch the three people working as Malachai and Vashti followed Ryan's directions without fail. They soon had the four ruined devices in working order, and Ryan had developed a protective layer of some sort of thick, liquid, film that he dipped them all into to coat the outer shell of the Portgens.

Ryan slightly turned toward Malachai and the others. "The Portgens just n..need to dry for the night, s..so that the waterproof c..oating dries well and hardens enough t..to keep water o..out o..of the insides of the d..devices."

Malachai replied, "Amazing, Ryan, thank you. We'll come get them in the morning and test them again to make certain they still work."

Ryan nodded his approval, returning to his work as the rest of the group left the room in search of dinner and another quiet evening of rest on their island paradise.

Jason noticed Oz headed his way with a look of determination upon his features and a sense of purpose in his walk.

"Jason." Oz came to stop in front of him.

Jason stopped to speak to the man as the others all filed past them. "What's up, Oz? You have a serious look about you."

"I'm sure I do." Oz waited for everyone else to be out of earshot. "I think I might know who th' b'trayers are."

"Really? Why so?"

"Las' night, Priss an' I saw Uriah an' Petra sneakin' 'bout the grounds after dark. I'm sure it was some sor' a' trys' they were havin', but still, why outside?"

"That is a good question, Oz. Sounds to me like they had private things to discuss and didn't want anyone else possibly overhearing what they had to say."

"Right. If it was jus' lover's chattin' then why go ta' all the trouble a' findin' a place ta' hide outdoors?"

"We need to call a meeting with the other leaders and make sure everyone else is up to speed on the situation. Hopefully, this is all just a mistake, but he does seem to be the most obvious person. I do have my other suspicions, but this is something we shouldn't ignore."

"Who else do ya" suspect?"

"My money is on Sofia."

"But she's one a' the leaders searchin' fer the trai'er."

"Yes, and that is something else that worries me. If she is one of them, then she knows everything that we discuss and every move we make."

"Why do ya' suspect her?"

"Too many coincidences that surround her and the key that went missing."

"I get that. I s'ppose you should jus' keep a watchin' Sofie then, and I'll keep my eyes on Uriah. Priss is watchin' Petra here. She said she'd keep a' close eye on 'er while we're all gone."

"Great. I suggest we tell everyone except for Sofia. If she is involved she could warn Uriah and Petra, if they are involved as well. If they aren't, then one less set of eyes isn't going to cause any problems."

"All right. Let's go an' find the others," Oz said as they turned to do just that.

"They're probably all headed outside for dinner," Jason said, the two of them walking out the door to the patio. They did indeed find the others and carefully motioned to them all to come meet with him and Oz quietly. Seth, Zaccai, Nick, and Zeke, all stood and nonchalantly made their way inside the house and toward the private meeting room they used before.

As Zaccai entered the room followed by the others, she turned noticing that Sofia wasn't present.

"Shall I go get Sofia?" she asked Jason.

"No. I don't want her included in this meeting," he said uneasily.

"You suspect her then?" Zaccai asked pointedly.

"Yes, I do."

"For what reasons?"

"I do have my reason's," Jason said. "Too many consequences surround her."

"I don't believe that she is involved in such a thing," Zaccai defended her old friend.

"I don't wish to believe it either, but perhaps you are too close to the situation, Zaccai, to be objective. You don't have to worry yourself with watching Sofia. I'll do that. And, I will not make any accusations until I know for a fact who the traitor, or traitors, are." Jason assured her.

"All right," Zaccai breathed heavily. "So, is Sofia the only person we are here to discuss?"

"No," Jason answered, "but I'll let Oz fill you all in on that."

They discussed what Oz saw and the other reasons that he had for suspecting Uriah. They spent the next thirty minutes going over everything they knew so far, and all they had seen and heard. After forming a plan of action concerning all the suspects, they then returned to the outside patio just in time for dinner.

Sofia watched them all exit the house, all at different points and times, trying to be nonchalant about it. She knew they must have had a meeting of the leaders without her, and she wondered why she had not been included. She sat and went over all the events that had transpired since she had returned to peregrination after leaving Zanchier. She realized that she did appear to look guilty of taking the key. She always seemed to be the one to find the thing or be in possession of it when it had disappeared and then reappeared. Plus, she lived on the very plane where it had been hidden in the first place. Even though it hurt to be excluded, and suspected of treachery, she supposed that she completely understood their motives. She supposed she too would have been suspicious of someone else had the roles been reversed. She ate her food as she swallowed past the lump in her throat. Some of these people were her friends and had been for many years before the new group of Peregrines came into play. It hurt that her friends might also suspect her, even if she did understand why.

During dinner, Uriah sat next to Timothy as usual. He could tell that something was on Tim's mind by the way he kept looking at him and grinning ever so slightly.

"Do you have something you wish to say, Tim?" Uriah asked him in an aggravated tone.

"No. Why do you ask?" Timothy tried hard to hide the grin spreading across his face.

"You're acting like a silly little school-boy with a great secret that he's trying very hard not to tell." Uriah laid down his fork and leaned toward Tim.

Uriah's response straightened Tim up a little as his sneaking smile disappeared. Perhaps telling Uriah that he saw him or asking about last night might not be such a good idea. But Tim feared it was too late. Uriah was no idiot and knew something was up. So, he might as well let him know what he saw.

"Nothing major, just more of a question for you." Tim cleared his throat and spoke in hushed tones. "I saw you and Petra last night."

Uriah's eyes grew large for a brief second as he quickly thought what to say. "What exactly do you think you saw?"

"I figure that you and Petra are having a fling. Or your actually in love with each other," he answered quietly, taking a bite of his food.

Uriah thought about the safest answer to give without adding more questions to the mix. "What difference does it make to you either way?"

"It doesn't. I just figured that a man like you to be void of feelings when it came to others."

"Why do you say that?" Uriah asked, growing agitated.

"You're pretty cold-hearted, Uriah. Especially when it comes to women. You don't exactly treat them as equals. You might fear,..." Tim changed the word he used when he noticed Uriah's expression turn to one of argument. "or respect some, like Zaccai. But I didn't think you capable of loving anyone."

"Right. Because you know so much about love yourself," he spat back quietly, slightly offended by Tim's words.

"More than you, I'm sure," Tim defended.

"Just because I refuse to let people walk all over me, doesn't mean that I'm *cold-hearted* as you say. It just means that I know my own value and I'm not willing to let everyone else tell me how I should live," he said brusquely.

"All right. Don't get your dander up. It was just an observation. So, what you're saying is, you do have a thing going with Petra then?" Tim stiffly smiled at him.

"What I have *going* is *my* business, not yours. So, keep your nose out of it unless I invite you into it. Understand?"

"Fine," Tim said in defense, yet still smiling ever so slightly. He had struck a nerve in Uriah. And he was curious just how deep that nerve ran. "Enough about Petra then. What do you plan to do, exactly, about *being told what to do*, as you say?"

"What makes you think I have something planned?" Uriah asked, unflinching.

"You must be thinking about something, Uriah. By your own admission, you aren't one to take all this lying down." Tim took another bite of his food.

"Why should you be so concerned with what I'm doing?"

"Maybe I want in." Tim's countenance suddenly grew serious.

"You sure about that?" Uriah asked cautiously, glancing around the table to see if anyone was watching them talk.

"I think so," Tim answered, a slight bit of skepticism lacing his voice.

"There's no thinking to it, boy. When you're sure, then we'll talk. And if I find out you spoke to anyone else about this little conversation, I'll kill you myself." Uriah looked him straight in the eyes.

Tim cockily smirked at him. "You think you could manage that do you?" he said, coolly. How did Uriah think that he'd kill him? He was virtually indestructible. Nothing had yet to pierce his skin since he'd received his gift.

"There are many ancient ways known to man on taking another's life. Do not make the mistake of thinking you're *indestructible*, Timothy," he sneered. "I've forgotten more things about killing men then you've ever *learned* in your whole, short, pathetic, little life." Uriah took another bite of his food, wiped his mouth and hands with his napkin, took one last drink from his glass, and pushed away from the table in a display of polite civility. Uriah walked away from the table and toward his room to escape any further *friendly* banter from anyone else for the evening.

Tim watched him go, knowing full well that Uriah would act on his word. Tim wondered what in the world he might have just gotten himself into. He knew Uriah to be a strong-willed, angry type of person, but he never suspected him to be the sinister, manipulative, cold, calculating type that would kill anyone who stood in his way. Tim may have made a very grave mistake by befriending the man. He only hoped that he could stay on Uriah's good side. A man like Uriah was very unpredictable and Tim certainly didn't want to find out what he was capable of doing.

Oz watched the two men talking quietly amongst themselves. He quickly averted his eyes to his plate when Uriah looked around the table. When Uriah's attention was turned back to the intense looking conversation going on between him and Timothy, Oz continued his side-ways glances as he watched them. It wasn't long before a definite transgression between the two of them transpired. Tim looked a bit worried as he glared at Uriah's retreating backside when he got up calmly and left the table. Uriah's intentions were becoming more evident the more Oz watched him. Uriah was hatching a plan of some sort. Oz just hoped that he could figure it out before it was too late. He looked around the table and noticed that Seth, Jason, and Zeke as well, had caught the exchange between the two men. They all looked at each other with questioning glances.

Oz took turns looking at the retreating back of Uriah, and the now irritable and worried looking Timothy. He wouldn't risk talking to Tim just yet about what just transpired, but he would definitely try to get closer to him to gain his trust. Perhaps Oz would be able to learn enough to figure out what was going on with Uriah.

As Uriah passed the library, Petra was exiting the room with a tray of used coffee cups from earlier in the day. He looked at her and signaled her to meet him in their usual place. She carefully acknowledged him with a brief glance, and they passed by each other without so much as a hello or smile between them.

Uriah would have to tell her they needed to be more careful. If Timothy Johnson had seen them together, then perhaps others had as well. They would have to get their stories straight about what transpired last night so there would be no further questions into the depths of their relationship.

Back outside around the large dinner table on the patio, everyone else enjoyed their meals, laughing and chatting with each other. Oz continued to occasionally gaze in Tim's direction. He noticed that even Timothy seemed to have shaken off whatever dark cloud had settled on him while Uriah was near. He chatted with Dominic, Wade, and Bridget about their hike into the upper mountain range and what they had done while there. He seemed to be genuinely interested in what they were saying, laughing along with them at whatever they were talking about.

Dinner was finished and Oz, Jason, Seth, Nick, and Zeke gathered around the fire pit on the patio to discuss what they observed at dinner. They chatted quietly but carefully so as not to draw any curious attention.

"Wha'ever had Tim's nickers in a bunch at dinner seems ta' 'ave faded now," Oz stated.

Jason answered, "Yeah, I noticed when Uriah left that he seemed somewhat put out."

Seth spoke up next. "I wonder what they were discussing so seriously?"

Zeke replied, "It's hard to tell with Uriah. He can offend just about anyone at any given point. Still, it did appear to be an intense conversation."

"An' we need ta' find out jus' what them two, or Uriah, is up ta'. We need ta' try an' play nice with Tim fer a while ta' see if he'll open up ta' us 'bout Uriah."

Jason answered, "That might be hard. Those two have been getting pretty close lately. Especially since they both feel betrayed since being removed from The Twelve."

Seth leaned forward. "Maybe so, but Tim didn't look very happy about whatever it was Uriah said to him just before he left the table."

Zeke said, "I noticed that. He actually looked angry and a little fearful at the same time."

Jason chimed in. "My thoughts exactly. I think we need to follow these two closely until we can figure out what's going on."

"Still think it might be Sofie?" Oz asked Jason pointedly.

"I'm not ruling anyone out just yet, Oz. I know you think she's innocent, and I pray you're right, but we have to make sure. This thing between Uriah and Timothy could be nothing more than two hard-headed bulls banging their horns together."

Nick cleared his throat to alert them to company as Caroline, Zaccai, Prisca, Sean, and Kristin all approached where they were sitting. They greeted them all as they joined them around the fire, and they spent the rest of the evening speculating about the underwater portals, how they thought the Staff of Moses, the Goddelikheid Crucible, and the Scroll of Rubric, were supposed to play into their next peregrination or the Final Battle. They talked well into the night, sometimes getting over-zealous and drawing the attention of everyone else, who then piled around the fire to join in the interesting sounding conversation being had by the others.

Simon, Nuncio, and Safra, being the only three left around the large table, sat watching the large group banter joyfully amongst themselves.

"Nuncio," Simon started, "we need to get to the ancient books and really start analyzing their contents. I feel the Final Battle isn't far off."

"Yes, I also feel that as well. I only hope the books reveal more about what we are to expect. We know very little yet about any of it really," Nuncio replied.

Safra, usually quiet, broke in. "Gentlemen, have we forgotten that God has supplied all of our needs so far? He has given us everything to guide us in the right direction, therefore we must rely on God to show us what we need to know. I am not against being prepared and looking through the books for answers, but we also must be careful not to rely on our own devices. We must let God lead us, now more than ever. He will show us what we need when the time is right."

Simon smiled at his wise old friend. "You are right of course, Safra. Sometimes I over think things, believing that God has given us all the tools and it is our job to unscramble all the mysteries. I forget to ask for his direction in all the hurrying and searching."

"What would we do without you here, Safra," Nuncio said, patting the woman's hand with his own. "You are a very wise leader. Much like your father Sage was for us all those years ago. Your council is much welcomed." He smiled at her.

Safra grinned and nodded to her friends at their kind words. Her father had taught her much from a very early age. It was up to her to carry on his legacy and guide where the Lord led her, but she felt a weariness in her very bones as of late. One that she couldn't explain or shake. She would have to venture to the prayer gardens tonight after everyone went to sleep. She didn't want anyone asking any questions of her until she fully understood the sense of foreboding that had taken hold of her mind, body, and soul. She would seek the Lord's guidance, spending the night in his very presence.

Therefore, I urge you, brothers and sisters, in view of God's mercy,
to offer your bodies as a living sacrifice, holy and pleasing to God —
this is your true and proper worship.

Romans 12:1

Chapter 8

Reader's Island

Very early the next morning, long before the sun's rays were due to paint the horizon, Safra returned from the prayer temple. She had spent the entire night praying and seeking God's favor for their futures. She prayed heavily for each person that was on the island, including the groundskeepers, housekeepers, and chefs. Her body and mind was exhausted, yet her night of praising and pleading had afforded her some knowledge as to why she felt such a sense of foreboding. She would return to her room at the main house, draw out the scenes revealed to her, then sleep for a few solid hours. After which, she would seek out the other Dragoman and tell them what God had revealed to her.

Safra sketched feverishly what God had revealed to her. The intense battle between good and evil which involved all sorts of strange-looking animals. Animals large in stature, unlike any she had ever seen. She was uncertain if this battle was what they had all been referencing as the Final Battle. There were certainly beasts involved in her vision. Could these beasts be the ones to which the prophecy spoke? She was unsure, but she knew that this battle would be an intense one all the same. She feared for her friends whose lives had been spent living as Peregrines and Dragoman.

This battle also showed her that all members of the island, no matter their current position, would have to fight in this battle to insure success, including herself. Safra saw herself on the battlefield as well. She had no special fighting abilities given to her by God. She could only assume herself to be a help to those who fell, helping Jason to heal them as quickly as possible.

Safra thought back to earlier days of aiding the Peregrines and Dragoman. The days when she aided her father, Sage, in helping them. Because of her father's association with the unusual people known as time-travelers, he had made certain that Safra had been trained to fight and fight well. She had been a skilled warrior in her day. She could still handle herself fairly well, even at 70 years old, but the attack on her in her Moroccan home by the teenaged street gang months back, had showed her she was weaker than she used to be. Could she handle herself in this battle? She was uncertain. Perhaps she would need to speak with Simon on how to best handle a situation like this. If God wanted her to fight, then she would without a second thought. But perhaps she should give herself a better chance, and one also for those whom she fought alongside. Safra grinned at the thoughts going through her mind. She would make certain that the path she envisioned was one sanctioned by God. If He chose for her to fight in her current state, she would do so. But if He wasn't against her giving herself and the others a better chance at success, then she would certainly take the steps to see it through.

She set her pens and papers down, satisfied with her depictions, and laid down for a few precious hours of sleep. Once awake, she showered, dressed, and headed downstairs to the kitchen for a late morning breakfast. While there, she also ran into Odessa who looked as though she also had a rough night with little sleep.

"Good morning, Odessa. You look very tired," Safra said sitting down beside her and piling food on her plate. She smiled up at Shannon, who brought Safra a cup of her favorite spiced tea, then sat a second cup of coffee in front of Odessa and left the women to talk.

"I am exhausted, Safra," Odessa said, nearly lying over on the large smooth polished table. She relished the coolness of it against her skin. The palms of her hands, the undersides of her arms, and the sides of her face.

Safra looked at Odessa curiously. She placed her hand on Odessa's skin, feeling her arms, and then her face. "You feel slightly warmer than you should. Are you feeling all right?"

"Other than not sleeping well, I think so. I'm just completely exhausted."

"Is there any particular reason you could not sleep?" Safra was curious as to what had kept her awake.

"Well, all night last night I kept having this fitful dream about a massive battle. Some of the images I saw were like none of the others I've had before. It would wake me in a fright, then I would quickly fall back to sleep, only to pick up where I left off."

"Yes," Safra said. "I too had a similar vision myself at the prayer temple last night. I've had a sense of foreboding for the last several days. One I couldn't quite understand. But it appears that the Good Lord is once again telling us something."

"Yeah, but you look rested," Odessa teased, smiling at her.

"Well, people my age don't require quite as much sleep as you young ones do." She smiled back. "Not to mention, that I'm not nearly as active as you are."

Odessa sat up straighter, using her hand to prop up her head as she sipped the second cup of steaming, caffeine laden coffee. "So, what did your vision reveal?"

"As you said, a massive battle which involved us all. Including the retired members of the island."

"I didn't see everyone else like that." Odessa was surprised at the differences. "Did you also see strange creatures involved?"

"Yes, but I was unsure as to their role."

"Well, in my dream, I saw the Keepers riding the backs of some of them."

"I did not see that part. God seemed to be revealing different things to each of us."

Odessa's demeanor changed somewhat suddenly, which made Safra very curious as to what else had been revealed to her.

"Go on. I sense there is something troubling you."

"There is," Odessa stated, swallowing hard. She took a deep breath and continued. "I saw someone fall in battle."

Safra could tell that whoever it was, had Odessa upset. She waited for her to finish. Safra looked at her in question at her silence.

Odessa knew Safra was waiting on her to speak, but she thought that perhaps if she didn't speak it aloud, it wouldn't come true. She took another sip of her coffee and knew she needed to get on with it.

"Alec. I saw Alec get struck and fall. But please don't say anything to anyone, especially not Alec. Perhaps it was just my overactive hormones, or feelings. Lately, Alec and I have had some problems between us and maybe my mind is just over playing things."

Safra's heart went out to the woman. It was hard enough to live this life without possibly seeing someone you love, get hurt and possibly die before it even happened.

"I understand, Odessa. I will not say a word. We don't want him worrying anyhow. He needs to keep his cool for battle. And perhaps what you saw does not mean imminent death. Perhaps it was just an injury."

"It just felt so real, so permanent," Odessa stated worriedly.

"Yes, but that could be the rawness of your emotions taking hold. Do not fear, dear. Whatever happens, the Lord is in control. Just remember that."

Odessa grinned at the wise, older, woman. "Thank you, Safra. You're right. Now, if I could just get enough coffee in me to be able to function today, things might be better."

"You still feel warm to me. I'm going to my room to get you some herbal tea that helps with such things. I'll be right back."

Safra got up, went upstairs, and returned with the tea, giving Shannon instructions on how to brew it for Odessa. After Odessa drank the tea, her body temperature returned to normal and the two women went in search of Simon to reveal all that they had been shown.

They found him and the others out on the training fields.

Simon turned to receive the women. "Good morning Ladies."

Safra spoke first. "We have some important news to share with you."

"All right, what is it?"

"I spent last night in the temple at the prayer gardens searching for answers to something that has been plaguing me lately."

"And did you get your answers?" Simon questioned her.

"Yes. God did reveal some very disturbing images to me."

"Yes," Odessa interjected. "To me as well."

Simon glanced back and forth between the two women. "Well, let's hear it then."

As Safra and Odessa explained to him all their dreams had revealed, Simon listened intently, his mind processing all they had said.

"Well, it appears that we need to gather the others at the house and fill them in on your visions."

"You seem very disturbed by this as well, Simon," Safra stated.

"I am. Most of these people haven't been in a battle since the one that injured them thirteen years ago, sending them into retirement here on the island. I'm not sure that most could even hold a sword or weapon anymore."

"I understand what you are saying, but surely God will provide as He always has."

"Yes, but what of Ryan. Was he plainly seen in either of your visions as well?" he asked, looking at them.

Safra looked at her old friend. "Yes, he was there also."

Simon sighed deeply and looked at Safra. He did not feel her unwavering faith. "Let us hope you are correct, Safra. Would the two of you join me in collecting all the others and bringing them here to the training fields? We'll tell everyone at once about your visions instead of making you repeat yourself more than necessary."

Odessa sighed. "Sure thing, Simon. I'll go and round up the groundskeepers." She bounded off to find them.

"And I will find the housekeepers."

"I'll talk to Clancy, Shannon, the other kitchen staff, Ryan, and Nuncio." They parted ways, and as Simon walked back up to the main house, he was worried about how the others who had been in retirement for years would take the news about taking up arms once again. More importantly, how was *Ryan* going to take the news. He had never held a weapon of any kind before. What would be his role in all of this?

Simon found the others and told them they needed to gather everyone else and head to the training fields for a meeting on a very important new development.

The large group of people began filtering into the fields, drawing the curiosity of the Peregrines training there. Everyone stopped what they were doing, watching the Island's staff approach Simon.

Seth looked at Jason who he had been sparring with. "What do you think that is all about?"

"I'm not sure. But if Simon has gathered the staff, then it must be something very important," Jason answered.

"Let's go check it out." Seth sheathed his sword.

The two men were not alone in their curiosity, as the others all began to do the same. Within a few minutes, Simon, Safra, and Odessa were surrounded by everyone on the island.

Seth walked over to Simon. "What's going on, Simon?"

"You shall see very soon, my boy." Simon grinned tensely.

He waited for the chatter and movement of everyone to stop before he continued. Simon looked around, taking a quick head-count.

"Is everyone accounted for?" he asked, looking at Safra and Odessa.

Odessa shrugged her shoulders. "I believe so. I have to admit, some of the groundskeepers I'm not really familiar with. Some of them kind of keep to themselves most of the time."

Safra put in, "Shannon and I found all the housekeepers."

"Good, Nuncio, will you take a quick head count of the island staff just to be certain everyone is here?"

Nuncio nodded to Simon to let him know that everyone was there, and Simon began the meeting.

"All right, everyone, settle down. Can you all hear me?" Simon said, as loudly as he could speak.

Everyone mumbled and nodded their replies to Simon. He explained to them about what Safra and Odessa saw in their dreams, much to the dismay, as he expected, of most of those retired.

Petra spoke up first. "How does God expect us to fight now? It has been so long since we have even had to think of doing so."

Clancy answered her. "True. We have been blessed to live a quiet existence for a good many years, unlike those of our friends who never could."

Shannon put in, "God never guaranteed that the remainder of our lives would be quiet ones. As Clancy stated, we have been blessed. But the time to use our gifts and abilities has come again, and I for one, if God wills it, am willing to fight for Him."

"But what if we are killed!" Petra stressed anxiously.

"What if we are?" one of the groundskeepers answered. "It is God's decision as to whether we live or die. And as a follower, I have no fear of death."

There were many shouts of affirmation to his words from those who once served, now ready to serve again.

"Well, I'm glad that you're all on board with this. However, I suggest that you all begin training again today. I'm a bit rusty myself, and I haven't been out of action nearly as long as most of you have," Simon chuckled.

"What about meals, and house upkeep?" Shannon asked.

"We can all pitch in there to help," Caroline suggested.

"Yes, we can all cook our own meals," Bridget said.

"And clean up our own rooms and do our own laundry," Kristin stated.

"There is still a lot of other things that need doing," Shannon stated. "And that many people trying to navigate the kitchen, even though it is large, would be quite difficult."

"We can all take turns cooking for everyone. We can team up and take different mealtimes," Sofia suggested.

"We divide and conquer on missions. We can certainly do the same here so that you can all train," Sean stated.

"I can try and work on a schedule for everyone," Zaccai said.

"And I'll help her with it," Nadia chimed in.

"I can help as well," Nick said. "Being a teacher for years makes you very organized. We should have the schedule done by lunch today," he said with a questioning look to Zaccai and Nadia, who shook their heads in agreement. "Then we can give everyone a copy and post a main view in the kitchen on the message board."

"And, since we will be at the main house working on the schedule, we will take care of preparing lunch today as well," Nadia said.

"Wonderful!" Simon exclaimed. "Now, to find you all weapons to use." He looked to the newly unretired warriors.

Clancy spoke up, "I don't know about everyone else, but Shannon and I still have ours from back in the day. They are stored in our cottage."

Others chimed in that they two had their weapons in storage, and only about five people needed to be fitted with a new weapon. Jason, Seth, and Zaccai took those needing weapons to the wardrobe and weapons room, the rest of the island staff went to their homes to liberate their stored weapons from the places they had been held for the last thirteen or more years. Once everyone returned, Simon gave explicit instructions to some of the active older Peregrines.

"All right, I want all of you more experienced Peregrines, to make sure everyone is up to speed on their training. They all likely still know what they're doing, but strength and agility might need some work. Nuncio, Malachai, Prisca, Vashti, and I will be training with you all as well."

"Simon, you and Malachai handled yourselves well back in Timna in the last demon war," Seth stated.

"Perhaps, but we could all do with more training. Especially if the magnitude of the next war is so large that our retired must take up weapons once again. Not only that, but Safra's drawings and Odessa's dreams, depict using large beasts as well. Meaning, we'll have to figure out how to get to Zanchier with the Keepers, and how to bring the beasts there, back to wherever we are to do battle. I must say, this is going to be hard to pinpoint. We weren't given a time or day when this massive attack would happen."

"Perhaps because it isn't near yet. Maybe God is giving us time to get everyone else into shape," Jason stated.

"Yes, that could be true," Simon said.

"But, if we're ta use the animals from Zanchier, gettin' the animals from one place ta another, will take som' time. Gettin' inta Zanchier might not be that hard but gettin' outa' there is harder an' takes some effert. It ain't som'thin that'll be easy er quick. It'll likely take hours ta' do that. 'Less you got some other way a' doin' it, Simon?"

"No, I don't," Simon stated, worried.

Bridget overheard them all talking and decided to let them know about her father's books. Uriah had said that he might have found an easier way to leave Zanchier, and it appeared that they needed that information now.

"Simon," she interjected, "my father's Dragoman books may have an answer to that problem."

Simon turned to her with a questioning gaze. "What do you mean, Bridget?"

"Uriah told me yesterday that my father had found an easier way to leave Zanchier. I never knew about it myself, but Uriah thinks that the answer could lie within my father's books."

"Is that so," Simon asked, now curious to get a good look at Hiram Burke's old books. "Do you have the books here with you?"

"Yes. When Caroline and I left Dover, I made sure to pack all of them."

"That is great news. Do you think you can show them to me tonight, after training and dinner?"

"Yes. They are in a drawer in my room."

"Well, it appears that things are shaping up nicely," Simon said happily. "Now let's just hope all of us older folks can whip up into shape just as quickly."

They all split up, with each currently trained Peregrine taking one of the others under their wing and working with them. Seth and Simon took Ryan to work with him. He was a very reluctant warrior indeed. He wanted nothing to do with touching a sword or gun. Seth decided that a gun would be the best weapon for Ryan to handle. He wouldn't even have to get close to a demon. He wondered if Ryan had ever even seen a demon before.

The remaining morning hours were spent training. Zaccai, Nick, and Nadia, having finished with the schedule, also prepared and brought lunch to the fields so they could take a short break and not waste time walking back and forth to the main house. After lunch, they resumed their training. All of them knowing that they weren't guaranteed any days to do so. Whenever they were called to leave the island they would have to go. It was uncertain what they were to do next, or where they were to go. So, they all decided to make the most of the daylight hours while they could. They trained long and hard all day while Bridget, Sofia, and Dominic took the next shift to cook dinner. They left the fields earlier than the rest to get the food started.

Jason looked about at the people, watching the older warriors learning new fighting skills. He was worried that some of them, especially those whose old wounds were still very troublesome to them, might not be able to handle a large-scale demon war. Adding those retired, Safra —who was nothing more than a civilian— and the current Dragoman, including Ryan who was in no way warrior material— to the fighting group, upped their total warrior count by another twenty-two people. Still, with the original current Peregrines totaling sixteen plus the three Keepers, he still couldn't imagine fighting a demon war larger than the last one. They at least had another two hundred warriors from Memnah's tribe that joined them in the fight and they still lost eleven people that day. One of which had been a gifted and chosen warrior of their very own. He prayed out loud looking over the group in training. "Lord, give us the strength and the protection we need to overcome this battle we are to face. I fear we will need you more than ever before. Grant us favor. Give us all strength."

Jason bowed his head almost in defeat already. His faith was shaken by this new revelation, and his marine-trained mind couldn't understand how they were to win a battle against the magnitude of evil forces that Safra and Odessa predicted. They had no count of course, but what they described seeing was much larger than the Timna fight. He once again wondered if it was all worth it. He needed to see Memnah once more. He may not get a chance to tell her goodbye if he didn't make it out of the next battle alive, and he wanted her to know why he never returned if he didn't survive this fight. Fighting his feelings for her were hopeless. He would either find a way for them to be together, or he would spend the rest of his life loving her, alone. He knew this to be true.

He decided that he would go to her tonight after the post dinner meeting. It may very well be the last time he would get to see her. Jason shook off the feelings and put up his guard, once again pushing his feelings to the back of his heart. He then stepped into the training field to give some much-needed pointers to those trying hard to teach the others, once again praying for the safety of his friends, but silently this time.

When sparring was done for the day the retired people all fought hard not to show how weary their tired bodies were as they made the one-mile trek back up to the main house.

Clancy and Shannon clasped arms, hoping to nonchalantly drag each other all the way back. Several of the others, including Nuncio, Safra, and Simon, climbed into one of the three available ATVs and rode back. Those who arrived first took showers as quickly as possible to make room for the others who would be returning within another ten to fifteen minutes.

Dinner was ready and quickly served outside beneath the full moon and the star-filled sky. Freshly bathed people slowly drug their tired bodies to the table as Bridget, Sofia, and Dominic worked diligently to get them served.

Clancy and Shannon sat at the table, their aging, out of shape bodies aching with the day's activities even after the hot refreshing showers.

"I hope I can move my arms tomorrow," Clancy stated with a chuckle.

Shannon grinned at him. "I'll rub you down with liniment tonight if you think that will help. You may need to rub me down as well," she laughed.

Simon joined in on their conversation. "I think re-training went rather well today. Especially with everyone's inactive status of the last decade." He smiled.

"Yes," Clancy agreed, "but I have to say, the groundskeepers were the superior of all of us old-timers. Those fellas sure do know how to keep in shape. I may have to exchange my frying pan for a rake," he laughed.

"Yes, I know what you mean. We housekeepers seem to never stop moving, but I don't think that vacuuming or sweeping gets our heart-rates up quite enough." Shannon smiled.

"Same goes here," Simon said, "and I stay pretty active myself."

After dinner, they all stayed put around the table, pushing the dishes to the inside while they sat and listened to battle strategies explained and organized by Jason. The next hour was spent going over a plan. Not knowing where they were to fight didn't afford much help, but at least they all knew what their job was to be, where they were to be stationed, and who their powers would work with.

After the meeting, everyone took their dishes to the kitchen themselves and helped wash, dry, and clean up. It took them very little time to complete the chores with the whole house helping out.

The new recruits all begged exhaustion and escaped to their rooms and homes early to get some much-needed rest. The younger

Peregrines and Keepers agreed to take care of anything else needing to be done before bed.

Jason grabbed his newly refurbished Portgen and took the opportunity to go see Memnah. He opened the Portal into 1840 Israel, as he had done so many times before, and walked through just a half a mile from Memnah's village. Little did he know that upon arrival in Timna Valley, he would be watched closely by two demon-possessed men who had been on the hunt for the people known as Peregrines. One of the last places the demons had encountered these Peregrines had been the Timna desert, and the humans that lived here had helped them fight.

Marnor watched the man walk out of thin air through a small bright light that vanished after he appeared. Was this man one of those Peregrine people? He had to be, but he thought they only appeared through storms. How was it possible for a man to appear from nowhere like that?

Marnor gritted his teeth against the searing misery. He was in excruciating pain at all times and the demon within him never let him sleep, tormenting his body and soul at all times. He watched Faigen who seemed to relish the new-found feel of power. He knew that Faigen also suffered the cruelty of pain and torment, but it didn't seem to bother him as much as it did himself. Marnor began to rethink the deal he had made to escape Zanchier. His life on this side of the portal had in no way been his own. He was forced to do the bidding of his possessor, and it made him angry, which only fed the evil spirit dwelling within him further. He would have stayed in Zanchier if he had known this was the life that awaited him on this side.

Marnor decided that he would find these Peregrines as quickly as possible. The demons searched for them constantly which was a huge benefit to Marnor. If he could find them, then maybe he could find a way to be free of the demonic spirit inside him. And now, he thought that his luck had suddenly changed with the appearance of this air-walker. Marnor and Faigen took off across the desert, the darkness covering them, toward the direction the man had been heading.

The Spirit clearly says that in later times some will
abandon the faith and follow deceiving
spirits and things taught by demons.

1 Timothy 4:1 (NIV)

Chapter 9

Timna Valley, Israel, 1840

Memnah had just cleaned up, washing the dust and grime of the day from her dark, desert-tanned skin. Loose strands of slightly damp tendrils of hair escaped the loose bun on the top of her head, the damp strands brushing her bare shoulders.

Her bathing tunic had been discarded, and the large, cloth, towel was wrapped tightly around her chest and waist. Her bare feet relished in the feel of the plush rug beneath her.

Memnah was just about to put her sleeping gown on when she heard a rustling outside her tent. She blew out the candle, distinguishing any light that might cast her shadow across the fabric of the walls. She grabbed her robe, slipped it on, and tied it tightly around her waist. She carefully took her large, curved, knife, slowly pulling it from its sheath, and quietly tip-toed toward the closed flap of her tent, waiting on the intruder to make his untimely entrance.

Memnah stood still, ready to pounce. The flap to her tent began to move as it was pushed inward, the shadow of a man's form cast across the floor of her tent, lit up by the burning torches placed about their camp. Memnah raised her blade, ready to strike, when she heard her name whispered into the room.

"Memnah," came the voice.

"Jason?" she questioned, as he turned toward her.

She could see the white of his bright straight smile in the dancing flames of the firelight as it cast shadows over his other half.

"You and that knife are going to be the death of me one of these days."

She smiled at him. "Serves you right sneaking around my tent like a thief."

"I only came to steal your heart." Jason smiled more broadly as he entered the tent and pulled her into his arms.

"Smooth talker." She giggled at him, leaning up to kiss him. They stood locked in an embrace for a few minutes before she broke the silence. "I'm so glad to see you. I've missed you terribly."

"I've missed you too." Jason let her go and took her by the hand to sit down.

Even in the dark, Memnah could sense something serious in him. "Jason, is something wrong?"

Jason, never being one to sugar-coat anything, knew she deserved to know the truth. "Memnah, I've come to let you know that two women, one of whom you might remember, Odessa, had a premonition about another demon war we will face soon."

"Surely your people will overcome once more."

"I'm not so sure about this one. The one we fought here was the largest I've seen yet to date. But the one coming appears to be even bigger."

"When? Where will you fight? Perhaps my people could help?"

"I doubt that Memnah. We have no idea when it is going to happen. Besides, I couldn't bear it if something happened to you."

"And how do you think I feel, Jason?"

"I know, Memnah. But this is my life. You know that."

"I do know that Jason. But what do you expect me to do? I fear for you just as you say you would fear for me."

Jason leaned over, touching her forehead with his, his right hand locked behind her neck, his left hand clasping hers. They sat that way for a minute, just being together. Jason sat back to look at her.

"Memnah, I just wanted to tell you that I love you. If I don't make it back here, I just…"

"Stop talking like that Jason. You will come back. You have to."

"I plan on it, Memnah. I just don't see how we can win against a demon army that large with the small band of fighters that we have."

"Surely the Lord will provide if you fight for him."

"I hope so. The visions also showed large beasts controlled by our Keepers, but even still, how many of them could there be?"

"Jason, it is very unlike you to talk this way. What else is troubling you?"

"I guess I'm just discouraged lately. I feel like what I'm doing is for nothing. Plus, I miss you. I watch the others together knowing we can't be. Then, with this impending war, I just wonder if it's all worth it. Even if we do win, we still may never be able to be together."

"I know, Jason. But would you be able to live with yourself if you gave it all up? Turned your back on your friends possibly leaving them to die? You have told me so many times how important it is for you to continue. That you are part of the Twelve chosen to fight. You would grow to resent me if you chose to stay with me instead."

"You're right. I couldn't do it anyway. As much as I want to stay with you, I know that what God wants from me must come first."

Jason's senses kicked in, as he held his hand out to silence Memnah, motioning for her to be quiet. He could sense demons. Why would they be here? Had he led them here, endangering Memnah in the process?

He stood, taking his gun from its holster and walked toward the tent flap. Memnah followed his lead, pulling her knife from its sheath once more and walking around the other side. They stood there waiting for someone to walk through the flap. Jason's demon sense slowly subsided and he cautiously stepped through the tent flap to the outside, scanning the area around him. Memnah's people were milling about their camp, undisturbed by anything. Jason turned to Memnah who had followed him outside.

"I'm not sure what's going on, but I need to get back to the island. I had intended to stay with you for a while this evening, but I think I'm endangering you by being here. I know I sensed demons a minute ago but now the feeling has left. I'm afraid I need to leave, maybe draw them away. But you need to stay on alert for a while."

"But what about you? What if they attack you in the desert alone?" she asked, worried.

"I do this all the time, Memnah, I'll be just fine. Just know that I'll love you, for eternity." Jason placed his hand on her cheek.

"And I you." She took his hand in hers and kissed the palm.

He leaned in and kissed her goodbye once again and set out into the night to find a hidden place to open the Portgen portal. If it were demons, he certainly didn't want them getting a hold of the Portgen. They could use it against them. He may need to see about having Ryan design a failproof switch or something that only allowed them to work based on the owner's DNA.

Jason found a stand of rocks and slipped in between them. He glanced around, just to make certain he wasn't being watched, and opened a portal to Reader's Island.

Marnor and Faigen watched the man disappear through some sort of hole that appeared out of nowhere. Looking through the large spyglass that he held, Marnor did notice that the man used some sort of small, hand-held device to open the hole. He thought back to the years before on Zanchier when they used to catch and torture these people for information on how they traveled, but he had never seen anything like the device this man carried. He also noticed that when they had followed him to the camp of the desert dwellers, that the man had acted like he knew they were there. He must have some sort of ability to sense things. What these things were, he didn't know. He knew that the demon that lay within him feared this man and his abilities. They quickly ran from the camp when the man and woman appeared outside the tent with weapons in hand. Perhaps it was the demons themselves that they sensed. An *evil* sensor so to speak. His sister Bridget seemed to think that her God was in control. Marnor had never believed in a higher power of any kind, but he supposed that if her God could give her the ability to speak to and control animals, then he could also give these Peregrines the ability to sense evil or danger. Marnor was growing even more frustrated. Would he ever be free of this creature within him? Or ever be able to get close to these Peregrine's again with it inside of him if they could tell they were there? Marnor and Faigen returned to their dimension in time to join the rest of the demons who seemed to be planning something rather large scale. Marnor only hoped that he could get free of his bondage, before whatever it was, happened.

Jason walked through the Portal to the other side. The hour was late and everyone else had crashed as early as possible. He made a mental note to speak with Ryan in the morning about the safety mechanism and headed straight for his room. He did not see the person sitting beneath the patio, under the cover of darkness, watching him.

Uriah watched curiously from the porch and the safety of the darkness as Jason walked by. He wondered to himself if there was some way that he could benefit from Jason's trips to the desert to see that tribal woman. He doubted so since she couldn't travel through the portal. Maybe *that* was the answer? He might be able to use her vulnerability to his advantage. If he could create a divide between the Peregrines and Dragoman, maybe get them fighting amongst themselves, he may not need Hiram's old books. Especially now that Bridget had handed them over to Simon and the other Dragoman to study. Then, perhaps he could use all these people and their *loving relationships* against them. Most people were willing to die for the ones they loved. And, since they weren't allowed to use their gifts against each other, then maybe it wouldn't be all that hard to do after all. He needed to get off this island and make contact with the demon-hoard leader to set his plan in motion. Perhaps he could ever use his Portgen the same way Jason did? Only, he would have to be very careful to hide his comings and goings, or he would be questioned. Uriah smiled to himself, got up, and walked into the yard behind a stand of trees near the house. He took out his Portgen, setting the coordinates for 1575, Dover, England. One year before Hiram had died. He just might be able to convince Hiram to come back before he was killed. He needed Hiram's expertise, even if Hiram had been out of practice for fourteen years before his death. Uriah had tried years before to convince him to return, but he had refused. With all the new information that Uriah had now, perhaps he could make Hiram listen. It had been very hard traveling to Dover before, but the Portgens made time-travel very easy indeed, and, made Uriah's plans so much easier to implement. He didn't know why he had never thought of this before now. He opened the Portal and walked through to Dover, England, to see his long-lost friend, Hiram Burke.

When Jason awoke the next morning, it was later than usual. He slept well last night; harder and longer than he usually did. He got up, got dressed, and went downstairs for breakfast and a quick chat with Simon and Ryan. He felt an urgency to have Ryan install some sort of safety feature on the Portgens. He ran into Simon at the bottom of the stairs headed toward the library, Jason assumed, for more book study.

"Simon, can I have a quick word with you." Jason bounded down the last flight of steps.

"Certainly, where would you like to talk?"

"How about while we walk to the computer room?"

Simon agreed to Jason's suggestion with a nod of his head, falling in step beside him.

"So, what do you wish to discuss," Simon asked, noting Jason's determined steps.

"A thought came to mind last night when I went to see Memnah. Do you remember back on Cyprus Island when Zaccai's Portgen was severed from its holder?"

"Yes." Simon was suddenly curious where the conversation was leading.

Jason stopped walking and looked at Simon. Simon halted his steps.

"Do you remember a demon picking it up and opening the portal that they vanished through?" Jason asked.

"Yes, I remember Alec explaining what he saw."

"Well, with the ease of Portgen travel, also comes the dangers."

"How do you mean?"

"Normal human beings may not be able to time-travel, but Demons can. If they happen to get a hold of someone's Portgen, that could be very bad news for not only us, but the world at large."

Simon's expression grew very dim. "I see your point."

"Well, since Ryan is a whiz at inventions, maybe he could make some sort of fail-safe based on everyone's DNA. So, the Portgens couldn't be used by anyone except who it belonged to."

"I can see how that would be beneficial, but I can also see where it could be detrimental for the Peregrine and Dragoman also."

"No more than it used to be. We've already taken Portgen travel for granted, Simon. We used to travel by storms only, and we dealt with whatever life threw at us in between." Jason took his Portgen from its holder and held it up. "These things are very handy but could also be the death of us if we aren't careful."

"Yes, I see what you're saying," Simon said. "I assume you were on your way to chat with Ryan about this now?"

"Yes. While I was in Timna, I felt a demonic presence. It was so strong and then it was suddenly gone. I don't know why it, or they, didn't attack. Maybe they were there just to observe. Perhaps they are learning more about us. Things to use against us in this new war that Odessa and Safra spoke about. If that's the case, we need to take extra precautions."

"Let's hope that Ryan can do what you are suggesting then," Simon said as the two of them entered the computer room where Ryan spent every waking moment, that is, until yesterday. He had been very reserved to leave the house at all. It was all Simon and Nuncio could do to get him to the training fields. Getting him to hold a gun had been such a chore that they almost just gave up. But Seth had a way with Ryan that few others ever had, and not only got him to hold the gun, but to shoot it as well.

They walked into the computer room and found Ryan, as usual, standing at the desk working on waterproofing all the Portgens. Jason explained to him what he wanted Ryan to make.

"Well," Ryan said, "I can maybe m..make them based on f..fingerprint scanning."

"How would that work, Ryan?" Simon asked.

"I c..can install two s..scan pads on each side where the th... thumb and first finger of the d..dominant hand would hold the Portgen. I can m..m..make it to where it will o..only work when the right p..person holds it. You will s..still need the on and off s..switch for s..safety reasons, but it won't o..open a portal without the o..o..owners b..bioscan."

"How long do you think it will take you to upgrade all of them?"

"I'm n..not sure. M..m..maybe a day or t..two."

Jason felt for the young man. When he had to talk a lot his stammer was heavy. "Do you think the water shield will cause problems with the bioscan being able to read through it?"

"N..no. The bioscan sh..should work o..on body heat. I will m..make it work."

"Great, Ryan," Jason said, patting him on the shoulder. "And all of us can help you get them ready. We will also need new Portgens for all the island staff here as well, including you."

"Yes. I..I already th..thought of that. I started m..making them last night."

Simon answered, "Great job Ryan my boy. We'll gather everyone up after breakfast and have them all meet in the large meeting room. Can you have something that will take everyone's fingerprint molds for you?"

"Y..yes. That w..will be e..easy to do."

"All right, Ryan. See you in there in two hours."

Ryan nodded his head in reply, apparently happy the conversation was over.

As Simon and Jason walked toward the entryway of the house where they would split up, they talked about recent events.

"Simon, when do you think we will be called to search for the next piece of armor? Surely, the entire island staff won't have to tag along on every mission?"

"I'm not sure, Jason. I used to think that I knew all the answers," Simon chuckled, "but it seems that God has put me in my place. Perhaps I was starting to get a big head?" Simon said, a small, shamed, grin upon his face. "I'm sure He will let us know what needs doing and when. He hasn't failed us yet."

"I understand that," Jason replied with a tight-lipped grin, "but another twenty-two people added to our regular travel party could make things very difficult."

"I don't think everyone will have to make those journeys. Truly, only the Chosen Twelve need to be present to locate the pieces."

"Yeah, but we also never know when demon wars will break out."

"True, but with the Portgens, the demons are easier to avoid."

"But if God is showing us a massive war, shouldn't we be ready no matter what we do or where we go?"

"Perhaps. But Jason, He hasn't even revealed the location of the third piece yet. Maybe God is giving us the time we need to be prepared. Such as getting the Portgens fixed, retraining the retired, gathering the necessary artifacts from our safe houses, and, getting a lead on who the betrayer might be. Do you really want to go into a demon war of that magnitude with one, or two, traitors alongside you?" Simon asked him in all seriousness.

"No, I don't. I suppose you're right, Simon. I mean, I know you're right." Jason took a deep breath and exhaled slowly. "I suppose we just keep on doing what we're doing and wait on the answer to come."

"I believe that is the best route to take here."

"Well, I'm going to get some breakfast then head out to the training fields. I'll talk to you later." Jason left Simon at the library door.

Simon turned into the library with the daunting task of yet another set of books to explore. Fortunately, he didn't have to do so alone. Malachai, Vashti, Prisca, and Nuncio were already hard at work, looking through the ancient texts they found hidden on the island. Hiram Burke's Dragoman archive books sat on the large table in the middle of the room, calling to him. He was very curious to see what he could discover between the pages of the books. Of course, Hiram had been no idiot. He wouldn't leave important information he wanted to keep hidden just stuck inside a book for anyone to find. No, he would have somehow hidden the information, even if he never expected anyone to ever see the books again he still would have taken precautions. The Dragoman decided they would spend the morning looking through the books, then head to the training fields after lunch. Then, when they returned tonight, they would spend more hours before bed perusing through the pages. Simon sat down at the table and took one of Hiram's books, threw up a silent prayer for guidance, and opened it.

Jason left the kitchen and headed out to the training fields with Seth, Caroline, Alec, and Odessa right behind him. It had been their turn to deal with the cooking, cleaning, and house laundry, such as the linens and towels. They all finished the chores in record time, having had the majority done early with only the kitchen remaining.

They all chatted and joked as they walked the distance to the fields. Odessa still had not had the chance to talk with Alec about her new-found feelings. But with the reoccurring dream of him being injured on the battlefield and not knowing how badly, she didn't want to visit the possibility of a relationship. What if he was killed?

Of course, if he were to die, shouldn't she spend as much time with him as she could. *Stop it Dee!* she admonished herself. The vision didn't show him dying only being struck. She was getting herself worked up for nothing.

"Dee? Are you all right?" she heard Alec call her name, shaking her from her thoughts. She looked up, realizing she had fallen slightly behind the others with Alec staying by her side.

"Yes, why do you ask?" she said, trying to be more chipper than she felt.

"You just look like something is troubling you very much." The obvious caring in his voice, and his thick, French, accent, washing over her like a soothing balm.

"I'm fine. I just keep having dreams about that impending battle." She didn't lie, her troubles did involve the battle.

"You know, that above all, you are my very best friend. If you need to talk I will always be here to listen, no matter what." He looked into her eyes. She wanted to melt right there. She almost told him how she felt but decided this was not the time.

"I know, Alec. Thank you, but really, I'm fine," she said, rubbing the side of his arm with her hand. They smiled at one another and picked up the pace, catching up with the others and involving themselves in the conversation that Seth, Jason, and Caroline were having.

They made it to the field and jumped into the training with the others. Lunch came quickly, then back out to the fields once again. By the time nightfall was upon them, everyone had a light meal, heard the new announcements about turning in their Portgens to Ryan again, then turned in early to bed once more.

As Seth got ready for bed, he thought about the day out on the training fields. He was impressed by the skills the retired people still possessed. Clancy and Shannon were skilled warriors, they may be a little slower from years of retirement and possibly age, but with proper training, everyone seemed to be progressing quickly. The people that took care of the island had just seemed like regular people to him. After watching them the last two days training and in sparring matches, they were still very formidable fighters and would truly be of great help in the next battle. Still, he had been talking to Jason who seemed to think that it still would not be enough.

Seth was relatively new to the whole believer thing, and wasn't very good at prayer yet, but he decided that he would give a bit more to that area during his personal prayer time before bed each night. If Jason were right, then God's favor was truly their only hope. Seth, and Caroline as well, had committed to pray for that favor in every prayer they prayed. The two of them knelt beside their bed, held hands, and prayed together for their friends and their futures.

The LORD confides in those who fear him;
he makes his covenant known to them.

Psalm 25:14

Chapter 10

Reader's Island, Present Day

Oz woke the next morning determined to talk to Bridget about becoming too friendly with Uriah. There was just something about him that wasn't right, and Oz was determined to find out what. And he certainly didn't want the man dragging Bridget down with him. Uriah had something up his sleeve when it came to Bridget. Oz had never seen Uriah be so obvious in trying to build a relationship. He wasn't the type to seek a person out first like he did with Bridget. It made the hair on the back of his neck stand up every time he saw Uriah talking to her. Which lately, seemed to be every chance he got.

Oz dressed quickly and went downstairs into the kitchen to try and catch her as early as he could. Fortunately, she was already seated at the table with her plate and Uriah was nowhere in sight. Oz grabbed himself a plate and sat down beside her.

"Good mornin' Bridget girl," he said with a genuine smile for the girl who had stolen his heart quickly back on Zanchier.

"Good morning, Oz," she smiled back. "It seems ages since we've been able to have a chat with just the two of us."

"That it has." He smiled, unsure how to broach the subject. "I noticed you an' Uriah seem ta be spendin' a lot a' time together lately."

"Yes. He's been telling me about my father and mother."

"Oh, well, ya' could a' ask'd me an' I would a' told ya' 'bout them. Well, whatever I could anyhoo."

"Yes, but Uriah offered. And he did know father very well, and even mother. Did you know my mother, Oz?"

"Not exactly, no. We never got ta meet 'er."

"Uriah said he did. He said he went to Zanchier with my father a few times where he met my mother. He even confirmed that Marnor, that horrid Scaither man, might actually be my brother."

"What's that!?" Oz exclaimed.

"Sorry, you're so easy to talk to, and I trust you so much that I forgot that I hadn't told you yet. Caroline is the only other person I've told. Dominic knows of course because he was there with me when I found out. You are the only other person besides them that I've mentioned it to. Besides, it's likely no one else knows who he is anyway. Please don't tell anyone else, Oz."

"A course not, girl. I'm sorry ya' found out a thing like that."

"Everything happens for a reason, right?" She sadly grinned.

"I suppose so." He grinned back. He decided to lead the conversation back to Uriah.

"Ya' know, ya' could a' ask'd jus' 'bout any one here an' they'd prob'bly tell ya' the same things that Uriah could. All the older folks here on th' islan' knew 'em perty well."

"Yes, but everyone sort of ignored me at first. They didn't even like me just because we shared the same last name. I suppose Uriah did to, but he at least offered to talk to me about him. He has good memories of my father. I don't think everyone could be so gracious."

"Ya don't know till ya ask," Oz encouraged.

"Well, it doesn't matter now. Uriah tells me enough."

"Bridget, I'm a lit'tl concerned 'bout ya getting' to close ta Uriah. I have a feelin' he's trouble."

"Why do you say that?" She looked at him curiously.

"Jus', ya know, the way he acts 'round ev'ryone. He likes ta stir up trouble. I jus' don't trust the man, an' I don't want ta see ya gettin' hurt is all."

"I'll be fine, Oz. I don't know why you're concerned over the two of us talking anyway. It's just conversation about things that I really want to know. My father never spoke to me about any of this.

As a matter of fact, he was vehement about avoiding the subject all together. I want to know all I can, so maybe I can understand him better. When I found out about this world, it was such a blessing to me. I was so lonely for so long, even when father was alive. I want to know why he refused to tell me about my destiny here. He must have had a very good reason for it, and I believe Uriah has the answers," she said stubbornly. "Besides, I can take care of myself. I did so for two years in Dover after father died, this is no different. And I am growing tired of everyone treating me like a little girl. I'm not you know. I turn seventeen next week. In Dover, that was marrying age."

"I understand, Bridget. We don't mean ta treat ya like a child. We jus' love ya' is all. Me an' Caroline both, an' you've made a lot a' friends here too that care 'bout ya'." Oz tried to calm the escalating tone of her voice and attitude.

"Yes, and Uriah is one of them," she said, no longer interested in her meal. "Excuse me, Oz, I have some things to take care of." She stood, ready to leave.

Oz reached out his hand, placing it on her arm. "Bridget girl, I'm awful sorry if'n I said som'thin' to hurt yer feelin's. I didn' mean ta do that. I'm jus' lookin' out fer the girl who cracked this big' ole heart a' mine open all those months back." Regret evident in his voice.

Bridget's attitude softened toward the man she saw as a grandfather. "I know, Oz. I'm sorry for getting all huffed up like a puffer fish. I don't know what is going on with me lately. I seem to be getting my knickers in a twist a lot these days. Thank you for your concern. I'll try to be careful." She leaned over and gave the man a peck on the cheek and left the kitchen.

Oz watched her go, concerned for her now more so than he was when he first sat down. She was going through something, but he wasn't certain what that was. He was going to have to enlist the help of Caroline, and Dominic as well, to keep an eye on her. And, he'll have to see about finding out exactly when her birthday was. She needed someone to make her feel special. And he thought he had just the ticket! He ate his breakfast going over things in his mind that might help in his plan with Bridget.

Seth and Caroline walked into the kitchen shortly after Bridget had left. Caroline sat next to Oz as Seth went to get them both some breakfast.

"Good Morning, Oz," she said happily.

"Am I glad ta see ya'," Oz said a bit flustered.

"What's going on?"

"Well, it appears our little Bridget, ain't sa lit'le anymore. She's dealin' with somethin' too, just not sure what."

"She mentioned something to me when they first got back from Zanchier."

"Yeah, she told me 'bout that fella' Marnor, but asked me ta keep it quiet. Can you imagine? Poor thing, findin' out that man's likely 'er brother."

"Yes, she told me as well. So, do you think something else other than Marnor is bothering her?"

"Yeah, I think so. I think she's tryin' ta grow up but feels like we all treat 'er like a lit'le kid. And I found out 'er birthday is next week," Oz stated in hushed tones.

"Really! What day?"

"She didn't say."

"You didn't ask her?" she said exasperated.

"No, I had other thin's on my mind at the time," he defended.

Caroline looked up and smiled at Seth who sat a steaming plate of eggs and bacon in front of her, turning to leave again.

"Well, we'll just have to find out somehow. Maybe I'll just ask her later when I see her. It isn't like we've all known each other for years and should know these things."

"Yeah, I s'ppose yer right 'bout that."

"We need to make some plans for a party. Maybe that will cheer her up. Seventeen is a big deal. She's basically a grown woman."

"Not ta' me she ain't. I know she ain't really my granddaugh'er, but she may as well be." Oz smiled brightly.

Caroline smiled and laughed at his protectiveness over Bridget. He was almost as protective of her too. If it weren't for her already being married to Seth, he would likely be just as much so. He reminded her of the father she had in her younger years before he passed. Her father had been more articulate and refined, being brought up as he had, and being the head of the library for years, but his kindness, sometimes gruffness, and protectiveness was much like Oz. She and Bridget had grown very fond of the large, burly, man from the Xantifal Mountains. He had tried to act all standoffish at first, but he had turned out to be a gentle giant.

Seth returned on his second trip to the table with two steaming mugs of coffee and found a seat next to her. The three of them sat for the next thirty minutes, planning out a surprise party for Bridget. Just as soon as Caroline found out the date, they would start working on it.

After their brief meeting and breakfast, they got up to go out and meet up with the others on the training fields, remembering the announcement after dinner last night to swing by the computer room first to turn in their Portgens to Ryan. He was making more upgrades to them and told them Simon would explain why when he finished with all of them.

Today wasn't much different than the last two days had been. The retired people were training hard and learning new moves and strategies quickly. They even had a few moves of their own that they taught to the newer people from back in the day when they were the ones traveling on missions.

Simon informed them all at dinner that Ryan would be finished with the new upgrades by the end of the day tomorrow, and everyone should have their Portgens back.

Jason was especially glad to hear this news since he hadn't gotten to see Memnah today. He wanted to check on her and her people, especially since he had felt the demonic presence near her village last night.

Odessa and Safra had no more leads yet as to the next piece of armor, or any more dreams or visions concerning the large battle they all faced somewhere in the relative future.

Uriah was still his stand-offish self but did seem to have mellowed out a little over the last few days.

Tim seemed to be back to normal, seemingly resigned to his fate and position.

Simon and the other Dragoman were still hard at work leafing through all the new books for any important information they might hold. They spent hours after dinner each night going through them, making necessary notations of any information they thought might be of use to them later.

Simon did find a code written within one of Hiram's books that Ryan was able to break using his computer and a cryptographic cipher. Hiram had used a series of letters and numbers to hide the instructions for entering and returning from Zanchier, without having to travel hundreds of miles from Storm Valley to the Dustbowl as Oz and the others had stated they had to do. Hiram apparently found another way to travel back and forth easily. Now Simon just had to sort through all the notes and make sense of it all. Simon was unsure as to why he went there in the first place. He must have some sort of journal somewhere that explained why he visited so much. He had to have a reason to go there to begin with in the first place. He only by happenstance met Mary while there. She wasn't his sole reason for going, at least Simon didn't think she had been.

Simon spent several more hours painstakingly looking at every detail of Hiram's books underneath a high-powered magnifying glass, hoping to spot some sort of hidden section somewhere within the books. He even tried using some magic spells to reveal any masked information contained within them with no luck. He decided to call it a night as it was well past midnight and his body and mind were exhausted. He would talk to Bridget in the morning to see if she might have left any of Hiram's books back in Dover. He might just make a trip there to look over things to make certain.

Hiram likely had things hidden that Bridget had no knowledge of. He had, after-all, kept the whole Peregrination thing from her for her entire life.

Simon took the books to lock them up for safety reasons and retired to his room for some much-needed rest. He was unaware that Petra had been watching where he had hidden the books.

Now, if she could just figure out how to get them out of the spell protected vault then she and Uriah could get Hiram's books and set out for Dover.

She watched Simon head upstairs, then sneaked back to where he had the books locked up, trying to pry the small vault door open. She spent the next ten minutes trying everything she could to get into it when she suddenly heard a noise behind her. She stopped and turned to see Prisca and Oz standing in the doorway, looking at her.

"Petra," Prisca stated coolly, "do you wish to tell me what it is exactly that you're doing?"

Petra couldn't think of anything to say to them. She just stood there, frozen in place, her brain a mass of jumbled replies.

"I think ya' need ta come along with us, Petra." Oz ushered her ahead of himself. He sat with her in the living area, while Prisca went to collect Nuncio, Simon, Malachai, and Vashti from their bedrooms.

When they all entered the room, Petra had refused to say anything. No amount of questioning was going to break her. She refused to say if anyone else was helping her, or why she even wanted the books.

Simon and the others spoke privately.

"Whatever it was that she was up to she's not telling," Prisca stated.

"We can't trust her enough to let her go. If she's not talking, then she's hiding something. She isn't even trying to deny that she was trying to take the books," Vashti said.

Simon glanced over at Petra. "Yes. I'm curious what she wanted with them? Was it just the new archives she was after, or Hiram's old books?"

Nuncio looked concerned. "Whatever it is, she obviously knows something we do not."

"She ain't workin' alone. I promise ya' Uriah's involved with this somehow. I jus' know it. 'Specially after that private meetin' between the two a' them the other night. I'm bankin' he put 'er up ta this in the first place."

Simon glanced at Oz. "Those are strong accusations to make, Oz. Uriah is already angry and put out with all the exclusions lately. If you're wrong, we could have an even bigger mess on our hands."

"Let's jus' make sure that I ain't b'fore we accuse 'im then."

Malachai stated, "He's such a hot-head that he is likely to mess up sooner or later. Especially now that we've caught Petra doing the dirty work. That is one ally on which he can no longer depend."

Prisca glanced over at the couch where Petra sat staring down at her clasped hands lying in her lap. "What do we do with her? We don't exactly have any holding cells here on the island."

"We can't exactly lock her in one of the rooms. They are all open to the balcony."

"I know a spell to place over the exits that will prevent her from leaving the room. We will just confine her to her quarters, and we will go by twos to check in on her, just in case she tries to pull any funny business," Simon said.

"Sounds like a plan to me," Nuncio stated. "I can't believe she was involved in all of this. I always thought her to be loyal."

Vashti looked at Petra again, a look of pity on her face. "Love can make a person do strange things."

They all looked at Vashti as it dawned on them what she was saying.

Simon never considered the fact that Petra was involved with Uriah. Of course, it seemed everyone on the island, whether newly arrived or old hands, had a secret or two and it usually involved another person here as well.

"All right everyone, let's take her to her room, then see if we can all manage a good night's sleep. We'll discuss further plans in the morning about trying to ferret out the other traitor before we make the announcement about Petra. We'll all meet before breakfast in the archival library, say at six?" Simon stated, sheer exhaustion starting to take hold of him.

Everyone nodded their agreement, took Petra to her room where Simon cast a holding spell barring escape through any windows or doors, and then all retired for the night.

Petra sat in her room as the weight of her decisions lay heavy on her shoulders. Surely Uriah would find a way to free her as soon as they announced her treachery to the others tomorrow. Then, the two of them would escape to a safe place where they could continue what they started so long ago. Perhaps they would soon be free of these self-righteous, pious people, and she and Uriah could lead NKRO together and rule the world.

Petra had spent her life working, slaving, and fighting for God for years before she discovered she wasn't good enough to be one of The Twelve. She thought the scar on her wrist was one of the symbols, just like the others back then thought their marks were as well. They all soon discovered they weren't the Chosen. Half of them were fine with it, and the other half were angry and bitter. That's when they started their plans for revenge fourteen years ago, but was interrupted by Hiram's sudden disappearance, and then death. Hiram was supposed to stick around and help them take control of Reader's Island, but he had suddenly just vanished, and all their plans had been ruined.

Uriah was now in position to be the New World Leader. A world they could create themselves by stopping the Peregrines and Dragoman from saving mankind and letting the demons have free reign, as long as they continued to honor their end of the bargain.

She just needed to be patient, keep her mouth shut, and trust Uriah to come through for her. She laid down on her bed in her makeshift prison and tried to sleep.

The next morning the Dragoman awoke early as planned and discussed catching Petra's accomplice. They chose to accept that Uriah was the most likely suspect since he was recently seen meeting secretly with Petra, and then fighting with Timothy one evening at dinner. They decided not to rule out anyone else, just to be watchful of the others as well. They also had another revelation once Odessa woke. As they walked into the kitchen to join the others for breakfast, she approached them with the news.

"Good morning, Simon. I had another dream last night about the next armor piece."

"Oh?"

"Yes, but I'm a little confused. I think we have to walk through one of the underwater portals."

"How are we to do that? You didn't see God parting the ocean, did you?" he asked jokingly.

"Well, actually, I sort of did."

Simon's eyes grew wide as he stopped eating and looked at her, giving her his undivided attention.

Odessa continued. "Gabriele was holding the Staff of Moses, and her shield gift surrounded the thirteen of us. Meaning, all of The Twelve, and you."

"I'm included in this vision and search?"

"I believe so. As I said, she held the staff and we all basically walked beneath the water through the portal, and into a huge cavern somewhere beneath the ocean on the floor where a city sits. I believe it is an ancient Grecian city based on what I could see."

"Well now, that is interesting. Do you know if we must walk through a particular portal or will any of them due?"

"I wasn't given that information."

"Hmm…for which piece are we to search?"

"Well, I'm a little unsure as to that too. I saw soldiers who wore many pieces of armor. So, I am uncertain which piece we are going after."

"Again, strange. Perhaps the next pieces are actually being used by an army?"

"Maybe," she replied.

"Could this army be the battle that you and Safra spoke of before?"

"No. This was totally different from that vision. I'm certain that one is a demon battle. But last night's dream was only about a handful of us, so perhaps we won't have to worry about the demon war just yet."

"Yes, you are probably correct there. Well, we'll meet with everyone later at the training fields. We have a few other things to discuss as well."

The two ate breakfast together and later joined the others at the fields where Simon filled them all in on all the latest developments, such as the Portgen upgrades, the reason for it, and Odessa's dream.

Simon addressed the group. "Odessa's dream revealed the location for our next piece. However, it only showed thirteen of us going after it. Everyone else will stay here on the island and train while we search for the next piece of armor. Hopefully this mission will not take us long."

Zaccai asked first. "Where is it, Simon?"

Simon took a deep breath. "Somewhere beneath the ocean floor."

Nick grew nervous over his dislike of deep water. "Simon, do all of The Twelve have to be in attendance?"

"Yes, Nick. Not only you twelve, but I must attend as well. For whatever reason."

"How are we supposed to get to a place somewhere beneath the ocean's surface?" Nick questioned again, beginning to sweat slightly from nerves.

"It has something to do with Gabriele and the Staff of Moses."

Sean noticed his friend Nick growing nervous, he would talk with him later to reassure him that he would not leave his side while underwater.

Gabriele spoke out next. "Me? What about me and the Staff?"

Odessa replied, "I'm not sure, Gabby. In my vision, it showed you holding the Staff and I think it was your gift of shielding that surrounded us somehow."

Gabby smiled broadly. "Cool."

Everyone chuckled slightly at her reaction. Everyone except Nick who was too caught up in his own discomforting thoughts.

Simon continued. "Also, Jason had the idea to add bio-scanning technology to the Portgens for added safety. After Zaccai and Zeke disappeared on Cyprus Island because a demon found her Portgen, we decided it was necessary. Now they only work based on each of your fingerprints."

"This next piece of information is a bit more distressing," Simon stated, growing slightly distraught. "Last night, we discovered a traitor amongst us."

Everyone grew quiet and he had their utmost attention.

"We discovered Petra trying to get into the vault where we kept the books. Even though she would say nothing, we believe she was trying to steal some, or all of them. For what purpose, we are unsure. She has been confined to her room under a holding spell. Whoever's turn it is each day for kitchen and cleaning duty, you will need to tend to her needs as well. She is not to be let out of the room except for restroom needs. Two people must be in attendance, never anyone alone; and I mean that strictly."

Simon noticed Uriah's expression turn dark and then quickly vanish. Oz might be right. Uriah could very well be her accomplice. He only hoped that Tim, who was on kitchen duty today with Uriah, was an honorable fellow and not in cahoots with them as well.

"All right, everyone, back to your daily duties, unless you are of The Twelve. You all need to meet with me again up at the house. If you have kitchen and house duties, we will rearrange that."

"Simon," Shannon spoke up, "I will handle all of that."

"Thank you, Shannon, that will be most helpful."

Everyone went about their duties, and training, while Simon and The Twelve went up to the house to prepare to leave for the mission. He and the other Dragoman spoke about watching things closely.

Oz gave Prisca instructions on keeping an eye on Bridget and Uriah's budding friendship, and their plans for her birthday surprise. He only hoped they would return before the big day.

They all packed lightly hoping for a quick trip, then went to the computer room to gather their Portgens and get brief instructions from Ryan on the new tech. After Simon retrieved the Staff of Moses they all walked down to the seashore.

Jason and Seth noticed Nick's profuse sweating as well. Seth walked over to speak with him.

"Nick, are you all right?"

Nick's nervous speech belayed his answer. "Sure," he said abruptly.

"Look, I've seen that look in many a new sailor's eye. You're afraid of water, aren't you?" Seth asked him without judgment.

"Sort of. I can swim, but since I lost my leg, I'm not too good at it. That amount of water just freaks me out, you know?" Nick answered, inhaling deeply and releasing the breath nervously.

"Look man, don't worry. I don't think we will actually be in the water. And if we are, I'll take care of you if you get into trouble."

"As will I," Sean chimed in, overhearing the conversation. He already knew of Nick's fear and was coming to walk beside him.

"Thanks, fellas. It's much appreciated." Nick was not too proud to accept help. That he learned when he returned from Vietnam with only half of one of his legs.

Simon gathered everyone near. "All right, let's all gather in closely. Gabby, I believe you are the one who is supposed to take the staff," he said handing it over.

She took it with one hand. "What am I supposed to do with it?" A confused look shadowed her features.

"I don't think Odessa's dream was that specific," he stated.

Odessa stepped up behind her. "I saw you holding it out in front of you with both hands, and your protection shield wrapped around and encompassed all of us."

Gabriele's eyes widened. "I don't know if my shield can do that. It covered the person next to me in the Timna Valley war, but I don't know if it will cover this many people, completely encompassed, underwater."

Simon encouraged her. "We won't know until you try."

"All right, here we go."

Gabriele took the staff in both hands and held it in front of her, the top of it at head level. She closed her eyes and concentrated on what she needed to do. Her shield powered up, but still fell slightly short of covering those in the back. She opened her eyes to look around, and realized it just wasn't enough.

Everyone encouraged her to try again. While she was trying to reopen the shield to make it expand, Jason turned on his Portgen to look over the enhancements. Her shield suddenly connected with his Portgen, bouncing the signal out behind him, and sealing the shield around them.

Gabriele felt the connection at that same moment and everyone else gasped in awe.

Jason was shocked and said in surprise, "Who knew these things could do that?"

"I don't think they were meant to. I believe it is just a provision from our maker." Simon grinned happily.

Gabby smiled. "Okay, now what?"

Odessa stated, "I think we all just walk together toward the water."

"All right, here we go," Gabby said, beginning forward, everyone staying close to each other. Jason kept his Portgen in hand to make certain the signal would stay open.

Nick took a deep, nervous, breath as Seth stood on one side and Sean on the other.

The band of time-travelers walked into the ocean waters as the staff parted the waters to each side, the shield keeping the water at bay. The sand underneath their feet was dry and smooth to walk on. The deeper they went, the higher the water rose, and everyone watched in wonder as the water closed in over top of them; their protective bubble keeping them dry. The water separated before them as fish scattered in all directions at their sudden appearance. They walked toward the portal which was located straight in front of them and passed through it to the other side. They continued walking forward, unsure where they were going, just trusting that this was what they were meant to do.

As they walked across the dry sandy bottom of the ocean floor, all manner of creatures darted away, startled by the strangers in their underwater world. Simon and the others looked around at some of the sunken vessels that littered the bottom, perhaps victims of the dreaded curse of the Bermuda Triangle. Otherwise known as the barrier to them.

They soon entered a large underwater cavern. As they continued on it was soon evident that they were walking upward, which meant they were likely to surface soon.

This made Nick very happy, he was feeling like he was having trouble breathing. Either from his nerves being under extreme duress, or from the possible lack of oxygen within their little protective bubble.

After about thirty minutes, the waters parted before them once more, revealing a city of some sort. Where they were was a mystery to all of them. They had no clue where they were going, unlike the other missions where their destinations had been evident before even leaving.

They continued their climb out of the water, the few people on the shore and docks scattering in shock and fear at the large group of people emerging from the sea.

They walked out upon the sand of the beach to be met by a man and a young girl, who instead of running away like the others, stood watching them with interest. They came to a stop and Gabby released the protective shield.

Nick released a deeply held breath of relief at being on dry land once more. Seth and Sean shared an amused look at his relief.

Simon stepped forward, looking around at the strange, ancient, city that lay before him as the strange man and girl approached them.

"Hello," Dekker said to the strangers. "We've been expecting you."

Simon smiled at the man and girl. "Thank you. Could you tell us where we are?"

"You are in Akrotiri, in the Sea of Crete," Dekker replied.

"Is that so?" Simon asked in awe. "Akrotiri aye…I thought it to be destroyed long ago by a volcanic eruption and Tsunami."

"Yes," Dekker replied, "As did we all." He smiled, hearing the surprise and wonder in Simon's voice. "My name is Dekker Smitt Vandenberg, and this is Annabelle Ellis," he offered.

"I am Simon Lane, and these are all Peregrines, time-travelers from other periods."

"Yes, as are we," Dekker smiled, knowingly.

Simon continued to introduce them all one by one.

Nick was suddenly struck still when the stranger introduced himself and the little girl by his side. She reminded him so much of his little Cassie. She looked very much like her and was even around the same age that Cassie had been when she had died.

Sean looked at his friend, curious as to the look on his face and why he seemed to be suddenly struck dumb.

"Nick? Are you all right?" he asked.

Nick was shaken from his state of mind. He glanced at his friend only briefly before his attention returned to the little girl who stood about twenty feet away from him.

"Yeah," he mumbled, "just seeing ghosts."

With introductions out of the way, they all followed their hosts through the streets of the city toward Dekker's blacksmith shop where he would put them up for the duration of their stay.

In this world you will have trouble. But take heart!
I have overcome the world.

John 16:33b

Chapter 11

Akrotiri, Sea of Crete

Nick followed along with the group, not really interested in the ancient buildings, statues, and people that existed around him. His focus was solely on the girl named Annabelle. She reminded him so much of Cassie that it was spooky. He knew Cassie was dead, but Annabelle's build, height, hair color and eye color, all matched that of Cassie's. Maybe he was just making too much of it? Perhaps it was simply because she was close in age, and she was really the only child he had been around for the last eight years. Even when he had taught school, pre-peregrination, he had chosen the older students. He was just unable to be around the elementary aged kids. They reminded him too much of what he had lost.

Annabelle looked back at Nick, realizing the man was watching her. She didn't feel afraid of him, just curious why he looked so surprised, and then sad, when he first saw her.

Nick noticed she looked back at him occasionally. He grew a little uncomfortable as the young girl smiled at him a time or two. He decided he needed to stop looking at her and try to concentrate on where he was and what was around him.

Sean also noticed the strange expressions that flit across Nick's face every time he looked at the girl. He wondered what had been going on with his friend lately. He supposed that he had been preoccupied with Kristin himself since Cyprus Island and that fateful ship voyage. He and Nick barely got a chance to talk at all anymore. Nick had never really shared much about his past anyway, except to tell Sean that he *had* a past with women and wasn't good at relationships. Now, with Nick's actions, Sean wondered if those relationships might have included children. And if so, was Nick forced to leave his family behind?

Sean thought about that for a moment. They all had left people behind to some degree for Peregrination, but he hadn't heard anyone mention a wife or children. From what he knew, everyone had either been single, or unmarried yet. Except for Seth and Caroline of course, but they were both brought to peregrination.

Sean looked at his friend once more. The obvious mental pain that was written on Nick's unknowing face was enough to give Sean pause. He quickly shook himself back to the present and continued walking, taking a few large jogging steps to catch up with the others. He inconspicuously glanced at Nick occasionally, his mind a flurry of questions. He was definitely going to have a chat with him as soon as he had a quiet opportunity.

Since Jason's Portgen had been on, he got a reading of their coordinates and the date once the shield had been dropped. The year read 2019. Jason's features contorted a little as confusion set in. They had never traveled into the future before this. And this place certainly didn't appear to be futuristic. It was more like history had preserved itself here.

Where exactly was Akrotiri in the world scope? he wondered.

Simon and Dekker continued to converse as they walked along the city streets; Dekker curious about their appearance and how they managed to walk out of the ocean without the need of gills.

Simon chuckled and explained their gifts to him, the underwater portal they walked through, and the use of ancient biblical artifacts that split the waters and allowed them to walk upon the sand at the ocean's bottom.

Dekker's eyebrows shot up. "You have the actual Staff of Moses?" he asked stunned.

Simon grinned. "Yes, we do. We acquired it on a mission to Israel before the temple of Solomon was destroyed."

"May I hold it?" Dekker asked.

"Certainly," Simon said, holding his hand out to Gabriele .

She smiled and handed him the staff, glad to be free of it for just a moment. Her hands and arms were slightly tired from holding it in the same position for the last thirty minutes. Not to mention the forceful charge she felt running through her body the entire time. She felt the same charge every time she used her gift to shield herself or someone else, but when her shield connected with the Portgen, she felt a jolt course through her body and the constant vibration of being highly, electrically, charged. She wasn't sure she liked that feeling. She felt a little tired after the ordeal. Of course, it could just be from the excitement of walking underwater and gazing at the ocean life that teamed all around them. They had just had the unique privilege of walking beneath the ocean's surface and seeing the wonder of it all without the aid of cumbersome equipment. It was like floating along in a glass submarine. It was all she could do to keep her focus and not allow her shield to go down. She was shaken from her thoughts as the awe in Dekker's voice brought her back to the present.

Dekker's hands wrapped around the staff as he felt every inch of it. "This is amazing. I can't believe that I am actually holding the Staff of Moses in my very own hands."

Annabelle watched her friend, grinning at his joy.

"May I touch it as well?" she asked Simon.

"Why of course, Annabelle." He smiled at her.

Dekker handed the staff to her, and she turned and twisted it in her hands before speaking again. "So, this is what Moses used to part the Red Sea?" she asked innocently.

"Well, in a sense, yes," Simon answered. "This was the staff that he used to perform many other miracles in Egypt as well. But we all know that the staff doesn't really have powers. The power comes from God, the staff is just the tool he used."

"That makes sense," she said matter-of-factly, smiling up at him.

Simon was very curious what a child such as Annabelle was doing here. She obviously was not a native of Akrotiri.

"So, Annabelle, where exactly is it that you come from?"

"Hawaii. I lived in an orphanage there for seven years. My parents died when I was little."

"And how did you come to be here in Akrotiri?"

"A hurricane hit the island and I woke up here, and Mr. Dekker found me."

Simon was shocked at what he heard. When Dekker had said, "as are we," he actually meant both of them. Simon assumed that there was someone else they hadn't met yet. Why would God bring a child of Annabelle's age into all of this? What could her purpose possibly be?

They walked into Dekker's shop as he swung the doors wide open. Simon realized what Dekker's profession was, or, had been.

"So, you're a blacksmith?"

"Yes. I was a blacksmith before Peregrination. And when I landed here there seemed to still be a need for one. Especially since my arrival sparked a panic in some."

"Why is that?" Simon was curious to his meaning.

"I was the first visitor these people have ever had since their city sank."

"Do you mean to say, that we are in an underwater cavern of some sort?" Simon asked, amazed.

"Yes, exactly that. Below and inside the very volcanic mountain that sank the city in the first place."

"I thought I read somewhere, in a more recent periodical, that they had found the city and was beginning excavations. How could both be the same place?" Simon wondered aloud.

"The ancients here tell of the highest part of the city being buried in the volcanic ash before the Tsunami hit and broke the land away. The lower part of the city was somehow preserved and was pushed inside this mountain."

Simon was shocked. "How in the world do they survive down here? Where does the sunlight or fresh water come from?"

"We aren't certain. It isn't exactly sunlight we see, but there is something that gives this place light. And the fresh water comes from streams within the base of the mountain.

"The water isn't tainted with the Volcanic gases in the mountain?"

"Some is, but there are fresh-water streams that feed pools all around Akrotiri. Having said that, the city and its people are not well. They have survived and managed for centuries, but they are weak, and disease is imminent. With every new generation, they grow weaker."

Simon thought for a moment. "You said earlier that you were the first visitor here."

"Yes, they had not seen an outsider for centuries. When I arrived, they soon realized that I was not a threat, but King Pyrrus did put an army into place to protect the city. I guess he figured that If I could arrive others could too. I am also certain that the guards will be here soon to assess your arrival and intentions."

"Yes, I noticed the terror our arrival caused. Normally when we walk out of a Portal, we are unseen. This is the first time we walked into a mission with no idea of where we were going. Hopefully they will not see us as a threat."

"You all wield weapons. I doubt that will be so," Dekker stated.

Simon looked at the others. "When the guards arrive, unless directly threatened, keep your weapons sheathed. We don't want them to see us as a threat, unless of course, things escalate."

Dekker looked around his shop. "Some of you are welcome to bed down here, others can use the limited space I have in my home. Between the two places we should be able to accommodate all of you. I can fit about five or so upstairs."

"Thank you, Dekker. Hopefully we will be able to retrieve what we came for quickly. We shouldn't be here for too long."

"Would that be the Shoes of Peace and the Helmet of Salvation?" Dekker asked Simon.

"Yes! They are both here? he said surprised. "How do you know of them?"

"Yes, they are. I believe that is why I was sent here. To locate the pieces first, which I have, but getting them will not be easy. They are worn by the top twelve commanders of the army. They believe them to be imbued with powers."

"Perhaps they are. It is the Armor of God after all," Simon stated. "How in the world are we to retrieve something that is in use?"

"You may have to fight them for it. The Akrotirians are a spiritual people, even if they do pray to false gods. If you tell them you were sent by God, perhaps they will bargain with you. But I seriously doubt they will hand over the pieces willingly."

"Yes." Simon thought deeply. "Perhaps there is a way we can get them without causing ill will. I'll think on it. All right, everyone," he said turning to the group surrounding them. "Five of you come upstairs with me, and the rest of you make your bunks here. When you are done, come meet the rest of us upstairs."

Dekker said pointing. "Second floor door up the staircase, just to the left side of my shop here."

Everyone agreed and split up. Seth, Caroline, Zaccai, Zeke, Jason, and Simon went with Dekker upstairs. The rest stayed to make their place in the shop.

Sean decided he was going to follow wherever Nick went. They needed to chat, and he was going to take advantage of the opportunity tonight during bed. He made sure to place his bedroll next to Nicks, with Kristin on his other side.

After setting their equipment down they headed upstairs with the others as Simon instructed. They walked into the small apartment home that overlooked some of the water and dock area, and some of the city on the other side.

Nick looked out over Akrotiri. It appeared to be a decent sized city. Very Greek and kept to the old ways. Of course, being hidden away from the rest of the world for centuries, not being introduced to new technologies and advancements would have that effect on a place. Parts of the city did appear to be crumbling. According to what Dekker had said, the city and its people were dying in their solation. While he stood looking out of the window of Dekker's home, he noticed a group of soldiers marching through the street below.

"I think we have company?" Nick glanced around the room.

Simon walked quickly to the window. "Yes, it appears you are correct. I'm certain we are who they are searching for."

"Yes," Dekker said, "and I'm sure they know where to find you."

There was a knock at Dekker's door, and he walked to open it. A man in uniform stood on the other side.

"Vandenburg," the man said, looking at the large gathering of people in the room. "We have a report of *visitors* to our city."

"Yes, Bartemus," Dekker answered, "as you can see, others arrived here just today. But they are peaceful and mean no harm."

"I will decide that for myself," Bartemus said, stepping into the room, a few other soldiers following behind him. He took stock of everyone there, looking to the weapons that hung from their sides and backs. "It is generally my experience, that those who come in peace do not wield weapons."

"Perhaps," Simon said, stepping forward, "but those who travel, do not do so without protection. We use our weapons for protection, not for anything else. My name is Simon Lane, and we have been directed to your city by our God."

"So, you are telling me you are messengers of the gods," Bartemus said, unbelieving.

"Not *the gods*. The one *true God*. The God of Abraham, Isaac, and Jacob."

Bartemus looked at Simon. He had heard stories of this God for years. Passed down by a few of the ancients, now long dead. "So, this God of yours, why would he send you here?"

"To retrieve some ancient pieces of armor that is sacred to our people. Armor that we need, to fight a great battle to save mankind, and that would likely end your people's isolation."

Simon's last statement got Bartemus's attention.

"What makes you think that our city is where this *armor* is located?"

"Because you're wearing some of it?" Dekker interjected, answering the question for Simon as he motioned to Bartemus's helmet and shoes.

"I will need to bring this, and you, before King Pyrrus. Your declarations must be reviewed and judged by the King and his council. You will all need to come with us."

"Certainly," Simon agreed.

"Leave your weapons here," Bartemus said.

Jason spoke at this demand. "No way."

"You have no choice," Bartemus said.

"We have every choice. They either come with us, or we don't go," Jason challenged him.

"My soldiers are highly trained. You will not win."

Jason stepped forward, now standing nearly nose to nose with Bartemus, "As are mine. And we are sent by God. You don't have a prayer, friend."

Bartemus looked around the room. "You have women warriors. What could they possibly do against a man?"

Zaccai stepped forward at that. "Would you like to find out what a woman could do?" She looked at him with a challenge.

Simon stepped in to interrupt the warring spirit that entered the room. "Now, now, everyone. Let's just take a moment here and relax. We need to go with Bartemus here to see the King, and we will be bringing our weapons. They do not leave our side when we are on missions. We will go willingly, but on our own terms."

Simon looked at Bartemus, who accepted the terms and stepped aside, letting them all pass before him out the door. Dekker and Annabelle were the last two out the door before Bartemus.

Bartemus, riding his horse-drawn chariot, led them through the maze of streets to the palace which sat at the highest point in the city. His ten, armed, men taking up the rear, either in chariots or on horseback themselves.

Seth and the others marveled at the scenery. Once through the ten-foot-high palace walls, they walked through lush gardens adorned with fountains and waterfalls that were fed by the freshwater springs that ran inside the mountain. The open-air, stone courtyards stood tall with columns that graced each edge of every pavilion. Stone benches sat beneath each pavilion and were scattered in different places in the courtyard where one could sit and gaze at the stars. Seth thought this ironic since now these people couldn't even see the sky or sun, much less the stars.

Caroline spoke his thoughts. "How sad for these people to be so isolated here for so many years."

Seth looked down at her. "Yes, but we really don't know how long they have been down here. We don't even know what time period we are in. I doubt that anyone knows."

"In a way, we are isolated from the rest of the world too, people I mean. But at least we aren't stuck in one place all the time with no way to see the sun, feel the wind on our faces, or hear the ocean waves lapping against the seashore." Caroline's thoughts took her somewhere far away.

Seth grinned at her, wrapping his arm around her shoulders. "You make it all sound so romantic."

She smiled up at him, wrapping her arm around his waist and squeezing.

They soon came to the palace doors which were already swung wide open. These people had little fear of invaders, so they had no reason to feel threatened enough to keep the King locked behind closed doors.

They entered the large hall of the castle's colonnade where the king sat on his throne on the other side.

They were ushered into the building, all taking the guards cue to bow before the seated king.

"So, you are the gods who walked out of the sea?" King Pyrrus stated abruptly.

Simon stepped up to speak. "Your highness, we are not gods, only men from the outside world where science, technology, and *our God* has provided us with many marvelous inventions."

"So, this ability to walk beneath the water can be done by anyone in your world?" he asked, a little nervous at the aspect of people walking out of the ocean and into his city.

"No. We have special gifts given to us by our God which allowed us to come the way we did. Others would need use of a special suit to breathe underwater."

"This gift, you all have it?"

"No, your highness, only one of us."

"The rest of you are like everyone else then?"

"We all have unique gifts, your highness, that allow us to battle a great evil in the outside world. That evil likely exists here as well."

The king looked at Simon, sizing him and the others up.

"What brings you to our world?"

"Our God sent us here to retrieve special pieces of armor that will aid us in winning a great battle to save all of mankind."

"Why would I care about such a battle?" the King asked.

"If we win, it may also end your people's isolation."

"How can you know this?" This grabbed the King's interest.

"A prophecy held within an ancient book that states that the veil between worlds will fall when The Chosen vanquish the great evil," Simon stated.

King Pyrrus pondered what Simon said. "How can I believe what you say to be true? Perhaps you lie to gain for yourself?"

"You have no way of knowing for certain, King Pyrrus. You can only have faith and trust."

The King watched them all, carefully sizing up each one of them. His gaze stopping and lingering at Odessa.

He turned to Simon once more. "Why do you think this *special armor* is here in Akrotiri?"

"Your captain of the guard wears two of the pieces. One on his feet, and the other, his head."

The King seemed to be on guard suddenly. "You come to take the imbued armor given to us by the gods?"

"We come to take the armor, created by the one true God. The God of the ancients, Abraham, Isaac, and Jacob."

"We do not know this God," the king stated proudly. "Why should we believe he created the armor. Our people have had the armor for hundreds of years; long before our city was sunken and preserved. The gods took pity on us and preserved our way of life beneath the sea. The armor belongs to us."

"It was created thousands of years ago by King Solomon of Israel. The pieces were stolen and separated. How did you come about the armor?"

"It was won in a great battle many years ago. The spoils of war."

"Yes, perhaps after it was stolen from the rightful people? Unfortunately, sire, we need this armor or all the world, above and below, will perish," Simon argued carefully.

"Why do you think you and your warriors are qualified to wear the armor? Only the best and most gifted of our soldiers are given the privilege."

"Because our God sent us here to retrieve it. We already have two of the other pieces out of the six that complete it. Perhaps you would like to battle for it then? Your best warriors against mine, the top twelve who wear the armor. If we win, we get the armor. If we lose, you keep it."

The King grinned. "Who will fight against my commanders? You only have seven men. Will some fight twice?"

Simon grinned. "No, your highness, our women are skilled warriors as well. They too have been called by God to fight for mankind's salvation."

The King laughed out loud, joined by many in his court. "Surely you jest," he said sobering slightly.

"No, I am very serious," Simon stated. "Do we have an agreement?"

King Pyrrus's countenance grew cocky as he looked around at the people standing before him, his gaze once again settling on Odessa.

"Yes. If your warriors win against mine, the armor is yours. But if we win, we keep the armor, and I take that woman as mine," he said pointing to Odessa.

Odessa's skin began to crawl, her anger at another man thinking that she was nothing more than property fueled her temper. Alec stepped up protesting the king's demands, but Simon stopped him quickly.

"I am sorry, King Pyrrus, but she is not mine to give. Odessa is a free woman who makes her own decisions. She is not property."

"In my world all women are property," he stated cockily.

"Perhaps, but we are not of your world," Simon stated coolly.

"No, you are not, but you are in my world now. And that is the deal, take it or leave it," the King challenged.

Odessa stepped up, her anger fueling her answer. "You have a deal, *Your Majesty,*" she spat.

He smiled at her, approaching where she stood. "You are eager to belong to me?"

She began to shake with anger. "Not at all. I'm eager to beat your warrior and show you that I belong to no man," she seethed.

He grinned at her spirit. "We shall see. We begin this evening." He turned to Simon. "At the coliseum. Each of your *warriors,*" he glanced at the women, "against one of mine."

"The rules?" Simon asked.

"There are no rules, only no killing. Our people have suffered enough death throughout the centuries due to illness."

"Agreed. My warriors are destined, and death would be an untimely event, one that I am certain our God will not allow," Simon said as he bowed.

The king turned to look at Simon, intrigued at the mention of his *God* giving them favor.

"My people have been chosen by the gods as well. We were spared from a great tragedy hundreds of years ago. Selected to survive here beneath the very mountain that wished to swallow us up. So, we shall see whose *gods* prevail. We meet at the arena an hour before sunset." He took his seat upon his throne once more, a smugness upon his features.

Simon and the others bowed ever so slightly, then turned and began the two mile walk back to Dekker's home.

Odessa still shook with anger at the king's demands. She would never become a slave to man again, especially a Greek king. She escaped the Grecian bondage of slavery fifteen years ago through peregrination. She would not go back, and she couldn't wait to wipe that smug look off the King's face.

Simon knew why Odessa was so angry, but he also knew she needed to control her anger, not let it control her. He would speak with her when they returned to Dekker's. Right now, the walk would give her time to cool down.

They walked into Dekker's smithing shop and Jason asked him, "where is an open place that we can warm up?"

"Well," Dekker thought for a moment. "There is a small valley just on the outskirts of the city. A small arena stands there back when the city thrived above ground. It is abandoned and lies in ruin but will suit your needs."

"Can you show us where?" Jason asked.

"Certainly, but you must all eat something to keep your strength up," he stated, worried. "I must prepare you all some lunch first."

"That can wait," Jason stated.

Annabelle stepped forward. "I can take them Mr. Dekker. I remember where it is."

They all looked at the young girl, most of them forgetting that she was even there under the circumstances.

Dekker smiled. "Thank you, Annabelle, that would be most helpful."

He turned to Jason. "I will pack a picnic lunch and bring it to the arena. But I suggest that you not train too hard. Reserve your strength for this evening. The guards are very skilled warriors. I have watched them train many times."

"I'll take your advice into consideration," Jason stated.

Simon spoke up, "I'll stay behind and help Dekker prepare lunch. We'll see you at the arena shortly."

The rest grabbed their water bladders and watched the young girl Annabelle, who quickly made her way to the side of Nick. He looked down at her, unsure what to make of her sudden attachment to him. Perhaps she sensed his uneasiness around her and decided to find out why he felt that way. He tried to ignore the girl as she peered up at him, but she suddenly grabbed his hand and pulled him to the front of the group with her. He was taken aback by her actions, and looked down at her small hand in his, unsure what to do. She smiled up at him, squinting against the light. He slightly grinned back; his brow furrowed in question, making her smile even larger.

She turned to the others. "This way." And began walking, pulling at Nick's hand to follow.

Everyone in the group exchanged glances with each other, smiling or shrugging their shoulders.

Sean whispered to Kristin. "I guess all of his years as a teacher make him more approachable than the rest of us." He smiled.

"Maybe." She smiled back. "But he looks terrified of her." She giggled.

Nick, overhearing their conversation, turned to scour at them. They both chuckled even harder at his obvious discomfort.

The person without the Spirit does not accept the things that
come from the Spirit of God but considers them
foolishness, and cannot understand them because
they are discerned only through the Spirit.

1 Corinthians 2:14

Chapter 12

Reader's Island, Present Day

Sofia, Nadia, Timothy, and Uriah had household and kitchen duty for the day, having to take the place on the roster for some of the Twelve that were out on peregrination.

Sofia noticed Uriah's mood and wondered what caused it. She may not have been around him for the past thirteen years, but she certainly had spent enough time around him before that.

Uriah grumbled at every task making the day drag on. Just the idea of covering for some of the others had Uriah in a foul mood.

Sofia decided she had had enough.

"Uriah, must you complain about every little thing required of you?" She asked pointedly.

"What's it to you?" He snapped.

"Everything," she answered back. "We're the ones stuck here with you having to listen to your constant complaining. Give it a rest, would you? You aren't doing anything more than anyone else has to do."

"Maybe not, but I should be out there on this mission, not stuck here like some reject."

"Hey, none of us have been chosen either," Nadia stated in frustration. "Yet you do not see us crying over it like a child. We have accepted our place, given to us by God. You would do well to do the same and let go of your bitterness before it destroys you." She stared at him in irritation.

Uriah glared at her. "Save your pep-talks for the others, they don't interest me. Besides, you are relatively new to this as well. I have given sixteen years to this life, and for what?" He spat.

Sofia stopped what she was doing and turned to face him. "Perhaps Nadia is new, Uriah. But I am not. I have been a Peregrine for far longer than even you, yet you don't see me whining about not being one of the Chosen."

Timothy watched the conversations with interest, wondering what Uriah's argument to Sofia's words would be.

"Well, unlike you, I'm not resigned to being second rate." He sneered.

"At least I don't consider myself better or above the others, like you do," she countered.

He stiffened, grabbed the prepared platter of food and drink that had been set aside for Petra, then said, "I'll take the food to Petra."

"Not alone you won't," Sofia interjected, "I'll go with you."

"Johnson can come with me." He motioned toward Timothy.

Sofia wasn't so sure about the pairing.

"Fine," Timothy said, dusting his hands on his apron then laying it aside. "I can go with him."

Sofia looked at Timothy. "She is not to be let out and no one is to converse or be left alone with her, understand?"

"Yes, I remember the rules," Timothy said irritably, following Uriah from the kitchen.

She couldn't have outright denied Uriah taking the food to Petra without letting on that they didn't trust him and were watching him. Besides, she doubted he would have listened anyway. She only hoped that Timothy wasn't involved as well and would report anything that Uriah might do or say.

Uriah and Timothy climbed the staircase that led to Petra's room. As a retired servant in the home she usually bunked in the servant's quarters with the other single women, located in the cottages behind the main house. But seeing as how that wouldn't be possible, they had imprisoned her in one of the bedrooms upstairs. Sofia had given up her room to stay in the servant's quarters with the others. The main house may have thirty bedrooms, but with the island having forty people, private rooms were sparse.

Petra's bedroom was the fifth door on the right about ten feet from the closest bathroom door. The holding spell that Simon placed on the room only kept her imprisoned if the door remained locked. Those tending to her could unlock the door to allow for food delivery and bathroom visits.

The key to her room was always placed on the tray on which her food was delivered. Uriah handed the tray to Timothy, removed the key, and opened the locked door. They found Petra sitting in a chair staring out the windows. The view she had was of the island landscape toward the beach, but not much else.

"Petra," Uriah said, catching her attention quickly, "we brought you lunch." Timothy carried the tray in, placing it on the desk that graced the wall of windows on the outside of the room.

Timothy noticed that she seemed about to say something to Uriah before she noticed him enter the room behind him. She quickly clamped her mouth shut.

Uriah spoke again. "If you need the restroom, I'll walk you over."

She shook her head yes, following Uriah to the door.

She stepped in front of him, and he grabbed her arm above her elbow to guide her without mishap. Timothy began to follow and Uriah held his hand up to stop him. "No need in both of us walking her ten feet."

"Fine, Uriah, but remember, no conversation." Timothy reminded him.

Uriah gave him a cocky look then turned to walk her down the hall while Timothy watched him closely.

He whispered close to her ear. "I'll come tonight."

She didn't respond, only entered the bathroom. When she exited, he returned her to her room, locking Petra behind the door once more. He then pocketed the key, pressing it into the small block of putty in his pocket. He removed it from his pocket before entering the kitchen and then handed the key to Sofia.

They all returned to their work in the house, with Uriah going upstairs to restock the restrooms and place the mold in his room for safekeeping. After cleaning they waited for everyone else to arrive at the house for lunch and then went to the training fields for practice for a few short hours, then back to kitchen and house duties. The day on the island was like any other day lately. Wake, cook, clean, practice, bed, then start all over again.

Uriah was growing weary of making believe that he was on friendly terms with everyone. His nerves couldn't handle friendly polite conversation any longer. He had grown to despise his life here on the island. His life as a Peregrine, traveling and doing the bidding of a God who could care less about his own wants and desires. He had been loyal for many years, even turning his back on Hiram years ago. He supposed that was the reason Hiram hadn't told him where he was going and had pulled away from their friendship. He supposed he couldn't blame him. It had taken Uriah much longer to see these people for what they really were. A bunch of mindless sheep being led about by the whims of a selfish God. Well, Uriah had had enough. He was going to do something about his future. He wasn't going to leave it up to God. He was in charge of who and what he wanted to be, and with Hiram's help, either physically or by way of his records and books, he was going to achieve what he wanted.

Uriah waited until he was certain everyone was asleep. He took the mold and snuck out to the stables where they fashioned the horseshoes. He started the fire under the forge and tossed a few pieces of iron in the melting pot. He waited for the metal to melt, then grasped the tongs picking up the small bowl and poured the molten liquid into the mold, fashioning himself a key to Petra's room. He dropped the key and mold into the cool bucket of oil to quick cool the metal, fished it out, popped the key from the mold, sanded any burs and pocketed it. He doused the forge fire, threw the mold into the trash, and went back to the house and toward Petra's room. He watched the hall to make certain that no one was around, crept toward her door, and carefully unlocked it, slipping inside her room and relocking the door from the inside.

Petra had been sitting on the bed waiting for Uriah to return. When he walked into the room, Petra stood and ran toward him flinging herself at him.

"Uriah, you came for me," she cried. "I knew you would come."

He grasped her around both biceps, pushing her away and holding her at arm's length.

"Not exactly, Petra." She looked at him with confusion. "What were you thinking trying to steal the books while Simon had them protected? You could have ruined everything."

"I..I was just doing what you asked me to do." She defended.

"I said, not to get caught." He hissed angrily, trying to keep his voice low so no one would hear them through the walls.

"I'm sorry, Uriah. What are we going to do?" she asked nervously. "Where will we go?"

"I'm not here to take you anywhere, Petra."

"What do you mean? You would leave me here, in prison?" she asked shocked.

"You got yourself into this mess, get yourself out."

"Surely you don't mean that, Uriah?" She whined.

"Of course I do. Besides, what do you expect me to do?"

"I don't know," she said, pacing. "We can leave tonight! You have a key. We can escape through the island grid. We can go anywhere we want. We'll never have to come back."

"You're daft woman. I'm not leaving, at least not yet. Do you really expect me to throw away everything that I've been working on and planning over the last six months?"

"Why did you even come here tonight?" she asked, hoping to lead the conversation toward his feelings for her.

"To make sure you keep your mouth shut about my involvement," he sneered.

"Uriah, don't you love me?" Tears began to fill her eyes.

"Why would you think that I loved you, Petra?"

"I thought…we've been intimate," she said, turning away.

"That's your mistake. That was just a bit of fun between friends."

"Fun?" her voice escalated, and Uriah grabbed her putting his hand over her mouth.

"Quiet woman, before someone hears you."

She calmed down a bit and he released her. "But you said we would rule the new world together." She reminded him.

"I never said together, you just assumed that part."

Petra began to back away from him. "I trusted you. I loved you, Uriah, and yet you would let me take the fall for everything? How could you do this to me?"

"Not only take the fall but plead guilty as the only one. If you tell anyone about my involvement, I'll kill you." His threat coldly placed before her.

Petra's eyes grew round with fear, knowing Uriah to be true to his word.

"They'll stop you, Uriah." Anger now fueling her words.

"They won't know it was me. I have my own key, remember." He smiled evilly.

Petra slunk onto the bed in a fit of tears. Uriah left her sobbing and once again locked her inside. He quietly and satisfactorily walked back to his room. Glad to finally be rid of the whiny, clingy, woman.

Timothy had been waiting for Uriah to make an appearance back at Petra's room. The long balcony that connected every room to the next made it easy for him to crouch outside Petra's bedroom window, looking inside and waiting for something to happen. He watched Uriah slink off to the stables earlier and saw the glowing of the light from the forge emanating from the barn.

Timothy had not gotten to where he had been in his professional career as the top lawyer in the state of California without learning to read people.

It was around three in the morning when Timothy saw Uriah enter Petra's room. He couldn't hear well enough to make out what they were saying, but he could tell from their body language that Petra was not happy. At first, she seemed very happy to see Uriah, then, whatever he said to her completely changed the atmosphere in the room. Tim could see that something Uriah said to Petra made her very fearful. Then, Uriah left her crying on the bed.

Timothy wasn't sure what Uriah was up to, but he knew it wasn't good. Now, he just had to decide what to do about it. Should he confront Uriah himself, or turn him over to the others? Timothy might not be happy about his personal situation either, but he didn't have it out for everyone the way Uriah obviously did. He decided there was nothing left to see tonight, and walked back to his room, closing and locking the balcony doors. He decided that he would start locking his bedroom door as well. He no longer trusted Uriah and didn't feel safe while the man was under the same roof. He climbed into bed for a fitful night due to the turnings of his mind.

The next morning, Timothy watched Uriah like a hawk, curious as to what else he might be up to. He was slightly tired this morning from the late night and the constant scenarios that ran through his mind. If he was going to keep up the Uriah watch, then he was going to need some help. Who could he recruit to help him? Should he go to the Dragoman or one of the other Peregrines? Or should he even bother with it at all? He was no snitch, but if Uriah was up to something that could get others injured or killed, then someone should know.

Timothy looked around at all the people still on the island. All the island staff were still training hard and getting better every day. He was surprised at how some of the older people could still move after so many years of retirement. Then there were the Dragoman,

Nuncio, Malachai, Prisca, and Vashti. And of course, the *non-twelve* Peregrines which included Sofia, Nadia, Uriah and himself. Then there were the three Keepers, Wade, Bridget, and Dominic.

Timothy supposed that he and Uriah really did get the short end of the stick here. Even the teenagers had a special title. Of course, all of these retired people were once active members who, at one point, thought that they too would be part of The Twelve. He supposed that God had his reasons. If only Uriah would see it that way. He thought that he and Uriah were becoming close friends, but after Uriah's threats after dinner the other night, Tim figured it best just to try and steer clear of the man. Uriah had an agenda, and it was all about himself. Tim was just glad he didn't get sucked into Uriah's plans the way Petra obviously had. Now, which of these people to involve. That was the question. Vashti was his Dragoman, so perhaps she should be the one? He decided that he would have a talk with her later, if he could manage to get her alone and out of earshot of everyone else.

That evening after dinner and the nightly devotional, Timothy managed to have Vashti meet him outside under the veranda to talk with her in private. Asking her to keep the meeting quiet and low key. He didn't want to draw attention to himself or have Uriah getting suspicious.

Vashti walked up to him, taking a seat next to him by the fire which burned in the pit.

"So, Tim, what's going on?" she asked pointedly.

"There's something I think you should know. I've sort of been watching Uriah and I think he's up to something?"

"Why do you say that?" Vashti asked curiously, trying to keep an expressionless face in case someone was watching them.

"Well, you know the rules concerning Petra. He's already broken a few of those. He even made himself a key to her room. I saw him in there last night talking to her. And whatever the conversation was about, Petra was none too happy. He's also been sneaking away at night for an hour or so. I'm not sure where he's going, but I think it involves his Portgen. I've seen the light when it opens flash on occasion. At least I think that's what it was. He was under the cover of bushes and trees."

Vashti's eyes grew large, as she listened to Tim, quickly trying to control her reactions. "Anything else you wish to report?" She was shocked that he hadn't come to her earlier than this.

"Not yet, except that I can't keep watching him on my own. I'm losing a lot of sleep and it's starting to affect my days."

"I will speak to the other Dragoman and we will take care of watching Uriah. You can rest easy."

"Thanks, but I'm sort of vested in it myself and curiosity has the better of me. I'll get more sleep, but I will ask questions. Will you be honest with me if I do?" he asked, watching her face for tell-tell signs of truthfulness.

Vashti passed the test with her answer. "I will do my best. As long as the other Dragoman have no problems with you knowing."

"Fair enough." Timothy stood up, stretching. "Well, it's time to hit the hay. After staying up most of last night, I figure I'll sleep like a log. Goodnight, Vashti."

"Goodnight, Timothy. And thank you for the information. It is most helpful."

Vashti sat in thought for the next several minutes before she was joined by Malachai who sat down next to her on the cushioned bench.

"What's got that pretty head of yours thinking so hard?" He handed her a steaming cup of flavored coffee.

She took it gratefully. "Just some things that Timothy filled me in on. We will need to speak to the others about this tonight. It's urgent. But we must act as though everything is fine. We don't want to alert anyone else to what's going on."

She definitely had Malachai's attention. "What *is* going on, Vashti?" he asked curiously, a bit concerned by the tone in her voice.

She sat and filled him in on what Timothy had told her, and the two of them decided that they would take the first night's watch. If they didn't get the chance to fill the others in tonight, then they would do so first thing in the morning. If they all suddenly disappeared into the house at the same time directly after she was seen chatting alone with Timothy, Uriah might catch on to the fact that something was happening. She didn't want to alert him in any way.

She and Malachai would both spend the night watching Uriah, deciding that it could be too dangerous for any one person to watch him alone. Uriah could be a rough person on his friendly days, and apparently, he had some dark secrets he didn't want revealed just yet; which could make him a very dangerous person indeed. If he was one of the betrayers, there was no telling what he was up to. And, he and Petra could have others in league with them. They couldn't risk letting him out of their sight for one minute. The future of man and the lives of their friends could very well depend upon it.

And I have filled him with the Spirit of God, with wisdom, with
understanding, with knowledge and with all kinds of skills —

Exodus 31:3

Chapter 13

The hour of the battle for the armor was growing close as the
Peregrines, Simon, Dekker, and Annabelle all marched toward the
large arena in the middle of the city. They could hear the trumpets
blasting their battle song, and the rhythm of the drums pounding
with each step they took.

As they entered the arena, they noticed people lining the stands,
ready for the evening of entertainment. The people of Akrotiri were
not new to these battles for the king held them weekly for training
purposes, pitting his soldiers against each other. However, the buzz
in the air let them know that this was different. The King's guard had
never had strangers to fight against before and the excitement of it
all charged the air around them.

Annabelle, Dekker, and Simon were soon escorted to the king's
private viewing box.

Simon looked at Odessa. "Keep your cool, Odessa. God will
prevail here today. Don't let your temper rule your head," he
warned.

"I know, Simon, thanks for the warning. My training with the
samurai for two years taught me that. At least we didn't have to fight
right after *the King* made his statement." She smiled at him as he
walked away, nodding his head to her with an amused look on his
face.

Annabelle grabbed Nick's hand before being led away, giving
him a reassuring smile. Nick finally smiled back at the girl.

"Don't fret little one," Nick reassured her.

"Oh, I'm not worried, I just didn't want you to be," she replied.

Nick chuckled softly at her faith. "Thank you, Annabelle."

"You're welcome. Besides, God wouldn't bring you all the way here just to let you die. He will give you all victory," she said, smiling broadly.

Everyone around them who heard the girl's words smiled and chuckled at her confidence. And she had yet to see them fight.

She waved goodbye as Dekker pulled her with him.

Nick smiled, watching her go. His demeanor quickly turning serious, wondering where she had come from and why God would choose one so young. He had thought that Bridget and Dominic were too young, but Annabelle was five years younger than Dominic. Why would God bring such a young child into a demon war? Nick couldn't understand what she could possibly be asked to do. He was soon shaken from his thoughts as Sean walked over and tapped him on the arm.

"Nick, are you all right?"

"Yeah, just lost in thought."

"Well, you better get your head screwed on straight. We're fixing to start."

The two of them caught up with the others as they were led to an area within the arena walls where they could stand and watch until called to fight.

They stood watching the stands fill with people and could feel the energy in the arena charge the air. The king's soldiers rode into the arena in chariots, riding swiftly around the grounds, loose dirt flying into the walls from the speed of the wheels as the chariots turned corners, some drifting from the speed.

The crowd cheered, roaring loudly at the thrill and excitement the thundering chariots evoked. Their favorites in today's battle, of course, being the home team; the King's guards.

King Pyrrus stood as eleven chariots came to a stop in front of the king's viewing box. They stood tall and proud in front of their king as the announcer introduced each of the four warriors that would begin the first round of battles.

Jason watched with interest, noticing the announcer introduced them from the lowest ranking officer and up. Beginning with the second lieutenant, first lieutenant, captain, and major. He then introduced the second group, which were the colonels, and lower ranking generals, then the third were his higher-ranking generals, which included Strategus Bartemus, army general, the man who came to Dekker's to bring them before the king. That still left one unannounced, which led Jason to believe that the last warrior to fight would be King Pyrrus himself.

Jason thought about the best order to place his people for battle. He looked at the Peregrines around him. They were all skilled fighters, but their gifts would not serve them here. Nor would they have used them. It would make it an unfair fight.

"All right everyone, he's ranked his warriors from the lowest of the guard to the highest. We need to figure out a lineup here. I'm going to try and pair you according to height, build, and strength. It's not an exact science, but it may make it more even."

Alec asked, "Jason, I only see eleven warriors on the arena floor. Where is the twelfth?"

"I believe the king himself will be the last to fight," he said with worry.

Odessa stepped up. "I want to fight the king," she said vehemently.

"That's not a good idea, Odessa," Jason stated.

"Why not?" she asked incredulously. "You don't think I can beat him?"

"Yes, I do think you are very capable of beating him. That's the problem. Women were never allowed to fight with the men."

"Because they see us as inferior!" she argued.

"Exactly, Odessa. Which is why you cannot fight the king. If you win, which I'm certain you will, it may not go over well at all. Could you imagine the backlash we would receive with a woman beating their king? Not to mention what they would have to live with here after we are gone. It might overthrow their entire government."

The argument Jason made did not sit well with Odessa, but she did understand.

"Let me fight him then," Alec said, ready to defend Odessa's honor.

"That's not a good idea either, Alec. You're too close to the situation. We cannot let our emotions be involved in this fight. We have to keep cool heads here people."

"Fine," Alec agreed.

Jason placed everyone according to what he thought best, leaving Bartemus strategus to himself, and Seth to fight the last warrior who was yet to be identified. Jason wanted a chance to fight the arrogant Bartemus after their earlier encounter at Dekker's home. He could tell Zaccai wanted the chance, but again, he left the highest-ranking officials to the men.

As the king's guard stepped down from the carts, standing side by side, they all realized that there was one very large man in the guard who's size hadn't been realized while standing in the chariot.

"Uh, Seth," Jason mumbled.

"I see him," Seth stated flatly.

"Maybe Zaccai should handle Bartemus and I will take on the unannounced warrior, while you deal with that guy."

"I think you may be right," Seth said, a glance passing between the two of them at the sheer size of the man. He appeared to be almost a head taller than Seth and nearly twice as wide.

Zaccai beamed from ear to ear. "Great. I want to have a go at this general." She smiled.

Jason looked at her. "Watch your emotions, Zaccai."

"Do not worry about me, Jason. I have always been able to control my feelings, especially in battle."

Jason grinned at her zeal and joy in getting to take on the pompous Bartemus Strategus.

The king set forth the rules for the games, which were very few. The only rules were no permanent maiming and no killing. Everything else was allowed. The first warrior to yield wins.

Simon, Dekker, and Annabelle were seated in the box next to King Pyrrus. One of the guards approached Dekker, speaking in Akrotiri.

"The girl cannot watch. She must leave the arena," he stated.

Dekker looked down at Annabelle. "You must leave the arena my dear. Children are not permitted to watch the games. I will take you to Heba."

"It's all right Mr. Dekker. I'll go down by the entrance and stand. You can stay here," Annabelle smiled. She looked up at the guard and grinned, then stood and walked from the arena. What they didn't know was that she had found a place within the arena to hide and watch the events. She wasn't about to miss this for anything if she could help it.

The fights began with two warriors from each side taking to the arena floor. The first two to fight from the Peregrines were Gabriele and Kristin. They fought hard and long for about ten minutes of intense one on one against their foes. But as expected the women won out. Kristin from sheer luck, and Gabriele from her years of intense training with her father. Murmurs of disbelief rippled through the crowds at the women winning.

The next two to fight were Caroline and Odessa. Odessa could feel King Pyrrus watching her as she walked into the center. Even if she won her battle, if anyone else lost, she would belong to the king. Her skin began to crawl again at the dark memories of belonging to a man. It fueled her anger and she had to breathe deeply several times to control it and set herself to rights again.

The two of them fought hard. Caroline sustaining a cut on her arm from her opponent's blade, making Seth flinch and want to run to her aid, only stopped by Jason's hand on his arm. In the end the two women were victorious, and the two losing men shamed by their commanders. Odessa walked from the field, glaring at the man who sat watching her every move. A small acknowledgement from him by way of a bowed head in her direction told her that he respected her win, but that it wasn't over yet. Again, their win drew disbelieving gasps from the crowds, but soon some began to clap and cheer for these strangers. Especially the women in the crowd who sat and watched the battles.

Next were Sean and Nick. They fought hard with Nick's opponent striking him on his prosthetic leg to the sound of a clinking noise, the man's sword vibrating in his hands. He stopped and looked down at Nick's leg, wondering why the man was not lying on the ground. Nick raised the leg of his pants to show the man the fashioned metal leg Ryan had made for him. Not only did the soldiers eyes grow wide in confusion, but those from the crowd who could see it also gasped in amazement. They had never seen anything like it. While his opponent was in a confused state, Nick struck out, making the man yield. His fear at Nick's obvious unhuman leg getting the better of him. This also aided Sean, for his opponent was curious as to the gasp from the crowd and the metal leg exposed for all to see. Sean swept the man's feet from beneath him knocking him to the ground in surrender.

As Sean and Nick walked victoriously from the arena center, Sean said, "Thanks, Nick. That was a very welcomed distraction."

"I guess you could say we had a *leg up*?"

The two men looked at each other and laughed heartily at Nick's joke as they passed the next two to fight, Alec and Zeke, on their way out. Wishing them good luck between belts of laughter.

Simon watched from his seat, his continuous prayers from the start lifting them all up to God as they each fought. Dekker watched as Simon's silent mumbling's drew his attention. He decided to help their cause by offering some of his own prayers up to heaven. The Bible did state that where two or more are gathered that He would also be there. Two praying saints couldn't hurt. With each win they praised Him for grace and victory, smiling with relief.

Alec and Zeke fought bravely and fiercely against their opponents. Alec's quick movements made him a hard target to strike. Zeke's opponent laid into his thick leather coverings with a few near-miss strikes leaving little more than bruised skin in its wake. The man he fought was strong and agile. A worthy opponent. Zeke's battle lasted longer than Alec's had, his quickly over within ten minutes due to his natural speed and agility.

Zeke and his opponent fought fiercely, each laying blow after blow to each other, strike for strike, punch for punch as their skin became bloodied, and the skin of their brows split as blood trickled down the sides of their cheeks. The man lunged at Zeke and he spun around striking him hard on the cheek one last time. Zeke then elbowed the man in the back between his shoulder blades, sending him face down into the dirt at their feet. The tip of Zeke's sword resting at the nape of the man's neck. He was out cold, his body unmoving upon the ground.

Some of the king's servants ran out to carry his limp body from the field as Zeke stood victorious. The crowd cheered emphatically for the new-comers and their impressive skills. Zeke exited the field as Seth and Oz entered. Their opponents were both emphatic and looking very self-assured.

Oz's opponent was an average-sized man, but young and agile looking, not much older than his early to mid-twenties. Oz offered up a quick prayer to the man upstairs as he shook his head, ready to fight. Oz hoped that skills and experience would aid him here. This man may be young, but he was also higher up in the king's guard which made him a skilled warrior at such a young age.

"Be nice now young fella'," Oz cajoled.

The young man smiled and said something in Greek that Oz could only imagine was meant to taunt him. It wasn't needed, he was already feeling unmatched. Strong as he was, he was not as agile as he used to be.

Seth and the giant standing before him looked at each other with apprehension; the giant was more convinced of his abilities than Seth was of his own. He wasn't used to being the small man in the room. And right now, the man before him was large enough to make Seth feel very self-conscious about his own abilities. The only thing that gave him sureness and strength was the fact that he was one of God's chosen.

"All right, big fella', let's get this show on the road," Seth said, concentrating on his foe.

The fighting began with all four men lashing out at their opponents. The younger man that Oz fought, quick in his movements, was keeping Oz on his toes. The boy could move so quickly that he could be on the other side of him before he knew it, slapping Oz on the behind with the flat side of his sword, taunting him and drawing laughter from the crowd. This only fueled the young man's playful spirit at making light of his opponent. It fueled Oz's agitation with each taunting slap.

The giant Seth fought swung at him with his mace, the air around Seth whizzing with the sound as his hair ruffled with the big movements and force of the man's swing. Seth laid a punch to the giant's ribcage, bending him over slightly. This gave Seth renewed confidence, knowing that his punches were at least felt by the large man.

The fight went on for at least fifteen minutes, with Seth dodging the man's mace while fending it off at other times with his sword. On one particular strike of the mace, Seth's sword broke, pieces shattering in all directions. Seth stood shocked for a brief moment then regained his head, dodging the man's swing once again. He quickly threw the sword from him, dodging another swing from the mace. When the force of the swing spun the giant slightly around, Seth was able to jump on his back, locking his arm around the man's throat and putting a choke hold on him. The giant struggled with all his might for almost a full minute, before Seth had him on his knees and falling forward into the dirt, out cold. Seth released his hold on the sleeping man, breathing hard himself as he stood to the roar of the crowd, which now stood and cheered loudly.

Oz was growing tired of the boy who was obviously toying with his older, less agile self.

"All right, young fella', I've had 'bout as much a' this as I can take." He reached out as the boy dodged past him once more, now striking the boy in the rear with his sword. Oz then managed to grab him by the back of his shirt, picked him up, and threw him to the ground about ten feet away. The boy rolled along the ground as Oz quickly trotted to where he had landed. The boy got up, slightly dazed at hitting the ground so hard and swung at Oz, missing him. Oz reached out, holding him at arm's length with one hand, and smacked him on the top of the head with the side of his other fisted hand, sending him to the ground in a limp pile, out cold.

The crowd erupted with laughter and cheering as Seth and Oz breathlessly walked off the field victorious.

Simon glanced at King Pyrrus, watching his reaction to all of his guards being beaten by the strangers; half of which were women. The king looked angry and slightly humiliated at the thought of each of his best so far, losing. The only two left to fight were Bartemus and the king. Simon prayed ever harder, knowing that beating the king could end poorly for them, but his God was greater and in control. He would deliver them regardless.

Zaccai and Jason walked onto the field, the last fight of the evening. The excited murmurings of the crowds dwindled as Bartemus and the king himself walked onto the fields. Zaccai and Bartemus stopped before each other as did Jason and King Pyrrus. Jason paid homage to the king by bowing ever-so-slightly to the man. The king acknowledged his actions with a slight nod of his head.

Bartemus spoke to Zaccai before he took his stance. "I have no wish to harm a woman. There is no disgrace if you bow out now."

"You have seen our *women* take the win against your soldiers so far. Are you frightened of me?"

Bartemus grinned at her words as the two took their fighting stances. "Not in the least. I am not as feeble a warrior as my men. I have no fear of a woman."

"Then I pity you. For I am no ordinary woman. I fight for my God, and He is my strength." She stepped forward and struck him; her strength making him stumble back slightly. His eyes grew large with surprise, then appreciation. He smiled at her and the two of them began to spar vehemently.

Jason and the king also began striking at each other, each realizing the other as a formidable opponent. Jason was surprised at the king's skills. The man obviously trained regularly with his soldiers. For Jason, that was the sign of a good ruler, one who fought by his men instead of sitting in rule over them with no idea as to what risks they faced in battle.

The fights went on for a good fifteen minutes, each pair being evenly matched in skill and strength.

Bartemus struck Zaccai with a punch to the chin, making her stumble backwards but staying on her feet. His eyes grew wide once again as she stood upright. He had hit her hard enough to knock her out. He was amazed that she took the punch so well. He had knocked out several of his soldiers that way. Not many withstood it. But this Nubian woman had taken it, shook it off, and was coming back at him. Bartemus had to admit, she was fit and strong. He himself was growing tired and weak from the battle against her.

Zaccai's chin ached as the skin had split and bled near her lip. She knew God was giving her strength. The man had hit her so hard she saw white light for a few seconds before her vision cleared. She felt renewed strength as she calmly walked toward Bartemus. Her staff spinning in her hands at her side. She watched as Bartemus seemed to grow a little nervous. So, she had commanded a little respect from the man after-all. At least enough to give him apprehension.

Zaccai spun in circles, her staff spinning around her, slicing the air between them as Bartemus shuffled backwards, trying to keep his eyes on her and the staff at the same time. He stumbled a bit and she took the opportunity to knock him to the ground, swiping his feet from beneath him with her staff and standing over him, the end of the staff at his throat. He had to yield as she stood too far away for him to reach her to retaliate.

The crowd erupted in applause as she helped him to his feet, and they both bowed an appreciative head to one another.

Jason and King Pyrrus had stopped their own battle for the moment when the crowd erupted in cheers. The king watching his general lying on the ground in defeat, beaten by a woman. He noticed his people cheering for the underdog, especially the women of his city. He turned back to Jason, they nodded to each other and began again, the crowd's cheering once again dwindling as they watched their king fight the last and final battle.

King Pyrrus's concentration had been broken by the wins of these women warriors.

Jason looked at the king as they sparred, and winded, said, "We could go on forever like this."

"Yes," King Pyrrus stated, winded also. "But someone has to win."

"We could call a truce. There is no shame in a king declaring a truce," Jason said striking again, as the two of them swung at each other once more, the weight of their weapons making their arms give out.

"I could not. We have never declared such a thing," the king defended, almost out of breath."

"Better a truce than to be beaten in front of your people, your highness," Jason offered.

"What makes you think you will win?" the king asked cockily.

"We have won already. The hearts of your people are with us. Our women have stirred a spirit in them. I have no desire to dishonor their king by beating you, but my God will not allow defeat. He called us here for the armor, and we will leave with it, one way or another."

The two of them were bent over, resting their weapon laden hands on their knees, trying to catch their breath.

The king looked at Jason, taking his words into account. What he spoke was truth. If he was beaten, then his people may not see him as a fit ruler. But if he declared a truce, showing humility and grace to these people, then the people would remain loyal.

Simon and Dekker, as well as the other Peregrines, noticed the conversation going on between the king and Jason. They sat almost breathless, waiting on what was to happen next, knowing the two men were exhausted after continuing the twenty-minute battle.

King Pyrrus stood, stabbed at the ground next to him with his sword leaving it stuck tightly, and walked toward Jason, his hand out in an act of acceptance.

Jason did the same as they locked hands in a handshake of civility. The king turned to the crowds who had erupted with cheers and elation, raising his and Jason's hands in the air with a hearty laugh and a smile on his face.

He turned to Jason. "The armor is yours. You may claim it tonight at the castle. We will have it ready for you."

King Pyrrus walked to his box and Jason walked off the field, back to where the others waited, the crowds still cheering heartily.

"My people," King Pyrrus spoke loudly, waiting for the noise to die down. "Today you have witnessed greatness like no other before it. Our new friends and my loyal soldiers fought bravely and with honor. We have learned humility today, and that the God of these people is a great God indeed. They have been given victory by their God. Tonight, we celebrate the joining of two vastly different cultures, banding together in friendship and civility. We feast and make merry throughout the city."

The crowds of people cheered again for their wise and just king, everyone excited about the festivities that would take place immediately as they exited the arena.

Annabelle came running into the area where the Peregrines had been waiting. She excitedly jumped up and down with joy, yelling, "We won! I knew we would win!"

Everyone laughed at her excitement and joy. Seth picked her up, spinning her in circles. "Yes we did, little one," he laughed setting her feet back on the ground.

She spotted Nick and ran over to him, throwing her arms around his waist with a squeeze. She looked up at him and stepped back. "You have a fake leg," she said, honestly and without judgment.

"Yes, I do," he grinned at her observation.

"How did you lose the real one?"

Nick couldn't help but laugh a bit at her earnestness. "In a war, a very long time ago. Long before God called me to fight this one."

She looked appeased by his answer with a nod of her head.

They all vacated the arena and headed back to Dekker's to bathe at one of the freshwater springs on the edge of the city. They dressed in the best clothing they had brought, none of which was by any means fashionable, but at least better than their battle garments. They had all learned over the years to be prepared for whatever a peregrination mission might throw their way.

They walked the distance back to the castle, as revelers clapped and congratulated them in passing. They couldn't understand what most of the people said to them, but they understood their meaning. People sang, danced, and drank in the streets, all the way to the palace walls.

Once they had passed through the walls of the palace, the party continued but in a more subdued manner. People still rejoiced, but the beaten soldiers were a little more reserved in their congratulations than the others had been. Particularly the men who were beaten by women.

Bartemus, seeing the shame in his men's countenance, decided to be the first to step forward and congratulate Zaccai and her people with true humility and acceptance. Perhaps if his men saw his graciousness and acceptance, they might follow his lead.

He gazed appreciatively on her appearance. She was a beautiful woman. Strong and gracious as well.

"Good evening, Zaccai," he said in English.

King Pyrrus and his soldiers all new English relatively well; the King insisting they all learn many languages.

"Good evening, Bartemus." She smiled coolly.

He grinned at her reply, understanding her reservations at speaking to him. "I wanted to congratulate you again on your win. I was mistaken in my thinking that a woman could not be an admirable opponent. I will not make that mistake again, thanks to you."

She genuinely smiled at him this time, revealing a perfect row of white teeth. She winced just a tad at the pulling of the now healing, but still raw split lip from the earlier fight.

The two of them laughed over the gesture, as they fell into step and spent the next few hours visiting and mingling in the crowd.

Zeke protectively watched the interaction, quickly falling in step beside the two of them and letting Bartemus know by the linking of his arm in hers, that she was taken.

Jason, Simon, and Dekker were met by the king as they entered the palace courtyard and walked toward the throne room.

"Welcome, my friends," King Pyrrus said smiling. He motioned to the wall where the Shoes of Peace and the Helmets of Salvation sat in sacks, ready to be taken. "Your rewards for winning today," he said sweeping his hand in that direction.

Simon said graciously, "Thank you, your highness."

King Pyrrus bowed his head in gracious reply. "I am a man of my word."

Simon asked, "How do you and your soldiers know English so well?"

"Being a king, I was educated in many tongues to prepare me to rule. Even though, none of those languages came in use until Dekker appeared many years ago, and now you."

Simon shook his head in understanding.

King Pyrrus noticed Odessa walk into the room at that moment. "Enjoy the party, my friends," the king said, walking away from them.

They watched him go, realizing where he was going. Fortunately, Alec, Seth, and Caroline were all with her.

King Pyrrus stopped in front of Odessa, who stiffened at the sight of him. He noticed her discomfort.

"Do not fear, my lady, for I come with humble congratulations," he said.

Odessa, still not happy at his nearness, did accept his words, even though they were not an apology.

"Thank you, Your Highness," she said with a strained grin.

"I do not wish to make an enemy of you, Odessa is it? Only, when I see such beauty, sometimes I forget myself."

Odessa, understanding what he said was meant to be his way of apologizing, smiled a bit more graciously. But she still remembered the years she suffered at the hands of Greek men like this king, and she could offer no more than what she already had.

"Thank you, your highness. Please excuse my friends and I as we visit with your warriors and pay homage for battles fought voraciously," she said with a slight bow.

Pyrrus grinned at her as she and the others walked away. He was not happy about losing the beauty, knowing she had not truly accepted his gracious apology. But he could do nothing else without inciting a war with these fierce warriors who had already proven themselves in the arena. If he could not win her over without force, then he must focus his attention's elsewhere.

The night drew late as people began to filter out of the palace grounds and to their homes. The Peregrines thanked their gracious host, took up the three sacks with the armor in them, and walked back to Dekker's for a good night's rest. They would leave Akrotiri in the morning, trying to use the Portgens first before retracing their steps through the underwater portals.

Praise the LORD from the earth, you great sea
creatures and all ocean depths,

Psalm 148:7

Chapter 14

Akrotiri, Sea of Crete

The next morning, people began to stir early. Seth was one of the first up and began waking the others. He stepped outside Dekker's door and walked downstairs. It was a strange feeling here, not to see the sun or what was the source of light that gave this place morning and night. The mornings weren't exactly brilliant, just a hazy sort of daylight. Seth stretched as he walked to the blacksmith shop to see if anyone else was awake yet. A few people were stirring and already getting up, Nick being one of them. Seth grinned, he had been wanting to speak with Nick about the new-found bond he and Annabelle seemed to have formed.

"Morning, Nick." Seth grinned as the man stepped outside the shop and the two of them walked away from the building, looking at the still sleeping, strangely beautiful, underwater city.

"Good morning, Seth," Nick replied. "Anyone else upstairs awake yet?"

"They're all getting around to it. I think everyone is a little sore from last night's *town entertainment*. That fella I fought sure gave me a run for my money." Seth chuckled.

"Yeah, I know what you mean. Fighting flesh and blood is different than battling demons. Especially when you're trying hard not to kill or maim the other person."

"Yes, it certainly was different, even from sparring with each other." Seth agreed.

"How's Caroline's arm?" Nick asked.

"Fine. Jason healed it once she returned from her fight."

"That must be hard, Seth. Watching your wife fight, get injured, and face death in every demon war."

Seth's expression turned serious. "Yes, it is. But I also have to remember what it was like when I thought I had lost her forever. I have to understand that God called her to this lifestyle, just the same as he did me, and He has a purpose for her. If I try to interfere with that, I go against the will of God, and my wife's. Besides, she'd kill me if I tried telling her what to do," Seth finished with a grin.

Nick smiled back with a slight chuckle.

"Nick, I noticed that you and Annabelle are becoming quite close."

"Yeah, go figure that one," Nick said with a lopsided grin.

"She seems quite taken with you. And I couldn't help noticing that you seemed quite shaken when you first saw her as well."

Nick's demeanor changed a bit to one of reserve and sadness. Nick took a deep breath and slowly began explaining.

"I've never told anyone here about my life before peregrinating. Everyone knows I was a high school science teacher, but they don't know that I was once married and that I had a daughter."

"Did you have to leave them behind?" Seth was suddenly concerned for his friend.

"No, not exactly. My wife and I divorced after nine years of marriage. My daughter, Cassie, died when she was eight years old from an incurable disease. It tore me *and* my marriage apart."

Sean woke and went outside. He saw the men chatting and went to join the conversation. Walking up behind them, he overheard Nick's explanation. He locked eyes with his friend who had heard his approach and turned to see who was coming.

Sean stood still, slightly shocked at what Nick had revealed. He looked compassionately at his friend and continued forward to meet them. Seth and Sean exchanged looks of understanding, offering Nick compassion. Both men placed a hand on Nick's shoulders as an act of comfort.

Seth said, "Sorry to hear that, Nick. It must have really been hard on you and your wife."

"It was. I drank too much, ignored my wife's pain because I was wallowing in my own, so we eventually divorced. Which brings us here and to Annabelle. When I first saw her, she reminded me so much of Cassie. Her age, build, coloring, everything. Well, everything except her spirit. Cassie was so sick for the last few years of her life. The illness had drained the joy and happiness right out of her. She hardly ever smiled, laughed, or played. It was all she could do to just wake up every morning and get through another day. In that respect, Annabelle is different. I look at her and see the vibrant child that Cassie might have been if she had been allowed to live."

Sean exhaled loudly. "Nick, I had no idea you were carrying such a burden all these years."

"Well, as you can imagine, it isn't something that I like discussing. I'd appreciate it if you two didn't mention this to anyone else. I don't want an all-out pity party happening on my account. Especially from all those women back there." Nick gave a small pain riddled grin.

Sean and Seth grinned knowingly right along with him, both men agreeing to secrecy.

"Still, it is curious how Annabelle has taken to you," Seth said as they all walked back toward Dekker's shop.

"Yeah," Sean said, "right from the start she was drawn to you."

"Probably because I couldn't stop staring at her," Nick stated.

"Maybe," Seth agreed.

Nick's expression became confused. "I just don't understand why God would call a kid that young? She's only ten years old and has to live like this. What is she going to do in a demon war?"

"Who are we to question the wisdom of God?" Sean answered.

The other two men looked at him and smiled. For someone so young, and who had a tendency to be immature at times, he sometimes spoke wisdom like few others could. Sean shrugged his shoulders and smiled, and the three stopped in front of Dekker's shop with the rest of the growing group.

The large group set about gathering their supplies, including Dekker and Annabelle. Dekker went into the Blacksmith shop to get his smithing tools. He would build another forge wherever they ended up on the next leg of this journey, but his tools were harder to replace. He slung the heavy bag over his shoulder, and Seth, noticing the slight stagger in his step walked over to him.

"Dekker, let me carry your bag for you."

"No, you have your own bags to burden you," he said, looking up to where the voice was coming from.

"My bags are a trifle to hold. Besides, my gift is strength, and your bag would be nothing for me."

Dekker could hear the smile in Seth's voice and yielded his bag.

"Thank you, Seth," he said, recognizing the voice. He had tried hard to place each voice with the name of each person. When Simon had introduced them, he made a mental note of each.

"Not a problem." Seth took the bag full of tools from the small man.

Simon stood in the center of the group. "All right, everyone, we are going to try the Portgens for return travel. All of you gather around here so we can be on our way."

Simon turned on his Portgen using the new fingerprint scanning technology and punched the home button. The portal did not open.

Simon sighed. "Well, that didn't work. Jason, try to use yours. Perhaps mine is broken."

Jason took out his Portgen, opened it and punched the home button. Nothing.

Jason said, "Well, it looks like we are returning the same way we came."

Odessa asked, "Why do you think they won't work from here?"

Simon answered, "Perhaps because this place is within another realm or dimension? We had no idea where we were going when we arrived here. We had no coordinates to pinpoint."

Jason said, "It could also be the interference from being so deep within the mountain."

"True," Caroline chimed in, "the rocks and metal minerals that likely vein through the mountain could interfere with the signal."

"Well," Simon said, "let's hope that Gabby can get us back the same way she got us here."

Gabriele stepped up and took the staff from Simon. Everyone gathered around her with Jason staying to the rear. She held the staff the same way as before, using her shield gift to connect to Jason's Portgen and they all walked into the water and out into the open ocean.

Annabelle was fascinated by what she saw. She couldn't believe this new life she was living. She only hoped that she didn't wake up from a dream. If it was a dream, it was the longest one she ever had. She looked at all the creatures in the water around her; many frightened off by their sudden intrusion into their world. She couldn't see very well due to the darkness of the waters in the cave. She could make out little trickles of light coming from somewhere in front of them. She also noticed the dryness of the sand which they all walked upon, knowing that to be God's provision. She looked up and watched the surface of the water get further and further away. Once they passed the outer edge of the underwater cavern where Akrotiri had been pushed back into so long ago, she could see the light of the sun's rays filtering into the depths of the ocean. The sea came to life in brilliant, sparkling shades. Corals lit the waters with their beautiful shapes and colors as the sunlight illuminated their shapes. Fish of all sizes and shapes darted in and out around them and they all seemed to focus in on her. Some very curious sharks decided to take a look at them, perhaps sizing them up as their next meal. As they walked along the ocean floor a large octopus inched its body up and over, slithering around the shield's outer shell spreading its legs out all around them, the underside of its body visible to everyone inside. Again, the creature seemed to focus its unthreatening attention on Annabelle. She smiled at the experience, looking at Nick.

Nick saw the sheer joy and lack of fear on Annabelle's face, and decided he should also enjoy the experience, without the fear that often overtook him. It was always amazing to him how much he could learn, especially from the younger generation. Even as a schoolteacher he had often watched the kids conquer their fears with determination and resolve. He took a deep breath, and released the tension in his body, marveling at God's creation. He realized that he had been running from God for so long that he had missed out on so much in life. This little girl was beginning to open his eyes once again. He was determined not to run any longer. When they got back to the island, he would sit down at the prayer temple and have a long-overdue conversation with Jesus.

They walked for about twenty minutes before they reached the spot where the gateway should have been..

"Simon," Seth said, "where's the gateway?"

They all stood there, looking all around them. Nick began to sweat once again.

"I think I know what has happened," Simon said, taking out his Portgen and punching in the coordinates of the gateway which they had walked through just yesterday. When he hit the button, a portal opened in front of them and they walked through, putting them on the third-dimension side of the gateway. Ten minutes later they were walking out of the water onto the shores of Reader's island.

"What just happened?" Kristen asked.

"Well, like the windows of the island above the water, the underwater gateways lead to ease of departure, but not so on returning. If we hadn't had those coordinates for the underwater gateway, we may have had a very long walk. I don't know if it would have been able to bring us here to the island, seeing as we were underwater," Simon smiled worriedly.

Simon turned to the two new-comers and smiled. He watched as Dekker seemed to enjoy the pleasures his senses were affording him.

Dekker could feel the warmth of the sun and the cool breeze on his skin. The brightness of the sun's rays illuminating the shapes and colors that he could somewhat make out. The scent of flowers and salt that wafted by on the breeze, and the sound of the waves upon the sand and rocks brought back memories from long ago of his homeland.

Annabelle laughed and giggled at the crashing waves.

"This reminds me of Hawaii," she said joyfully.

Simon smiled down at her. "I'm sure it does. This is our home and it's called Reader's Island. The island sits in the middle of the Bermuda Triangle."

"Really? Where all the ships and planes always disappear?" she asked incredulously.

"Exactly," Simon answered. "The barrier you see all around is the reason those ships and planes disappear. If they come in contact with any part of the barrier during certain phases of the moon and tide, they are transported to other worlds or dimensions."

"Cool!" Annabelle replied.

Simon and the others laughed at her exuberance and awe.

The others who were already on the practice fields noticed the arrival of the group and stopped their training to meet them on the beach; each taking turns introducing themselves to the newcomers. All of them curious as to the purpose of the young girl.

They walked the distance up to the big house, the Peregrines who just returned turning down requests to practice.

Seth said, "I think I speak for everyone here by saying that we have had enough fighting for a day or two."

Those who were with him all mumbling their agreements as they all walked toward the house to stow their packs in their rooms. Simon showed Dekker and Annabelle where they would be staying, then met everyone else in the kitchen for a hearty breakfast.

Many of those that stayed on the island were there having breakfast as well, along with the ones who had already gone out to the training fields earlier. They were all anxious to hear about the mission The Twelve had gone on yesterday and how they found the armor pieces so quickly.

Simon watched the cheerful chaos for the next forty minutes as several of The Twelve took turns telling the story, especially those who were involved the most like Odessa, Jason, and Zaccai. Still, questions about Annabelle and Dekker's presence were asked, with no available answers as to why she was here. Simon did have a clue though about Annabelle's position with them based solely on his observations of the water creatures that tended to follow or be curious about her. He figured that she was yet another Keeper. The youngest ever to peregrinate that he knew of, but they hadn't fully delved into all the ancient texts. There was so much work needing to be done, and so little time. Simon would have to get Annabelle and Dekker, plus all the island staffers to be fitted for the chipping devices, and have Ryan make two more Portgens. That young man was certainly busy these days, but he enjoyed doing it so it wasn't like work to him.

Simon went to sit by Annabelle.

"Well, Annabelle, do you have any idea why you might be here?"

She turned to look at him. "Not really. Mr. Dekker said it was because God had a very special plan for me."

"He is right. We just need to figure out what that is so we can help train you."

"Oh, all right. What do I do?" she asked enthusiastically.

Simon smiled at her. "I'm curious to know whether or not you have a special bond with animals?"

Annabelle's face scrunched up in thought. "I don't know. We didn't have any animals at the orphanage. I've never been around them much, but I do love them a lot."

"Well, we have some very special young people here on the island who I'd like you to meet. I believe they can help us figure out if you are meant to be what we call a Keeper."

"What is a Keeper?"

"It is someone who can talk with the animals and sort of control them. The animals often do as the Keeper asks."

"That sounds like fun!" She emphatically clapped her hands in excitement.

"Perhaps, but it is also a great responsibility."

"Oh yes sir. At the orphanage, the teachers always said I was very responsible. I will do a good job."

Simon laughed. "I am certain you will. But first, we must figure out what job you are called to do."

She smiled brightly at him, excited to begin this new journey in her life. Simon called Bridget, Dominic, and Wade. They came over to where he and Annabelle sat.

"Good morning, Simon," Bridget said, a questioning look on her face as they all stopped at the table.

"Everyone, I would like you to meet Annabelle. Annabelle, this is Bridget, Dominic, and Wade. They are our Keepers, and I would like you to go with them to see if you are like them."

"Okay, Mr. Simon," she said, standing.

Simon looked at Bridget. "Just take her and do what you all do. Let me know if she is to be a Keeper."

"Certainly, Simon. We will be back later."

They all left the kitchen and the teenagers were chatting with her and asking her all sorts of questions.

Bridget and the others walked outside and into the woods just by the main house. They could see deer and other forest creatures grazing there. Bridget told Annabelle what to do.

"Now, Annabelle, as Keepers, we communicate with the animals by thought or speech. Why don't you try it?"

Annabelle shook her head in acknowledgement. She looked at the deer and spoke out loud, calling it to her.

"Hello. Can you come to me?"

The deer raised its head and looked at them. It slowly started walking toward them and Annabelle got very excited.

"Look! It's coming!" she said, jumping up and down.

The deer stopped suddenly.

"Annabelle, you must stay calm. I believe your excitement is frightening her," Bridget said.

"Oh. I'm sorry." Annabelle stood still and tried to control her emotions. "Come on girl, I won't hurt you," she said in a soft tone.

The deer approached her cautiously still, but soon was close enough for Annabelle to touch. Annabelle grinned broadly, stroking the soft fur of the deer's head and neck.

"Well, that test is positive. Let's try the ocean creatures," Bridget said as they walked toward the beach.

"You mean that we can also speak to them?"

"Yes," Bridget answered.

"How exciting!"

Dominic, Wade, and Bridget all laughed at her exuberance. They all remembered feeling the same way when they first realized they could talk with the animals.

When they reached the water, they all waded out just a bit.

Dominic said, "Okay, Annabelle, think about a creature and call to it."

Annabelle stood in the gently lapping ocean waves; her eyes closed as she focused on the creature in her mind.

Soon, they were all surrounded by starfish. Their tendrils tickling their toes.

They all giggled at the sensation.

Dominic asked her, "Why starfish?"

She smiled. "I just love them. They are very interesting things."

For the next hour they all laughed and played around in the warm island waters, calling all manner of sea creatures to them, and teaching Annabelle about her gift and the possibilities that came with it.

The Dragoman took the house chores for the day while the rest of the island people took to the training fields once more. The Dragoman briefed Simon about the recent events involving Uriah, Petra, and Timothy as they tidied the kitchen.

Simon asked the group, "Have any of you thought about speaking to Petra about it? If she is as upset as Tim seems to think, perhaps she will be more forthcoming with us about what Uriah is up to."

Nuncio replied, "It did occur to me, but we just got wind of the whole scenario last night. We haven't had time as of yet."

"What say you to going and talking with her now?" Simon asked.

"Now is as good a time as any. We can speak with her when we take her breakfast to her."

The five of them went to her room, unlocked the door, and walked inside. She lay curled up on the bed, unmoving."

"Petra," Nuncio called, "your breakfast is here." Prisca carried the tray to the desk and swapped it for the other one.

She didn't move, only lay there staring out the window.

Vashti sat on the bed facing her, waiting for her to acknowledge them. They all gathered around her bed.

"Petra, we really need you to cooperate. It will go so much better for you if you do," Vashti spoke softly to her.

She simply looked at them, unmoving.

Simon spoke, "Petra, we know that Uriah came to see you last night."

That got her attention a bit more. Simon could read a sudden nervousness in her body language.

"We also know that he has a key to your room. Is he threatening you somehow?"

Petra sat up, leaning her back against the headboard. Her hands nervously fidgeting in her lap.

She glanced up at the people in front of her, but still said nothing, swallowing hard.

Prisca asked her, "Petra, we can't help you if you don't tell us what's going on. If Uriah is involved in something, we need to know what. A lot of people could get killed again, Petra, and it will all be for nothing, because God is the author here, not Uriah. He will be stopped one way or another. Now, if you've helped him, you must pay the price for that. But that price may be easier going if you tell us what he is up to?"

Petra stared down into her lap, wringing her hands. "He said he'd kill me if I talked."

Everyone looked at each other as she continued. "I loved him so much. He just used me."

Prisca put her hand out to Petra, placing it on hers. Petra looked up at Prisca, her eyes full of tears, her broken and battered heart spilling out as the tears fell down her cheeks. She continued to speak.

"He said we would rule the new world together." She sobbed.

Simon, Nuncio, and Malachai exchanged looks of dread.

"What do you mean, Petra?" Simon asked.

"Hiram started a new order long ago called the NKRO — New Kingdom Rulers Order- and Uriah plans to resurrect the plan."

"What exactly is the NKRO, Petra?" Nuncio asked.

"I'm not sure. I just know it involves using demonic forces to take over." She sniffed. Then the crying started again as she continued. "We were supposed to rule over everything together. He promised me. Then he said that it was my imagination and if I told anyone about him being involved that he would kill me."

"Don't worry, Petra, we will protect you," Nuncio said. "We must move her to a different room without Uriah knowing where."

They all agreed and decided to move her to the smaller conference room in the back of the house until they could figure out another accommodation. After they had her locked inside, they went back out to the library to discuss, in private, what should happen next.

Simon said, "We will set a trap for Uriah tonight. We will let him overhear us talking about speaking to Petra tomorrow morning. We'll say that she requested to speak with us. That might make him think she is going to betray him. Then we will hide in her room and wait to see if he comes to make good on his promise to kill her."

Malachai said, "Sounds good. What time shall we all arrive?"

"We need to make sure Uriah is in his room before we all go to Petra's. Prisca, you and Vashti keep an eye on him after dinner. When he retires to his room, let us know and we will all slowly make our way to Petra's room. Let's just hope we can catch him before he implements whatever crazy scheme he's planning."

They went to the practice fields and made sure that Uriah was in earshot of their conversation, making it appear that they were trying to keep it quiet. As the day progressed, any time Uriah disappeared, someone would make sure to intervene and turn him back to the training fields or say they needed to use the restroom as well and walk with him.

At one point, when the Dragoman walked with him back up to the main house to prepare lunch, Simon could tell that Uriah was getting agitated by the inability to be alone today. They made sure that they showed no interest in him directly, just a mere coincidence.

Simon said, "You know, I really need to go through the archives some more, especially since I went on that last mission. I think I'll stay up here at the house today. I'll also start preparing dinner for tonight so no one else will have to worry with it."

Malachai replied, "I'll stay and help you, Simon."

"Great. Two are better than one." He smiled.

Uriah rolled his eyes in frustration. He would have to get to Petra tonight after everyone went to bed. He couldn't chance her talking to them. He was stupid to threaten her. He should have just strung her along a bit longer until he could begin to implement his plans. He would go back to talk with Hiram once more tonight and explain the urgency. Maybe he could convince him to return before it was too late. Then, hopefully, after hiding Hiram somewhere, he would return and take care of Petra.

Simon and Malachai kept watch over everyone who came and went through-out the day. Uriah, not making another attempt to come to the main house until dinnertime. After dinner and night Bible-study, Uriah quickly left and retired to his room.

Vashti watched him enter his room from the hallway, noticing the tell-tale light of the Portgen's energy opening a portal, and then darkness. She wondered where in the world he had gone. It worried her a bit, and she looked down the hallway to Petra's room to see if the Portgen's light could be seen underneath her doorway, but there was no light visible.

Well, at least he didn't jump to her room, Vashti thought. *But if he didn't go there, where did he go?* "What are you up to, Uriah Mose?" she whispered to herself.

She went to inform the others, who nonchalantly slipped away one by one, bidding the others a good night. They all took their place in Petra's room and waited to see if Uriah returned. Vashti stayed in her room, located just a few doors down from Uriah's, and kept watch to see if he would return soon.

If you remain in me and my words remain in you, ask whatever
you wish, and it will be done for you. This is to my Father's glory,
that you bear much fruit, showing yourselves to be my disciples.

John 15:7-8

Chapter 15

"Simon," Malachai whispered, "we've been here for hours now. I'm
not sure he's coming."

"Perhaps, wherever it is he went he hasn't yet returned," Simon
whispered back. "Prisca, are you still awake?"

"Yes. Do you really think I could sleep knowing someone could
walk in here any minute to try and murder me?" she whispered back
from beneath the bed covers in disbelief, mumbling something in
French.

"Just making sure," Simon said apologetically.

"Shh…" Malachai said, "I think I hear something.

As they all quieted down, they could hear a key turning the lock
in the door. The door opened, and they could hear the soft, cautious
footsteps of someone walking across the wooden floor. The
floorboards creaked just a tad and the person stopped suddenly.
Realizing there was no movement from the bed, they continued
toward it. The moonlight through the large windows and doors cast
a shadow of the person who grasped one of the pillows from the bed
and held it out.

Simon and Malachai sprang forth from their hiding place at the
same time Vashti had stepped into the doorway. She flipped on the
light switch just as Malachai yelled, "Stop right there, Uriah!"

Prisca sat upright in the bed and Uriah froze. He was shocked
to see them all there. He suddenly realized that he had been set up.

They had already spoken to Petra and she had probably told them everything. Uriah scanned the room, looking for a way to run, but the protection spell was still on the windows and balcony doors, and Vashti stood in the door to the hallway. He threw the pillow toward Simon and Malachai and suddenly bolted toward Vashti, slamming into her and pushing her backward onto the floor of the hallway. She reached out to grab him but couldn't hold on. The men and Prisca ran after him, through the upstairs hallway and down the sweeping staircase, only to find Oz standing at the bottom holding Uriah by the scruff of the neck. Uriah belted and fussed, swinging, and kicking trying to escape Oz's hold. Oz rolled his eyes, tired of the man's complaining and fighting. With the balled fist of his other hand, he hit Uriah on the top of his head and knocked him out cold, dropping him to the floor.

Simon, Malachai, Prisca, and Vashti stood looking down at the man, all smiling at their good fortune.

Prisca walked past them and planted a kiss on Oz's cheek.

"I am so happy to see you, Wendal." She smiled.

"Well, ya' didn' think I was gonna' let ya' take on this maniac alone did ya?"

Simon grinned. "I am very glad you were here, Oz. If you hadn't been, we may have never caught him."

Malachai looked at Vashti.

"Are you all right, Vashti? Did he hurt you?"

She replied, "I'm fine, I think. I may be a bit sore on the backside tomorrow, but I don't think any more damage was done."

Oz asked, "So, what do ya' want ta do with 'im?"

Simon answered, "Well, the first thing we do is search him for that extra key and any weapons. Then we'll confine him to his own room and move Petra back into hers. After that, we'll have to think of a more permanent place for the both of them."

Oz and Malachai picked Uriah up, carrying him upstairs to his room where Simon placed another confinement spell on Uriah's quarters. They then found the key and all of Uriah's weapons and left the room, locking the door behind them.

Vashti and Prisca had gone to retrieve Petra and return her to her room, telling her that they had caught Uriah in the act of trying to suffocate her with a bed pillow. They again locked her in her room and then all retired to their own to try and rest for the remainder of the night.

Simon sighed as he walked into his room, grateful that the betrayers were caught, but broken-hearted at the same time. *How could Uriah and Petra do what they had done?* He prayed for their very souls, knowing that they weren't saved. To be able to turn their backs on God and what He had asked of them meant that they truly didn't believe. They may know God is real, but they hadn't put their trust in Jesus. Simon climbed into bed in the early morning hour, weary and exhausted, to claim what precious little sleep there was left to the new day.

When Simon and the other Dragoman woke that morning, they all met in the kitchen for breakfast where he announced to everyone else there about Uriah and Petra. He asked if anyone knew of any strange behavior by either of them, or noticed anything unusual lately, to let any of the Dragoman know.

Uriah had been up to something, and they still had to figure out if he was somehow able to implement his plan, whatever that was. The Dragoman would speak with him again later and try to make him talk, but they would hopefully not have to lead into interrogation, only plead to his sense of decency, that is if he still had any.

Everyone went about their day which turned out to be quite a pleasant one under the circumstances. Oz and Caroline, along with a handful of others continued to plan for Bridget's surprise birthday party in just another four days or so. They never knew where they would be in four days, so the party may have to wait.

During the evening hours each night, Oz would disappear into the horse stables and work on fashioning a necklace for Bridget from some of the precious metals he had brought with him from Zanchier. When he lived there, he had kept some stashed in his travel bag no matter where he went. It had become a habit over the years because the metals were worth a lot there, and he used them to barter and purchase much needed supplies. Between that and the colorful feathers of the Kabihanxu that he sometimes found lying on the forest floor, it made some beautiful jewelry. Just like his and Prisca's wedding bands.

When he and Caroline discussed a birthday party for Bridget, he decided to make her a special gift to let her know what she meant to him.

While Oz was working on her necklace tonight, Dekker had come into the stables to see the forge.

"Evenin'," Oz called to him.

"Good evening, Oz." Dekker smiled at the very familiar and unforgettable voice of the man. Then thanked the groundskeeper for escorting him down to the stables.

"I'll take 'im back ta' the house, Rourke," Oz stated with a wave. The man waved back and left.

"Whatcha doin' all the way out here?"

"I just wanted to check out the forge. Simon told me that there was one in here. He said it was used for the horseshoes."

"Yeah, it is, 'mong other things. Sometimes we use it ta' fix a broken sword blade, er knife."

"So, who here is the forge master?"

"I s'ppose that'd be me. I sort a' got used ta' usin' one back in Zanchier."

"Is that where you are from, Oz?"

"No. I was trapped there fer 'bout thirteen years after a coo was staged years ago."

"I see." Dekker was curious as to the design of the forge. "Do you mind if I feel around a bit?"

"No, not at all. Help yerself."

"Do you mind if I ask what you are working on?" Dekker walked the room feeling the tools and equipment.

"Oh, jus' a surprise fer a very special young girl here. Her birthday is comin' up nex' week, an' she's been a bit down lately. We are surprisin' 'er with a par'y. I'm makin' 'er a nec'lace from some materi'ls I brought back with me from Zanchier. Really perty stuff."

"Do you mind if I feel the materials?" Dekker sat beside Oz on an obliging log he had felt.

"Not at all." Oz handed Dekker some of the metal and feathers.

"Goodness!" Dekker replied in disbelief. "Is this a feather."

"Yeah, from a' creature back in Zanchier. Big birds that'll roast ya' first with their fire-breath, then eat ya' in one big bite," he said menacingly, but with a smile.

Dekker could hear the teasing in his voice and wasn't sure if he was pulling his leg or not.

"Really?" he asked to make certain.

"Fer sure," Oz said honestly. "Biggest birds ya' ever did see." Oz suddenly felt a little sheepish because of his words. "Sorry, didn' mean ta' say that."

Dekker laughed. "Not to worry. I'm not offended at all. I used to be able to see not too long ago. I started losing my vision about five years back. I can still see a bit, but it is very blurry, shadowy images."

"Did ya' ever try glasses?"

"Not really. I've been in Akrotiri for most of that time. Do you think spectacles would really work?"

"Don' know. But it's worth a try. I bet Simon er Ryan could fig're out how ta' make ya' a pair."

"That would be amazing to be able to see again. I'm not getting my hopes up though. It would take a powerful prescription to make me see again."

"Well, let's hope they can do it. Er at least take ya' to a time period where ya' can get a pair."

"Let's hope." Dekker took the metals in his hands. "What sort of metal is this, Oz?"

"That there is Rhenium an' Ruthenium, both highly prized back in Zanchier. They like ta' use it in their armor. The firebirds have a hard time burnin' through the stuff."

"Is that so?"

"Yep. From what I gathered while livin' in Zanchier, was that years ago the people there fought entire wars over the stuff."

"Hmmm…a metal that could resist heating up and boiling you alive inside an armored suit would be highly prized."

"Yep. 'Specially with them big fire-breathin' birds flyin' 'round. Not ta' mention the giant cat-like creatures that roam the moun'ains. It's hard ta' dent as well."

The two men sat and chatted for the next hour while Oz finished Bridget's necklace. Then Oz escorted Dekker back up to the house and the two of them went in search of Simon. He found Nuncio instead.

"Evenin' Nuncio. Have ya' seen Simon anywhere?"

"I believe he turned in early tonight. Several of them didn't get much sleep last night."

"Right," Oz said.

"Is there something I can help you with, Oz?" Nuncio asked.

"Well, we were wonderin' if maybe Dekker here, might jus' need a pair a' glasses? Is 'ere some way ta' find out?"

"Well, we could take him to a current time period tomorrow and see if we could get him fitted. It may take some time. Time which we never know if we will have or not," Nuncio answered.

"I fig're it'd be worth a try. Specially since he has ta' live like the rest a' us."

"Very true. Sounds like a plan then. When Simon wakes tomorrow, I'll discuss the trip with him. Perhaps he or one of the other Dragoman can take you into a town, Dekker," Nuncio said. "I personally don't go to many places. I suffer from a very bad hip injury."

"That would be fine, thank you. However, I don't have any way to pay for the glasses."

"Not to worry there, Dekker. We Dragoman have things like that under control. No one here worries about money. Those who came before us, and we ourselves, learned how to navigate around our way of life. We have amassed quite a fortune between all of us throughout the years. It is necessary for what we do. God has blessed us tremendously in that area."

"Thank you. I do appreciate that. I just hope that glasses will work. It would make blacksmithing, and navigating this new world, much easier."

"Yes, well, I must bid you gentlemen goodnight. I am tired myself." Nuncio stretched and yawned.

"'Night Nuncio, see ya' tomorra'," Oz replied. He then turned his attention to Dekker. "Do ya' need help getting' ta' yer room?"

"No, thank you, Oz. I've spent the last two days walking the house and I have the front of the house here memorized. Thank you for all of your help, and your company tonight." Dekker began the climb up the stairway to his room.

"Night." Oz watched the man walk up a few steps, then he went in search of Prisca. He found her in one of the sitting rooms speaking quietly with Bridget.

"Hey there you two." He smiled as he entered. Prisca's face looked a little concerned and Oz looked from her to Bridget, now noticing the look on Bridget's face as well. "What's goin' on, is som'thin' wrong?"

Prisca looked up at Oz, but Bridget just stared at the floor.

"Bridget is having a hard time dealing with the arrest and confinement of Uriah," Prisca explained to him.

"Oh, well, there ain't much we can do 'bout that, Bridget."

"I know, Oz." Bridget stood up and looked at him in frustration. "But why is it every time I want to find out something about my parents, the people I get close to, who know the most, are suddenly removed from my grasp?"

"Bridget, that ain't no one else's fault but Uriah's. He was up ta' some bad stuff. The Dragoman didn' have much of a choice," he defended.

"I know that Oz. I'm just trying to understand why so many people that I get close to end up being bad." Tears began to form in her eyes.

"We ain't bad Bridget. Me, an' Priss, an' Caroline an' all the others, we're yer friends too. Ya' still got all a' us."

"I know and I am grateful for all of you. But Uriah was the one person who knew my father and mother the most. And now I can't ask him anything else about them. He even knew a little about Marnor being my half-brother. I'm just so tired of being linked to all the really bad people. Either by birth or by friendship." She swiped at a lone tear that began to slide down her cheek. She stormed away, angry and frustrated.

"Bridge…"

"Let her go, Wendal. She just needs some time to sort things out. She'll be all right, eventually." Prisca placed a staying hand on his arm.

"I jus' ain't never seen 'er so upset b'fore. It makes me worry 'bout 'er. She jus' ain't 'er usu'l happy, easy' goin' self lately. All this stuff is really getting' to 'er. I'm jus' curious what Uriah might a' told her 'bout 'er parents?"

"Well, we are planning on speaking to him in the morning. We just didn't have the strength to do so today. If you want, you can ask him about Bridget once we are done questioning him."

"Thanks, love. I think that might jus' be what I'll do. If'n he'll talk ta' me at all."

"Let's hope and pray that he thinks about the consequences and is forthcoming about his plans." Prisca was worried that he would do just the opposite.

The two of them headed off to bed, Oz wondering if he would ever get to sleep tonight. He was worried about Bridget's state of mind. He had never seen her so unhappy before. He decided he would say a special prayer for her tonight and every night until she returned to her old self. He pulled the necklace from his shirt pocket, showed it to Prisca who beamed over the beauty of it, then he laid it on the dresser. The two of them changed into their bed clothes and knelt beside the bed to pray.

Bridget ran from the house, past the patio area where people were still gathered and into the night. Caroline called to her and was about to go after her when Seth stopped her with a hand on her arm and a shake of his head.

"Seth, I need to see why she is so upset," Caroline said worriedly.

"I saw her talking with Oz and Prisca just a little while ago before I brought out the coffee. I think that whatever she is going through, she needs to sort out for herself. If she wanted to talk with you, I'm sure she would seek you out."

They watched her hurry past the stand of trees and disappear into the night.

Bridget ran all the way to the water's edge where she collapsed onto the sand into a fit of tears, sobbing heavily for a few minutes. The weight of all that she had learned about her past, what her father had done and been like, what her mother had done to her then fourteen-year-old son, and her horrid brother — who she figured had a right to feel the way he did — had all built up to a boiling point where she couldn't control her emotions or feelings anymore. She finished sobbing and looked up to the heavens.

"God? Why is my life, and my past so full of awful people and things? I've tried ever so hard to be a good girl, but everything I've learned about my family seems to be soured. I'm not complaining mind you. But I can't take it anymore. I was beginning to learn some about my mother and father. Things that weren't awful. But even that has been taken from me. Help me to deal with all of this. I'm failing drastically at it."

Bridget sat on the beach for the next hour, her arms curled around her legs as she watched the rhythmic rolling of the waves upon the moonlit sands. The movement, the refreshing salty breezes, and the peacefulness of the night, acting like a balm to her wounded soul. She finally got up and walked back to the main house, passing by several people who were still up. Several looked her way, wondering at her unusually quiet demeanor. Dominic, Gabby, and Wade, exchanging concerned looks between them.

Caroline and Seth were still up, waiting for her to return from wherever she had run off to. Caroline stood and walked toward Bridget calling out to her.

"Bridget? Are you all right?" She stopped just in front of her.

"Not really, Caroline. I'm just so tired of the horror of my family's past, and now all of this with Uriah. We were growing very close, you know. He was showing me better sides to my parents."

"I know. And I'm so sorry. Do you need to talk about it?"

Bridget just shook her head no.

Well, if you do, or if you need anything else, then just come and find me anytime, day or night. Okay?"

Bridget nodded yes, shrugged her shoulders, sighed heavily, and walked into the house and up to her room. She collapsed onto her bed, her mind still reeling until she fell into a restless sleep filled with one nightmare after another.

Dominic watched her go, worried about her. She hadn't been the same person since they returned from Zanchier almost a week earlier. He always thought her to be an annoyingly happy pest before he learned of some of her heartaches while in the Tintagel forest. Now, he feared she would never return to her happy self after the month that she'd had. He missed her jovial attitude about life and everything in it. Maybe tomorrow he'd try to get her to talk to him. Her birthday celebration couldn't come soon enough. She needed some serious cheering up and he would spend the night trying to figure out how to do just that.

Everyone soon dispersed from the veranda area, depositing their coffee cups, drink cups, and dessert plates in the kitchen and washing them quickly before heading upstairs.

Dominic passed by Bridget's bedroom and listened briefly at the door. He wanted to make sure she wasn't sitting up crying alone in her room. There was no sound and he assumed that meant she had managed to get to sleep. He thought about their time in Zanchier and suddenly had a brilliant idea. He would talk with Simon and some of the others about it in the morning.

He smiled to himself hoping that what he wanted to do would work. If so, Bridget would have an amazing birthday celebration, and he hoped that it would lift her spirits and bring back the old Bridget they all knew and loved.

He walked to his room, wondering if he would be able to sleep now that the excitement of his idea kept rolling over in his head. His mind was sifting through ideas so quickly than he feared he would forget them. He grabbed his sketch pad, curled up Indian style on his bed and began drawing one of the images that he remembered vividly of Bridget back in Zanchier. He would surprise her with two gifts if possible. His drawing was a sure thing. The other, not so much. He hoped and prayed that his idea would work.

A heart at peace gives life to the body,
but envy rots the bones.

Proverbs 14:30

Chapter 16

Simon and Nuncio met early for breakfast outside on the patio beneath the veranda, discussing some of yesterday's events.

Nuncio began with, "Simon, I was speaking to Dekker and Oz last night and Oz questioned whether glasses might help Dekker to see."

"It's quite possible that glasses may help him. We can take a trip into a current city later this afternoon," Simon answered.

As they sat visiting and chatting, Dominic appeared through the double glass doors of the patio, headed toward them.

"Morning Simon, Nuncio," he greeted them sitting down. "I have a question to ask."

Simon looked at him. "All right, ask away."

"Well, you know how Bridget has been really down lately, she was crying last night. I wanted to know if we could bring Han and Cho and maybe even Mother and Paxton here to the island. Just for the day, for her birthday?"

Simon was taken by complete surprise. "Dominic, I've never encountered these creatures. I have no idea what they are or are capable of, and I doubt they would be able to travel through the Portgen."

"The horses can. They even passed through the portals during regular storms, which you all thought wasn't possible. Most people might not be able to pass through, but apparently animals can."

Nuncio and Simon exchanged glances. Nuncio spoke up. "Still, how would we even get them here to the island. These animals you speak of may not be able to tolerate our world. We don't know how they will react."

"The creatures know several of us already besides Bridget, and with the Keepers being able to communicate with them, we should be able to control them."

Nuncio was very uneasy about the idea. "That is a lot to ask just for a birthday party."

Simon reflected on the dreams he had been having as of late. "Nuncio," he broke in, "do you remember me telling you about large creatures fighting in this large demon war for which we have been preparing?"

"Yes,'' Nuncio replied, reflectively.

"Perhaps these are the very creatures I have been seeing. Dominic may be correct here. We may very well need to bring them here to our world. I doubt seriously if this battle is to be fought in Zanchier, a world where most of us have never before been."

"You have a point," Nuncio stated, looking at Dominic. "How do you propose to get them here? Who would go to bring them back?"

"Well, we can't tell Bridget even though she was the closest to them. From what she told me from when they lived there, Oz and Sofia were pretty close to them and even used them when Bridget and Caroline left. Caroline, Seth, and I have also been around them. All of us could go get them," he said excitedly, waiting on their reply as he sat on the edge of his seat.

"What if something unexpected happens while you are all there and you can't get back?" Simon questioned.

"Bridget and I got back all right. Oz and Sofia, and even Caroline know the area well too, and they made it back also. And, since Ryan has been working on the location of Zanchier with coordinates since me and Bridget returned last week, we may be able to use the Portgens to leave there more easily than before."

Simon and Nuncio exchanged worrisome glances, then with a shrug they accepted the challenge.

Simon said, "All right, my boy, let's go see who we can round up for this little adventure."

Simon and Dominic stood and went into the kitchen in search of those that Dominic mentioned, finding Oz, Prisca, and Sofia at the breakfast table.

"Good morning," Simon said, he and Dominic approaching them. "Oz, Sofia, Dominic has an idea we would like to run by the two of you." He and Dominic both took seats.

Simon and Dominic took turns explaining his idea to them. Oz and Sofia looked a bit apprehensive but did relay that they thought the animals would be cooperative. They had grown very used to them after Bridget and Caroline had left, and Oz and Sofia knew how to handle them.

They made a plan to leave the next morning, planning on getting back in time for her party that afternoon. They would have Annabelle and Wade distract her with training Annabelle some more, while the rest prepared for a lunch time bash. Oz, Sofia, Dominic, Seth, and Caroline would leave for Zanchier in the morning and hope that Ryan had the Portgens online with the strange, untraceable, world of Zanchier.

Simon and Oz went into the computer room after breakfast to see Ryan about just that.

"Ryan, my boy, good morning."

"Good morning, Simon," Ryan answered.

"I was curious to know if you happened to find coordinates on the world that Oz and Sofia were trapped in before they returned here? The place called Zanchier?"

"No. I think it is on a wh…whole separate plane. One we haven't discovered y…yet."

"Well, I can check Hiram's books again. I did find a code that I was working on translating. He used a cipher to hide messages in his books. I think we have that worked out. Perhaps the answer is in there. Hiram apparently made regular visits to the place."

Oz said, "I'll go gather up Seth an' Caroline an' explain what's goin' on." He then left the room.

Simon looked at Ryan. "I'll see what I can find and return later, if I feel it is something that you can use to help us."

"Okay," Ryan said, turning back to his desk and computer once more.

Simon left the computer room and headed toward the archival library where Nuncio and the others were to gather after breakfast. Nuncio and Malachai were to bring the books out of the vault to the library for further study. As he entered, he noticed everyone seated in the center, spread out amongst the oversized chairs, wingbacks, and small couches. He approached and sat amongst them.

Nuncio looked around and began. "I suppose the first thing that we need to discuss is the fact that we need to speak to Uriah first thing this morning. We sort of ignored the subject yesterday due to lack of sleep from the capture the night before."

Simon replied, "Yes, we need to see if he will tell us anything about the NKRO that Petra mentioned. And we need to see if we can find out where he peregrinated to last night."

Vashti spoke this time. "Last night wasn't the first time. Timothy saw him leave a few nights back as well. Who knows how often he has left or where he went, or with whom he has been meeting?"

Prisca replied, "Perhaps I should speak with Uriah. We used to be fairly close before the disappearances. I know he still has some feelings for me, whatever they may be, because of his comforting words when Dina passed. Maybe he will talk to me?"

Malachai said, "We can try that to start. But if he won't talk to Prisca, what are we going to do? We can't exactly torture the man, it isn't Christian."

"Yes," Simon replied, "I've thought that myself. I have no idea how to approach the situation. Are we to keep them confined to their bedrooms for eternity?"

Nuncio straightened in his chair. "I have a thought. Once we speak to them, we can banish them to someplace else. Take their Portgens, and weapons, leaving their chips on them to possibly keep track of where they are and what they are doing."

"What if they remove the chips?" Malachai asked.

"I'm hoping they've forgotten that they are there," Nuncio replied. "I know I often forget about them. The only time I remember them is during discussions like this, or when Ryan is tracking someone who is missing."

Simon sighed. "Well, if they do remove them, then so be it. I think banishment would be a good plan. But where do we send them?"

Prisca squirmed a little. "How about Zanchier. From what Oz and the others have said, it isn't an easy place from which to escape."

"Yes, I have heard that, but it is possible," Simon answered.

"Anywhere we send them, they can still peregrinate through storms," Vashti said.

"Yes," Malachai replied, "but they can't navigate where they want to go very well without the help of a Dragoman."

Prisca said, "What about Petra though. We said we would protect her from Uriah's threats."

Simon answered, "We will have to send them to different places, far away from each other."

Everyone looked uneasy about it all, but knew they had no other choice in the matter.

Simon said standing, "All right, let's get this *chat* with Uriah over with." They all followed Simon's example and stood, leaving the library, headed for Uriah's room.

Uriah of course was unresponsive and would not cooperate in any way. They explained to him what they would eventually be forced to do with him and Petra, whenever God called them to leave the island.

Uriah fumed. "You can't do that. God called me to peregrination. Only He can dismiss me."

Simon looked at him in disbelief. "Uriah, if your belief in God was true, then you wouldn't have betrayed everyone for your own agenda. Banishing you is God's way. If it were up to me personally, I don't think I would chance setting you free at all."

"So what? You want to kill me then?" Uriah asked with a sneer.

"It's no less than you offered to Petra," Simon said seriously.

Uriah just looked at him. A hateful glare on his face.

Simon continued. "It's either banishment, or death. We don't have the manpower to keep you imprisoned for an indefinite amount of time."

"So, to be rid of me you'd strand me anywhere and in any time in the universe?" he asked in disbelief.

"Yes. We'll let the Lord deal with you in his own way. Your fate is in his hands."

"You can't do that, Simon. I could wander the earth and realms forever. How am I supposed to live?" Uriah spat.

"Perhaps you should have thought of that before you decided to betray us," he answered.

"God betrayed me!" he yelled in anger. "I have spent sixteen years doing His bidding, and for what?"

"That's your problem, Uriah. You see it as a job. One where if you do enough you should get rewards or points. It doesn't work that way. But without Jesus in your life, you'll never see it the way you should. I really feel sorry for you, Uriah. You had everything you could possibly *ever* need. And you threw it away because you couldn't recognize the value of it."

"I don't need your pity, and I certainly don't want it."

"Then what could you possibly be worried about by being left to your own devices?" Simon stated. Uriah didn't respond, so Simon and the others left the room.

Prisca said, "Oz had wanted to speak to him about Bridget's mood, but I don't think he'll be any more receptive to him than he was for us. I have to say, I think Uriah is a completely lost cause."

Malachai pulled the door closed and locked it before replying.

"Sadly, Prisca, I believe you are right. I just don't know why he feels as strongly as he does."

Simon shook his head at the loss of a one-time friend and ally.

They all returned to the library to, once again, look over Hiram's Dragoman books. Simon picked up the list of possible ciphers that Ryan had discovered on the computer. He would try and match up the ciphers to the one used in Hiram's books. Simon and Malachai spent the remainder of the morning deciphering hidden messages placed in one of them. They were addressed to any followers of the NKRO. Apparently, anyone who followed the same beliefs, after a period of proven loyalty, was given the ability to decipher the code.

Simon realized that the code spoke of a special place that resided on a plane, that lived within a storm portal. If the storm reached a magnitude of a six to seven on the scale, the special portal would open. The place was known as Zanchier and was rich in important minerals known as Rhenium and Ruthenium. Zanchier was run by a band of cutthroat outlaws known as the Scaithers. These people liked money and could be persuaded to help the cause. Hiram apparently amassed a personal, small fortune by visiting this place and trading up for these minerals.

Another area stated that to enter and exit Storm Valley, you must visit during the fall and winter seasons. Only during certain phases of the moon and during these seasons, could you leave by way of the valley. Otherwise, you would have to travel to a place known as the Dustbowl to leave Zanchier.

The last code they deciphered spoke of an ancient archival book locked away deep withing the islands interior. Within this book, it spoke of the way to defeat the great evil and return the earth and all realms within to a peaceful existence. Also deciphered was, how the Rhenium and Ruthenium found on Zanchier were to be used to strengthen the Armor of God to defeat the four dragons in the final battle.

Simon and Malachai stopped decoding and looked at each other.

"Good grief!" Simon said. "The Twelve must battle four dragons to save mankind. Is that how you read it as well?"

"That's what it sounds like to me."

"Do you think it literally means four dragons?"

"Let's hope not," Malachai replied, fearing the worst.

"We have to figure out the language code in the *Book of the Keepers*. The answers must be in that book. This must be why Petra and Uriah were trying to steal the books. Perhaps they didn't want our side to win. I can't imagine what sort of world they were planning if we failed."

Malachai looked at Simon. "Neither could I my friend."

Simon gathered the books and decoded cryptographs. "We need to gather everything we have together in one place. Now that Uriah and Petra are locked up, we should be able to lay everything out and see if we can make sense of it all."

"Sounds like a plan, Simon. I'll grab the rest of Hiram's books." Picking them up, he looked around the room and spotted Vashti. "Vashti, clear the large table please."

Vashti looked up shaking her head in agreement. "What are you two doing?"

"Gathering everything in one spot. We've found some very interesting hidden messages in Hiram's books."

"All right," she said, "I'll grab the ancient archive books we found in the cave."

Once they had all the books, keys, and the bag of jewels found wrapped in a cloth with an ancient text written on it, they studied what they had.

Vashti picked up the jewels, untying them from their bonds and laid the wrap open, exposing them to the light. Nuncio entered the room at that moment, curious to what they were up to.

Vashti was stunned by the beauty of the gems. "Simon, do some of these jewels look strange to you?" She picked one up and held it against the light.

"How do you mean, Vashti?"

"I'm not sure. I've just never seen anything like some of them before. Plus, they all appear to be flat on one side. Like they were attached to something."

Nuncio stepped up to the table to peer at what had her interest. He was surprised by what he saw. Then he counted how many jewels there were.

"I think I have an answer for you, Vashti," Nuncio said with a slight smile.

They all three turned to him.

"I believe these jewels were once part of the Swords of the Spirit. I read somewhere in one of the recently found ancient archive books that the swords were dismantled by thieves. The jewels were separated from them and sold. No one ever found them again."

"When did you read that?" Simon asked in disbelief.

"I think when you were all off on one of your adventures. Possibly in Tintagel."

"Why did you never tell me, or any of the others?"

"An aging mind, I guess. I never connected that wrapped parcel of jewels with the Swords of the Spirit. We've never really looked at them," Nuncio offered as an explanation.

"True," Simon said, looking to his old friend. "I believe you're right, Nuncio. These must be the jewels that belong in the hilt of each of the swords."

They all looked at each other and smiled.

Simon sighed in relief. "I believe that we are getting answers to the many questions which have formed over these last months. Now, we just need to take a trip to Zanchier, gather enough Rhenium and Ruthenium to coat all the armor pieces, then have our newly found blacksmith to forge the Swords of the Spirit once again."

"Amazing that he would show up just at this time, don't you think?" Vashti said in awe.

"Not amazing, Vashti. Devine appointment I believe are the words you are searching for," Simon replied.

They all smiled at one another. Then Prisca chimed in.

"We still do not have the last two pieces of armor. We still need the Shields of Faith, and if there are any remnants to the Swords of the Spirit, perhaps we need to find them as well?"

Simon looked at her. "True, but I believe that we must fight in another battle before we continue our search for the pieces. Why else would God be preparing everyone for it without us having all the armor yet. My friends, I believe we have some very busy travels ahead, along with two problems on hand. We can't leave them locked in their rooms while we all go traipsing over and through all the worlds." Simon referenced Uriah and Petra. "We need to devise a plan of action. We may need to divide and conquer soon, but first I believe this large demon battle must come first."

Malachai agreed. "I think you are right, Simon. Perhaps we need to get back to the training fields. We've taken the last few days to look through books and catch the thieves. Now, if we are to be of any use in war, then we must prepare as well."

"Yes, you are right, Malachai," Nuncio said. "But we must also take care of the loose ends here."

Simon replied, "We'll just have to burn the midnight oil then. I do suggest though, that one or two stay and keep watch over the books and gems. Uriah and Petra may be locked up, but Uriah is a very resourceful man. I don't trust leaving everything out in the open as long as he is under the same roof."

"Point taken," Nuncio said. "Since I can't train much anyway, perhaps I should stay here and look over things. I'll study the information you have found so far and continue looking for answers."

Everyone agreed and they all went to the kitchen for a quick lunch then off to the training fields, minus Nuncio, to get in a workout.

The Dragoman heeded Jason's strategic know how, Alec's expertise with weaponry, and made plans with the others using their gifts and abilities to their advantage in any way possible.

While walking back up to the main house for dinner, they heard a sort of explosion. Everyone ran for the house, wondering what could have happened.

The first few ran through the front doors and into the kitchen. Thinking that the kitchen crew for the day may have had an accident. Simon noticed that Nuncio was standing at the bottom of the stairs beginning to climb them.

"Nuncio, what happened?" he asked him.

"I think it came from somewhere upstairs. I was just going up to see what it was."

"Stay here and watch the books and jewels. You too," Simon pointed at Malachai and the other Dragoman. He ran upstairs followed by Jason, Seth, Alec, and several others, and ran down the hallway between all of the bedrooms. He stood outside Uriah's room for a moment just listening. He unlocked the door and stepped inside, quickly noticing the hot melted handles of the patio doors. Uriah had used his gift of electricity to generate enough heat and power — apparently using the outlets in the room from the looks of the charred sockets— to overpower Simon's containment spell. He must have jumped off the balcony and ran.

Simon sighed, wondering where he could have gone, and worrying about him returning to the island sometime in the future.

"This is all we need," he said to those behind him in the room. "He's obviously gone through the windows."

They all left the room, going to check Petra's room first.

"Petra?" Simon called, unlocking the room. As the door swung open, he saw her sitting on the bed, her arms curled around her knees in fear.

"Simon," she said in relief. "I thought you were Uriah."

"No, he is gone though. He escaped his confinement. You wouldn't happen to know where he's going would you?"

"No. I'm afraid not," she said moving to the edge of the bed. "Do you think he'll come back here?"

"Do you know of a reason he would?"

"None other than to kill me for betraying him." She hugged her arms and tried to rub away the sudden chill that crept up her body.

"What about the books. You did try to steal them before. What does he want them for?"

"I don't know, Simon. Honestly. He just said he needed Hiram's books, and also, one of the ancient archive books, but he didn't say which one or for what."

"Well, it appears we are back to locking up the books once again."

Jason asked, "Do you really think he would chance coming back here?"

"I wouldn't put anything past Uriah," Simon stated. "Maybe we can still find him. I'll have Ryan track his chip."

Simon went downstairs to the computer room.

"Ryan, does the chipping system show where Uriah is?"

"Yes," Ryan replied. "The front lawn just past the patio area."

They all ran to where Ryan said that the chip was pinging. They found Uriah's chip lying in the grass. Not only could they not track him now, but they had no idea which portal window he went through.

There, in the presence of the LORD your God, you and your families
shall eat and shall rejoice in everything you have put your hand to,
because the LORD your God has blessed you.

Deuteronomy 12:7

Chapter 17

The next morning, Simon took Dekker into a modern city to see if
they could get him an eye exam to find if glasses would help his
vision. They returned several hours later, stating that they did
indeed find a doctor who would rush to order an extra thick pair of
glasses for Dekker. His eyesight was very poor indeed, but he wasn't
going blind as he thought. He just needed a special prescription.

Oz, Caroline, Sofia, Seth, and Dominic went back to Zanchier as
early as possible so they would make it back to Reader's Island in
time for Bridget's birthday celebration. Everyone else did their part,
either distracting Bridget or getting things prepared for the party
that would take place at lunchtime.

Prisca, Malachai, Jason, Nadia, and Nick hung decorations
beneath the veranda. Mixing the colorful decorations in amongst the
fragrant hanging flowers. The kitchen and house staff sat up the
table decorations and prepared a special lunch and birthday cake.
Everyone else busied themselves with the smaller details.

Prisca and Vashti wrapped a few gifts that were gathered for
Bridget. Mostly from Oz and Prisca, Seth and Caroline, Simon and
Nuncio, and Dominic. Everyone was very anxious to see the
creatures that Oz and the others would returned with. Most of them
had never seen anything too out of the ordinary before, so this would
be very interesting.

As Bridget, Annabelle, and Wade wandered through the lush
greenery of the island's forest, teaching Annabelle how to use her

gift, the lunch hour started to grow closer and Bridget begged one last time to be able to return to the main house to get something to eat.

"Annabelle," she said exhausted, "there really isn't much more to show you. Your gift will come naturally. You're telepathic abilities will grow stronger as will your gift. Now, can we *please* return to the main house? I'm starving. I barely got to eat breakfast at all before you two pulled me out of the kitchen." She threw an annoyed sideways glance at Wade.

"Well, I guess we can go back now." He glanced carefully at Annabelle.

Just as Annabelle was going to speak, the trio heard a loud squawk split the air and reverberated through the trees and underbrush.

Bridget's head snapped up toward the sky. She knew that squawk better than any other sound in the world.

"Han?" she breathed, beginning to run out of the underbrush, searching the bright blue sky above.

Wade and Annabelle smiled at each other and ran after Bridget.

Bridget stood out in the open, spinning in circles as she searched the sky. She started running toward the main house as fast as her feet would allow her to move. As she ran, she heard it again, and the low catcalls of the Pagorinx. Bridget's heart raced as her feet pounded the soil of the island, quickened by the excitement of the possibility of seeing her friends again. She didn't think, she only ran toward what she hoped wasn't her vivid imagination taking her to her happy place in the midst of the mountain of sorrow she had faced lately.

As the threesome ran around the rear of the house toward the front, Bridget suddenly stopped, almost making Wade bump into her.

Everyone was standing outside in the yard and patio area, gazing in awe at the massive animals being ridden by the four Peregrines and one Keeper. Alec saw Bridget come around the house and alerted the others.

"Bridget's here!" he yelled, and everyone turned to look at her.

"Happy Birthday, Bridget!" everyone yelled in almost unison.

Bridget was in shock. She was surprised by the party and everyone who stood there wishing her happiness. But the most shocking of all was the fact that Han, Cho, Mother, and Paxton stood in front of her. She smiled the biggest smile anyone had seen yet and ran to the animals as tears of joy streaked her cheeks.

"Han!" She ran up to the massive bird and wrapped her arms around his beak as he nuzzled her lovingly. She took turns loving on and communing with each of the animals, ending with her sweet Paxton.

"Oh, Paxton, how I've missed you all so much."

The cub, now almost as fully grown as his mother, purred loudly, and rubbed against her to the point that he toppled her to the ground, lying down beside her. Bridget erupted in a fit of giggles. As she lay there, the rest of the group took the opportunity to get up close and personal with the unbelievable creatures.

Bridget soon stood and looked at her friends. She couldn't believe they had done this for her.

"Thank you all so much. I can't believe you brought Han, Cho, Mother, and Paxton here for my birthday," she said amid tears and a choked-up voice.

Oz stepped forward. "Well, a' course we did. We love ya' girl, an' don't ya' ferget that."

Bridget smiled up at the large man she had come to know and love like a grandfather.

"Thank you, Oz." She smiled at him.

"How ever did you manage it? I thought Zanchier wasn't easily found?"

"Well, same way as always, we caught a' storm. But now 'cause Simon found some info in yer pa's books we know how ta get there easier."

Simon stepped up. "Bridget, everyone has taken part in preparing this wonderful party for our brand new seventeen-year-old. We know your birthday isn't for a few more days, but with our way of life, we never know when we will be called to leave the island. And we know how sad you've been lately, so, we chose today to celebrate. Clancy has made some wonderful food, and a beautiful cake."

Bridget looked around at everyone there, still smiling. "Thank you all so very much. This means the world to me. Especially bringing the animals here."

Simon said, "Well that part was Dominic's idea."

Bridget looked at the boy who had become a very good friend to her over the last month. She walked over to him and gave him a big hug.

"Thank you, Dominic, for thinking of me so much. This means the world to me," she repeated again, and smiled as another heartfelt tear streaked her cheek.

"Your welcome, Bridget. I guess it cheered you up," he said with a grin.

"Yes." She giggled and sniffed. "Very much."

Everyone gathered around her, giving her a hug and birthday wishes. Then they all sat down to have lunch and cake, Bridget's eyes straying to the animals who lounged on the front lawn peacefully. She looked around the table and smiled, realizing she had the biggest and best family ever. She would always remember her father as a good man, the way he had been with her. But she knew she had a new life now, and the people in her past, and present, that weren't exactly good or kind, were just that. People in her life. They did not define who she was or who she was supposed to become. Only God could do that. And her participation in what He wanted from her was her choice. She was not controlled by her past or those in it.

Oz stood to speak. "Bridget, me an' Priss got ya' a lit'le somethin' fer yer birthday." He took the wrapped package and walked over to where she sat.

Bridget smiled up at him thoughtfully, surprised by yet another gift. "Thank you, Oz, Prisca," she said, looking at the woman.

Bridget opened the package to reveal a beautiful heart-shaped necklace that was open in the center and hung from a beautiful silver chain. The colors in the necklace matched the colors in Oz and Prisca's wedding bands. The streaks of red, orange, gold, and turquoise, melding together around the surface of the heart. She looked up at Oz. "Did you make this for me?"

"A' course I did. You were the first ta' open up this ole' froz'n heart a' mine after years a loneliness. I want'd ya' ta know what ya' mean ta' me, an' Priss," he said looking at his wife. "An' ta let ya' know that no mat'er what, I'll always be there ta protect ya', an' pick ya' up when yer down an' out." The big man quickly swiped at a stray tear that rolled down his cheek.

Bridget's eyes filled with tears again as she quickly jumped up into her chair and wrapped her arms around the large man's neck.

"Thank you, Oz. I love you ever so much." She sniffed and gave him a peck on the cheek as he patted her back, trying to control his emotions. He then went to sit down with Prisca again. There wasn't a dry eye around the table at the show of obvious adoration that the two shared for one another.

"Seth and I have a gift as well." Caroline stood, grabbed the package, and walked over to Bridget. "It isn't much, but we thought you could use it." She handed the package to Bridget and inside was the most beautifully embellished knife she had ever seen. She pulled the blade from its sheath to look at it. The knife was the length of her forearm, the blade was straight except for a slight curve at the tip, and the handle was made of a highly polished, silvery metal and was inlaid with a beautiful sea-colored jewel in the tip.

"Oh Caroline, it's beautiful!" she exclaimed. "Thank you so much." She looked across the table at Seth. "Thank you, Seth. It's absolutely perfect." She and Caroline exchanged hugs and Caroline made her way back to her seat.

Dominic, who sat next to Bridget said, "My turn."

Bridget looked at him. "But you've already given me a gift. A spectacular one at that."

"Yeah, I know, but I wanted to give you something that you could have forever. The animals will have to go back to Zanchier eventually."

Bridget realized this and a small bit of sadness at the thought entered her eyes but was quickly replaced by the gift Dominic placed in her hands. She smiled at him and opened the large flat package.

She held a beautifully framed sketch of her, Han, and Paxton. Apparently created from a memory of Dominic's from the three days they had spent there almost two weeks ago. She was standing on the largest platform of the treehouse, her back to Storm Valley. Han was to her right and Paxton to her left. The drawing nearly took her breath away.

"Oh, Dominic, it's gorgeous. It's the most beautiful picture I've ever seen. Thank you so much." She turned to him and gave him a tearful hug.

Dominic beamed with pride and joy as everyone asked her to pass the large twelve by fourteen image around the table.

He said, "Rourke made the frame out of some of the islands wood."

Everyone commented on the expert drawing and the beautiful wooden frame as it passed from one person to another.

Simon stood next. "Nuncio and I have one more gift for you Bridget." He handed her another flat package. As he watched her open it, he explained. "It isn't much, but we thought you should have it. We came across the photo a few days ago, hidden in the lining of one of your father's books."

Bridget looked down into another framed picture. But this one was an actual photograph of her father, Hiram Burke, and a woman whom she assumed was her mother, Mary Draiwood Burke. She had never seen a picture of her mother before this. She looked at Simon with a questioning stare.

He knew what she was asking. "Yes, that is your mother. We only saw her one time." Simon not wishing to say that it was when she had died trying to come through the portal. "She was a beautiful woman. You look very much like she did." He grinned, a tad sadly at her, knowing her emotions were likely wreaking havoc within her at the moment.

She looked up at him and glanced at Nuncio before turning to him and saying, "Thank you. I shall cherish this photo forever." She held the framed photo to her chest, wrapping her arms around the back of it.

She grinned, placing the photo on the table, then stood up.

"This has been the absolute best day I have had or could possibly ever have." She smiled as she looked around the table at her friends and family. "Thank you all so very much."

The revelers celebrated far into the afternoon, with Bridget and the others who had ridden the animals before, taking anyone else who wanted to experience riding them on a trip around the island.

Oz had grabbed several strings of the dried meats that still hung in the root cellar of his treehouse back in Zanchier, to bring with him for the animals to eat. He knew they would need nourishment of some kind. After feeding them some of the meats, they took them to one of the springs in the center of the island where fresh water flowed from somewhere beneath and let the animals drink till full.

The sky began to grow dark, and Bridget knew her time with the Zanchier creatures was coming to an end.

She looked at Oz. "Will you take them back tonight?" Knowing that to do so would be a long journey for him and whoever else joined him.

"Yeah. They need ta be in their home-land. Ya' know that, right?"

"Yes, but it will be a long trip."

"Yeah, but we'll jus' stay in the treehouse tonight, then have Han an' the others take us ta the Dustbowl tammara' mornin'."

"I would like to go with you, if I may."

"Sure ya can go." He smiled down at her.

Oz yelled to Sofia and Dominic to join them to return the animals. He grabbed his weapon from the table, knowing Zanchier to be a treacherous place. Everyone gathered around them to say their goodbyes to the magnificent creatures, as Oz, Bridget, Sofia, and Dominic, mounted the backs of the animals. They waved goodbye, stating their return early tomorrow morning since it wasn't quite the correct time of year and phase of the moon for a return journey tonight.

Simon instructed Oz to the correct window in which to walk to find an appropriate storm to Zanchier, and they walked the animals through to the other side to a remote area where the animals wouldn't be seen by anyone else.

Everyone watched them go, then set about cleaning up after the party. Caroline took the two pictures given to Bridget for her birthday to her room. Bridget had worn the necklace instantly and had place the sheathed knife on her belt. Everything had been cleaned up within the hour and they spent the rest of the night relaxing around the firepits before heading inside for bed.

Zanchier

Their arrival in storm valley had once again been a turbulent event. However, they did get through it quickly as they were already on the backs of the animals. They were deposited on the lowest and largest platform of the treehouse and dismounted. They all said farewell to the creatures. The others turned and went inside while Bridget stayed where she stood, breathing deeply of the night air and the scent of the late-summer to early-fall flowers that bloomed in the forest around them. The moon shone brightly in the night sky over Storm Valley as the rain began to disperse. She was glad to be back. She considered the Xantifal Mountains her home above any other. She breathed deeply once more and walked into the treehouse. In the morning, they would call the animals back and be taken to the Dustbowl to return to the island. She only hoped they didn't run into the Scaithers while they were here. She didn't want to see Marnor Draiwood ever again.

She dried off and changed into some of the clothing that Sofia had left behind in their hurry to leave Zanchier months back. She and Sofia would share the larger bed in her old room, and Dominic would sleep in the twin-size bed. The very room she and Dominic had stayed in just two weeks ago. Oz of course slept in his old room. After putting on dry clothing, they all fell asleep quickly.

Early the next morning, they used Oz's Tarphamor horn to call to the Kabihanxus for one more journey to the Dustbowl then home to Reader's Island. Oz and Dominic rode on Han while Sofia and Bridget rode Cho. They dropped them near the Dustbowl then flew away once more. Bridget watched them go, wishing she could stay in Zanchier with them. As much as she loved her new family and friends, she loved this place and the animals that lived here even more.

They ran into the Dustbowl being swept up into one of the constant tornados that gave the area its name. They were tossed out on the other side, then quickly pushed the home button on Oz's Portgen.

It was around ten a.m. when they arrived back on the island. Most everyone else was already on the training fields so they went down to join them. The day was a regular normal day on the island. Yesterday's festivities were a nice break from their normal routine, but today was all business once again.

Simon and the other Dragoman were still trying to figure out what to do with Petra. Should they take her with them when they left, or banish her as they discussed? With Uriah in hiding, he could return to the island at any time. Simon and the others were trying to decide how to protect the island from just such a problem. If they all had to leave, it would be the first time in hundreds of years that the island had been left unattended. They had no fear of leaving except for the fact that Uriah might return and wreak havoc or try to steal the books and keys. Their only surety was that the demons could not step foot on the island. It was protected by God and sacred. It was the one place on all the earth, and in all the realms, the demons could not go.

Simon, Nuncio, Malachai, Vashti, and Prisca decided that they would take a break from fight training today to hash out all the unanswered questions. They would also search much deeper through the sections of the books they marked as important, hoping to find some more answers.

After the others returned from Zanchier, Simon and Dekker returned to the time period where he had his eye exam to see if his glasses were ready for pickup. They were indeed, and when Dekker put the bottle thick glasses on, he was amazed at what he could see.

The eye doctor said, "It's going to take you some time to adjust to them. You can expect the usual headaches and eye tiredness that usually accompanies a new pair. Especially ones this thick since your vision was so bad. Your basically considered blind."

Dekker replied as he looked all around the room, a smile on his face. "Thank you, Doctor. I appreciate it very much. It's been years since I've been able to see like this. I feel like a new man."

The three men said their farewells, and Simon and Dekker returned to the remote place where they entered this time period and returned to the island.

Dekker couldn't stop smiling as he took in the beauty that lay all around him as they walked. "My goodness. Would you look at this place? I tried to imagine it from the sounds and smells, and the descriptions you all gave me, but it is far beyond what I could imagine."

Simon chuckled. "Yes. Reader's Island is a mystical place. Beautiful beyond anything else. I imagine the Garden of Eden to have been much like this."

Dekker chuckled. "Are you sure this isn't it?"

Simon laughed. "Well, since God shut the garden up, I doubt it. But He certainly has provided greatly for those He chose to live this way. We used to only use the island for meetings and a temporary respite. We feared the temptation to stay and never leave to be too great. But this new generation of Peregrines seem to handle it all very well. They know their place, and their duty, and it seems nothing will stop them from fulfilling God's wishes."

"Good thing I'm not one of them. I don't know if I could ever leave here," Dekker stated.

"Oh, but you are, Dekker."

"How do you mean? I'm no Dragoman, and I'm certainly not a warrior. Just a humble blacksmith. I have no idea what I'm supposed to do here."

"I believe that God has called you to remake the Swords of the Spirit."

"Do you really think so?"

"Absolutely. You said so yourself that you weren't a Dragoman or Peregrine, so why else would you be here? We've found the first four pieces of the armor."

Dekker thought for a moment. "So, why do you not think the swords are out there somewhere?"

"Because we found a bag of jewels that apparently fit into the hilt of the swords. And a secret message in one of the books that state that the swords were dismantled and melted down. Then, of course, God sends us an A-1 blacksmith." Simon finished, smiling at Dekker.

"How do you know I'm that good," Dekker asked, teasingly.

"God called you to it, did He not?" Simon smiled.

"Well, isn't that something." Dekker smiled back. "I knew God had a plan for me, I just wasn't certain what that was, till now."

"Yes, now, we just need to figure out the materials that we are to use to fashion these blades. The Chosen Twelve are to battle dragons in the final battle."

The two men walked into the main house, and everyone commented on his glasses. He was finally able to put faces with names and voices. Dekker went off to the training fields to see the others while Simon went into the library to look through the books once again. The other Dragoman were there with all the books they needed to search, spread across the extra-long table in the center of the massive room. Simon looked at the five beautifully ornate ancient archive books and their equally unique keys that unlocked their secrets. Beside them on the table were the four books that once belonged to Hiram Burke, listed as *Historical Events, Book of Codes,*

Geography, and *History of Storms.* These books weren't much unlike the sets that each Dragoman kept themselves. The only one missing in his collection was his archive book listing all those that he mentored. Perhaps it had been lost, or perhaps it might be somewhere in his home back in Dover, England, in the late 1500s.

Simon picked up one of the last ancient archive books to be opened, the *Book of Lineage.* He wondered if there was more to it other than who did what, and when? He needed to search the books to make certain that the cryptograph he decoded in one of Hiram's books was correct and not a hoax. He walked to the kitchen, grabbed a large mug of steaming coffee, and went back to the library. He sat down at the large table and took the lineage book and began reading where he left off, praying that God would guide him in the right direction.

For it is by grace you have been saved, through faith — and this is
not from yourselves, it is the gift of God —

Ephesians 2:8

Chapter 18

Dekker was truly enjoying his glasses. He hadn't realized just how bad his eyes were getting until he lost his sight almost completely. He had made the rounds at the training fields, putting the remaining voices and names with their faces. One thing the lack of sight had afforded him was the ability to remember things well and quickly.

He decided to walk back up to the main house to see what he needed to do next. It seemed that everyone on the island was busy doing something, and he felt he should be as well. He walked into the archive library where the Dragoman were hard at work studying books. He found Simon sitting at a large table in the room's center.

"Simon, I hate to disturb your work, but I was wondering if there was anything that I could help with?"

Simon looked up from the book, grateful for a respite to rest his tired eyes. "Hello, Dekker. I'm certain we can find something for you. I don't know if you would recognize anything that we might be searching for in the books, but you're welcome to try." Dekker sat and Simon grabbed one of the books and handed it to him.

"If you come across anything in this that looks to be important or some sort of instruction, then mark it or make a note of it."

"I can do that. It's been years since I've read a book." He smiled and took it in his hands just staring at the cover while moving his hands across it, feeling the cool, smooth leather.

Simon grinned before returning his attention back to his own book. They spent the next several hours hunched over the table, sticking papers anywhere they thought might be important.

It was soon time for a late lunch. Everyone had been so engaged in whatever they were doing that those responsible for today's lunch and chores had missed it by an hour. Everyone gathered in the kitchen to help expedite a quick meal, starving from the day's activities. They took a bit longer for lunch than usual with everyone just sitting and enjoying the coolness of the large, inside dining room. Even though the island kept a comfortably stable temperature, that only aided you when your body was in a regular state of being. When training, their body temperatures would still heat up to the point of extreme sweating.

At about just after two pm, the groups went back to their assigned spots for the day with the assigned group taking care of the house and kitchen, deciding they had better get a jump on dinner.

Dekker found something of importance concerning the armor pieces that he thought should be brought to Simon's attention sooner than later.

"Simon, I have a question. Where are we to get the iron that is to be used to forge the swords?"

"Well, we can get that just about anywhere, why do you ask?"

"It says here in this book, that the armor was fashioned from a very special metal. And that when the swords were stolen and destroyed, and the gems sold, that whoever had taken them apparently had a very hard time melting the metal down. Whatever the swords were made of must have been some very heat resistant stuff."

"Hmm, I haven't read that yet. Nuncio mentioned that he read about the swords being stolen and disassembled. But he never mentioned that part to us."

"You know, I was talking with Oz out in the stable the other night about a type of metal that was highly sought after in Zanchier. Oz said that the metal resisted heating up and had a very high melting point. If the Peregrines are to battle dragons, and these dragons may or may not breathe fire, then perhaps we should get some of this Rhenium and Ruthenium to make the swords with and recoat the Armor of God as well."

"You make a very valid point, Dekker. Perhaps this is the purpose of our continued returns to Zanchier? God may be leading us to something there that we may need." Simon grinned at the discovery. "Good work old boy!" Simon slapped him on the shoulder. "Now, if we could just figure out a better and faster way into and out of Zanchier, it would make acquiring the metals much easier. We will need quite a lot of the stuff. Then we will have to put it through the process of separating the metals from the rock. The Goddelikheid Crucible should do quite nicely for that." Simon smiled, seeing all the work over the last four months coming together, and the why's behind retrieving certain artifacts.

Simon's elation came to a halt and his expression turned serious. "I just thought of something else. We have almost acquired all the armor pieces, but I was remiss about one small detail. In the *Book of Armor*, where it describes the pieces, it also spoke of colorful cloaks representing each of the twelve tribes of Israel. We haven't found any cloaks with the armor pieces so far. I don't see how fabric could survive for thousands of years anyway. I wonder if we are supposed to have the cloaks remade as to the specifications in the book?"

Dekker asked, "Do you have an expert seamstress here?"

"I don't think so. I'm not even certain where we would find the material as listed. Sure, we have access to anywhere in the world at our fingertips, but this was very special material and finding an exact match may be impossible."

"Well," Dekker said, "I know an expert seamstress. Her name is Heba. She lives in Akrotiri."

"I'm not certain we should chance returning there," Simon said questioningly.

"The King is a good and honorable man. A pompous one, like most kings, but a good one none the less. If he let you leave once, I don't see it being a problem again."

"Well then, perhaps we could pay her to make the cloaks. But first, we need to find the material to use." Simon racked his brain, trying to think of where to find their match. They would likely have to return to ancient Egypt or Israel to find what they needed.

The men made the necessary notes so as to not forget what they came up with, then continued searching the books. Malachai, who was still trying to decipher the language in the *Book of the Keepers* walked over to Simon with the book in hand.

"Simon, do you recognize this symbol from any of the ancient languages you've studied? It is another one that is not part of the code Ryan found online. If we can only translate half the book, then I don't see what good it is going to do us." He laid the book on the table between Simon and Dekker.

"No, I have no idea what it means," Simon said exasperated.

"That looks to be ancient Akrotirian," Dekker stated, catching the attention of the two men.

Simon asked astonished, "Do you mean that you recognize this language?"

"Yes, well sort of. I'm not skilled at reading it, but many of the old ones in the Akrotirian city know this language. Heba is one of them. Her father taught her long ago. The city has adapted a newer way of writing and speaking now, but some, very few though, still use this ancient way of writing. I saw several hieroglyphs before my eyes became too bad."

Simon and Malachai looked at each other and grinned broadly.

Simon said excitedly, "Praise the Lord, things are truly beginning to come together!" The three men grinned and laughed at his exuberance grabbing the attention of the others in the room. The rest quickly made their way to the table where the three of them sat, as Simon and Dekker explained what they had found.

Nuncio smiled. "It appears that we are headed out for some very interesting expeditions. Ones that we all must make, because we never know when this impending demon battle will strike."

"True," Simon said. "Let's keep digging until God gives us the day and time to leave the island. Next on the agenda I'm afraid is dealing with Petra. We can't leave her here, locked in her room for days or weeks on end."

Prisca spoke, "Perhaps we should just take her with us?"

Malachai said, "It might be difficult to watch her at all times?"

"Maybe not," Simon answered. "The Peregrines have a very good system of checks and balances in place when they travel. They always have two guards on duty that change out every two hours. It shouldn't be difficult at all to watch her."

Malachi said, "What about during a battle? There is no way we could watch her, and no way we should give her a weapon. She could turn it on any one of us."

Vashti said, "We'll just have to take her along, *not* give her a weapon, and pray that God takes care of the rest. Unless we elect to send her to Zanchier?"

Nuncio stated, "That might be easiest. But how do we do that and make certain that she gets there and stays there? She's heard all of the stories about how to leave the place. What if she comes back to the island?"

Simon looked at him. "Then that's her decision. If she returns, we will have no choice but to *deal* with her."

"Simon," Prisca said astonished, "we can't take a human life! It is forbidden!"

"Then let's hope and pray that she doesn't return. We'll explain it to her, and she must make up her own mind and deal with the consequences. I won't allow what happened thirteen years ago to happen again."

They all looked at each other, shaking their heads in uncertain agreement. After the brief impromptu meeting, they went to Petra's room to explain their decision to her.

She begged them to change their minds. "Please, don't banish me to that place? I'm done with Uriah. He used and betrayed me. I hold no loyalty to him any longer. I promise to be loyal to the cause."

"Petra," Simon said, "there is no way that we can trust you again. You were working with Uriah to destroy all of us and the work the Lord put us to. Do you really expect us to believe that you've suddenly just turned over a new leaf? If your loyalty is so fleeting, I'm pretty certain that I don't want that sort of loyalty on the team."

Petra looked at him, knowing he was right but argued her case anyway. "I've learned my lesson, Simon." She looked at all of them. "I'm willing to work for God again. The life Uriah and Hiram promised is a memory, and a bleak one at that. *Please*, don't send me away. I promise to be loyal. You won't hear a peep out of me or have another issue with me ever again."

They all looked at one another. Simon sighed and answered her, "It isn't that simple Petra. You're not a child caught in an infraction. What you and Uriah were planning, and I'm still not completely certain what that is, was destructive to us all and all of the human, and non-human race. I'm sorry, but it would take an act of God, in your favor, to make me trust you again. And frankly, God only favors His children, which I seriously doubt you ever took to heart."

Petra shrank onto the bed, fear gripping her body, knowing that she had stepped way over the line with these people she once called friends. She sat looking at them as they quietly discussed something on the other side of the room. Prisca and Vashti throwing her looks of concern every so often.

Simon returned to her bedside. "Against my better judgment, the others have decided to take you with us."

Petra's excitement grew, but Simon stopped her from speaking. "I'm not finished yet, Petra. You will still be a prisoner. Watched *every* second of *every* day. If we get into a battle with the demons, you are on your own. We can't protect you and we won't give you a weapon. You either accept these terms or banishment to Zanchier it is," he stated sternly.

"I agree. I'll be good and helpful, I promise. I couldn't make it on my own in a place like Zanchier if what Oz and the others say is true. Thank you, Simon. Thank you all."

"I promise you, Petra, if you make me regret this decision, I'll deal with you myself, and hang the consequences," Simon threatened.

Petra could see the anger behind his eyes and written in the stressed lines of his face. She had never before seen Simon so angry or stern. She had never heard him threaten death to anyone before either. She knew he meant what he said. She shook her head in agreement, grateful for a chance to redeem herself.

The Dragoman left the room, securing it once again. They returned to the library where Dekker was still looking through books and they all continued the work once more.

Simon went to the large, front windows of the library for a moment alone. He gazed out at the lush, serene landscape of the island and breathed deeply, trying to control his temper. He about lost it with Petra. If there was one thing that burned him up it was lack of loyalty. He hadn't been this angry in a long time. If it had been up to him alone, he would have turned her out on her own and left her to fend for herself with nothing but the clothes on her back. Traitorous behavior deserved nothing less. Accept, possibly death. Simon shook his head to clear it. His emotions were beginning to rule his head. He would never intentionally take another human life, but he was seriously considering doing so where Petra and Uriah were concerned. Perhaps it was his Irish blood and upbringing that was making his temper flare. He needed to sit and pray about his attitude as of late. With the business of their current lives he had been neglecting his daily commune with God and it was beginning to affect him negatively. Simon sat for the next ten minutes in silent prayer, knowing it was vital for the rest of his day to go better.

Simon returned to the archive library and the table full of books, his temper under control and feeling much calmer now. He picked up the *Book of the Keepers* and asked Dekker if he could make out any of the symbols himself.

Dekker shook his head no.

"I know they are Akrotiri but I don't know what any of them mean. I'm sorry I'm not more help."

"Not a problem at all, Dekker. I suppose the first trip we need to make is to Akrotiri to speak with Heba. We need to know what this book says. There is also a message on a piece of cloth written in the same language that we'll need to take to her for translation as well. We'll discuss this with the Peregrine leaders tonight after dinner. Perhaps one of them knows where we can acquire the material for the cloaks, and we can make one swift trip of it. Akrotiri isn't as easy to get to as most other places. A long walk across the ocean floor takes a bit of doing."

"Perhaps it would be easier to bring Heba here to the island?" Dekker asked.

"Unfortunately, those not called by God will die if they try to Peregrinate. She cannot come with us. No, we will have to travel back to retrieve the cloaks once she is finished sewing them. That is, if she will do so in the first place."

"I'm certain she will. That is what she does in Akrotiri after all."

"Well then, let's talk with the others about that material and we'll go from there. It's nearly dinner time now anyhow. We might as well stop until after dinner or possibly even tomorrow morning."

Simon turned to the rest of the Dragoman. "I'm going into the kitchen to see if the others need any further help readying dinner. I suggest we all give our tired eyes and backs a break for the next several hours."

"I agree," Nuncio said, standing carefully due to the pain in his hip and stretched his long frame.

Everyone else followed suit while Simon disappeared into the kitchen area. He realized that today's kitchen volunteers were none other than Jason, Oz, Seth, and Caroline.

"Well, just the people to whom I wanted to speak." He looked at Jason and Oz.

"Simon." Jason greeted him with a nod. "What do you need with me?" He stood up straight from his position over the few remaining dishes in the sink.

"I was curious to know, if in all your recent travels, do you remember seeing any ancient fabrics? Such as the ones that are described as being representative of the twelve tribes?"

"Hmm…I'm not sure. It isn't often that we go to markets while we travel. But Seth and I did go to one when we went to Israel for the Staff of Moses. We had some time to kill before the storm blew in that brought us home. I can't say for certain there was materials like you need, but more than likely there is since it was during the time of Solomon's Temple."

"It may be difficult to find the exact materials used in the armor when King Solomon had it made." Simon pondered.

Oz overheard their conversation as he was standing at the stove stirring the large pot of roast, vegetables, and gravy.

"Er', Jason, do ya' remember the large panels a' fabric hangin' in King Sol'mon's private chambers? Each one was a' repr'sentation a' one a' the twelve tribes a' Israel. Maybe Memnah's people, now they know we ain't thieves, would be willin' ta' give us a bit a' each panel ta make new cloaks? It wouldn't take much at all. An' that fabric is lik'ly the very same that King Sol'mon used in the firs' place."

Simon smiled widely. "Oz old boy, *you* are a genius."

Oz beamed under the praise of his friend. "Well, try tellin' that ta Priss." He laughed.

The other men chuckled along with him.

Jason looked at Simon. "I can go see her after dinner tonight and ask if it would be possible."

Simon beamed once again. "That would be most helpful, Jason." *My how things were coming together*, he thought. "See you boys in an hour. I'm just going to walk to the fields and call everyone in for dinner." With that, Simon left the kitchen, and with a renewed spring in his step, walked down to the training fields enjoying the scent of the flowers on the evening breeze.

On the way to the fields, he encountered Odessa coming up to the house, a troubled look on her face.

"Odessa, what is it?"

"I just had an awake vision. Like the one I had when we were warned of the last demon war in Timna Valley."

"And?" Simon asked, disturbed.

"The demon war we've been preparing for the last week, it's going to happen two days from now."

"Where?"

"Timna Valley," she said confused.

"I wonder why we fight there again?"

"I think it might have something to do with the raising of an army. For some reason, in my vision, I saw men rising from the ground, like they appeared out of dust."

"Like skeletons?" Simon asked curiously.

"No. Flesh and blood."

"Could it have been Memnah's tribe again?"

"No. All I saw were men, coming up from solid ground. Like they just suddenly stood up. And there were thousands of them, Simon."

"Well, this is very interesting indeed." He scanned his memory, searching for some clue from the Word. "I suggest we all start getting prepared then. Can you go back to the fields and inform the others that we will have an early dinner? I need to go back to the house to research something about what you just told me."

"Certainly, Simon." Odessa turned and headed back to the training fields.

Simon rushed back to the main house, grabbed a Bible from the library table, and leafed through the book, searching for answers to Odessa's vision. He found what he believed to be the answer in the book of Ezekiel, chapter 37, where it speaks of the dry bones.

Simon smiled. "Lord you are great!"

He went into the kitchen to tell the others what Odessa had seen and what he found in the Bible.

Jason was silent for a bit, feeling small-minded and unfaithful.

"You know," he said to the men standing there, "I've been very concerned about this coming war. I didn't think we stood a chance with the few amount of people that we have fighting. Not even with the added strength of the Zanchier creatures. I didn't think any of us would survive it. Now I feel like a fool not trusting that God would provide for us. Do you really think He'll do what it says in Ezekial?" Jason still felt a bit apprehensive.

Simon said, "Well, if what Odessa saw in her vision is true, then yes. We even have to return to Timna Valley to fight."

Jason said, "You know, if we go back to Timna, Memnah's people are going to want to fight with us. They claim the valley as what they are to protect."

"Odessa didn't mention seeing them in the war," Simon stated.

"She also didn't mention seeing them in the last one we fought with them either," Jason said pointedly.

"True," Simon stated. "Well, if they wish to join us, then they may do so. As long as they have God's blessing."

The men all stood in the kitchen, smiling at one another with knowing. God had provided for them once again. They would have an equal army with which to fight.

Simon wondered how the event was to take place. Was someone meant to read from the Bible? Would God just raise them up when He saw fit to do so? He decided that he wouldn't worry about the details. God was obviously in control and providing them with the answers they needed when they needed them.

He went about helping Jason, Oz, Seth, and Caroline get dinner served outside, and the tables set up with dinnerware. They would share one last meal together as a group here on the island. In the morning, they would prepare for the days that lay ahead in the Timna Valley desert. Preparing for a battle unlike any they had ever faced before. But with God's help and provision, Simon prayed that each and every one of them would make it back alive.

When everyone had a chance to clean up, they all met outside on the patio beneath the veranda. Simon filled everyone in on the newest development concerning the massive demon war in which they must all fight. Some of the island's long-term inhabitants, groaning about how quickly it came about.

Someone said, "I'm not sure I'm ready at all. We've had less than a week to prepare."

Simon answered, "Ready or not, we have no choice. We must leave."

Someone else replied, "What if we don't go and just stay here. If the battle is to take place somewhere else, then we'll be safe here. Why fight at all?"

Simon sighed. "I know all of you who have lived here uninterrupted for the last thirteen years, or longer, don't see why this battle must take place. You've gotten used to the lure of the island. But don't forget, you were all once great warriors. Fearsome, strong, and true. You fought long and hard for God once long ago. Now He's called you all to it once more. Don't turn your back on the mission now. I can't force you to fight, but just remember that you were called to this life a long time ago. You've just been fortunate to have a nice respite from it for a great many years."

"Yes, but what about our injuries received thirteen years ago? How can we fight well with them?"

"God called you to fight, and I am certain He will strengthen each and every one of you. Besides, you all still have your gifts. You have used them and practiced with them over the last week. And should anyone perish, be comforted that you will be in the Father's arms. What more could we ask? Our future is secure people. We should have no fear of death."

"Here, here, Simon," Nuncio said, standing to toast his lifelong friend. "I've missed the action for far too long. I sit here on the island, day after day, watching the adventures you all take. Wishing that I could still do so myself. Don't get me wrong, I know my purpose was here for a time, but I for one am ready to fight once again. And if it is to be my last fight, then I shall go out in a blaze of glory. God will provide for us all. You shall all see the miracles of the Lord once the battle begins. He has shown Odessa and Safra many miracles already concerning this fight. Rest easy, my friends and be strong, for God wins in the end. We have the book that tells us that He does." He held his glass up before taking a long drink.

Everyone at the table raised their glasses in the toast along with Nuncio, turning their glasses up to drink also. People's fears may not have been erased, but perhaps they were less burdened by them after Nuncio's rousing speech.

King Solomon was greater in riches and wisdom
than all the other kings of the earth.

1 Kings 10:23

Chapter 19

Reader's Island

The next morning was spent gathering supplies, saddling all the horses in the stables, and realizing they were very short on supply with the additional people. Rourke, the head groundskeeper, suggested taking the four ATVs they used on the island, which they had never before thought of using. They had spent so many years traveling by foot, then by animal, they never thought about vehicles. They could be quite useful. With four ATVs seating at least four people each, that would help with the shortage of horses. Then Simon remembered something. His dreams of the Zanchier creatures. Those creatures were to fight in this war as well. He would have to send another team to get the animals. This time, it would be the Keepers. It was their time to be of use where their gifts were concerned.

Simon called to Bridget, Dominic, Wade, and Annabelle. When they all gathered around him, he explained.

"I'm going to need you four to bring the Kabihanxus and the Pagorinxes to Timna Valley on the day of the battle."

Bridget was confused. "Why, Simon?"

"I've been having dreams that depict these animals fighting in this war. You were riding them during the battle. They are very important to the success of this fight. You must bring them without fail."

Bridget asked, "How many should we bring, Simon? There are more Kabihanxus and Pagorinxes other than the ones to which I am closest."

"I'm not certain. I simply assume many will follow you when you call to them."

Bridget replied, "All right then. Once camp is settled in Timna, the four of us will return to Zanchier and bring them back. I suggest however, that you warn Memnah's tribe if they are to fight with us. I don't want anyone attacking the creatures and being eaten alive."

"You have a very good point. I'll see to it that they are forewarned."

The four teens went back to work, packing their own packs and helping to prepare needed kitchen supplies.

It was past noon when the large caravan was ready to set out. Petra had been handcuffed to one of the ATVs siderails in which Nuncio, Rourke, and one other staffer would ride.

The journey was very short. Literally opening the portal and passing through to the other side. They had the coordinates of the last cavern where they stayed and decided to make camp there once more. They were very familiar with the area and the cavern was large enough for everyone.

The decision to come a day early was a strategic one. Jason needed to see Memnah and inform her people of what was happening. They also wanted to gather some of the fabrics from Solomon's secret chamber for the cloaks, which Memnah's people agreed to allow.

Jason said to her, "Memnah, to speed things up, we need to go to Solomon's Pillars using the Portgen. Do you trust me with your necklace, the star of David, to open and reseal the chambers?"

"Yes." She removed the chain from her neck and handed it to him. Jason knew what a tremendous amount of trust this took on her part. She alone amongst her tribe was trusted with the medallion.

"Thank you, Memnah." He stared appreciatively into her deep greenish-brown eyes.

She grinned at him slightly, and Jason almost went weak in the knees.

Jason, along with Seth, Caroline, Alec, and Odessa, all walked through the Portgen's portal to Solomon's Pillars sixteen miles across the Negev Desert.

Jason opened the cavern's hidden entrance once more, and the five of them entered the ornately decorated passage that led to the cavern and once temporary throne room of King Solomon. The others were overwhelmed by what lay inside the throne room. Jason had to jar them from their stupor.

Fortunately, the long pieces of materials hanging against the back wall of the room started at the ceiling and ended in small heaps upon the cavern floor. They only needed about eight feet by four feet for each cloak. Each piece of hanging material was so wide and long that they had to remove very little of the fabric for their needs. Once finished, they packed up the materials in their packs, left the throne room and cavern entrance, resealed the hidden door, and reopened the portal for camp.

It was nearing late afternoon as the Peregrines sat making plans for the next day's battle. Memnah and her people wanted to fight the great evil with them, and she returned to her village to prepare her people for the next day. After she had that taken care of, she returned to the cavern to spend as much personal time with Jason as she could.

She walked in and sat down beside him during the meeting.

Jason looked at her and grinned, asking, "All ready?"

She grinned back after a deep exhale. "All ready."

"You and your people don't have to do this, Memnah."

"Oh but we do. It is our duty to fight evil and protect this valley."

"But you lost so many last time."

"Yes, and you lost one of your own out of so few people already. We know the costs, Jason. Just as your people do. Of which, I see you have added another twenty or so people to the fight. Are they all called by God as well?"

"Yes. They've just been in retirement for the last thirteen years."

"So these are the survivors of the betrayal you once told me about?"

"Yes. They stay on the island where we are all now based. I wish I could show you that place, Memnah. It's very beautiful. So much so that at times it takes your breath away. Much like you do to me." He looked over her face, taking in every line and contour.

She smiled broadly at his compliment, nudging him playfully with her shoulder.

They returned their attentions to the matter at hand. They were planning a battle strategy for tomorrow and Jason wondered how that would include Ryan Halloran. The guy never left the computer room, but they at least got him to hold a gun. He hadn't liked it at all. Especially the loud noise it made. If that noise set him on edge, how was he going to handle an all-out war? It appeared that Simon already had that thought out. He reached into his bag and pulled out a heavy pair of earmuffs used in shooting sports. Simon handed them to Ryan, whispering something in his ear. Ryan nodded and smiled slightly. Still, how was he to fight?

Simon stood to quieten the murmurs flying around the large group.

"Everyone, please, listen up. When we went to Akrotiri by way of the underwater gateway, we discovered something purely by accident. Gabriele's gift amplifies off the Portgen somehow. Now, I had Ryan develop a large generator of sorts that will connect to Gabby's gift and bounce to each of your Portgens, possibly giving you all a bit of protection. But for that to work, we would all need to stay within a certain proximity to each other. I believe it will work at the beginning of the battle, but once things get into full swing, you may not have it anymore. But you still have your God given gifts to use against these beasts, and we have Memnah and her people who will also help in the fight, as they did last time." He tipped his head to her in appreciation. She returned the gesture. "Not only that, but the Keepers will travel to Zanchier first thing in the morning to bring back the creatures you all met the other day. Memnah, you and your people will need to familiarize yourselves with these creatures. However, I wouldn't get too close without one of the Keepers nearby. I understand the animals are meat eaters."

Memnah looked at Jason with large eyes. "What does he mean by this?"

He smiled at the look on her face. "You'll see tomorrow."

She shrugged it off and continued to listen once again.

A staffer asked the question, "That still isn't a lot of people to help fight, unless Memnah's tribe has thousands of warriors? Are we supposed to handle it all by ourselves?"

Simon sighed. "No, actually, Odessa's vision yesterday revealed an act of God, a miracle we will all witness tomorrow. When or how, I'm uncertain. I just know that we will have help tomorrow."

"When will the battle begin?" Wade asked.

"I'm not certain about that either. Odessa did say the sun was pretty high in the sky, so I'm assuming mid-day." Simon looked around the cave at all the people. "Are there any more questions?"

No one spoke up and they dismissed the meeting.

The groups sat around the fires that were built earlier in the day and lit when the sun began to go down, making the desert much colder. The early fall days cooled the temperatures of the desert even more.

Simon sat looking over the information they had compiled from the books. He also reread the Bible passage from Ezekiel. His brow furrowed in concentration and confusion. Safra noticed this and went to speak to him.

"Something troubles you," she stated, sitting beside him.

"I never could hide anything from you, could I?" He smiled.

"No," she stated simply.

"It's this passage from Ezekiel. I know God will raise an army tomorrow, but in the passage, Ezekiel spoke over the army. I'm uncertain as to who here will fulfill that role."

"There you go again doubting God. He will provide all that is needed when the time is right."

Simon chuckled at her. "Oh, Safra, what would I do without your level-headed, faithful guidance. You have been a rock to me for so many years. I value your friendship above all else."

"And I yours." The two exchanged affectionate looks.

Simon secretly feared for Safra. She was older, and although she was still a fierce warrior, she had no special gift like the others to protect her. She was just as vulnerable as Memnah and her people. He didn't know what he would do if he lost her. He didn't know when she had become so valuable to him, but she had.

They sat in companionable silence for a while longer before Safra excused herself and went to bed. Simon too, soon turned in, and he noticed that several others were doing the same. Hoping to get a good night's sleep for the battle ahead. Simon passed the open flap of Jason's tent, noticing he and Memnah curled together on top of his bedroll. It appeared that no one had changed out of their clothing for the day. Everyone wanting to be ready for whenever tomorrow's war would begin. He slid into his tent, closed the flap, and prayed himself to sleep.

Safra watched until Simon went to his tent and closed the flap. She then took the Portgen she had Ryan make for her, went outside the cavern, and opened a portal to Morocco, in 1926. She prayed hard, hoping that she could travel this way without the aid of another Peregrine or Dragoman, closed her eyes, tensed up ready to die, and stepped through unharmed to the other side.

"Whew…" she said relieved. "Now, to find my younger self." She set out walking to her father's shop where their home was always located it the rear of the store. She hoped that she didn't frighten her younger self by appearing. She only went back to her forty-five-year-old self; the age when she was in her prime as a warrior. She was old enough to have had experience, and logic, yet young enough to still be able to kick some rear.

She entered the quiet shop, knowing her father would not be there. He had passed on long ago and Safra had spent the remainder of her life in this quiet little shop, alone, except for her friends, the Peregrines and Dragoman who frequented often. The familiar jingle of the bell above the door made her smile. She hadn't heard that sound in three months. Ever since Simon brought her to the island after the street gang destroyed it and the demons began attacking more frequently. She heard a woman call out.

"Be right with you."

Safra stood there, knowing to whom that voice belonged. It was only a few more seconds before she came face to face with her younger self. Her younger self, who looked at her confusingly.

"Do I know you?" she asked.

"Yes," she said simply.

"Are you one of the Peregrines or Dragoman my father and I help. I feel I've met you before."

"Oh, you know me well, Safra. For I am you, many years from now."

Her younger self stood still in shock, realizing why the old woman seemed so familiar to her. "How is this possible?"

"You know very well how?" She admonished her younger self.

"Yes, I..I know. I've seen many travelers from the future and the past, but I never thought that I would see myself."

Safra grinned, understanding.

"They need you."

"If you are with them, then they have me."

"They need a younger me. A large demon war is set to take place tomorrow. I am old. I can no longer do the things that you can. You will take my place tomorrow, and I must leave this world."

"You're dying," she simply stated, sadness and realization audible in her voice.

"Yes."

Safra's younger self locked up the shop, grabbed the few things she would need, and left her home with the older version of herself. The older Safra explained to the younger one everything she needed to know. The bio-scan technology worked for the younger woman since they were one and the same person. The younger Safra delivered the older to the island where she could see to setting her life in order before walking through one of the windows that surrounded the island and disappearing forever.

The younger Safra returned to Timna Valley, Israel, in the year 1840, slipped into Safra's tent and would wait to battle the next day. How she was going to explain this to Simon was beyond her. Luckily, they had known each other for a few years already at the age she was now. She had known Nuncio and others before him a bit longer. Peregrines and Dragoman sifted in and out of her father's life for as long as she could remember. Her father had been a devout advocate for their cause, and she became one as well.

She laid down and swiftly drifted off to sleep, knowing she would need it.

The night was a quiet one, the sounds of whispered prayers echoing throughout the cavern as people either prayed before going to sleep or prayed themselves *to* sleep.

When everyone began stirring the next morning, Safra stepped from her tent and frightened the life out of some of the others who were already up and preparing breakfast. Odessa jumped up, pulling her katana from its sheath, and wielding it toward the woman.

"Who are you, and what did you do with Safra?" she asked, confused by the woman who just walked out of Safra's tent. She did look like Safra, but she certainly was not the older woman who she saw go into the tent just eight or so hours earlier.

"I am Safra, from an earlier time period. Your Safra from the current period in her life, came and got me last night."

"You have got to be joking? That can't be possible!" Odessa said stunned.

"Sure it is. Safra, me, or older me, has lived a full life. There are past versions of us throughout history. We were never pulled out of history by God the way you all were. Your history stopped when you all Peregrinated. If you returned before that time, you would find younger versions of yourself before the period from which you left. Safra, or I, lived in the first-dimension world my entire life, except for the times when someone, mostly Simon, brought me through a storm portal to convene on Reader's Island with the other Dragoman."

"Why would she do this? Bring you here, now, and then leave us?" Odessa asked unbelieving.

"She knew that she could be no help to you at her present age and state of health. She's dying. At this age, I am in my prime. Mentally, physically, and skillfully. The older me may be much wiser than I am now, but in her wisdom, she knew she would be a hindrance today."

"So, she, or you, is gone forever?" Odessa asked sadly.

"Yes. But I am not going anywhere. I will always be here unless God decides otherwise. We shall see what He decides about that today, shall we not?" Safra walked away grinning nonchalantly, like what just happened was completely normal. Odessa sat staring after her backside as it disappeared out the cavern opening and into the desert beyond, wondering if she was going crazy, as were the ten others who stood in shock at the revelation and conversation they had just overheard.

Odessa stood there, looking at the cave opening, wondering if she had dreamed it all. After fifteen years of peregrinating, she had seen a lot of things, but this one took the cake.

"I'm not a drinking woman, but if I had a bottle of anything right now, I could be convinced to start." She shook her head and went back to cooking breakfast, glancing occasionally at the cavern's opening, wondering if the apparition would return. The others gathered near her mumbled their own agreements with her statement.

As everyone finally woke, and began to move about the camp, Safra reentered the cavern. Most everyone reacted the same way as Odessa had, even the Dragoman who had known her for much longer.

Simon nearly dropped his coffee cup.

"Safra?" He stood as he questioned what he saw.

"Hello, Simon. Good to see you at this stage. You look good. You always were a handsome man, but you've improved with age."

"How…" his voice trailed off in confusion.

"Sit back down and I'll tell you all about it." She took a seat next to him. She had the attention of the entire cavern, minus the ten people who had already heard her tell it.

Ten minutes later, everyone was gathering around the breakfast pan, spooning large helpings onto their plates, most stealing unbelieving glances at the new and improved version of Safra.

Zeke and Nick stood chatting as they watched her.

"She was some kind of woman back in her day," Zeke said appreciatively.

"How old do you think she is now. I mean, this version?" Nick asked.

"I don't know. But she sure is fit. I always saw the beauty behind Safra's wrinkles, but I had no idea she used to look like that?" Zeke shook his head in pleasant surprise.

"You and me both, brother," Nick replied as the two men finished their plates and went to meet the others outside.

Simon quickly dispersed the Keepers to Zanchier as soon as they had finished off their breakfast. Telling them to make it as quickly as possible. The battle should take place around noon, so that gave them approximately five to six hours to make the journey.

They made sure that Petra was securely chained to a post that had been driven into the rock before they had to leave to fight.

As the large group of Peregrines and Dragoman gathered outside to prepare for battle, another two-hundred men from Memnah's tribe appeared on horseback. As they pulled up close to the Peregrine army, most of the men were shocked to see the four-wheeled contraptions called ATVs. They dismounted and looked at the vehicles, amazed by what they saw, asking many questions. Some saying hello to those who they remembered from the last time they were in the Negev Desert.

Memnah translated for her people who did not speak English, as Simon reiterated the battle plan for their benefit.

"Gabriele will stay on the left of the battle-field, and Ryan, along with a driver of an ATV, will stay on the right. They will try to keep the same pace to keep the force-shield up. Each of you spread out allowing Memnah's men to be in between for the protection of the shield as well. Dekker and Nuncio will be in another of the ATVs somewhere near the center. Each of you must turn your Portgens on to bounce the signal across to each other, reaching Ryan on the end. Be prepared should Gabby be unable to hold the shield and fight as well. This is an unprecedented event. We're doing things we've never before tried."

"Simon, when is this army that is supposed to help us, arrive?" someone asked.

"I'm as clueless as you on that," he replied. "We must just trust God's timing."

"Is this where we are to fight the demons?" another person asked.

"Again, I am uncertain," Simon answered, exasperated.

Jason replied, "Last time, we saw a dust cloud kicking up, alerting us to their position."

Everyone looked to the horizon, watching, and waiting.

Jason stood up to talk. "All right everyone, let's get into formation now so that when it's time to leave we'll be ready.

The people all began moving toward a more open area so that they could do just that, all anxiously awaiting the call to move out.

Zanchier

Bridget, Wade, Dominic, and Annabelle walked out of the intense storm into another one in Storm Valley. She telepathically called to each of her animal friends, willing them to their position. They ran into the middle of the large field scanning the rain filled sky.

Suddenly the shrieks of the Kabihanxu filled the air between booms of thunder. The Pagorinxes, Mother and Paxton, bolted through the rain in their direction. Wade and Annabelle climbed onto the backs of Mother and Paxton, while Bridget and Dominic waited on Han and Cho to land so they could do the same.

Once she was situated on Han's back, Bridget said, "No treehouse today Han. Fly us over the mountain area so that we may call the creatures of Zanchier to aid in the battle." Bridget and the other Keepers began calling to all the Kabihanxus and Pagorinxes in Zanchier to aid them in the fight. They quickly flew and ran over and through the thick forest, the four Keepers telepathically calling out to the large creatures of Zanchier.

Annabelle and Wade had a hard time holding on to the backs of the Pagorinxes. They had never ridden on the animals at this pace. The creatures could sense their unease and behaved accordingly, trying to ease their discomfort.

As they bolted down the mountainside, and across the vast, open, planes of Bakrashan headed for the Dustbowl, Pagorinx and Kabihanxu alike began to join them in the race across the valley. Dozens of Pagorinx and Kabihanxu appeared like magic out of the lush, thick, massive trees of Zanchier.

They ran as quickly as possible toward the Dustbowl which was still hours away.

Annabelle called to the other Keepers telepathically.

"We need to make sure the animals all get something to drink before we get to the dustbowl. They still have a war to fight in."

Bridget replied in kind, *"You're right, Annabelle. There is a small river thirty minutes from here in that direction. We'll stop there but only for a few minutes."*

The people of Zanchier who were out and about, took notice of the animals and the four riders racing through the planes. They had never before seen anything like it.

The Scaithers who were camped at the edge of the planes had seen it before, and they all ran for their lives screaming in fear. Afraid that the girl who spoke to the deadly creatures may turn them against them once again.

They ran on for a while longer, stopping only briefly at the river to let the animals drink their fill.

Timna Valley

As they stood in formation, nerves drawing tightly, horses prancing from the tension that laced the air, someone yelled.

"There!"

Everyone turned to look where he pointed. In the same area the last battle was fought, the demon army was apparently moving in.

Simon threw up a prayer. "Lord, if you're going to deliver us that army, now would be a good time."

They began to move out, headed toward the cloud of dust far out into the desert.

Dekker yelled to Nuncio, "I need to talk to Simon."

"Rourke," Nuncio instructed, "take us near to Simon."

"Sure thing, boss," Rourke replied. He gassed the ATV, breaking formation and looking for Simon somewhere in the massive line of people. He was on horseback somewhere, that much he knew.

"Hurry," Dekker yelled. "It's of the utmost importance."

"I'm trying!" Rourke yelled back over the roar of the noise around them. "Do you see him anywhere?"

Dekker scanned the crowds, his instincts and his glasses giving him victory. "There!" he shouted and pointed.

Rourke sped the ATV toward Simon, pulling up beside his horse.

"Simon!" Dekker yelled, grabbing the man's attention.

"What is it, man?" Simon asked a bit frazzled.

"I think I'm supposed to call on the army!"

Dekker now had Simon's full attention. "Where, how?"

Dekker pointed to the ridgeline of an adjacent mountain. "I believe up there!"

Simon turned his horse while Rourke turned the ATV and the four of them took off up the mountainside toward the ridgeline that overlooked the valley in which the war would be fought. Simon hoped and prayed they were doing the right thing. Getting this far away from the others left them four people short, but hopefully, very soon, there would be thousands to take their place.

Simon looked out across the valley, watching the dust in the distance grow thicker. He could hear the sounds of trumpets and drums belting loudly, trying to intimidate the enemy, which in this case was them.

"Please hurry, Bridget," Simon said by way of a prayer, searching the sky for any signs of the four Keepers.

As in the days when you came out of Egypt,
I will show them my wonders.

Micah 7:15

Chapter 20

Timna Valley, Israel, 1840

Dekker and Simon stood on the ridgeline, Dekker picking up the Bible laying in the back of the ATV and turning to Ezekiel 37:1. He looked out over the valley before them and read as loudly as possible, looking to the heavens.

"The hand of the Lord came upon me and brought me out in the Spirit of the Lord, and set me down in the midst of the valley; and it was full of bones. Then He caused me to pass by them all around, and behold, there were very many in the open valley; and indeed they were very dry. And He said to me, "Son of man, can these bones live?" So I answered, "O Lord God, You know." Again He said to me, "Prophesy to these bones, and say to them, 'O dry bones, hear the word of the Lord! Thus says the Lord God to these bones, "Surely I will cause breath to enter into you, and you shall live. I will put sinews on you and bring flesh upon you, cover you with skin and put breath in you: and you shall live. Then you shall know that I am the Lord." So I prophesied as commanded; and as I prophesied there was a noise, a rattling sound, and the bones came together, bone to bone. I looked, and tendons and flesh appeared on them and skin covered them, but there was no breath in them."

When Dekker reached this part of the reading from Ezekiel, just as it said in the Bible, there was a great rattling from the ground. The bones that lay upon the desert floor and beneath, sprang forth rattling and came together. As the men watched from the ridgeline, and the rest of their small band of troops watched from the ground, the bones came together, forming bodies. Then sinews — as Dekker had read — formed on the skeletons, then came the flesh, followed by clothed, armed, men. It was like watching decay in fast-forward but reversed. Soon, lying before them where they were formed, was a great and vast army of thousands of soldiers, called from the dust of the earth. Their very breath stopped in disbelief waiting on the army to stand.

Simon murmured to Dekker, "Keep reading."

Dekker shook his head in compliance and continued. "Then he said to me, "Prophesy to the breath; prophesy, son of man, and say to it, 'This is what the Sovereign LORD says: Come, breath, from the four winds and breathe into these slain, that they may live.'" So I prophesied as he commanded me, and breath entered them; they came to life and stood up on their feet — a vast army."

Winds blew from all directions, over the mountain ridge and across the valley floor. The army from dust stood up at that moment as living, breathing, beings, ready to fight the great evil that approached the valley from the other side. Their shouts and battle cries roared throughout the valley, echoing off the surrounding mountainsides.

Jason and the others sat in their saddles and ATVs unable to utter a single word. The miracle that God had performed for them before their very eyes leaving them all speechless and in utter awe of the God that they served. Jason felt humbled and ashamed of the fact that he had spent the last week worrying about how they would overcome such a large army of demons. He felt unworthy to serve the Lord, but he would do so with renewed hope, laying his previous worries aside.

You could hear the shock and awe in the language of Memnah's men murmur throughout the group.

Jason couldn't take his eyes from the army in front of him. He humbly stated, "I shall never doubt you again, Lord."

The horses began to prance and dance nervously at the charged air that now hummed with the war songs of the recently risen army.

The clash of the steel blades of the swords they held, beating against the shields as they prepared to run at the advancing demon hoard.

Dekker, Simon, Nuncio, and Rourke all looked at each other in complete awe and shock. Soon to be replaced by rejoicing, smiling, laughing, dancing about, and hugging each other. They all praised the Lord on the top of the ridgeline for a minute before leaving to join the rest of the army on the ground.

The army in front of them seemed to be waiting on something. Jason wasn't sure if he was supposed to give the call to advance, so he pulled his hand-gun from its holster, pointed it at the sky and fired.

The army in front took off like a shot, running and yelling their battle cries, and the rest behind them followed suit. Gabby opened her shield protection and it connected one by one to the Portgens of all the other Peregrines spread out within the army of less than three hundred. The last connection it made was to the generator type receiver that Ryan and one of the other groundskeepers had strapped inside the back seat of an ATV. They stayed to the far outside of the line to catch the end of the signal and amplify it back to Gabby, making the shield stronger and covering their entire troop.

Ryan sat on the passenger's side of the ATV, buckled to the seat wearing a helmet, earmuffs, and holding a handgun. The others insisted on him having something with which to protect himself. He didn't like guns, and when he went to fire it, he closed his eyes and just pointed it randomly in front of him. Brian, the driver of the ATV, shouted to Ryan over the noise of the battle-field, tapping his arm to get his attention. "Open your eyes when you shoot, Ryan. You might actually hit something. Besides, we don't want you taking out any of our warriors!"

Ryan cracked one eye open but kept the other closed with his head cocked down and sideways. He pointed his gun at a demon flying far out front of the advancing demon hoard. It flew overhead and he fired, closing his one open eye at the same time. He hit it directly between the eyes, and watched it fall and crash to the desert floor, sliding to a halt as their ATV sped by. Ryan leaned out slightly to watch the demon's body begin to dissipate as they continued forward in battle.

The roar and rumble of demon upon man filled the air, the clash of steel on steel, and the battle cries of the warriors roared as they met their enemy in a massive collision.

Simon, Dekker, Rourke, and Nuncio finally caught up with the tail end of the army as Simon's and Nuncio's Portgens connected with the shield, throwing a protective haze out around them.

As they rode and drove as fast as they could to join the fight, Simon felt a massive swoosh of air overhead and he looked up to see the sky filled with soaring, fire-breathing, Kabihanxu. Simon gave a loud shout of joy, throwing his fist into the air. He was soon joined at the rear by a large number of Pagorinxes, running past him as though he were almost standing still. Annabelle and Wade sat on the backs of Mother and Paxton, the two he recognized from having been brought to the island. Simon was again dumbfounded. The creatures were huge and made him and his horse look like dwarfs in comparison. The cats leaped over the majority of their army, pushing off the shield that surrounded them. Simon could see Memnah's men startle, trying to make sense of it all. They quickly realized these creatures were on their side. Memnah and her people were new to all of God's visible miracles and His unexplored creation.

The Kabihanxus flew through the sky and over the opposing army, laying fire to the beasts below, then snatching them from the ground and ripping them to shreds, slinging the remains out across the desert.

Some of the Pagorinxes bit at the demons, shaking them ferociously while others swatted at them, sending them flying across the desert and slamming into nearby boulders, the bodies shattering.

The Peregrines and Dragoman fought with renewed strength and vigor, knowing that they were not alone. God had supplied amply.

Odessa had made certain to position herself close to where she could keep an eye on Alec. The images from her dream of him falling in battle had continued to haunt her constantly over the last week.

She still had not taken the opportunity to tell him how she felt about him. She finally realized, at the prospect of losing him, that she did in fact love him, and not just in a friendly manner.

She shook her head to clear her thoughts just as a demon was bearing down on her. She would have seen it coming if she could just stay focused on the task at hand.

The demon came straight down at her leaping into the air, its weapon pointed in a downward position at Odessa.

Alec saw the attack and teleported in front of Odessa, knocking her aside. The demons blade made contact with his left shoulder. The blade running all the way through, protruding from his back. The demon withdrew its blade and made the move to strike again to sever Alec's head as he fell to his knees in pain on the battlefield. Odessa could do nothing, the whole event taking place so quickly as she tried to stand to stop the demon.

As the demon began to swing at Alec one last time, to Odessa's great relief, Jason appeared on horseback. Not having a clear shot, he raced forward and kicked the demon in the face with his boot, sending it sprawling backwards. He jumped from his horse, shot the demon between the eyes, and quickly ran to Alec. Others nearby saw what was happening and went to fend off other demons trying to attack them while Jason tried to heal Alec's wound. Odessa fought with all she had, anger and fear now gripping her soul as she tried to protect the two men.

The poison from the demon's blade was already beginning to invade Alec's body. Jason knelt beside him, both hands on either side of the wound as he prayed hard and fast. People fought off demons all around them, trying to give him time to tend to Alec.

Within twenty seconds, Alec's wound was almost healed, enough for him to stand and fight again. Jason didn't have the time to heal him completely, but at least he thought he was able to draw out the poison. Jason whistled to his horse which came to him and he mounted it again, taking off in the midst of the battle, shooting with both hands locked around his automatic pistols.

Seth sliced at the creatures around him with his long, curved, blade, punching at others, grabbing some from the air with his hand as they flew overhead, throwing them to the ground then killing them.

Caroline flipped and jumped, slicing at and laying waste to the demons that were near her.

Many were amazed to see the younger Safra move. They were all used to such things within themselves, but they had never seen Safra this way. She was every bit as agile as any of them, without the added gifts and abilities given to her by God.

Sean, still at a disadvantage with his water abilities, had to rely on skill alone to fight the demons, but Kristen fought by his side and opened the ground beneath several, enough to throw them off balance, enabling Sean and herself to be able to slay them.

Zaccai, using the surrounding plants and trees, threw forth branches and vines to entangle and ensnare the beasts, giving those nearby the ability to destroy them.

Nick threw balls of fire to burn them where they stood, then shot them through the heart or head.

Nadia turned what internal moisture their bodies held into ice, freezing them in their place so she could kill them.

With each strike to Timothy's body, the demon's blades and maces broke or shattered. He felt the pressure of the hit, just without consequences, turning and slaying the beasts in turn.

Oz's ability to manipulate their molecular structure instantly killed several as he basically turned them inside out. While Sofia had the advantage of her ability to disappear only to reappear elsewhere for a surprise attack.

Simon and the other Dragoman used their gifts to have victory over those they fought as well. He, Malachai, and Nuncio all had the gift of the Magi, using their magic to their benefit.

All the gifts of the newly unretired Peregrines and Dragoman returning in full force to the benefit of them that had them.

Memnah and her people only had their weapons to aid them, and fought fiercely, being of immense benefit to the war. Most of them knowing full well what they were up against after the first and last battle in which they had fought the demons. They too had renewed strength and hope after being witness to God raising an army of the once dead to life in their favor.

The battle continued on for the better part of an hour, the Peregrines fighting hard, the demons, scattering and dying.

Jason spent much of his time stopping to heal those who had been wounded, unable to reach everyone, but trying with all his ability to do just that.

Oz was fighting a demon when he realized that his power would not work on the creature. Oz tried again, confused about why he couldn't kill the beast with his molecular manipulation. Then, he got a closer look at the demon. There was something familiar about it. Oz suddenly realized why the beast would not die. He struck it and it fell to the ground, wounded. Oz laid his sword to its throat.

"Marnor?" he asked shocked.

Marnor lay there, his hands over the stab wound to his side.

"Who are you?" Marnor asked, confused and in pain.

"I know ya', from Zanchier." Oz was shocked that he was seeing a Scaither outside of Zanchier.

Marnor pleaded with him. "Please, kill me. I'm in constant pain. This existence is miserable." He gritted his teeth.

"I'm afraid I can't do that."

"Why not? I'm begging you to," Marnor cried as the demon fought against his pleadings.

"That decision is up ta' God." Oz left him lying there as he ran off to fight another demon.

Marnor lay there, his body dying a slow, painful, death. The demon that had possessed him felt the death and rose to leave him.

Bridget and Han were flying over-head and she witnessed the beast leave his body, realizing who it was that was laying there on the ground.

"Han, down." She told him exactly where to go with her mind.

Hand flew to the ground, reached out with his large front talons, and picked Marnor up. Bridget searched frantically for Jason, finally spotting him and directing Han toward him.

"Jason," she screamed, grabbing his attention.

Jason ran to where Han landed and looked at the man lying there. "Bridget, who is this?"

"He's my half-brother."

"The Scaither? The one who is a horrid person?"

"Yes." She stood over him, looking at him lying there, so pale and almost dead.

"You want me to heal him?" Jason asked her in disbelief.

"I know it's a strange request, Jason, but he's the only real family I have left." She looked at Marnor who looked back at her, tears of pain running from his eyes into his hairline.

"All right, Bridget. I just hope you don't regret this."

Jason placed his hands on Marnor's wound, praying hard and loudly that God grant the man grace.

To Marnor's utter shock and amazement, his wound began to heal, he could feel his body grow stronger. He looked back and forth between Jason and Bridget in disbelief that these people were helping him.

When Jason had finished, Marnor's wound had stopped bleeding, but the scar remained.

"You're going to be tired for a while. I sealed the wound, but I can't replace the blood loss," Jason said to Marnor. He turned to Bridget. "Take him somewhere on the ridgeline away from the battle.

"Thank you, Jason." She then turned to Marnor. "Come with me, now." She climbed on the back of the massive Kabihanxu. Marnor was slightly apprehensive as he stumbled his way toward the bird. Bridget extended her hand down to him.

Marnor looked at her hand, then up at her face, knowing full well he didn't deserve to be treated with such grace and forgiveness. He took her hand, and she helped him get onto Han's back. Han quickly ascended into the air, flying them to the base of the mountain. Bridget put Marnor leaning against a rock.

"Stay here," she instructed him, "I'll return when the fight is over."

Marnor couldn't speak, just shook his head in agreement, still holding his stomach where the wound had been. When she flew away on the massive bird to rejoin the battle, Marnor lifted his shirt and looked at the pink scar that now graced his stomach. He swallowed hard, slid to the ground as he watched his half-sister soar through the sky, and broke down into tears. Grateful for the second chance that he knew he in no way deserved. He sat crying as he watched the bravery and thought about the grace of those he spent so many years helping Riglan torture. People he tortured himself. Some of those very people who survived it all, out there on the battlefield at this very moment. He watched his younger sister soaring through the air on the beast that obeyed her every command, because it trusted her.

Han flew through the air, snatching demons up and pulling them apart with his massive claws and beak. The battle was slowing as he threw one demon to the side and went to grab another. Just then a large molten boulder, covered in spikes, flew through the air straight toward him and Bridget. He turned quickly to keep the boulder from hitting Bridget and took the brunt of the hit. Screeching in pain, Han spun through the air unconscious, and he and Bridget hit the ground hard, knocking her from his back. Bridget rolled across the desert floor, unconscious as well.

Caroline saw her and the large bird take the hit and fall from the sky, running as quickly as she could to where Bridget lay. She contacted Oz through telepathy, asking him to help her.

"Oz, Bridget, and Han are injured, I need your help. Bridget is unconscious and I can't move her myself."

"Be right there, girl," Oz replied.

Oz ran to where he saw the large bird lying on the ground, battling his way across the field. When he got to where Bridget lay, he handed his weapons to Caroline, picked up Bridget, and ran to the safety of some outlying rocks and placed her on the ground.

"Take care of 'er, Caroline. I'll try ta' fin' Jason an' send 'im over." Oz took his weapons back from her and ran back out, searching frantically for Jason, with no luck. Oz went to the large bird lying on the ground. Han didn't move. Oz couldn't tell if the bird was just unconscious or dead. As he stood looking over Han's burned feathers, he saw a large, charred, area on his side and wing, and deep puncture wounds created by the burning boulder that had dislodged when they hit the ground. Blood trickled through the thick cracked skin, staining Han's beautiful, colorful, plumage.

"That don' look good at all," Oz said in disbelief. He had never seen one of the birds injured in this way before. He believed them to be invincible.

He turned, still trying to find Jason, finally spotting him across the field doing battle. He ran to him as quickly as he could. Once he reached his side, he helped him fend off a few demons before turning to speak.

"Jason, Bridget's over by those rocks, 'ere," he said pointing. "She took a hard fall. Her an' Han both. She's unconscious but alive. I don' think the Kabihanxu made it."

Jason looked at Oz then looked at the large fallen bird lying on the ground. He looked at Oz once again, knowing this would devastate Bridget.

"I'll go check her out." Jason ran toward where he saw Oz point. He saw Caroline wave to him. When Jason approached, Bridget was still lying unconscious on the ground. He bent over, moving his hands along her body, hovering just above it. He couldn't feel anything in her. He checked her head and felt a massive lump on the back of her skull.

"I think she'll be okay, Caroline. But I don't think Han made it. Stay with her until she comes to." He then left to return to the fight.

A few minutes later, Bridget began to stir from her stupor. She slowly sat up, looking around her. She suddenly remembered where she was and what had happened to her, and Han.

"Han," she said looking around frantically, wincing at the pain in her head.

"Sh…Bridget, take it easy. You had a nasty fall," Caroline said, trying to calm the girl.

"Caroline where is Han?" She looked into the woman's eyes for an answer.

Caroline looked at her, not sure how to tell her the news.

Bridget could tell something was wrong. She stood up on wobbly legs and pushed passed Caroline who tried to stop her.

"Bridget, wait! You're hurt!"

Bridget ignored Caroline's pleas as she ran, fumbling along the ground to the bird that lay unmoving upon the sand.

"Han." Bridget could barely choke out, as tears began to streak her cheeks.

"Han!" She screamed as she got closer, running around the large bird's frame. She slowed, panicking at the large, charred, area of his chest and wing. She ran to his head, falling to the ground near his massive beak. His eyes were closed and unmoving.

"Han?" She wept as she stroked the birds head, pushing at him to try to get him to move. "Han, wake up!" She screamed at him. But the bird didn't move. Bridget sat there, stroking the bird's feathers, and laying upon his massive head and neck soaking his feathers with her flowing tears. Bridget sat there unmoving, the war still waging all around her.

As the battle died down and the last demon was laid to waste, they began to take stock of the damage. They stumbled, tired, beaten, and some injured along the battlefield. The remains of all the demons that had been slain last, beginning to dissipate and float off, carried away by the slight breeze that drifted suddenly across the valley. Several of the large Pagorinxes had been killed along with a few of the Kabihanxu's. One of those being Han. Dominic went to sit with Bridget, throwing an arm around her shoulder to comfort her, as she continued to sob into his shoulder.

Many of Memnah's people had been killed, and many more had sustained injuries. Memnah and the others helped them form a line for Jason to heal the worst of the injured right now. They would deal with the lesser injuries back at the cavern.

Fortunately, none of The Twelve had lost their lives. Some of the retired Peregrines and Dragoman had not been as fortunate. Nuncio was among them.

In all, the body count for those that perished in the war were forty people and eight Zanchieth creatures, plus about six of their own horses and about a dozen of the tribal men's horses. Also, the army raised from the dust had all perished, but had given them a great advantage. However the army from the dust returned to dust, as though they were never there. Unfortunately, the remains of those who died would not be carried away upon the desert winds as did those of the demons. So, the rest of them, with the help of the Pagorinxes' massive paws, spent the next hour digging graves large enough for the animals. Bridget had refused to allow them to lay decaying upon the desert floor. The others all agreed. The animals deserved a proper burial for their sacrifices. Cho, Han's mate, sat by his side, gently nudging him, trying to get him to move. She made soft cooing noises, then let out one loud shriek into the heavens as though she were in pain at the loss of him.

It was at that point that Marnor staggered toward them. He had been making his way slowly, back across the desert, ever since he saw Bridget and Han fall from the sky.

Caroline saw the man's approach and knew him right away, confusion at how he got there written across her face. She raised her bow, ready to let an arrow fly into his evil heart. When Marnor saw her raise her bow, he held his hands out in front of him, cowering, and hit the sand on his knees.

"Caroline, stop!" Jason yelled to her.

"Why?" she asked him shocked. Not taking her eyes off the man. "Do you have *any* idea who this man is?" She seethed.

"Only that Bridget asked me to heal him, and that she called him her half-brother."

Caroline's head spun around to look at him.

Marnor cowered before her on the ground. "Please!" he yelled. "I'm sorry! Just...give me a chance! I'm sorry! I'm truly sorry! For everything!"

Caroline slowly let her bow and arrow fall to her side. She walked up to the man and said, "One wrong move on your part, and I won't think twice about putting an arrow through your thick skull."

Seth walked up to her and placed a hand on her shoulder, whispering to her to relax. Not sure she would, or why this man vexed her so much. He knew he was the Scaither called Marnor, but not much else. He wondered how he got here, and why he vexed his wife so much.

Everyone watched the scene with curiosity, but not willing or able to do much else, or ask questions. They were all spent, physically, mentally, and emotionally.

The Keepers returned the creatures back to Zanchier where they belonged, dropping them all at Storm Valley. Bridget wasn't yet ready to leave, wanting to stay with Cho for a bit. The keepers went to Han and Cho's nest with her. Once there, they saw they had three eggs. They sat in the nest with her for the next half hour, looking at the eggs, and comforting the large bird. Soon they had her fly them all to the dustbowl to return home.

While most finished burying the animals, the bodies of the deceased people were laid across available horses by the others and taken to Memnah's camp for ceremonial burial services. After Memnah's people prepared their bodies, along with those of their own people, the fallen Peregrines and Dragoman were returned to the cavern to be taken to Reader's Island, soon to be laid to rest beside the prayer gardens next to Dina. Petra sat, chained to the unforgiving post in the ground and sadly watched the scene around her. Many of the fallen had been her friends for the last thirteen years. Including Nuncio.

Jason and Memnah said goodbye once more as God's chosen walked through the Portgen onto Reader's Island, their dead in tow.

Memnah's heart broke for her people, and for Jason's. They had won a great victory today, but at a terrible price.

A person's wisdom yields patience. It is to
one's glory to overlook an offense.

Proverbs 19:11

Chapter 21

Reader's Island

The return to the island was, again, a somber event. By the time they finished in the valley and returned to the island, the Keepers were returning from delivering the creatures to Zanchier. They were already tired from the fight and the burial of the animals. Now, they had to do it all over again. Much of the island staff was no longer there to handle the burdens of the task at hand. Many of them now lost to death. They were in a much better place, but the burden of their passing lay heavily on those left behind.

Simon and Malachai put Petra back in her room and again put a protective shield over it. Everyone pitched in, making the digging of the nine graves go quickly.

Bridget had finally stopped crying, coming to terms with Han's death.

Tomorrow they would make grave markers for those that perished. Tomorrow Simon would go about recording the event in the archive historical books. Tomorrow they would take the day to mourn and rest. Tomorrow. Another day for them to push on.

He had lost a great many friends today. All people he had known for many years. Though none so close to him as Nuncio. Simon smiled painfully at the memory of the man. Nuncio had said that he wanted to go out in a blaze of glory, and so he had. A stray tear streaked his cheek as the memories of battles fought, stories shared, past friends lost, and a lifetime spent in each other's company flooded his mind. Thirty years they had been friends, and he would miss his oldest and dearest friend most of all. He also had friends in many of the people who had worked on the island, and they all would be missed. Their loss felt strongest by the once retired warriors.

Shannon and Clancy were battered and bruised, but no worse for wear. After the dead were laid to rest in their graves, the two of them sat on the benches in the prayer gardens mourning their life-long friends and colleagues, grateful to still be able to hold each other.

Safra respectfully allowed them all to mourn their losses as she busied herself tending to the needs of others. She, with the help of Dekker, and the apparently, strange newcomer, Marnor, prepared meals, cleaned up, and brought people coffee and snacks. She noticed the odd reaction from the one called Caroline toward Marnor. She wondered what that was all about. She sighed. If only her older self could have been able to give her a bit more information about this new life she led now before she disappeared. Still, she wasn't certain if she would return to her time or stay here with Simon and these other people indefinitely. She would decide that tomorrow. Tonight, she would do whatever was needed of her to help those who were hurting. She had known some of the fallen people, and she was certain that her older self would have mourned just as hard right next to the others. But the only one lost that she truly knew was Nuncio, and she had only met him a handful of times. The only person on the island that she honestly knew well was Simon, and her heart ached for him and the pain that he was going through. As people passed through the kitchen, Safra handed out coffee mugs.

Odessa and Alec were two of those people, and they thanked her and took their mugs outside to relax, finding one of the large outdoor couches unused. They sat down and took soothing sips from their steaming mugs. Odessa looked at Alec, seeing the paleness of his normally tanned skin. She had realized that the reason he was injured was because she couldn't stop worrying about him. Which in turn put her own life in danger, causing him to step between her and the demon that hurt him. Because of that sacrifice, she knew without a doubt that she loved that little Frenchman. Now he would need rest, and a lot of it. After Jason healed him earlier, he continued to fight, expending all of his energy due to the blood loss. Now that they were back on the island, she intended to make certain that he rested and allowed his body the time that it needed to heal properly.

"Alec," she said, looking at him, "when I saw you get injured, I thought I would lose it. In my vision last week, I saw that happen, all the way up to the part where the demon almost decapitated you. Only, my vision didn't show me anything past that." Her eyes began to tear up and she could barely speak the next words. "I thought you were going to die, and there was nothing I could do to stop it. I thought I was going to lose you forever." She sobbed heavily now.

Alec reached out and pulled her into his arms, comforting her as a friend would comfort another.

"I am fine, Dee, you see?" He looked down into her tear-filled eyes. "God provided for us both. I will always be here my friend. Even if you cannot see me."

Odessa sat back a little to look him in the eyes. "Alec, I just want you to know that I love you."

"Yes, I know. And I love you as well."

"No, Alec. Not a friendly love. I mean to say that I truly love you. Romantically."

Alec stopped for a minute and pulled back a little. He was in deep thought. "Dee, I do not want you to say that you are in love with me, just because you are afraid that you might lose me. That is not the way a relationship should start. It might not be real, but only appears to be out of fear of loss."

Odessa shook her head, her spiraled short curls swinging around her face. "No. It isn't like that, Alec. I promise. The truth is that I realized it when we went camping on the mountain peak last week. When I saw you and Gabby laughing together and having a good time, it made me jealous of her. It made me realize that you have other options here. Very young, very attractive women who you can have a life with. It made me realize that I wanted to be that woman to you."

Alec grinned from ear to ear. "Why did you not tell me this at the time?"

"Because it was that night that I had the dream about your dying. And I didn't want you to have to worry about me if we were in a relationship. I wanted you to be able to think and concentrate."

"Good grief, Dee! Do you not know that even though we have not been a couple, I have always worried about you and looked out for you? It is *my love* for you that keeps me going. That gives me the determination to go on. The hope that one day, this would happen." He smiled, wiping a stray tear from her cheek.

Odessa broke down in tears again, throwing her arms around his neck. "Thank you for waiting for me, Alec. I know I've been hard-headed."

Alec sat her back, looking into her eyes again. "I had no other choice, my love." He smiled at her and then kissed her gently, embracing her in a hug once again. They sat together, just holding one another for the rest of the evening.

The evening on the island was one of quiet reflection by all who survived the battle.

Timothy sat thinking about the day and his life up till now. He had liked Nuncio, and several of the other retired men who had kept the grounds on the island, and those who had worked in other parts of the house. He had gotten to know some of them pretty well over the last week during training. He was beginning to fully understand loss and pain like he never had before. He realized that he may be near impossible to injure during a battle, but those that he cared about were not. It would truly be a miserable existence if all he had to live for was himself. He decided to start making a change in his life and his attitude. He tended to be jaded when looking at life and those around him. He figured he should start praying more and study his Bible. The only time he got anything from the Word, was during the nightly Bible study after dinner, and then, he barely even listened. He decided that after what he saw today, and the experiences that went along with it, he needed to work on himself, a lot. He got up and walked over to the firepit to join the younger ones who sat there, talking quietly amongst themselves. Gabriele grinned up at him as he sat down beside her on one of the couches.

Gabrielle, Dominic, Wade, Bridget, and Annabelle sat around the outside firepit, reminiscing quietly about the animals; some concerned about how quiet Annabelle had been since the battle. She was very young to have seen the things that she did today. The others could tell that something was bothering her. Gabriele remembered the connection she had with Nick and decided to go find him. She left the group, promising to return. She found Nick sitting in the kitchen, a cup of coffee in hand, staring at the table.

"Nick?" Gabriele said, entering the kitchen.

Nick looked over at her. "Hey Gabby."

"Hey. Um, I know you and Annabelle have gotten sort of close since she and Dekker joined our group, but she seems really sad. I think someone she knows better than anyone else should maybe talk to her. She seems to be taken with you, so I figured you'd be best to speak with her. She's *really* young to have seen what she did today and I think it is bothering her."

Nick's expression seemed thoughtful for a moment, then he sat down his coffee cup. "You're right about that. Take me to her." He follow Gabby back outside.

Nick walked up to Annabelle and quietly sat down next to her on the couch. She didn't say a thing or even look up at him. The two of them just sat there next to each other staring into the dancing flames of the firepit. It only took moments for Annabelle to lace her arm through Nick's and lean against his arm, as small tears trickled down her cheeks. She sniffed and Nick wrapped his arms around her small frame, and she climbed up in his lap, laying her head in his shoulder. He sat there holding her as she silently cried, eventually falling asleep, secure in his arms.

Everyone watched the scene before them. Bridget and Gabby both tearing up at the tenderness of it, knowing she was feeling sad and lonely.

Across the patio, another person watched the scene. Nadia sat looking at the tenderness of heart the large man displayed to the small child. She had noticed Nick was a kind man. He never said much, only when what he needed to say was important. She also noticed a sadness within him. She saw it back when Dinah had died, and she noticed it more times since. She had come to like him. He was a good man, and her opinion of him grew even more tonight as she watched him with the little girl. She was so young to be called to deal with the things that most of them as adults had trouble understanding. Nadia knew that God knew what He was doing. She figured that Annabelle being called here wasn't only for what God wanted from her for His work, but also for what Nick might need as well. She smiled as she sat and watched him just simply hold Annabelle on his lap, leaning back against the couch and staring up at the stars. She stood up, walking over to the firepit where they sat. She took the blanket she had been using to cover herself and laid it across Annabelle, then sat down beside him leaning back against the couch. He looked over at her and grinned. She grinned back at him, then turned to gaze up at the stars too.

Everyone around the fire grew quiet following their examples, and just sat and stared at the night sky until most of them fell asleep curled up against each other on the large, overstuffed, lawn furniture. Needing the comfort found in one another.

Caroline, Seth, Jason, Oz, Prisca, Zaccai, Zeke, and a few others spent the evening unsaddling the horses and tending to the needs of the animals, quietly going about the tasks at hand. Putting the tack away, brushing down all the horses, feeding and watering them, and making sure all the horseshoes were intact and in place. Jason looked them all over to check for any injuries.

Safra, Dekker and Marnor all walked out to the stables carrying large trays of drinks and refreshments to those working with the animals there.

When Caroline saw Marnor enter the barn she instantly stiffened. Seth noticed her reaction and walked over to her, placing a hand at her waist.

"Caroline, are you all right?"

"Yes," she said shortly.

"Who is that man to you?"

She turned to look at Seth. "I'll explain later. I'm going to shower." She walked away from him and out of the barn toward the house.

Seth watched her go. He had never seen her take a dislike to anyone that much before. He stared at the man, who watched Caroline leave the barn. Seth walked over to him, looming tall and menacing over him.

"I don't know who you are, but my wife doesn't like you and that is good enough for me," Seth warned.

Marnor looked up at the massive man in front of him. He remembered hearing her talk about a husband. Marnor swallowed hard. He was *way* out of his element here and he certainly didn't want to make *this* man angry at him. Not after what he had witnessed the man was capable of on the battlefield today.

"I promise, man, I ain't gonna' cause any problems for anybody here."

Seth bent over Marnor, nearly touching nose to nose, and said, "I'll make sure of that." Then he turned and walked away, following Caroline inside the main house.

Marnor let out a breath he didn't know he was holding. He simply wanted to apologize to the woman. He needed to make amends to a lot of the people here. Sofia being another one whom he had done awful things to. How was he going to go about doing that was another question all together? He hoped that once they figured out who he was, they wouldn't make him leave. He wanted to be near his little sister and get to know her. He needed to understand what made her the way she was. She was different than anyone else he had ever met. He figured, much like the majority of the people on this island they had brought him to. Bridget had saved his life, the one they called Oz had spared it, then Jason had healed him. He wanted to know what made them do the things they did today. No, he *needed* to know.

He turned to find everyone in the barn watching the interaction between him and Seth. They all looked at him as though they weren't even sure why or what he was doing here. They all returned to their work as Safra, Dekker, and he passed out the snacks.

When finished with the chores, Safra looked at him and said, "All right. Come with me. You need a shower and some clean clothes. You smell like you've been living in a sewage dump."

Marnor looked down at his shabby clothing. "I suppose I sort of have. I've spent the last two weeks or so possessed by a demon."

Safra turned wide-eyed at his statement. "Well, now, that's not something you hear every day. How did you get out of that one?"

"The battle today. Oz refused to kill me when I begged for death, and Bridget begged the one called Jason to save my life when the demon fled my dying body."

"That's some story you have to tell. Don't waste the gift you were given today." Safra looked at him pointedly.

As they walked out of the kitchen, Shannon and Clancy entered the house. Safra asked her where to find a place for Marnor to sleep and some clothing for him to wear.

"I'll show him, dear," Shannon said. "It's on the way to our quarters." She turned to Clancy. "Be there in a bit, dear."

Shannon showed him to a room in the servant's quarters and instructed him where he could find some clothing that apparently belonged to one of the deceased gardeners, along with a new toothbrush and tube of toothpaste that they kept in stock in a bathroom cabinet.

Marnor thanked her, grabbed some clothing out of the dresser she showed him, and went in to clean up in the bathroom. It took him a minute to figure out the shower, but he soon stood beneath the wonderfully hot water and let it wash over him.

Back at the main house, Safra entered the library where Simon sat alone, looking tired and worn down. She placed a cup of herbal tea, the kind she knew he liked, on the table beside the chair where he sat. She sat down beside him and waited to see if he wanted to talk.

Simon looked over at her. "Thank you, Safra. This is very kind of you." He took the cup in his hand and took a long drink. He smiled ever so slightly at the delightful taste and aroma. He looked over at her and took one of her hands in his, giving it a squeeze.

"It's going to take some getting used to seeing you like this," he stated with a lopsided grin.

Safra smiled at him. "I understand that. However, I'm uncertain if I should stay here. I'm not sure what effect that will have on history, my history, or actually the future in particular."

"We can discuss such things tomorrow." Simon sighed. "I'm weary, and I think I shall turn in for the night. After I finish my tea that is."

Safra and Simon sat in companionable silence for the next ten minutes before Simon got up to go to bed. Safra followed him up the stairs asking him to show her to her room. Simon obliged, and Safra kissed him on the cheek. "Goodnight, Simon."

"Goodnight, Safra," he said, wearily grinning after her as she entered her room and shut the door. Simon trudged to his own room, gathered some clothing for a quick shower, after which, he returned to his room and collapsed into his bed, completely exhausted.

Kristen and Sean had hung around the prayer gardens, visiting Dinah's grave for a bit. They sat in the gardens and prayed together for all the people who had lost their lives, and all those they left behind. Afterwards, they walked down to the beach and sat together on the sand well into the night, just talking and holding hands. Sean and Kristen lay back in the sand, Sean's arms up behind his head, Kristen doing the same.

"Sean, do you think we'll have to face another demon war like that one?"

"I certainly hope not." Sean sighed heavily.

Kristen turned to look up at him. "Me too. I don't think our little group could survive many more like that."

He looked back at her. "Yeah, I know what you mean."

"What do you think will happen next?"

"Well, we still have two more pieces of armor to find."

"Right. The Shields of Faith and the Swords of Truth."

"Maybe they will both be together like the last two pieces," he said, rolling his head to the side to look at her again.

"I doubt we'll get that lucky twice." She grinned lopsidedly.

Kristen continued. "What do you think the Final Battle Simon and the other Dragoman are always talking about will be like?"

"I have no idea, why?" Sean asked puzzled, hearing worry in her voice.

"I just feel like I'm not really supposed to be in that fight. I mean, Tim and Uriah are both much more experienced than I am. What if I can't handle the fight? There are only going to be twelve of us."

Sean leaned up on one elbow and turned to face her. "First of all, God chose you for this, so I'm gonna' say that you'll do just fine. You aren't the only one who has been at this a short time that was chosen, Gabby's like you too. Second, I'd say you kicked some behind pretty well today in that demon war. You did make it back alive."

"Yeah, but probably only because God has other plans for me."

"Kristen, that's the only reason any of us made it back today. God's plans for all of us aren't finished yet. It wasn't because we all have these amazing gifts. It helps, yeah, but we survived because God willed it. No one is any better than the other in that respect. We all have a destiny to fulfill. Once we do that, it's still up to God whether or not we survive the Final Battle."

Kristen looked at him in all seriousness. "How do you always know the right thing to say?"

"I guess I'm just blessed, with looks, charm, and wisdom," he teased her, puffing out his chest, and bulging a bicep.

Kristen giggled at him, knowing he was joking. They lay there for the next thirty minutes, picking at each other and giggling at one another's silly comments. They curled up together on the sand to watch the stars twinkle in the night sky and soon fell asleep.

Forty feet away from them, Vashti sat upon one of the long lounge chairs by the shoreline, wrapped in Malachai's arms, staring out at the lapping waves. The white tips that broke the surface of each gentle wave glistened in the moonlight.

They sat silently, enjoying each other's company. Happy to still be alive and together. It had been many years since they had to fight in a war. And never one of that magnitude.

Vashti asked, "Do you think Uriah will return to the island?"

Malachai sighed. "I really don't know. The life he led before peregrination, I'm sure, is a vague memory. This life is all he has ever really known. He's been doing this a long time."

"I always thought that I knew him, you know," she said sadly.

"As did I, Vashti. Just goes to show you how deceitful people can be. It makes me wonder what else he's hidden from us all these years. If we hadn't found out about his treachery, today's battle might have turned out differently. All of us might not have ever returned."

"It's such a scary thought. I mean, I know God is in control, but He was in control thirteen years ago too. People can interfere to some degree I suppose."

"Perhaps, but nothing happens without His knowing. You know that."

"Yes, I suppose I do. I just wish that He would sometimes let us know ahead of time."

"It's called Faith, Vashti," he said, planting a kiss on the top of her head.

"I'm glad yours is stronger than mine. At least I have you to lean on." She smiled at him. They sat for a while longer, then walked to the main house to turn in for the night. Tomorrow was another day, and life did not stop. Not even for death. They passed by all the ones asleep on the lawn furniture, walked inside, and upstairs to their room.

Everyone else finished out at the stables, and slowly made their way to the house.

Zeke looked at Zaccai, the strains of the day evident on her features.

"You okay, Lady?"

"Yes," Zaccai said sighing. "Just a very long day, mixed with the emotions of the losses."

Zeke reached out, wrapping an arm around her shoulder, and pulling her to him. She leaned her head on his shoulder wrapping an arm around his waist as he laid his head on hers. They walked slowly toward the house, relishing the comfort of each other. When they reached Zaccai's room, she turned to Zeke and placed her hands on each cheek. She kissed him lightly on the lips, stepped back and looked him in the eyes.

"Goodnight, Ezekiel."

"Goodnight, Zaccai." They looked at each other with compassion for a moment longer before Zaccai dropped her hands and turned to enter her room. She closed the door and Zeke turned to go to his own room. He grabbed some clean clothing and went out to shower, noticing that most of those who were at the barn —including Zaccai— were doing the same.

They took quick showers to wash away the grime of the day before heading off to bed. Soon the main house and surrounding servant's quarters were quiet. No one stirred due to exhaustion by all on the island. The night would bring a brief respite and renewal needed by all of them. The night stars twinkled down on Reader's Island, the world around them oblivious to the aching losses felt by the worlds protectors over the sacrifices of so many. The only sound heard throughout the island were the sounds of the gentle lull of the ocean waves lapping at the shoreline of their one, true, safe-haven.

Book 5

The Peregrines are in search of the last piece of armor known as the Sword of the Spirit. The Dragoman now know they were in fact destroyed, and the jewels that once sat in the hilts were found wrapped in a cloth with an ancient text written on it and hidden with one of the ancient text keys. Without knowing where or when, they can't go back into time to prevent it so they must figure out another way.

Seth and Caroline find themselves separated once again. The Final Twelve must split into teams to take on four different beasts to do battle against, to save the world.

All the realms are unknowingly dependent upon the Peregrines, Dragoman, and the ever-important Beast Keepers to fulfill the prophecy revealed to them in the *Book of Armor*.

The swords have been refashioned by the blacksmith who was appointed by God to forge them once more for the battle to end all battles. If they can succeed, the new world will live in peace for a time and they can finally be at rest to live normal lives as rulers over all the lands and realms of the earth.

About the Author

S.G. Boudreaux is a stay-at-home mom who has homeschooled her three children for the last twenty years. She has been married to her husband for twenty-four years, and they reside in Louisiana where her husband was born and raised. They, surrounded by two dogs and a cat, live in the country. Her idea for the books called the Peregrination Series were inspired by the constant and recurring storms that seem to be escalating in number and severity. God gave her the vision in the summer of 2017 to write a five-novel fiction series based on biblical values, Christian morals, and fun, true-to-life characters. Her family is very active in their local church where they serve in an array of areas.

For more on her life and current events that she is involved in, visit her website at www.sgboudreaux.com or her amazon authors page at amazon.com/author/sgboudreaux

Other Book in the Series

Other books by author

Zanchier Series of Books

Book 1: Earth
Subjugation Book 1

Book 2: Wind
Uprising Book 2

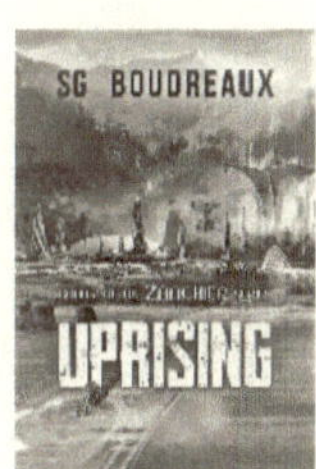

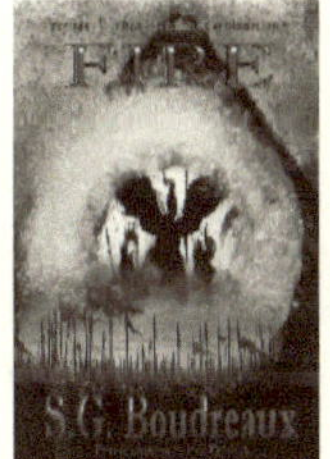

Book 3: Fire

Anarchy Book 3

Book 5 The Final Battle;
Battle of the Beasts

Search other Nonfiction books by
Shawna Boudreaux